A NOVEL

Becoming Darkness is published by Switch Press
A Capstone Imprint
1710 Roe Crest Drive
North Mankato, Minnesota 56003
www.switchpress.com

Library of Congress Cataloging-in-Publication Data
Brambles, Lindsay, author.
Becoming darkness / by Lindsay Brambles.
pages cm

Summary: Toward the end of World War II Hitler unleashed the Gomorrah virus, which wiped out most of humanity and turned the rest into vampires, except for those who, like seventeen-year-old Sophie Harkness, carry a genetic mutation that makes them immune — but when her best friend is murdered and attempts are made on her life, Sophie sets out to discover the dark secrets that lie at the heart of Haven, the last refuge of the Immunes.

ISBN 978-1-63079-017-2 (paper over board) -- ISBN 978-1-63079-034-9 (ebook pdf) -- ISBN 978-1-63079-037-0 (reflowable epub) -- ISBN 978-1-63079-074-5 (paperback)

1. Vampires--Juvenile fiction. 2. Virus diseases--Juvenile fiction. 3. Conspiracies--Juvenile fiction. 4. Secrecy--Juvenile fiction. 5. Murder--Juvenile fiction. 6. Alternative histories (Fiction)--Juvenile fiction. [1. Vampires--Fiction. 2. Virus diseases--Fiction. 3. Conspiracies--Fiction. 4. Secrets--Fiction. 5. Murder--Fiction.] I. Title.

PZ7.1.B75Be 2015
813.6--dc23
[Fic]

2015001579

Photocredits: Shutterstock

Book Designer: K. Fraser

Printed and bound in China.
009707F16

BECOMING Darkness

BY LINDSAY FRANCIS BRAMBLES

I opened my eyes, and
there was only darkness.

PROLOGUE
THE INSTRUMENTS OF DARKNESS

You can see them in the background of photographs and motion pictures from before the war. They resemble shadows, though they cast none. Often wraith-like, they are hard men, mean-faced men, soulless and cruel. They're there with Hitler, dressed in black, aloof, close to the Führer, yet never quite *with* him. They're part of the Gestapo and the SS and the handful of others who were the architects of a reign of terror that changed the world forever and very nearly destroyed it. They look oddly different — not truly alive. Rumors swirl about them: that they're older than the pyramids, as ancient as dust; that they're wanderers, moving through space and time, searching for something and quite willing to destroy everyone and everything to find it.

You know them immediately by the hollowness in their eyes, echoed in the pinched features of their angular faces. They are living death: waxen of skin, with hawk-like noses, neither human nor animal but something in between. A studied contrast to Hitler's notions of an Aryan race. But there's no mistaking their power — or their place at the apex of the hierarchy of horror that was and is the Third Reich. It speaks from out of the past, from out of those very photos, which serve as an unpleasant reminder of the events that led to the world as it is today.

Wherever there is power there are men like these; they are the instruments of darkness, the harbingers of despair.

In school they teach of the atrocities that befell humanity in the bleakness of the 1930s and 1940s. When the world spun out of control and war raged across it — just before the dark stain of the plague spread around the globe and changed everything. To some that time is known as The Fall — the end of the world as it was and very nearly the end of all humankind.

For those who lived through it, the Second World War was a nightmare to begin with, but when Hitler and his Nazi goons released Gomorrah, it turned the entire planet into a living Hell. Asia, Australia, Africa, and the Americas were all but laid to waste by the virus. Their populations were driven into extinction, their cities — except for New York — crumbling, abandoned ruins. Only in Europe, home of the Nazi war machine, did order rise out of the chaos, and there, in a dozen or so cities, the Third Reich survives, the dominion of all who were transformed into vampires by Gomorrah.

If there'd been any justice, the Führer would have perished along with the billions of others who succumbed. But he didn't, and now what is left of the world exists under his cruel tyranny, slave to a madman and the dark forces behind him. The vampires reign, except in Haven, the last bastion of humanity — the last outpost of hope.

Of the entire world's population, we Havenites are the few who are genetically immune to Gomorrah. To the enemy, we're the Untouchables, the Undesirables, their curse and their bane. Our blood is toxic to them. Poison. As deadly as the sun, more lethal than the sword. But the odds are in their favor — we Immunes are but a mere two million while they, the immortal Undead, number one hundred times that.

Back in the forties, they fought hard to be rid of us, and then in '48 the fighting stopped. Just like that. We pretend we were victorious, that we somehow frightened them into a truce. But the truth is that they let us live for reasons that have remained a mystery to all but a select few. The idea that they'll one day change their minds and finish us off is the fear that haunts us all. That they haven't done it yet may say more of us than it does of them.

It's said that peace seldom comes without a price. Perhaps we sacrificed more than we should have in order to maintain it. Perhaps on the day when the war ended and the truce was struck, *all* of humanity was lost. Perhaps on that day, it wasn't only the vampires who were no longer human.

PART ONE: HAVEN

CHAPTER 1
THE MURDER

The words came out of the blue.

"Sophie," Camille said as we walked barefoot along the beach, "I've been thinking."

"About boys again?" I asked.

Camille scowled. "No. About New York. I'm thinking of taking a trip there."

I blinked and gaped at my best friend in disbelief. "You're *what*?"

"You know, one of those tourist junkets. See how the vamps live. Visit the sights. We're not getting any younger."

I thought she was pulling my leg. "We're only seventeen. And besides, what sights are you talking about? Why on earth would you want to go someplace where you'd have millions of vamps staring at you like you're some sort of contagion, wishing you were dead and probably wishing they could do the honors?"

"Don't be silly. People are always going there and everywhere else in the Third Reich — London, Rome, Berlin. All the big vamp cities. There are even Immunes working there. I mean, it's not like the war just ended yesterday. Everything's different now."

"Not everything."

"What's that supposed to mean?" Camille asked.

"Just —" I started to say.

"Just what?" she interrupted, cocking her head and giving me her puzzled-kitten look.

I shook my head. "Nothing. Never mind. It's not important."

"Come on. Spill."

I laughed nervously. "There's nothing to tell. Really."

"Yeah. Right."

I just smiled and looked out to sea, where the waves curled up and rushed onto the strip of white sand. Their hiss and roar was deliciously soothing, a constant reminder of how the vastness of the Pacific Ocean served as a barrier between the three equatorial islands that constituted Haven and the rest of the world. *Us* and *them.* Immunes and vamps.

Farther down Coral Beach, where the playhouses of the rich stood against a backdrop of palm and acacia, I could hear the cry of a frigate bird and in it, the echoes of a time when everything had been so much different. A time long before I was born. A time that too often seemed as though it must have been a dream.

Closing my eyes, I breathed deeply and tried to lose myself for a moment or two in my surroundings. But even the warmth of the sand and the gentle ocean breeze weren't enough to make me forget the secret I'd lived with for far too long.

For nearly four years I'd been keeping it from Camille, and now hardly seemed the time to start confessing. Why risk ruining things when we only had a week left of our summer vacation? A week before we had to get back to the real world, to the city and school and all that other stuff we'd left behind for the luxury of her parent's ritzy beach house. Just the two of us sharing one of Haven's most coveted vacation spots. Besides, I wasn't sure my best friend would understand. Half the time I wasn't sure *I* did.

I could feel Camille studying me, trying to gauge whether or not to pursue the matter. I waited for the inevitable barrage of questions; waited for her to give me that look of hers that always made me want to blurt out everything. But the questions never came, and when I looked back at her, I could see her thoughts were elsewhere.

"Do you ever wonder what it might have been like?" Camille asked, catching me off guard.

I hesitated a step and stared at her. "What *what* might have been like?" I asked.

"You know? The world. Do you ever think about what it might have been like if there'd never been a war? If there'd never been any vamps?" She brushed her hair back behind her ears, but a gust of wind tugged it free. For a moment it was a bright gold halo about her head, and in that instant, standing there in her two-piece bathing suit and yellow chiffon robe, backlit by the late afternoon sun that reflected off the sea, Camille resembled one of those pinup girls from the war — all curves and long legs and sex appeal. It was no wonder the boys drooled over her.

"Well?" she said.

I shrugged. "Doesn't everyone? But there's not much sense in dwelling on it, is there? It is what it is."

"But maybe it didn't have to be," she went on. "I've been reading this book."

"A *book*?"

She rolled her eyes. "Yeah, a book. I do read, you know."

I smiled. Camille voluntarily reading a book was kind of like people gladly paying taxes.

"Anyway, this *book* was written ages ago by some guy on the islands. I think maybe before we were born. He describes this world where the virus never existed. No Gomorrah, so no vamps. Cool, eh? In the book the war ends in '45, with the Third Reich falling to the Allies."

I sniffed dismissively. "Sounds pretty farfetched, if you ask me. What's this book called?"

"*No Haven for Darkness.*"

"Seriously?" I couldn't help laughing.

Camille looked annoyed. "What does it matter what it was called? What's important is that the author says it was Gomorrah that changed everything."

I shrugged. "Maybe. And maybe the Third Reich would have won anyway, and there'd have been billions under their thumb. You know what they always say: 'Better dead than Undead and in bed with Hitler.' And at least we have Haven."

"Yeah. Sure. Haven." There was a sour note in her voice. She blew out a breath and looked wistfully across the waves.

"Don't be so glum," I said. "We have it good."

"Do we?"

I squinted at her; it was unusual for Camille to be so morose. "Whatever has gotten into you?"

She seemed to vacillate, undecided, and then blurted out: "It's just that the world's so big, and there used to be so many people. I mean, take Jimmy Stewart, for example."

I wasn't sure where she was going with that, so I said, "Isn't Stewart a vamp?"

"No."

"I'm sure he is. The one in that vamp film we saw last week."

"That was Cary Grant," Camille argued.

"Oh."

"That's not the point, anyway." She frowned at me in frustration.

"What is the point, Cam?"

"It just makes me sad."

"Why?"

"Because most of them are gone. Stewart and so many others. Clark Gable. Gregory Peck. Bette Davis. All those great actors. Almost all of Hollywood."

"Most of them would be dead by now, anyway," I said, even though I knew it was a stupid point to make.

"But at least they'd have had all those years to make more films."

"Well, the ones who turned into vamps did, didn't they? They just do it in Berlin and London now." I paused and gave her a bemused look. "Is this really all about movies?"

Camille huffed impatiently and looked at me as though I were an idiot. "Of course not. It's about the fact that we can't do what we want, that we have all these stupid rules and all these obligations." Her hands fluttered expressively. "It's like we're prisoners or something. If it was like that guy's book, then everything would be different. It'd be better. Our lives wouldn't be confined by so many restrictions. We wouldn't have to carry stupid ration books everywhere we go, for one thing. We'd be able to buy whatever we want, whenever we want and not have to hand over coupons for practically everything but the air we breathe. Imagine not having to choose between whether you were going to have a pound of sugar or get a new dress."

I refrained from pointing out that as a child of the Westerlys, one of the wealthiest families in Haven, Camille seldom had to make such choices. If you had enough money, you could usually get around most of the rationing restrictions. It had never been my impression the Westerlys wanted for anything.

But naturally, Camille was oblivious to this. She continued, her tone impassioned. "Think of it," she said. "In a world without vamps, we wouldn't be stuck on these stupid islands, out in the middle of nowhere, trying to pretend everything's okay. We'd have the whole world to live in. We could do whatever we wanted — be whatever we wanted. We wouldn't be forced by the government to pick damned potatoes or whatever for half our summer. We wouldn't be worrying every day about the vamps invading us or blowing us into oblivion. We wouldn't be *alone*."

"I don't think things are so bad," I said. "We have peace, and the vamps aren't showing any signs of breaking the truce. The population of Haven is growing. Things can only get better. And let's be honest, it's hard to be alone with two million other people on our side."

Camille muttered something unintelligible and said, "I just wish things were like in that book is all. That's the kind of world I want to live in. I'm tired —" She made a face and swept her arms wide in a demonstrative manner, as if to encompass the islands. "I'm just tired of *this*. I mean, look at us, Sophie. In a year we have to start thinking about getting married and having kids, for pity's sake. Kids! Eighteen years old and starting a family. My grandmother didn't marry until she was twenty-seven and then only because she chose to."

"I thought you *wanted* to get married and have kids."

"I just don't want to feel like I *have* to," she said. "I want to have a choice. I don't want the government telling me it's my obligation to the state to pop out four or five babies like I'm some sort of machine. It's the twenty-first century, and we're worse off than our grandmothers were sixty years ago."

Camille glanced at me, and I could tell she was really riled. "Things are different from what they were back then," I said. "We have to keep rebuilding."

"Rebuilding?" She snorted with unbridled scorn.

"Yeah. Strength in numbers, remember?" But even as I said it, I knew I was just spouting the government line, the same old propaganda I'd been taught since I was a little girl. The truth was, the whole getting married and having kids thing bothered me just as much as it did Camille. Maybe even more — though for entirely different reasons.

"It'll be centuries before we can ever challenge the vamps," Camille argued. "And since they can't reproduce, you know damn well they'll never let us get to that point, anyway. Why do you think they keep us stuck here? They know there's a limit to how many people these bloody rocks can support. Every time we ask to open up a colony on the mainland they turn us down. Hitler knows what'll happen if we ever get too strong."

It slipped out before I could catch myself. "Not all the vamps are like Hitler and his cronies."

Camille gave me an odd look. "How on earth would you know? When did you ever meet one?"

I looked away, toward the far horizon, imagining a place I'd never seen. Imagining the place where he sometimes lived, the place he called home.

I met him for the first time on New Year's Eve, 1999, a little more than a month before my fourteenth birthday. I could never forget it, because that was the night the insanity had started.

* * *

It's hard to believe it was less than four years ago that my eyes were opened to a world I'd never really understood. Back then, I knew little more than anyone else about vamps, despite my father dealing with them frequently in his capacity as head of the Presidential Security Service. He'd never discussed such things with me, other than in the most perfunctory manner, and it's likely I'd never have learned any more about them had I not been with him the night he was summoned.

Because it was New Year's Eve, we'd gone out for dinner. It was a long-standing tradition for my father and me and one of the few occasions I could count on us eating together. My mother had died giving birth to me, so for all my life he and I had only had each other. But he was a busy man, always on call, and despite occupying the same house, the moments we shared were few and far between.

We'd been dining at Castelano's Restaurant, located in downtown Caelo, Haven's capital city, when the call came in. The waiter brought the phone to the table on a silver platter, dragging its long cord between the tables and setting it down before Father as though it were the next course in the meal.

Father reluctantly picked up the receiver, his face darkening as he spoke. He tried to beg off, insisting he couldn't deal with the matter because he was with me. But whoever was on the other end was persistent and made it clear this was something that couldn't wait.

At one point Father said, "A 302 is a local matter. Not my business. Let the police handle it."

My ears pricked up at that, because as much as my father had tried to shield me from his work, I knew enough to recognize a 302 was a homicide — murder.

Father hung up soon after. He sat, resting his hands on the phone for a moment, then sighed and dialed another number. Though he kept his voice low, there was no missing the mention of vamps and the Embassy during the brief conversation that ensued.

In Haven there's but one embassy, the overt reminder of Hitler's power and home to the only vamps permitted residence on the islands as agreed upon in the treaty between the Third Reich and Immunes. If Father was talking to the Embassy, that meant a diplomatic angle and possibly a whole mess of trouble.

When he finished, he turned to me. "I'll get you a taxi," he said, confirming our evening was cut short. The waiter retrieved the phone, and Father asked for the check. A few minutes later, we were outside in the rain trying to flag down one of the black-and-white striped electrics ubiquitous in Caelo's downtown core. Unfortunately, given the New Year's Eve holiday, every cab that passed by had its sign lit, indicating it was occupied or already called to business.

"Goddammit," Father cursed. "There's never a bloody zebra when you need one."

"It's a busy night," I said. I waited a moment, then added in the most casual tone possible, "I could come with you."

"No."

Usually with Father, "no" meant no, and there was no getting around it — which isn't to say he was a hard or cruel man by any stretch of the imagination. Admittedly, to look at him you might think otherwise. With his broad shoulders, lantern jaw, and perpetual five o'clock shadow, Camille always joked that my father resembled a movie gangster. And it was true he could sometimes be gruff and too often aloof. But despite the fact that I often felt I didn't really know him, there were occasions when he would show me his gentler, more compassionate side. That was when I'd think to myself, *This* is the real Jonathan Harkness.

While Father's determination to keep his work out of our relationship as much as possible had been a constant in my life, he'd never been particularly successful. He'd be off on some presidential assignment for days at a time, leaving me in the care of Grace, my maternal grandmother. Hence nights like tonight, which were "our" time and not to be interrupted by anything.

"I'll stay in the car," I promised. "I won't be in the way, and at least we'll get to spend a bit more time together."

"Fine. But you just —"

"I know," I said, smiling and taking on a severe look as I mimicked his gravelly tone. "Do what I say and keep out of trouble."

Father grunted but then smiled back at me. "Just remember this isn't one of your adventures."

"Of course," I said innocently. But naturally I was thinking that was exactly what it was — an adventure I could later blab about to my friends. There was never a lot of excitement in Haven, and anything having to do with vamps would be a goldmine.

Despite the downpour, Father and I avoided getting drenched on our way to the BMW, and as soon as we settled inside we were off. The car was a rare imported internal combustion job, the engine brutish compared to the anemic whine of the dilapidated electrics that were more common throughout Haven. It was always a thrill to drive in; it felt fast and powerful and everything that so much of Haven wasn't.

Father hunched over the steering wheel as he drove. "When we get there you don't move from that seat unless I tell you to," he said, giving me his patented steel-eyed scowl. "You got that?"

I nodded. I knew that in all likelihood the remainder of the night would be incredibly boring, but catching even a glimpse of a vamp would make it worthwhile. I'd never seen one, except in pictures and newsreels and the occasional report on TV, and to nab a look in person would make Camille incredibly jealous.

It took about ten minutes to reach the scene of the crime, and by the time we arrived, a crowd had already gathered. Red lights flashed on police cars and the lone ambulance, and a barricade had been set up to hold back the growing mob of onlookers now milling about.

The nose of the BMW nudged toward the edge of the bystanders, and as we advanced, a policeman stepped toward us from out of the rain, flashlight in hand, pointing the beam into the car. Squinting, father rolled down the window a few inches and looked out at the young cop as the sounds of rain, machines, and people rushed in.

"Can I help you, sir?" the constable asked, looking past Father to me and then back again.

Father flashed his badge, and the young constable immediately straightened and said, "Very good, sir. Go right on in." He stepped back a pace and started shouting and gesturing to the nearest members of the crowd to clear a path.

We parked next to the ambulance, and Father stepped out into the pelting rain. It quickly soaked his suit and slicked his hair, but he seemed insensible to it as he leaned back into the car. "Stay put," he said, stern-faced. "I mean it, Sophie. I don't want you getting out under any circumstances."

"But I can't see anything from here," I argued, crossing my arms and slumping in my seat.

"That's the point."

"You never let me have any fun."

Father stared hard at me. I tried to play the game, glaring back at him, but there was no beating him when he was serious.

"I should have taken you home," Father said under his breath. With that, he shut the door and dashed off toward the men standing in the alley just beyond the cordon of vehicles. Another constable ran up to him, holding an umbrella. Father took it and moved on, quickly merging with the other men gathered about and soon lost from view in the shadows.

The rain drummed loudly on the roof of the car, an ominous soundtrack to the scene beyond. I strained to see what was happening, but everything was a blur through the downpour. After a few minutes I began to regret having come. The initial excitement had quickly evaporated — especially since it appeared there were no vamps involved after all.

I sat there, wilting in the humidity, hoping Father would hurry up and get back before I expired from the heat. It was becoming really unpleasant in the car. Outside the air stank of garbage and wet tarmac, and what little I could see beyond the windows was a strange, elusive mystery of fuzzy streetlamps, strobing lights, and shadows that seemed to stretch and tear like fat blobs of oil spreading across the surface of a puddle.

After a few minutes the rain eased, and I was able to see a bit more clearly. The glare of headlights behind me caught my attention, and I looked back over my shoulder to see a stretch limousine pulling up before the barricade. The constable who'd met us earlier ran up to the car, but he'd barely leaned toward the Mercedes before he froze, his face turning ashen as he quickly backed away.

The barricade was moved aside, and the limousine rolled forward on its whitewall tires, pulling up beside our car. I wiped at the fog that was beginning to form on the windows, but the view wasn't much improved, so I cranked the passenger window down a notch or two to get a better look. A fine mist of droplets flew through the narrow opening, peppering my face and beading on my eyelashes, forcing me to blink.

I sat there, staring at the Mercedes, my whole body aquiver with curiosity. In all of Haven there were only two cars like that — one belonged to the president and the other to the Third Reich Embassy. The swastika flags and Nazi emblem on the car beside me were clear indications this one *wasn't* the president's.

A policeman dashed by, vanishing into the alley, and a moment later Father reappeared. At first I thought he'd finished his business and was returning to the car, but instead he headed straight for the Mercedes. As he approached the limousine, the back door closest to me opened, and a tall, lean man stepped out. His face was hidden in shadow, but I didn't need to see it to know what he was.

The treaty that allowed for the presence of the Third Reich Embassy in Haven clearly stipulated that there are never to be more than thirteen vamps residing on the islands at any given time — exclusive of the zeppelin crews restricted to the aerodrome. Of those thirteen, few had ever been seen beyond the fortified walls of their Embassy. And yet there one was, in the flesh, just a few feet from me, apparently summoned by Father in the call he'd made from the restaurant.

Father moved forward to greet the vamp, his expression like none I'd seen before. It was fleeting and vanished as quickly as it had appeared, leaving behind the all-too-familiar visage I'd come to associate with his work.

I watched them, holding my breath, not sure what to expect, and eagerly hoping for what I'd come to see. I got my wish when a series of lightning flashes lit the scene as brightly as if it were day. In that brief interval, the shade of night was stripped away, and for the first time, I saw the stranger clearly.

While I'd not said anything, it was as though he'd heard me gasp. He twisted slightly toward me, his eyes meeting mine. In the instant we exchanged looks, I had the oddest feeling — as if I'd been in a deep sleep and someone had slapped me hard across the face, jolting me awake. Without warning, my world was turned upside down. One moment I was a child, and in the next, it was as though I'd been transformed. I was full of thoughts and feelings that up until that point had only been at the periphery of my consciousness.

I fumbled for the handle on the door, rapidly cranking the window shut and huddling deeper in the shadowed interior of the car. My heart banged wildly in my chest, and for a few minutes I just sat there, bewildered, wrestling with the strange sensations that had overcome me, not quite sure what to make of them.

It had been a mere glimpse, but his face was frozen in my mind. I closed my eyes, and there it was: a man who appeared to be no more than seventeen or eighteen, his features framed by blond, short-cropped hair, a weariness and sadness in his green eyes. He might have been one of the boys who worked on the farms, except he lacked the deep skin tones that came from hours spent in the fields. His face was unmarred save for an unusual scar on his left cheek, just below his eye. Shaped like an inverted crescent moon, it lent his face character, and I was certain there was a story behind it that had nothing to do with the thing he'd become.

He wasn't what I'd expected and not at all what I'd been taught to believe. I hadn't thought a vamp could seem so alive. With nothing more than a fleeting look, he'd made me feel exposed, as though every secret I had was on display, every feeling out in the open for anyone to see. But at the same time, he'd left the impression of being just as vulnerable.

It wasn't supposed to be that way. Vamps weren't supposed to be anything like us.

I don't know how long I sat in the car, trying to reconcile what I'd seen with the myths I'd been taught. After what seemed an eternity, Father and the vamp returned. They paused beside the Mercedes, ignoring the rain and standing deep in conversation for a minute or two before shaking hands and parting.

As he climbed back into his car, the vamp turned in my direction again. There was nothing casual about it; he was looking at me intentionally. I kept my eyes focused ahead but felt that stare as though it were a hot brand on my cheek.

Out the corner of my eye I watched him disappear into the Mercedes, and shortly thereafter, it drove off into the chaos of Caelo's crowded streets. I thought that was the last I'd ever see of him.

Father got into the car, wet and disgruntled as he settled in behind the wheel. He smelt of damp cloth and rain and didn't look in the mood to talk, so as we retraced our route through the city, I kept dutifully silent. But all the while I was wrestling with the need to get answers to the questions badgering me, and the longer his silence was drawn out, the more impatient I became.

Finally I couldn't hold my tongue any longer. "Who was he?" I burst out.

"Who?"

"The vamp. They don't often come out of the Embassy."

Father glanced at me but didn't answer.

"Do you know him? I saw you talking. I saw you shake hands." I wondered what it would be like to hold a vamp's hand, if it was really like holding a dead fish, the way the stories said.

"I shake hands with a lot of people," Father said.

"But why was he there? What did he want?"

"You ask too many questions."

Undaunted, I forged ahead. "What would a vamp be doing at a local murder?"

Father looked at me sharply. "Who said anything about a murder?"

I gave him the look, the one that said I wasn't stupid. "Come on, Dad. A 302?"

He ignored me, eyes fixed on the road.

"Dad!"

"Remind me never to tell you any more stories from when I used to be on the police force."

"You're avoiding the question."

"I've no intention of answering it," he growled. "It's nothing that concerns you. And I don't want you saying anything about this to your friends."

"What? But, Dad —"

"Sophie." Father looked at me hard. "You promised."

"I promised not to get into trouble. But you've got to let me tell my friends. At least Camille."

"Absolutely not."

"Why? Is it a state secret?"

"Look," he said, "this is an extremely sensitive matter. The security of Haven could hang in the balance."

"The security of Haven?"

"Yes."

"That's so cliché." And far more melodramatic than usual for him.

"Just let it rest."

There was something in his voice that made me realize he was serious. I couldn't recall ever having seen him so out of sorts. Had I not known better, I'd have said my father was actually afraid.

Baffled, I looked out the window of the car into the bleak night, wondering what he'd seen that could have rattled him so. It couldn't have been the vamp; he'd been around them plenty. One thing was certain, though — whatever had happened in that alley had been more than just an ordinary murder.

* * *

By the time I finished my story, the sun had dipped low to the horizon. Deep reds and oranges bled into the rapier-like clouds in the west, smearing across the darkening line where sea met sky. Beside me Camille was silent, and I could tell by the look on her face that she was hurt it had taken me this long to confide in her.

"I can't believe you never told me this before," she finally said.

"Didn't you hear me? My father forbid me to."

"Your father's been in the looney bin for the past six months."

"Camille!"

"Well, it's true."

"You know very well it isn't. Clarkson isn't —" I struggled for words. "Well, it isn't for crazies."

"Okay, then that place where they keep all the old farts with addled brains locked up."

"You're so insensitive," I said, glaring at her.

"Sorry." And I could see she was — insofar as Camille could ever be sorry about anything. "It's just that I'm your friend. You could have told me long ago. I mean, it's not like you always did everything your dad told you to do, anyway."

I opened my mouth in protest, then closed it. I had little ammunition to argue the point.

"You know I wouldn't have blabbed to anyone about it," Camille continued. She narrowed her eyes. "Besides, it's not like it was that big of a deal." An eyebrow arched, her look probing, searching. "Or was it?"

"No," I said hurriedly. "No big deal at all." But I couldn't look her in the eye, and I felt my cheeks go hot.

"Oh my —" Camille stared at me wide-eyed. "You're not serious. You can't expect me to believe you fell in love with him after just one glance."

"Of course not! Don't be ridiculous. I wasn't even fourteen, for pity's sake."

She raised an eyebrow again.

I felt sheepish and said in a tiny voice, "Look, it just sort of happened . . . gradually. I mean, it's not like I *wanted* it to happen."

"Gradually?" The eyebrow went higher. "Just sort of happened *gradually*?"

"Let's just drop it."

"Oh, no, sister. Not on your life. You don't get off that easily."

"I don't know why you're making such a big production about it. You fall in love at the drop of a hat."

"But we're not talking about me. This is *you* — the girl who doesn't have time for boyfriends because she's too busy being the perfect student. And we're not talking about any old boy, are we? I mean, he's a vamp! A v-a-m-p."

"I know how to spell."

"But do you know what it means?"

I didn't like thinking about it myself: a Havenite in love with a vamp. There weren't many people here who would understand that. I wasn't sure Camille did.

"So let me get this straight," she said. "You see this vamp once, and then what? You just *happened* to bump into him again? And again? And then suddenly you're what? Going steady?"

"It wasn't suddenly, and it's complicated."

"Complicated?" Camille wrinkled her nose at me and made a dismissive noise. "People only say that when they have no real excuse for what they're doing."

"You don't understand."

"I understand that this is Haven. I mean honestly, Sophie, what were you thinking? Falling in love with a vamp? In Haven?" She shook her head, then added, "Is that why you were always turning guys down?"

I didn't say anything, but my face betrayed me.

"Wow!" She grinned foxily and shot me a licentious look. "So how long have you two been, you know . . ."

"It didn't really start getting serious until a year ago," I said. I felt her eyes on me and realized telling her all this was a lot more uncomfortable than I'd imagined it would be. Somehow, in this light, the whole affair now seemed somehow sordid and wrong, which admittedly wasn't the first time I'd been made conscious of that.

"No wonder you did so well in *foreign* relations last term. Looks like you were getting some private tutoring on the side."

"Camille!"

There was laughter in her face as she stepped up to me and slipped her arm through mine, drawing me close. "Who would ever have thought prim and proper Sophie Harkness had such a deep, dark secret. You're going to have to tell me all the juicy details."

"You have to keep this to yourself," I pleaded.

Camille's expression sobered, but her eyes remained merry. "Aye, aye, Captain," she said, snapping off a jaunty salute. "Mum's the word."

"Camille, please. I'm serious. If —"

"If anyone found out they might not be so keen on the idea?" she interrupted. "Yeah, I'm not stupid. I get the picture. I mean, it's not exactly *normal*."

"Hey!"

"Well, the vamps did try to wipe us out. Some would call what you're doing consorting with the enemy — although I'm sure the people who thought up that term never imagined it in quite such lurid terms."

Camille chuckled, but I just glared at her, not seeing anything funny about it.

"Oh, lighten up, Soph. You've got to admit this is pretty out there."

I grimaced. It wasn't easy dealing with the fact that the man I'd become involved with had been part of what the history books described as "the murdering horde that slaughtered most of humanity." And sometimes, like now, I was almost ashamed I could ignore it.

"Come on, now," said Camille, "give me the rest of the goods."

* * *

In the week following the alleyway murder I saw almost nothing of Father. If he slept at all, it wasn't at home. On those occasions when he did put in an appearance, it was merely for a quick shower, a shave, and a change of clothes. Then he was out the door with barely a spoken word.

I remember desperately wanting to know more about what was going on, but even if Father had been around long enough to ask, I'd never have been foolhardy enough to pose the question. So I scoured the newspapers, listened to the radio, and watched the evening news for any hint of the murder. A crime like that would have been a big deal in Haven, so I expected it to be front and center, but it barely rated a mention in the papers, and the radio and television offered only brief references to it. There was no word about who the victim was or how he'd died, and I got the feeling that the whole thing was being quietly swept under the rug.

Even by normal standards, Father's absences during that time were abnormally long and his mood even more taciturn than usual. Coming directly on the heels of the alleyway murder, it was hard not to conclude that it was all somehow related. And if that were the case, then it was unlikely to be some simple cut-and-dried homicide best left to the police. The head of Presidential Security Service certainly wouldn't have been involved, and he definitely wouldn't have called a vamp from the Third Reich Embassy to the scene unless there'd been some reason to — a really big reason.

Add to that the fact that the incident was clearly being kept from the public eye, and one could be forgiven for assuming that whatever had happened that night had spooked some people in high places. Spooked them enough that they'd brought out the big guns and put a lid on the whole shebang.

For the umpteenth time I read the *Haven Herald*'s account of the incident, which I had cut out and saved, hoping I might spot something I hadn't seen before:

Police were called to the scene of a homicide in an alley off Carthage Street in downtown Caelo yesterday evening. Sources say the body of an elderly male was found lying half hidden in garbage, apparently the victim of a robbery. Police have yet to reveal details or possible suspects, but there are suggestions the murder was simply the result of a disagreement between two local vagrants.

There was a bit more from a police spokesman, assuring everyone that it was an isolated event, that murders were rare in Haven, and that there was no cause for alarm. Essentially the article was a lot about nothing. But it was what it didn't say that had me wondering. There wasn't a single word about my father's involvement or the vamp's presence at the crime scene.

I knew there had to be more to it, but what that might be I couldn't begin to speculate. There was little I could do with the limited resources I had, so after a few weeks of getting nowhere fast, I reluctantly abandoned my investigation and filed the whole business away in the back of my mind. I moved on to other things, and almost a year later, when I had my second encounter with my vampire, I'd pretty much accepted that I was never going to know the truth.

CHAPTER 2
VALENTINE

"I remember that time," said Camille as we continued along the beach. "You always seemed so preoccupied. I recall thinking something was going on between you and your dad." She pursed her lips pensively for a moment before adding, "Don't you want to know the truth?"

I frowned at her, confused. "What are you talking about?"

"The murder, of course."

"What does it matter now?" I said, throwing up my hands. "That was ages ago."

"But surely you're curious? It's an unsolved case."

"I don't know that it *is* unsolved."

She crooked an eyebrow. "So you think your father . . . ?"

I shrugged. "If he knew the answer, he never said. And now . . ." I looked away, clamping down on the pain that flared up inside me. "Well, you know how he is."

"Yeah. Sorry."

"Yeah."

"So I guess you'll never know," Camille said, trying to make it sound like she didn't care when I knew perfectly well she did.

"I guess not."

She knit her brow but didn't say anything more. Camille was never silent for long, however, and a few minutes later she blurted out, "So when did you see him again?"

"What?" I blinked at her, caught off guard.

"You know? The vamp. When and where? I mean, it's Haven. It's not like you could be open about it. When did all the secret rendezvous start?" She prodded me with a finger. "Come on. Out with it, missy."

I wanted to tell her to forget it, that I should never have said anything about any of it in the first place. But I knew she wouldn't stop pestering me until I'd told her everything, so as we headed back to the beach house I grudgingly resumed my tale. Once you've opened the bottle and let the genie out, it's next to impossible to put it back in.

* * *

After the night of the alleyway murder, I suppose I kept thinking about him largely because he was a vamp. Seeing one of them in the flesh had made me feel like I'd done something daring. It was akin to reading one of those banned vamp novels that are smuggled into Haven and sold on the black market. You know you'll get in a heap of trouble if you get caught with one, but you just can't help yourself. Forbidden fruit and all that.

It was just over a year later, during a visit to the local branch of the Caelo Library, when I saw him again. The library was a frequent haunt of mine, a place where I could retreat from the constant fussing of my grandmother and the loneliness I sometimes felt around my father. I always enjoyed its peace and tranquility, surrounded as I was by vestiges of a lost time. You could pretend the world was a different place. The sort of place it was before the Fall. The sort of place some said it should be.

There were few staff members on duty as I wandered about that day, and they remained close to the service desk at the front, tending to returns and other administrative chores that had been set aside during the busier hours. I made my way into the twentieth-century history section, amidst books whose contents I'd grown familiar with on previous occasions. As I surveyed the shelves, looking to see if there was anything new, one book in particular caught my eye.

I'd never seen it before, and the volume seemed completely out of place. It was drab and battered looking, with no title on the spine, and when I examined it more closely, I realized there weren't any library numbers pasted to it either. It was such an odd thing that it was impossible to resist, so I pulled it from the shelf to get a better look. The cover was made of old leather, worn soft and smooth by years of handling, the touch of it almost evocative — though in ways I can't explain.

There were no external markings, so I opened the book to the first page and promptly gasped. The name *Mary Wolstencroft* was written across it in a bold and elegant script.

Seeing my mother's maiden name left me stunned and breathless. I staggered back, bumping up against the opposite shelf and almost dropping the book in the process. For an instant it was as if time stood still. I was frozen, my heart in my throat.

It took me a moment to recover, and when I did, I turned another page. There was more of the same graceful penmanship, its loops and strokes all done in a leisurely, feminine style. It resembled calligraphy, the flourishes suggesting someone with a romantic outlook. The sort of woman my father had described to me on those rare occasions when he'd spoken about my mother at all.

I'd never known my mother, but one of the few mementos I had from her was a letter she'd written to me the day she discovered she was pregnant. Over the years I must have looked at it hundreds of times, to the point that it was now frayed at the edges and coming apart along the creases. The brief passages of love and hope and expectations for the future had been burned into my memory, and so, too, was her handwriting.

Standing there, book in hand, I felt as if I were touching the spirit of the woman who had died the day I was born. This was something of *hers*, a part of her. These were *her* words. And with them I was as close to her as I'd ever been. Perhaps as close to her as I could ever hope to be.

The book clearly didn't belong here, and I couldn't for the life of me figure out how it had come to be in the library. I was about to take it to one of the staff and inquire about it when it hit me that maybe this was more than a bit of serendipity. Maybe I hadn't simply stumbled upon the book at all. Maybe someone had put it there on purpose so I'd find it. Someone who knew Mary Wolstencroft was my mother and knew my habits well enough to know which section of the stacks I frequented most often.

That's just plain crazy, I told myself. Who would do such a thing? Certainly not my father. And definitely not my grandmother. Grace wasn't the sort to engage in subterfuge; she'd have been more direct.

If I'd had any sense, I'd have left well enough alone right then and there. But when you're fourteen you don't always weigh the pros and cons of a situation. The lure of the book was too powerful to resist; the desire to read my mother's words far too compelling. So instead I sank to the floor and opened the mysterious volume in my lap. Its handwritten words glared up at me, a challenge and an enticement that had me on edge.

I ran a hand over the pages as if there was something to learn from their texture. There was no telling what the book might contain, yet I hesitated to read, wrestling with my emotions. Eventually I was able to focus on the words rather than on my feelings. But before I could read a single line, a shadow crossed the page. Looking up, I found myself staring into the face of the vamp from the alleyway murder — *my* vampire, as I'm inclined to think of him now.

I swallowed and felt myself flush as my pulse shifted into high gear. Words eluded me, and all I could do was stare at him, recalling that first encounter.

There is something about vamps that immediately sets them apart from humans. It's not something easily explained. They don't look dramatically different from us — though strangely, when you see them in photos, you can immediately distinguish them. It's true their skin is paler and sometimes has an almost porcelain quality to it. And in certain lights there's an almost unnatural bioluminescence to their eyes. But what really sets them apart are the intangibles, the things for which there are no simple explanations. The things I felt the first time — the ones most evident when you encounter them in person. They have — for want of a better word — *a presence* about them. It's as if an aura surrounds them, so that if they walk into a room, you're immediately conscious of them. Maybe it's some sort of energy they radiate or a chemical like pheromones. But whatever it is, there's no getting around it when you experience it firsthand. I doubt any Immune would ever mistake a vamp for a human. And I daresay the same goes the other way.

That said, in the dim light of the stacks, my vampire seemed as close to human as one of his kind could probably ever get. The soft illumination suited him, and even his eyes seemed more natural in that setting. I realized then that it wasn't the physical sense of him that was so alluring but rather an air of enigma and individuality that made him seem so mature and self-assured. You didn't find that in Haven boys; they were too caught up in themselves, always trying to impress. My vampire, however, knew who he was and didn't need to convince anyone of it.

"May I?" he asked, holding out a hand.

At first I didn't know what he meant. Then I realized he wanted to see my mother's book. Glancing down at it, I instinctively tightened my grip, clinging to it possessively. But before I could open my mouth in protest, he had it in his hand, his movements so fast they were little more than a blur.

He held it lightly, indifferently, examining it with a casual regard, as if it meant nothing to him — though watching his eyes, the reality was clearly otherwise. He opened the journal and riffled through the pages in a way that made me certain he was already familiar with the contents.

"Words are powerful things," he said. "Sometimes quite dangerous." He looked up from the book, setting his eyes on me.

I was finding it difficult to breathe; for some reason, all I could think about was my father shaking hands with this man. Though it was crazy, and the sort of thing that would have scandalized Camille, I found myself wishing he'd touch me. I wanted to feel a vamp's skin, and the only thing that kept me from reaching out to him was the fear that the stories I'd heard about vamps while growing up would be proved true. Haven was rife with tales about how they were like the vampires in Bram Stoker's *Dracula*, how they didn't need to breathe and didn't have a pulse. They were the Undead, according to some — though it wasn't actually true that any of them had ever died and been resurrected. They'd all simply been infected with Gomorrah and transformed.

The vamp seemed to be waiting for me to speak, so at last I said, "Words are only dangerous to those who fear the truth."

The faintest of smiles tugged at his lips. "There are many shades of truth, Sophie."

I'd no idea how he knew my name, and at that moment I can't honestly say I cared. All that mattered was the way he said it — speaking as Paris might have spoken when describing Helen of Troy.

He reached out to me, brushing aside a lock of hair that had fallen across my forehead. For a moment he hesitated, then bent lower, closer, his face not far from mine. I could see the scar on his cheek clearly, the slight pucker of the flesh, oddly symmetrical, begging to be touched.

My eyes locked with his, and he moved his hand, caressing my cheek, his thumb brushing my lower lip. His palm was cool and pleasant feeling, not at all like a dead fish. As though driven by instinct, I leaned into it, closing my eyes, savoring the gentleness, not wanting it to end. It was almost hypnotic. I should have been afraid, but I wasn't.

"Sophie," he said again in that voice.

I felt things that left me confused.

Because he was a vamp.

Because I wasn't.

And then, just like that, the moment passed, and he stood over me, studying me, as though he wasn't quite sure what to make of me. As though he was trying hard to restrain himself.

Neither of us moved in the uncomfortable silence. Finally I said, "There isn't anything to be gained by lying." My words were a whisper, but I was surprised at how audacious I sounded. "They say the truth will set you free."

His face changed, his expression relaxing, and he laughed. Cynically. We both knew I wasn't talking about the book.

"They may say that," he said. "But what do *they* know?"

"So you don't agree?" I said.

"You've a great deal yet to learn about life." He glanced at the book in his hand. "You remind me of someone I once knew. She believed far too strongly in the truth as a means to an end. She thought it could be liberating, but more often than not it's simply another prison." He seemed stricken, as though haunted by a memory.

"I don't believe that."

"Of course you don't. But you will. One day you'll have to." For a moment the look in his eyes was reminiscent of my father's when he spoke of my mother. "When you've lived as long as I have, you realize there comes a point when you must shed your delusions and your ideals."

"As long as *you* have?" I said, almost laughing. "You're only a few —" I stopped short, realizing the mistake I'd made. He might appear to be barely eighteen years old — hardly older than I was —

but that was only because he looked the age he'd been at the time of his transformation. For all I knew, he might have been one of the first infected when the plague had struck in the early forties.

"You see," he said, smiling again, seeming more melancholy, "the truth isn't always so pretty."

I didn't know what to say. With my back still against the shelf of books, I eased myself to my feet, the palms of my hands sliding across textured spines. My knees felt weak, and my stomach was doing calisthenics. "Did you leave that book for me?" I asked.

"No."

"Do you know who did?"

"What makes you think someone left it for *you*?" There was an arrogance to his tone, accented by the slight rise of an eyebrow.

"Because —" But I halted, mouth ajar. I'd no real reply, other than to argue it could hardly be coincidence.

He turned and started to leave, walking a few steps toward the end of the aisle.

"Wait!" I called after him in a voice too loud for a library.

He paused in midstep and looked back, his eyebrow raised again, this time in query.

"How do you know who I am?"

At first he just grinned. But he didn't seem amused so much as sad. "I've known your father since before you were born," he said. "He's spoken of you often over the years."

It sounded reasonable, and yet I felt that even if he wasn't actually lying, he also wasn't telling me the entire truth.

I frowned at him. "Just who are you, really? What's your name?"

"Does it matter?"

"Is it a secret?" I countered, perhaps a little too boldly.

"Valentine," he said, as though it truly didn't matter. "I am Valentine."

"That's it? Just Valentine?"

"It's enough."

"Well, *Valentine*, I want my book back." I advanced a step and thrust out my hand expectantly, trying to look fierce and determined but not doing a very good job of it.

He glanced down at the journal he held. "I think not," he said, tucking it under his arm. "It isn't yours to have."

"I found it," I said with a flash of indignation.

"Surely you don't think that means it belongs to you?"

"If anyone has a right to it, I do." I didn't elaborate, though I'm not sure why.

"You're making assumptions. That's a dangerous thing to do."

I felt a spark of anger. "You have no right to take it!"

"I have more right than you can possibly imagine," he said, his voice lanced with pain. "For the moment I'll just hang onto it for safekeeping. You're not ready for what's in here." He patted the book. "Maybe you never will be. There are some truths better left unsaid, Sophie Harkness."

"Don't you think I should be the judge of that?"

"Not yet, I don't." He looked at me in the oddest way, as though with regret, but also with something that made me backpedal into the shelves behind me. Not from fear, but because I was sure I saw in him some reflection of the emotions running rampant in me.

"Soon you'll be a woman," he said.

"What does that have to do with it?"

"Your whole world will change. What's in this book would only complicate it unnecessarily."

With that he walked away, gone before I'd even taken another breath.

* * *

By the time I'd reached this point in my story, Camille and I had arrived at the beach house. As we let ourselves in, she looked at her watch and swore. "Hell's bells," she said. "I forgot about my date."

"Date?"

"Yeah." She shrugged and grinned sheepishly. "That cute guy at Del Cano's. Remember?"

I shook my head. "Not really. Does cute guy have a name?"

"Danny." Camille started toward the stairs, stopped, and looked back. "Maybe I should cancel."

"You? Cancel a date?" I feigned astonishment.

"I want to hear more about your vampire."

"We've plenty of time for that," I assured her. But really I was of two minds about continuing. Now that I'd started, a part of me wanted to finish. Mostly because I knew that if I thought about it too long I'd chicken out and not tell her just how far things had gone. On the other hand, the voice of reason kept telling me that would be a good thing. Maybe this was something I should keep to myself. After all, what if Camille inadvertently mentioned it to someone? To her parents, maybe. I shuddered at the prospect. They'd always been so kind to me — they were practically family — and I couldn't imagine what they'd think about me carrying on with a vamp.

"Hey, you should come," she said.

"On your date? No thanks. Three's a crowd and all that. Anyway, I have some reading I want to do."

"You sure?"

"Positive. My book and I will be fine."

We were going through the ritual we'd established over the years — Camille would ask, I'd refuse, she'd press a little, I'd make the appropriate noises, and then she'd run off, her conscience clear.

"You promise to tell me everything when I get back?" she said.

"Cross my heart." I made the motion with me hand.

Camille left to get dressed, happily humming to herself as she made her way upstairs.

While I waited for her to come back down, I sat at the kitchen counter, snacking on a sandwich and leafing through an old '40s issue of *LIFE* magazine. Camille had purchased it from a scavy at the local market, paying an outrageous sum for the thing, and I wasn't sure I could see the point. I always thought it eerie (and rather depressing) looking at these salvaged relics of a lost world — especially when you happened upon a picture of someone who'd become a vamp and realized that person didn't look any older now than when the picture had been taken decades before.

Of course, the magazine was just the tip of the iceberg when it came to this sort of thing. Haven was practically built on the remnants of the past. In the early days of the Republic, shiploads of scavengers had bravely ventured beyond the U-boat patrols to coastal cities like Sydney, Vancouver, and San Francisco. They'd brought back useful stuff — as much as their holds could contain — and that, along with the scrapped freighters and ocean liners on which the first Immunes had arrived, had helped lay the foundation for what too many of us now took for granted.

Salvage was less crucial to our survival these days. Now it was more about knickknacks and bric-a-brac: china, furniture, paintings, and old magazines, like the issue of *LIFE* I was looking at. There was a growing market for nostalgia, with people paying good money for anything that came from the pre-Fall era. But the risks were great, and only the most daring and foolhardy scavies still engaged in the practice.

After the Fall, the Third Reich had imposed severe limitations on our movements throughout the world, and going anywhere near the mainland was a violation of those restrictions. The only city Haven ships were actually permitted to sail to was New York City — which was why the Haven government frowned upon scavenging. But so long as there was profit to be made, the boats would go out — and they'd keep bringing back reminders of a world people like me could only ever experience vicariously. Personally, I thought that sometimes it was better to let sleeping dogs lie.

"So what do you think?" Camille asked as she swept into the kitchen some time later.

I looked up from a black-and-white still of a pre-vamp Rita Hayworth kneeling on a bed in a lace-trimmed silk nightgown. "Where on earth did you get that?" I asked, eyeing Camille up and down.

"It's one of Mom's." She struck a pose, arms flung up and wide, presenting herself and the dress in the best possible light. In her gown and slingbacks, she looked as though she could have stepped from the pages of that *LIFE* magazine. "I found it in the closet," she said, running her hands down the dress, over the swell of her hips. "These, too," she added, stroking the necklace of gold plates that draped flatteringly toward her bosom and fingering the dazzling earrings that matched.

"Good thing your mom's not here," I said. "She'd have a fit if she thought you were off clubbing in something that expensive. It must have cost her a whole month's clothing ration."

Camille shrugged. "She's probably completely forgotten about this stuff."

"Well, regardless, you look fantastic."

"Except my hands." She held them out before her, making a production of examining her fingers. "They still haven't recovered from all that potato picking we did for our Mandatory Labor Service."

I grimaced at my own recollections of that time. Everyone in Haven had to put in a stint with the MLS each year. For students it usually meant farmwork, which was why we'd been picking potatoes on South Island all of July.

"Our MLS was a month ago, Cam," I said. "You should have well and truly recovered by now. Besides, believe me, nobody's going to be looking at your hands."

That elicited a giggle of satisfaction.

I've always thought Camille resembled her mother to a remarkable degree, but never had she been more the spitting image of Amelia than in that moment. Younger, yes, but in a softer light you'd have had a hard time telling them apart. Of course, that was as far as the resemblance went — Camille had none of her mother's drive or ambition.

Amelia's father had been one of the first settlers in Haven and one of the architects of its constitution. His daughter had followed in his footsteps. She'd trained as a medical doctor (though she no longer practiced now that she was a member of the President's Council), and she was married to John Westerly, the owner of Island Transnational Shipping, Haven's largest transportation company.

Amelia was a powerful and influential figure in Haven politics and was always on the go — so much so that Camille would sometimes joke that we were both motherless. It was an exaggeration, because despite her busy schedule, Amelia had always been a caring and affectionate parent. Ever since kindergarten, when I'd first met Camille and she'd pronounced me her "best friend for life," Amelia had become a sort of substitute mother for me, occupying that blank space in my life that I'd desperately wanted filled. I'd become so comfortable with her and her husband that I'd long ago taken to referring to them as aunt and uncle — even though we weren't technically related. In actuality, we couldn't have been further from it. The Westerlys were one of the wealthiest families on the islands; the Wolstencroft and Harkness lines . . . not so much.

"We'll talk when I get back," Camille said as she turned and sashayed to the door. "And not just about that delicious vamp of yours." She gave me a saucy look and winked. "I've a surprise for you."

I didn't ask what it was; she was always foisting gifts on me. "You go have fun now," I said, meaning it.

Camille's eyes sparkled with mischief. "Oh, I intend to, darling." She blew me a kiss, and then she was gone, her laughter ringing in my ears.

CHAPTER 3

A FIGURE IN HIDING

They found her body on the beach. The edge of the surf had reached her, soaking her gown so that it clung to her flesh, making the thin layers of material almost transparent. The retreating water had clawed at the sand around her but hadn't had the strength to drag her into the sea. So there she lay, partly buried, her long blond hair fanned out around her head and grains of sand plastered against her exposed cheek. Her eyes were closed, and there was a peacefulness about her that made it appear as though she were asleep.

There were no overt signs of trauma, no immediate explanation for her death. No motive, either. She still wore her jewelry, and her handbag had been found nearby, loaded with cash and the even more valuable Ration Book.

Now I stood looking down at her, a dispassionate inspector beside me. Other police officers wandered about the crime scene, chatting in a clinical, emotionless fashion. I stood there in the sand and couldn't believe she was dead. I wanted to say, "Camille, wake up. Stop joking around."

The police had come pounding on the door a few minutes earlier, asking questions about her. They had roused me from sleep, and maybe I'd still been a bit fuzzy, because at first I hadn't really understood what was happening. But when the inspector had asked me to come and identify the body it hit me. I'd felt my legs buckling and thought I'd be sick. I hadn't wanted to go with them. I had wanted Camille to come in the door of the beach house and wake me from this nightmare and tell me all about her date with Danny.

After I'd identified Camille, the inspector and I went back to the house, and I sat in the living room near the windows that overlooked the beach. They questioned me. Rigorously. It was only natural, given that I'd been the only other person at the beach house. From their perspective, I was a suspect. And for the time being, one of the few they had.

As the daughter of a man who'd started his career as a cop, I had a pretty clear idea of where I stood. Unless the police found evidence to the contrary, I might soon be charged with murder. But that was the last thing on my mind as I watched the dozen or so officers milling around outside, circling Camille's lifeless body while a growing crowd of gawking spectators gathered to point and gossip behind a barrier that had been set up at the periphery of the beach.

I wanted the police to hurry up and finish with their forensic work so they could cover her up and take her away to somewhere she could rest with some dignity. I hated seeing my best friend like that. And I hated watching as the police photographer — along with the dozen or so reporters just outside the barricade — snapped photo after photo of her, flashbulbs going off like strokes of lightning. It horrified me to think that in the morning papers there'd be images of her like this for all of Haven to ogle. I kept imagining how terrible that would be for Aunt Amelia and Uncle John, and I wanted to phone them but I didn't have any idea what to say.

It was only when someone finally covered Camille with a sheet that it truly sank in — she was dead and gone forever. I broke down and wept hysterically until finally the onsite medical examiner gave me a sedative.

I slept and didn't awaken until the next morning, when the sun had risen and the crowds had melted away. The beach directly in front of the house was now deserted, save for a lone constable keeping watch over the strip of flashbulb-littered sand where Camille's body had been. I lay there on the settee, looking out to sea, dazed and disconsolate.

I was watching the waves when a plainclothes policeman stepped into view. A well-built man in his mid-forties with graying hair at the temples and a cynical cast to his eyes, he looked as though he'd witnessed a lot of life, and perhaps not the best parts of it. He reminded me of my father. Havershaw was his name; I remembered it from the night before. He had grilled me earlier — apparently not to his satisfaction.

"How are you feeling?" he asked.

I sat up slowly, unsteadily, still groggy from the sedative and a bit spent from my hysterics. I wondered what he expected me to say.

"I can call the doctor if you like," he offered.

"No," I said, waving the suggestion aside.

"I'd like to ask you a few more questions," said Havershaw. He walked over to where I was sitting, pulling a small notebook and pencil from the inside pocket of his rumpled gray jacket. He sat down in one of the armchairs opposite me, flipped open the notebook, and consulted the contents. "You've known Miss Westerly a long time," he said, without looking up.

"Yes."

"Forgive my saying so, but the two of you don't seem likely friends."

"I don't."

He looked up from the notebook, visibly puzzled. "I beg your pardon?"

"I don't forgive you for saying so," I said, glaring at him.

Havershaw didn't say anything, just scribbled in his damned notebook. "Was money ever an issue between the two of you?" he asked.

"What? No. Never."

"Boys?"

"No! Of course not."

"No need to get upset."

I glared at him even more fiercely, but he ignored me. "Are we through?" I asked.

Havershaw sighed, lowered the notebook. "I'm just trying to do my job, Miss Harkness."

"Then do it better. While you're wasting time with me, there's a killer out there roaming the streets."

"We're combing the area for possible suspects."

"Sure you are."

More scribbling in the notebook.

"Am I under arrest?" I asked.

He cocked an eyebrow and a grin flirted with his lips. "Should you be?"

I sat there, staring balefully back at him.

Finally he broke my gaze. "You know Miss Westerly's parents?"

"Yes."

"Know them well?"

"Very. They're like family. But what does that have to do with Camille's murder?"

"We don't know for certain it was a murder," Havershaw said. "We won't until the autopsy is complete. I'm just trying to get a broader picture of things."

"Look, if you feel so strongly about me as a suspect —"

He held up a hand to silence me. "I imagine it would cause quite the scandal were I to throw you in the nick on a hunch. I'm quite familiar with the fact that your father is the former chief of the PSS."

"My father isn't the man you think him to be, Inspector."

"I'm sure he still carries considerable influence in the halls of power."

"He's sick," I snapped. "Some sort of dementia. They think maybe early onset Alzheimer's. He lives in Clarkson now." It was out of my mouth before I'd actually thought it through. That was private information I'd kept close to me — a secret I'd only ever shared with Val and Camille. And now Camille had taken it to her grave.

Havershaw's face had blanched, and if I'd made him uncomfortable I was glad. "I'm sorry to hear that," he said.

"Not as sorry as I am."

"When?" he asked.

I almost said, "It's none of your damn business," but caught myself. "Not long ago," I told him. "It was very sudden." It had seemed to happen almost overnight — though maybe there'd been signs I'd overlooked because of the distance that had grown between us.

"That would explain the early retirement," Havershaw muttered, more to himself than to me. He jotted something down in his notebook.

"Given the circumstances, I think you'll agree he's beyond influencing anyone — not that he'd ever have used his position in that way regardless."

And maybe he'd have just let me rot in jail, I thought — especially after what had happened a year ago, when he'd found out about Val and me. It still hurt to think about it. That had been the worst argument we'd ever had. In many respects, it was the last one we'd ever had.

* * *

"You're just like your mother!" Father had shouted at me that day.

The way he'd said it, there was no mistaking that he didn't mean it in a good way. I didn't have a clue what all that was about, and at the time I didn't care. I was too intent on having it out with him. We'd engaged in a no-holds-barred, knock-down, drag-out row after that, until I'd finally had enough of the yelling and stormed out of the house to go stay with Camille.

It was never the same between us after that. Father hadn't trusted me, and I hadn't been able to understand him.

When I returned home a week later, we picked up where we'd left off, railing against one another, shouting till we were blue in the face. God knows what the neighbors must have thought of it all.

"You know him," I said at one point, meaning Val. "You've worked with him. You know he's not a Nazi."

"I couldn't care less about *that.*"

I blinked and stared at him in disbelief. "I never thought you'd be so narrow-minded and prejudiced."

"Have you gone mad?" Father said, his whole body tense with rage. "Have you not given this any thought, Sophie? Don't you know where you are? Look around you. No one will ever accept this. *No one.*"

"It's not illegal."

"That doesn't make it right!"

"I'm not ending it," I said, defiant. "It's my life."

"You're sixteen years old! You don't have the first clue about life."

"And what do you know about it, Dad?" I sneered. "Just your goddamn job, is what!"

That stung him, but all he said was, "There can be no future with him, Sophie. Not here."

"Then maybe we'll go there."

"Don't be an idiot."

"It was obviously a mistake to come back here," I said. "I should have stayed with Camille."

With that, I turned and stormed toward my bedroom, my thoughts all messed up. *Maybe I'll just run away or something*, I mused. *Maybe go live with Camille forever.*

Of course I completely ignored the impracticalities of such an idea, not least of which being that Father would never let it happen. I had nearly a year until I could legally be free of him, which meant I was stuck with him, whether I liked it or not.

"Please," Father begged, calling after me. "You have to end this. It'll never come to any good. Trust me when I say that he'll only bring you pain."

I stopped and whirled around to face him, rage and a deep hurt boiling inside me. "Well, guess what, Dad, you've got a head start on him."

And that was that. Father could have forbidden me to see Val, and I could have threatened to leave for good, but in the end we both knew that neither was going to happen. So we settled into an uneasy armistice, the two of us pretending like none of it had ever happened.

But it was a sham. We lived in the same house, but it was as though we were strangers orbiting one another from a distance, never able to overcome the forces steadily pushing us further and further apart.

I couldn't understand how a relationship could sour so quickly and so utterly. My father turned to the bottle; I, on the other hand, got more wrapped up in Val, even as I became increasingly conscious that that, of course, was the root of it all — we'd ruined everything, my vampire and I.

It was all downhill from there. Maybe it even contributed to my father's illness. And that made it all the more untenable, because it meant I was at least partly to blame. It's never easy living with the knowledge that you've so thoroughly destroyed someone you love so profoundly.

I should have ended it with Val. I knew it, even then. But I couldn't. And it wasn't just that I didn't want to. I knew that I loved him, but it was more than that. At times I almost had this sense of him being a sort of sickness, an addiction — though perhaps that's an oversimplification of something that was far more complicated. Too complicated for me to really understand.

What I did know was that there were moments when I was certain that even if our histories had taken different paths, eventually and inevitably they'd have converged. It brought to mind one of my grandmother's pearls of wisdom: "Some things are just meant to be, and no matter what we do to avoid them, they'll come to pass. The Universe has a plan, and we simply don't have the power to overcome it."

* * *

"Miss Harkness?"

I started and looked up. Havershaw was eyeing me curiously. I'd obviously been lost in my memories for quite some time.

"I have something I'd like you to look at," the inspector said. He dug into one of the large side pockets of his jacket and pulled out some glossy black-and-white photos. He handed them across to me.

"What am I supposed to be looking for?" I asked as I glanced at the first of them. Relief rushed through me when I saw they were only shots of the crowd that had gathered near the crime scene the night before.

"Just keep looking."

I shuffled the top picture to the back of the pile and looked at the next one. More of the same but showing a different group of people. I stared at the image, scanning faces. "I don't recognize them," I said.

The photos were all basically alike: snaps of the perimeter of the crime scene, most of them with dozens of people pushed up close to the barricade. I was about to toss them aside when I saw what I was sure Havershaw wanted me to see — a man standing apart from the rest of the crowd, lurking in the background, almost hidden by shadows. And though I couldn't see the details of his face, I knew he was a vamp. And I knew which one. In Haven there were few possibilities — and only one who was comfortable enough to be out and about like that.

I must have gasped, for Havershaw's eyes gleamed, and he leaned forward in his chair. "Someone you know?"

I didn't answer.

"Is it someone you know, Miss Harkness?" This time, his tone was far more commanding.

"Yes," I said, the word scarcely audible.

"What do you suppose he was doing here?"

I shook my head. "I've no idea."

That was the truth. I hadn't seen Valentine all summer. It wasn't like our relationship had ever been normal. We had no rhythm, no routine; we came together when opportunity struck. It was Haven, after all, and we couldn't exactly be open about things. In that respect my father had certainly been right. Besides, Val was always off somewhere, flying to New York or Berlin without warning. "Embassy business," he'd say.

Shortly before my summer vacation had started, he'd left abruptly, dashing all hope we'd had of spending a few weeks together. It had been a bitter disappointment. "Can't be helped," Val had said. "There's something I have to attend to in New York. But you'll be the first to know when I get back."

Apparently not, I thought. Seeing him in the photo was definitely a shock. I felt a little miffed that he hadn't bothered to get in touch with me, because I'd given him the number of the beach house phone before he left and had made sure to tell him where I'd be.

"Look at these," Havershaw said, producing a second batch of pictures.

I froze when I saw the first one. I didn't need to ask where they'd been taken; I remembered that night as though it had been yesterday.

I felt Havershaw's eyes on me. "Why are you showing me these?" I asked.

"The next photo," he said, by way of an answer.

I slid the first behind the rest and stared at the second in the pile, my heart beating faster. The image showed Val and my father talking in the rain, almost exactly as I'd seen them nearly four years ago on the night of the alleyway murder.

"It's the same vamp," said Havershaw. "Curious, don't you think?"

"No, I don't." I tried to sound indifferent. "He's the liaison officer for the Third Reich. He's really the only one of them who goes outside the Embassy grounds with any regularity. I'm sure he's been to a lot of places in Haven. It's his job."

"Hmmm."

I looked up at Havershaw, a tremor passing through me. "I'm not sure where all this is leading," I said as calmly as I could.

"Don't you? You don't think it's strange a vamp would be present at two local murders? We don't have a lot of homicides in Haven, and I don't recall the vamps taking an interest in any of them. Except these two."

"I'm sure I don't have an explanation." And I didn't, though I sure as hell wanted to get one from Val. "Maybe you should talk to the vamp."

Havershaw sat back and chuckled drily. "I don't suppose I'd get a straight answer. And since he has diplomatic immunity, there's no way I can press the matter. You, on the other hand, Miss Harkness . . ." He smiled darkly. "Upon you I can bring the full weight of the law."

"It's not a crime to associate with a vampire," I said. But I knew it might as well be. That's what Father had been trying to get into my head, and I only needed to think of my grandmother's antipathy toward vamps to know what people would think of me and Val. The older generation pretty much despised the Undead, and though some members of the younger set were a bit more open, I don't think even they would ever approve a match between a human and a vamp.

"No, it isn't a crime," Havershaw agreed. "Unless, of course, the vampire you associate with has been engaged in a felony and you happen to be aware of it."

I couldn't hide my shock. "You think he had something to do with Camille's death?"

"Let's just say I'm curious to know why he'd be hanging around the scene of the crime . . . on *both* occasions."

"You can't seriously think Camille's death and a murder that took place nearly four years ago are connected."

"They are by the very fact of his presence, Miss Harkness. That's enough to pique my interest."

"My father called him to that murder scene in the alley. And the fact that he's here now . . . well that's just a coincidence."

"We'll see."

I put the photos down beside the others on the coffee table. "I'm not feeling well." It wasn't altogether untrue. I wanted to get out of this house and back home. Back to where I could try to forget about Coral Beach and what had happened here. I felt as though I were drowning, and the harder I struggled to come to grips with what had happened, the deeper I sank.

Havershaw gathered the photos up and slipped them back into his pocket. "I'll call the doctor."

"I just want to go home," I said, my voice breaking. I sounded like a little girl, and suddenly I was crying. It was all too much. Camille's death, Val being here, the inspector and his stupid questions and veiled insinuations, and the realization I was alone, that my best friend was gone forever.

Havershaw handed me a handkerchief and rose to his feet, flipped the notebook closed, and put it in his inside pocket. "We can continue this another time," he said. "When you're feeling more up to it."

I nodded, wiping at my eyes, just wanting him to go away and leave me alone.

"I'm posting a couple of uniforms outside," he continued. "For your safety." With that he turned and made his way to the front door. "Good day, Miss Harkness. I'll be in touch."

And then he was gone, and I was alone in that empty beach house, the echoes of Camille all around me.

CHAPTER 4
CAELO

Speaking to Camille's parents was one of the most difficult things I'd ever done. I was grateful it was a quick conversation. They said all the right things, of course. Aunt Amelia told me how much I'd meant to Camille and thanked me for being such a good friend to her daughter. Uncle John assured me he'd make certain the police understood I couldn't possibly have had anything to do with the murder. He said he'd even get me a lawyer if necessary.

I thanked them and told them I'd see them at the funeral. But as I hung up the phone, I couldn't shake the feeling that something wasn't quite right about them. They'd sounded rather mechanical, as though they'd rehearsed it all.

In the end I dismissed it, not wanting to read too much into it. They'd just lost their daughter, after all; of course they'd sounded a little off.

Havershaw had decided it was safe to let me go home. Not much of a gamble on his part, given the nature of Haven. It wasn't like I could just up and leave for some other part of the world. It was all vamps outside of the islands, and besides, a flight to somewhere like New York, or Paris, or London, where the vamps accepted a few Immune tourists, cost a lot more than I could ever afford.

With the official okay to depart, I hurriedly packed my things, and by nine o'clock I was out the door. I wanted to get away from the beach house and back to the comfort and familiarity of my flat. When my father had taken ill, my grandmother had pushed for me to come live with her, but that had been out of the question. As much as I cared about Grace, we were fire and ice, oil and water. A few weeks of living together and I'm pretty sure we'd have been at each other's throats. I had tried staying on in my father's house — the only place I'd ever known as home — but after a few weeks it just hadn't felt right. I'd quickly been consumed by the need to get away from it and put it behind me. Too much bad karma there, I guess. Or just too many memories — good *and* bad — to haunt me.

In the end, after a great deal of argument, Grace had reluctantly relented and let me sell the house, and I'd moved into a third-floor flat near Haeden University. The proceeds from the sale went into trust for me, a monthly stipend that helped pay my rent and cover the cost of food and other essentials.

It was a cozy arrangement for me and had made me feel more independent than I'd ever felt before. I liked it. I liked it a lot. Maybe even more so because Camille had envied it; Amelia would never have let her be on her own at seventeen. But I have to admit that I also sometimes felt guilty knowing it had come at the expense of my father.

A police electric carried me from the beach house to the train station, a short drive that seemed to last an eternity. The whole way there I had the uncomfortable feeling the two officers accompanying me were more than just escorts.

Havershaw's doing, I thought. I wondered if this was how it'd be for the foreseeable future — until, at least, he had his pound of flesh.

The police watched me right into the station, and I was glad to get lost amongst the crowds and be beyond their scrutiny. I was catching an earlier train than I'd been booked for, however, so I had to use a coupon from my RB — my Ration Book — to pay the processing penalty for having my departure bumped up. I hated doing it, because it meant having to skimp on something else later on. But I really wanted to get home and decided that going without a meal or having to walk to school wasn't such a high price to pay.

When I went out onto the station platform a few minutes later, I found it crowded with teenagers my age, all awaiting the arrival of the ten o'clock to Caelo. Camille's absence loomed large as I observed the girls and boys lollygagging in groups, chatting excitedly about their holidays and laughing breezily.

I drew back into the shadows, putting distance between us as I ambled toward the newsstand. It was a big mistake. The first thing I saw was the headline on the *Coral Beach Gazette*, boldly proclaiming the murder of the Westerly heiress. There was a grainy black-and-white photo of the crime scene right on the cover, Camille's body exposed to gawkers while the police photographer did his bit. The *Caelo Times* and the *Haven Chronicle* were just as bad. I shuddered and turned away, feeling like I wanted to throw up and fighting hard not to cry.

The train couldn't come soon enough, and when the battered and aging electric rolled into the station, I dashed for the nearest door and scrambled aboard. I found my seat and settled in by the window, closing my eyes in relief, glad to be on my way.

A few minutes later we departed, the sounds of the electric a hypnotic symphony as we rolled along the tracks, threatening to lull me to sleep. I made an effort to read for a while, but the harder I tried to concentrate, the more my mind focused on the very thing I was trying not to think about — Havershaw's suspicions and the pictures of Val.

At last I gave up and put my book aside, staring out the window and watching as sugarcane gave way to scrub and rock as we neared the southern coast of North Island. Within minutes we crossed Union Bridge, a long span that seemed to leap across the Narrows, joining North Island to Central Island.

I pressed my face to the window and looked down past the web of trestles, staring into the foaming, rocky ribbon of turbulent sea that separated the two islands. The Pacific spread far and wide to the east and west, the distant horizons sharp lines etched against a perfect sky. Beyond one lay what had once been the Americas; beyond the other, Australia and Asia. All now desolate — except for New York City, the only enclave of the Third Reich that existed outside of Europe.

I turned my gaze away, focused forward, and moments later Central Island spread before us. The Blue Mountains rose in the distance, dominating the center of the island, their slopes shaded by forest and jungle. The electric line turned east, and the train rumbled along in the direction of the small coastal town of Peele.

We were still a ways from Caelo when the lights overhead flickered and died. The whine of the electric motors faded away, and the train ground to a halt. A collective groan went up from the passengers.

"Bloody blackouts," someone seated in front of me cursed. "This is the second one today."

"Sorry for the inconvenience, folks," the conductor said as he came down the aisle. "I'm sure it'll only be a few minutes. If it gets too stuffy, you can open the windows."

More groans.

We'd come to a stop in the middle of a field, and there was nothing around us but pasture, a flock of grazing sheep, and a wind farm to the north. I stared at the windmills, at the filigree of their derrick-like towers and the rusty blades that whirled in an almost poetic symmetry, generating thousands of kilowatts of hydro for the city while just a few miles away we sat here without so much as a spark. Talk about irony.

I couldn't recall a single day of my entire life in Haven that hadn't been marked by blackouts and brownouts. The government was always saying that the demand for hydro on the islands had exceeded generating capacity and that we needed to conserve. But on a hot day like today, with fans going and the wealthy using their air conditioners, blackouts were inevitable — regardless of the strict rationing.

I leaned my head against the window, and in the warm sunshine my thoughts drifted. I was transported back to a moment between Val and me that had occurred more than a year and a half ago . . . a moment that had changed the context of our relationship forever.

* * *

It was quite a while after our meeting in the library that I began seeing Val with increasing regularity. It took time and a lot of effort on my part, but eventually it seemed he was as drawn to me as I was to him — although initially I'm not sure it was for the same reasons.

I quickly acquired the ability to fool my father and grandmother into believing I was locked away in my room, industriously engaged in schoolwork or some equally innocuous enterprise. And when it wasn't safe to use that ploy I would just tell them I was going to a friend's or to the library.

Val seldom had trouble finding me, no matter what out-of-the-way place I chose for our rendezvous. "I could track you by your scent," he once joked. "Everyone has a unique smell."

"Do vamps?" I asked.

"Yes. But vamps and humans smell distinctly different."

"Different in what way?"

"For vamps the Immune scent is rather unpleasant."

"Are you saying I stink?" The idea that I might smell revolting to him was mortifying to me.

Val just laughed. "I have never found your scent to be anything other than intoxicating," he said.

"So what? You're saying I'm different?"

"Haven't I always?"

I never pursued the matter after that, but I wasn't sure he'd been telling me the truth. After all, I was an Immune, he was a vamp, and if all Immunes smelt unpleasant to vamps, it followed that my scent must be disagreeable to him. It made me terribly self-conscious, and for a while I took to wearing perfume — a lot of it — until finally he begged me to stop.

"It's overpowering," he complained.

"I don't want you turned off by my smell." Even talking about it made me want to go scrub myself with scented soap.

"I told you, I'm not. I love the scent of you."

I let it rest, and eventually I forgot about it. It certainly never became an issue, even when our relationship grew decidedly more physical and intimate.

Whenever we met in those early days, it was usually after sunset and always away from the public eye. We weren't oblivious to the dangers of our relationship — the same ones my father would later drive home in the argument that split us apart. Val and I were both well aware that a vamp consorting with an Immune girl was anathema to pretty much everyone in Haven. Sure, it might not be illegal, but history and long decades of prejudice made it — in the eyes of many — immoral and treasonous.

Val was never anything other than a gentleman, and for the longest time all he ever did was sit with me and talk and listen. Usually I did the talking, and he did the listening. It seemed to be an arrangement that satisfied him, but as I got older, I found that I wanted more from him than mere friendship.

The night we met in the park near Haeden University I'd decided it was time to push the boundaries of our relationship. I'd just come from the birthday party Camille had thrown for me, and I was feeling like I'd made an important transition in my life.

"I'm sixteen today, Val," I began. "And I —"

"Sixteen," he said, shaking his head. "That used to be such an important milestone in one's life."

"It still is, but the really big one's next year."

"Ah, yes, when Haven officially recognizes you as a woman."

"I'm a woman now," I said indignantly. "And that's not what I want to talk about, anyway."

"Oh? And what is it you wish to discuss?"

"I want to know . . ." I hesitated.

"What?"

"It's just that we've been meeting regularly for more than a year, and I feel like you're still an enigma. I want to know more about you. I want to feel we're going somewhere."

"Going somewhere?" Val angled an eyebrow, regarding me quizzically.

"You know? This. Us."

I felt myself beginning to blush and realized that for as much as I'd fantasized about us being a couple, it was quite another thing to have it be a reality. I'd reached a point where I couldn't bear the thought of him not being in my life, yet I worried that if I pushed things too far too quickly it would ruin everything. I wasn't even sure he came anywhere close to feeling for me what I felt for him.

Needless to say, this was all new territory for me. Most girls I knew had someone they could turn to for advice when it came to the whole boy-girl thing: an older sister, a close friend, a mother. But I had no older sister, I wasn't about to admit any of this to Camille, and if my mother had been alive I was pretty sure she'd have been just as shocked and disapproving as anyone else in Haven. After all, my situation was hardly normal.

"You think I'm an enigma," Val said, ignoring the rest of my words. He chuckled and shook his head. "It sounds very mysterious."

"Well, you are. All I know about you is that you're a vamp, that you work for the Nazis, and that you have a home in New York."

He shrugged. "What more do you need?"

I gave him a blunt stare. "You're kidding, right? How about where you were born and what you did before —"

"I wouldn't want to give you nightmares," he interrupted.

"Don't joke."

"I'm not." And there was that look in his eyes, the one I'd first seen in the library, that sadness that made me want to wrap him in my arms and console him.

"Look, you don't have to worry about turning me off or anything. I know all about how vamps used to drink human blood. It doesn't bother me."

That wasn't completely true; it was more like I chose to pretend it had never happened. And the truth was, the whole idea of Val drinking blood — *any* blood — was the one aspect of our relationship that still troubled me. Sure it might be animal blood vamps drank these days, but it remained unsettling all the same and more than a little gut-wrenching if you gave it too much thought — which I tried my hardest not to.

Still, you couldn't ignore the fact that until all the non-Immunes in existence had been wiped from the face of the earth, vamps had preyed on them for their blood. The Undead had only resorted to animals — mostly livestock — out of necessity. Blood was their sole sustenance, and it had to come from somewhere. Given that they couldn't drink Immune blood and non-Immune humans hadn't existed on the planet since the end of the war, that left animals as the only viable alternative. The Third Reich raised cows and pigs by the tens of millions.

"Remember what I told you about the truth, Sophie," Val warned. There was something disconcerting in his expression, and I wondered if it was because he felt ashamed of that whole drinking-human-blood episode of vamp history.

"I'm not afraid to know the truth," I said.

"Maybe I'm afraid to tell it."

"Please," I begged, slipping my hand into his. "As a birthday gift." We'd rarely made physical contact up to that point, and there'd been plenty of times when I'd wondered why. What was holding him back? It certainly couldn't have been because of any signals I was sending. "If our relationship is going to get serious . . ."

"Whoa!" Val gently extracted his hand from mine. "Sophie —"

"Is it me? Aren't you attracted to me?"

"It's not that at all. Far from it. But . . ."

"But what?"

"You know the world we live in. There's no place for that kind of relationship."

"The world doesn't have to stay the same, Val."

He laughed softly at that. "It's refreshing to know there's someone in this day and age who can see the possibility of better things. I suppose if anyone could change things, it would be you."

I was sure he was teasing me. "Yeah. Right," I'd said. "I'll just go get myself elected president."

"I wasn't being facetious, Sophie. You're quite . . . extraordinary. You just don't realize it."

I blushed and said, "Well, if I'm going to change the world, I can start here."

Val smiled forlornly. "How exactly do you propose to do that?"

"One step at a time." I gave him a telling look and put my hand on his again.

"I am what I am, Sophie. And you . . ." He turned his head and peered off into the distance. "Well, maybe you're just too optimistic."

"So you don't believe this can go anywhere?" I said, feeling hurt.

"I didn't say that. I'm just trying to be realistic. I'm trying to do the right thing."

"Then what are you saying? That you want to end it?"

Val jerked, startled. "No. Of course not. But . . ."

"But what? What is it that's holding you back? Just tell me already."

"I wish it were that simple. But you and I, Sophie, we're complicated."

"We don't have to be."

"Don't you see? I have a past, and you're only beginning to make one."

"I don't care about that."

"I'm not sure you'd say that if you knew the things I've done. The sins of our pasts cast long shadows, Sophie. And sometimes it's impossible to get out from under them. All too often they can darken the lives of others."

"Sometimes shining a little light sheds a new perspective."

Val shook his head. "I don't think so. Not in this case."

"You won't know unless you tell me."

If vamps had been inclined to sigh, I'm certain he would have. "Oh, Sophie, you can't even begin to imagine . . ."

We sat in silence for a moment or two, Val staring across the park, studying the domed edifice of Haeden's library, the Margollieau Camera. Finally, as though he were talking about someone else, he said, "I was born Vladimir Arghezi. My grandparents were immigrants from the Ukraine who settled on a farm not far from a city called Regina."

"Where was that?"

"Before the Fall it was a city in a country called Canada. Out on the prairies, in a province called Saskatchewan." He flashed a grin. "You should take your history and geography lessons a bit more seriously."

"Hey!" I gave him a playful punch to the shoulder. "I'm an A student, I'll have you know."

Val raised his eyebrows. "I suppose there wouldn't be much point in teaching you about the parts of a world that have long been dead."

"I know where Canada used to be," I said imperiously. "It was just that Saska-whatchamacallit that tripped me up."

"Saskatchewan," he said again.

"Right." I repeated the word, letting it roll off my tongue. "I'm sure I've heard of it." I tried to recall exactly where. And then it struck me — that was where Grace was from.

I contemplated asking Val if he'd known her, then realized how ridiculous that was. What were the chances? After all, Haven wasn't very large, and most people here had only a small circle of friends. If you asked a random person in Easthaven if they knew a particular person in Caelo, it was highly unlikely they would.

"I would have been a farmer," Val continued, "but the war broke out, and I was eager to be a part of it. I wanted to fight the Nazis and end Hitler's tyranny. Of course, my parents wouldn't hear of it. I was only seventeen, for one thing. And my older brother had been injured in a farming accident a year before, so they wanted me around to help out. But I was determined. I borrowed my brother's birth certificate and lied my way into the army." The tones of his voice grew warmer, richer, more emotionally charged with the memory.

"They were happy to have bodies, because things weren't going well. The Russians were taking heavy losses on the Eastern Front and wanted the Allies to open another in the west. So a guy named Mountbatten came up with this idea for an assault. Test the Nazi defenses, I suppose. I got to England just in time to be part of the force sent over to Dieppe, on the coast of France. I shouldn't have even been there. I was the greenest of the green and hadn't trained like the rest of them, but they sent me over because I could speak German and French. Fortunately I knew how to use a gun, and I could carry more than my fair share of supplies, so I ended up on a boat crossing the English Channel. There were about five thousand of us Canadians, and the remaining thousand or so were mostly Brits. I remember it as though it were yesterday. That's one of the curses of being a vamp: you can never forget anything. Not even the things you wish you could." His expression gave me the sense that there was a lot he wished he could.

"It was August 19, 1942," Val continued, his voice cracking. "We started the assault at five in the morning." He shuddered, and I almost told him to stop, to forget it, that it was too emotionally taxing. But I didn't, because a part of me knew that if I didn't get it from him now, I never would.

"That was the first time," he said.

"The first time you saw combat?"

"No." He closed his eyes, clenched his jaw. "The first time I tasted human blood. I had stepped out of the landing craft and slipped on the stones. I fell face first into shallow water. The guy ahead of me had been shot through the head, and there was this red stain spreading out from him. Waves washed it into my mouth, and I couldn't help swallowing. I was too scared to think about it much. There was chaos all around. Machine guns firing, men screaming and falling, mortars turning the rocks on the beach into shrapnel. And the tanks were getting bogged down, stuck on the rounded pebbles and stones.

"Someone grabbed me by the scruff of the neck and hauled me ashore. He dragged me to the seawall, where about a dozen others were already crouched, and I just huddled there, scared out of my wits, thinking that any minute I was going to die. I watched others trying to make it ashore, most cut to ribbons the moment they left the landing craft. A few made it as far as the beach, but they got pinned down or shot.

"We heard one of our tanks rolling along above. When it got close enough, the lot of us scrambled up over the seawall and ran through a hail of bullets. I watched men to the left and right of me ripped to shreds, blood everywhere. Ahead of me was a machine gun nest, and without really thinking, I tossed a grenade into it."

He paused and put his hand to his cheek, fingertips tracing the outline of the scar. "That's when I got this. A piece of shrapnel from the blast. I should have been dead, but somehow I escaped the worst of it. The German soldiers manning that nest weren't so lucky. Those were the first two people I killed." His tone clearly suggested they were far from the last.

I gestured toward the scar. "I thought vampires just sort of . . ."

"Regenerated?" He shrugged. "This happened *before* my transformation. While blood is a restorative, it won't heal or erase all wounds. Even less so with the animal blood we feed on now."

Sickened, I turned away for a moment, hiding the look on my face.

"About six hours later it was all over." Val's voice was so faint at that point that I had to strain to hear it against the traffic. "Some managed to make it back to England, but there were a lot who died or were taken captive. I spent the rest of my war in a German prisoner-of-war camp called Stalag VIII-B."

"So you were there when they unleashed Gomorrah."

"Yes. The Nazis experimented on POWs and the Jews in the concentration camps. But there was an outbreak of flu in the camps at the time, and that was the beginning of the Fall. Gomorrah was a mutation of the original virus they'd injected us with. The flu virus somehow combined with the original virus and became airborne. After that it spread like wildfire."

Val's face was drawn. "I had thought Dieppe was a horror of inhuman senselessness, but it was nothing compared with what followed. The only reason everything was saved from becoming a total nightmare was that Hitler and most of the Nazi hierarchy were transformed." He looked askance at me. "A cruel irony, don't you think? They managed to maintain control and became more ruthless than ever. They were among the closest to ground zero, so they were part of the first wave to be turned. That gave them time to get reorganized. When people started hunting vamps down, the Nazis used the chaos to their advantage. They swept through Europe, quickly seizing command because that was really the only viable power structure amid the mayhem. Then they moved on to Russia and Britain and the Middle East."

"When did you . . ." I started to ask.

He wiped his face with a shaky hand. "I didn't join them right away. I'm not a Nazi, Sophie. Truth to tell, few vamps are. But you have to realize that in the end there was nowhere else for us to go. The Immunes were hell-bent on killing all vamps. It didn't matter that many of us had been on their side and that we'd still have fought with them against Hitler. We were the enemy now. We were monsters. And we had to be destroyed.

"I tried to escape. I wanted to get back home, get back to people who knew me. There was a girl I'd left behind . . . we were going to get married."

At that, I tensed, overcome by the oddest sensation. At first I wasn't sure what it was but then realized it might actually be jealousy.

"I wanted to find her," he continued. "I wanted to see if she was all right. It was crazy, of course. Tens of millions had already died in North America, and more were falling every day. The chances of me finding her . . . of her still being alive . . ." Val closed his eyes and pinched the bridge of his nose. "The madness was even more intense back home, because the Nazis hadn't arrived yet."

He looked sidelong at me, ran a hand over his hair, then arched his neck and closed his eyes again, as though marshaling his thoughts.

"There were others who wanted to get back, so we joined forces, found a ship, and took off for home. I arrived back in a country that didn't want me; a country that didn't want any of those who'd been changed. They were terrified of us and did their best to destroy us. In most cases they succeeded. Even as we steamed into Halifax, they firebombed the ship. I barely made it off, and most of the others didn't. I heard later they were doing this everywhere. In New York they were herding infected people into subways and setting them on fire. In some cases they just bombed entire towns until there was nothing but ash and dust."

I shuddered at the images. There wasn't a lot about *that* in the history books. Mostly it was about the valiant resistance Immunes had put up, about how we'd overcome overwhelming odds and forced a peace on the vamps, and what a glorious thing it was that we'd saved humanity by creating the Republic of Haven.

This was probably the first time I ever truly considered the possibility that not all vamps were diehard Nazis. In Haven we were inclined to convince ourselves they were all the same. It was easier that way; easier to justify the past and to continue our enmity toward them. The more inhuman you make your enemy, the easier it is to stand against him. But after spending a bit of time with Val, I was beginning to question all that.

"When the Nazis arrived and bludgeoned North America into submission, there really wasn't much left," Val said, rousing me from my thoughts. "Most of the cities were rubble, and most of the transformed had migrated to New York, which was one of the few places still relatively intact. By that point it seemed easiest to let Hitler and his bunch take control. They offered a chance for some sort of normality. Law and order. Protection. Work." He wore a look of resignation as he glanced at me.

"I never knew it was so bad," I said. But that wasn't completely true. I'd heard accounts from the Immune side of the equation, from my grandmother's perspective. The terror; the Nazi concentration camps in Alberta and Montana; the long train ride to Vancouver; the moment they'd thought they were going to be executed, only to find the vamps were shipping them out in boats to some remote Pacific archipelago on the equator — what eventually would become Haven. But Grace had always made her tales epic and heroic; they'd been grand adventures on a massive scale. They'd never seemed quite as real as what I'd just heard from Val.

"You think what I've told you was the bad part?" he said.

I looked at him, waiting for him to elaborate, not pressuring him.

"There are things I had to do," he said, his voice tight. "Things I did to survive . . ."

Val paused, clearly somewhere else, remembering something awful. And even though I suspected what, I didn't want him to tell me. I wanted to pretend none of that had ever happened. I thought back to that encounter in the library, when I'd found the book and he had told me there were some truths better left unsaid — a warning he had reiterated only minutes ago.

"That's all in the past," I told him, trying to make my words sound genuine.

"That doesn't mean it didn't happen." He bowed his head, staring sightlessly at the ground. "At least I can be thankful vamps don't really sleep, otherwise my dreams would always be nightmares." He flicked a look in my direction. "There's a reason they call us monsters."

I touched his arm. "You're not."

Val laughed, but there was no mirth in it. "Have you ever thought about what I am? I mean, truly thought about it, Sophie?"

I didn't tell him that there were times in the past when I'd thought of nothing else. I had thought about what he was and what that meant for us. We came from different worlds, and there was no denying that in mine he'd never truly be accepted. And even if we could get past that issue, there was another truth — Val would live forever but never appear to age. I'd continue to grow older, and although it wouldn't make a lot of difference at first, over time it would become an unbridgeable gulf.

I shuddered inwardly and pushed the thought from my mind. I refused to believe we couldn't have a future together. When you loved someone there always had to be a way.

"I don't care what you are," I said. Those words didn't come out as easily as they should have. I could tell myself it didn't make any difference, but the fact was that right then and there, it was almost impossible to look at Val and be with him and *not* think on some level about what he'd become and the things he might have done.

"You're unusual," he said.

"I'll take that as a compliment."

He cracked a grin. "Yes, you would. It's what I love about you."

"Ah, so you do love me."

He didn't answer, but I didn't need him to.

"So what's the problem? Kiss me, already." It just came out, shocking me as much as Val. But I said it because I wanted to take his mind off the horrors of his past and distract myself from dwelling on them. And because I was afraid that if we didn't do it now we never would. All that baggage would get in the way, and it would never happen.

I sat there, my heart fluttering, and began to regret my impulsiveness. I wasn't sure what to expect if he actually did it. It struck me that it was a giant leap. We would be going from mere friendship into a whole other dimension. It would be crossing a line, and once we went that far, there could be no going back. We could never be the same again.

Val turned to me, leaned a bit closer, and I felt myself involuntarily shrink from him.

"You're afraid," he said. There was a hint of hurt in his voice, and I hated being the cause of it.

"No," I said quickly. "I'm not afraid. I just —"

"It's all right," Val said, wearing a false grin as he eased back. "It's better this way. Better that we not . . ." He suddenly grew distant, staring sightlessly through the trees toward the whitewashed, Mediterranean-style buildings of Haeden. Behind us, through a screen of bushes, I heard the hum of electrics buzzing this way and that along Wellington.

You're such an idiot, I scolded myself.

Seconds seemed like hours. And then it just happened.

Slowly at first.

Tentatively.

I took his hand in both of mine, lifted it, caressed it, touched my lips to it. Then I turned to him, shifted closer until my thigh was pressed against his, and reached up to angle his face toward mine. For a moment we just stared at one another, and all I heard was my breathing, quickening with anticipation.

Val's hand slid under my skirt and up my thigh to my waist. I shivered at the sensuousness of it, never having been touched in that way before. I found myself moving closer to him, pressing against him, reacting instinctively.

"To hell with it," I breathed. And then we kissed.

I'd imagined doing it almost since the first time I'd seen him, and I'd visualized it down to the last detail, until it seemed so real to me that I wasn't sure reality could ever measure up. I was wrong.

He smelt of spice and tasted of honey, and his lips were like a soothing balm. It wasn't what I'd expected, and I realized I'd always feared kissing a vamp might be so awful I'd never want to do it again.

After a moment of hesitation his lips parted. He slipped both arms around me, pulling me even closer against the hard muscles of his chest. I ran my fingers through his hair, down his neck. My heart was pounding, as loud and active to him as his was still and silent to me.

His body drew warmth from me, and I was so hot and feverish that I had plenty to spare. I don't know how long that kiss lasted, but for me the universe froze, contracting into that solitary moment. The only thing in the world for me was Val, and I believe in my heart I was all that existed for him.

The kiss became more than a kiss, and I didn't want it to end. If I could have lived like that for the rest of my days I'd have been happy. From then on, our relationship was something else. Different. Better. But it remained burdened by one incontrovertible truth — Val was a vamp, and I was not. There was nothing we could ever do to change that.

* * *

The train jerked, knocking my head back against the seat and jarring me from my thoughts of the past. Startled, I sat up and looked out to see that we were on the move again. The shadows were long, and to the west the sun was beginning to dip behind the mountains. A weary cheer rang out from the other passengers as we gathered speed and headed toward the city. I yawned and stretched, settling in for the last part of the journey, and watched the countryside change until the cityscape rose above the horizon.

For all its many shortcomings, I loved Caelo. I loved its quaint charms and its quirky mix of Mediterranean, gothic, and postwar architecture. It didn't look anything like the pictures and films I'd seen of the vamp cities; it always seemed they were gray and dull and overwhelmingly oppressive. Not Caelo. Sometimes you could be there and forget for a while that there was a time, not so long ago, when the world had almost ended, when everything human had come very close to being lost forever.

Caelo sprawled around the inward-most tip of Resolute Bay, close to the foothills of the mountains, and not that far from the heart of Central Island. It was intimate and warm and full of life. A stark contrast to a vacation spot like Coral Beach, where everything was laid-back and unhurried and very provincial, Caelo was busy and loud and crowded. There were always people going somewhere in the city, always doing something.

Val had once said that was what he liked best about it; it never stopped. "It's as though people are trying to pack as much life as possible into a short time."

That was yet another reminder of how we were separated by our differences. Time meant little to him because he had so much of it. The days were long, the nights eternal. But for me they were all too brief and would one day cease altogether.

The train passed through the rundown industrial sector and edged closer to the harbor. Through the openings between warehouses and factories I saw the turquoise and blue waters of Resolute Bay. Decades ago Haven had had its beginnings out there. After the truce had been signed, the surviving Immunes had boarded hundreds of creaky old ships and had sailed into the Pacific, to where the antimeridian and the equator intersect. There they'd found the archipelago we now call Haven.

I couldn't begin to imagine how they must have felt back then when they'd first looked upon these shores and known these islands would be their only home for the rest of their lives. I'd never known any other existence, but they'd come from a world so much wider. They'd sailed from ports around the globe to a place none of them had ever heard of. Most had come from North America, Australia, New Zealand, and Japan, because those had been the last to suffer the plague. In many other countries, Immunes had died of famine or disease or had simply been wiped out by the Nazis before the hostilities came to an end.

"We were all refugees," Grace had told me once. "And Haven was the biggest refugee camp in the history of humankind."

That made me think of Camille and of how trapped she'd felt here. I realized that in some respects we were all prisoners, the sea a wall that enclosed us. Some would doubtless have argued otherwise, that Haven was our fortress, and the sea a protective moat.

The train rolled to a squealing stop inside the aging scrap-iron edifice that was Victoria Station. I collected my luggage and trundled toward the exit on Harvard Street, bypassing the zebra stand and making my way out into the broad expanse of the avenue. Electrics hummed by as I dodged through traffic and joined a knot of people waiting at the transit stop.

Within moments I was struggling to board one of the old streetcars the scavies had brought back from San Francisco. I tried to lug my bag up the worn wooden steps, and a few passengers moved to assist me. But the cheerful, kindly demeanor of their faces dematerialized as they looked beyond and shrank from me as though I were a leper. I turned to see what had startled them and found myself face to face with Val.

CHAPTER 5

FEELING LOSS

I fought for breath and forgot about everything else. The murder. Havershaw. The photos. The pain and the emptiness Camille's death had left inside me. Standing there in the aisle of the idling streetcar, seeing him before me, it was all wiped away.

Almost every inch of his body was covered in clothing. Though it was a sweltering day, he wore dark trousers, a long jacket, gloves, sunglasses, and a broad-brimmed fedora. The collar of his jacket was turned up, leaving only the smallest portion of his face visible — all in the interest of protecting him from the lethal sun. It varies from vamp to vamp, but most will die and turn to ash within a few minutes of exposure to direct sunlight. It's a grisly end that Immunes exploited to good effect during the war.

"You're looking well," he said, reaching for me.

"'You're looking well'?" I repeated, staring at him dazedly, heedless of the other passengers who were beating a hasty retreat. "You're gone two months, don't tell me you've come back, and all you can say is 'you're looking well'?"

I twisted in his grasp, but he was far too strong for even my best efforts. And truth be told, I was at war with myself, one side of me wanting to step into his arms and be as close to him as I could, while the other was angry and hurt and wanted to push him away.

Val grinned, and I knew that behind his sunglasses there was laughter in his eyes. "Should I tell you how beautiful you are?" he said. "Or that every minute away from you was torture and that only in this moment have I felt any peace at all?"

"You're such a liar," I said. "That might work if we lived in one of those dreadful romance novels, but I'm not buying it." I glared at him, making it clear I wouldn't be so easily pacified.

"But it's true," he protested.

"For pity's sake, keep your voice down. Do you want the whole world to know?"

"Would that be so bad?"

"Whatever has gotten into you?"

Val's only answer was to slide his hands down my arms, gather my hands in his, and raise them to his lips. He kissed each in turn, softly, sensuously. "You can't imagine how much I've needed you these past few weeks."

"Stop that!" I hissed. "People will see."

"I think it's a little late to be concerned about that."

I pulled away from him, backed farther into the streetcar, and only then noticed it was empty — except for the driver, who was doing his level best to pretend he didn't exist.

"You sure know how to clear a place," I said.

"One of the perks," Val said, straight-faced.

"What are you doing here, anyway?"

"I told you — I couldn't be without you. I was thoroughly miserable."

I rolled my eyes. "Right. Apparently not miserable enough to forego your *business* trip. We missed the best part of the summer together, you rotter."

Val had the good grace to look contrite. "I know. I'm sorry. But I really did have urgent matters to attend to in New York," he said.

"Wouldn't have had anything to do with those rumors of rebellion among the ranks of the vamps that keep cropping up, would it?"

He laughed, but I couldn't help but think there was a false ring to it. "Wherever do you get such notions?" he asked.

"Don't you ever read the editorials? I thought part of your job for the Embassy was keeping up on the local gossip?"

"Haven writers have such vivid imaginations. You know as well as I do they've been talking about that sort of thing for decades. There's no more foundation to it now than there ever was."

"Well, regardless, you left me in the lurch."

"Weren't you picking peaches or something this summer?"

"Potatoes. And my Mandatory Labor Service only lasted for a month. That's not the point, anyway."

The corner of Val's mouth quirked up in an elfin grin. "At least give me credit for risking my life to see you. It's not every day you'll find a man willing to walk through fire to see the woman he loves."

I could see a small blister on his left ear where the sun had caught him for a moment too long. It was already healing, but I felt a chill go through me all the same.

He pulled me to a seat and settled beside me. Up ahead the driver glanced nervously back at us. Val shot him a look and the poor man practically jumped out of his skin.

"We've paid our fare," Val called to him in a frosty tone he rarely used around me. "Drive on, please." The driver swallowed, bobbed his head in a nervous nod, and turned to his task.

Out of the sun, Val doffed his hat and undid his jacket. His face was as inscrutable as ever, and not for the first time did I wish I could read minds. But it didn't take a psychic to know he was hiding something from me.

"Why are you really here?" I asked. "I thought we promised to be discreet."

"I thought it time for a change."

"Like hell."

He flashed a dazzling smile. "You worry too much."

"Fine for you to say. You don't have to live here."

"Yet I do. And I want to be able to see you whenever I want to."

"Really." I regarded him cynically. "Is that why you were up at Coral Beach?"

Val's expression faltered ever so slightly, a momentary slip I might have missed had I not known him so well. "Whoever told you that?" he said, as though it were utter nonsense.

"I had a delightful little chat with an Inspector Havershaw. You may be familiar with him; he certainly is with you."

Val displayed a sudden interest in the buildings we were passing. "Haven isn't a large place. As liaison officer I'm acquainted with a great many people."

"I'm sure. But Inspector Havershaw seems especially interested in you."

"Is he now?" Val seemed entirely unconcerned.

"He also seems to be under the impression I may have murdered my best friend." I heard the catch in my voice and struggled against the sudden surge of anguish and the tears that wanted to break free. "You were there. I'm sure the details didn't escape you. Especially not with all your connections."

Val raised an eyebrow. "Havershaw thinks you had something to do with the murder? Seriously?"

"Yes, 'seriously.' I got the distinct impression he's not the sort to kid around."

"You're worried." It wasn't a question.

"Hell, yes! Why wouldn't I be?"

"But you're innocent."

"Of course I am," I said, bristling with indignation.

Val shrugged. "Then I'm certain you'll be cleared of any wrongdoing."

"That's it? That's all you have to say?"

"I've observed that justice works quite well in Haven."

"You make it sound so simple."

"It is. The police will look into the matter and find there's no reason to believe you had anything to do with it." He grinned disarmingly. "I know you, and I know you're capable of many things" — he said that suggestively — "but I don't think murder is one of them."

"Remind me not to call *you* as a witness if there's a trial," I said, slouching in my seat and crossing my arms.

"Relax, Sophie. Everything will be all right." He patted my arm.

I stared at him in disbelief. "How can you sit there and say that?" My jaw tightened, and again I felt the searing emotions that kept swirling just beneath the surface whenever I thought of Camille. "For pity's sake, Val, I could be charged with murder. I don't know what it's like where you come from, but we take that sort of thing very seriously around here." I felt tears well in my eyes again and hated it. Hated that I was so afraid. Hated that I could be overpowered by thoughts of Camille at the most unexpected moments and nearly lose it.

The streetcar jerked to a halt, but one look at Val deterred anyone from coming aboard. With a rattle and a clank, we started moving again, climbing the steep hill toward the downtown core. Ahead of us a handful of stubby, plain-faced skyscrapers jutted into the cloudless sky, and beyond them I could see the distant slopes of the Blue Mountains.

"You have quite the way with people," I said, trying to be nonchalant as yet another crowd of waiting passengers balked at joining us.

"I do well enough with you," he said, giving me a little nudge.

I felt myself grow hot. "Maybe I just don't know any better."

"Your father would agree."

"Yes. Would have." I didn't try to hide my distress.

Val's expression sobered. "Yes. I suppose so. It might have helped you right now if he wasn't . . ." He didn't finish.

"He'd never have interfered with a police investigation," I said, reminded of how I'd said as much to Havershaw. "You know that. Even if it was someone in his family. Once a cop, always a cop. He believed in the system; it was his life." Too much of his life, I'd always thought.

"You'd be surprised at what people will do for the ones they love." It didn't sound as though he was speaking hypothetically.

"So about Coral Beach," I said, hoping to catch him off guard. "Why were you really there?"

"I was worried about you."

"Worried?" I said. "You just told me I shouldn't be worried."

Val looked as though he regretted having said anything, and I half expected him to prevaricate, the way he often did when he didn't want to talk about something. Instead he said, "I think you should be careful. This murder . . ." He glanced away, visibly uncomfortable about something.

"What?"

"I just think you should be careful."

"Careful? Careful about what?" I asked.

"There are complications in my life," he said.

"What sort of complications?"

"A problem from my past."

"What does that have to do with me?" I pressed.

He seemed to weigh this for a moment, then said, "There are things happening right now that it would be better you weren't involved in."

"Do these things have anything to do with why you went to New York?"

He didn't answer, which I took to be an answer in and of itself.

"You say I shouldn't be involved, but this had something to do with Camille's murder, didn't it? So how can I not be? She was my best friend."

"She was also the daughter of some very important people."

Now I was puzzled and intrigued, and judging by the look on Val's face, he realized he was just digging a deeper hole.

"Surely you're not suggesting the Westerlys are involved in something —"

"No, of course not," Val said a bit too quickly. "I'm just suggesting you be careful."

"No," I said, shaking my head. "No. You don't just drop a bombshell like that and leave me hanging."

"Look, the less you know, the safer you'll be. I'm sure your father would tell you the same thing if he could."

"You're beginning to frighten me, Val."

"Good. I hope I frighten you enough that you'll listen to what I say for a change. Keep your nose out of this. Let me handle it."

"Handle what, for pity's sake?"

"Your friend's death, among other things. I know you, Sophie. You're willful and impetuous, and you don't always think things through before you act."

"Gee, thanks for the compliments."

"I'm serious. Listen when I tell you not to go digging."

"Jesus, Val, lighten up. I hadn't intended to get any more involved than I already am. I'm not Nancy Drew, you know."

He looked at me as though he didn't believe a word I'd said.

"I swear on my mother's grave."

The expression on his face was the oddest I'd ever seen; it vanished almost as soon as it appeared. "You look like you've seen a ghost," I said, partly in jest.

Val quickly recovered. "Just make sure you keep out of this." His tone was firm, his manner blunt, and I could tell he wasn't joking.

I was full of questions, but the streetcar was slowing, and Val was getting ready to leave. "Your stop, I believe," he said. He glanced toward the driver, then leaned down and kissed me. It made me forget the questions, which I suspect was the whole point.

"I think for a while we should keep our distance," he said as he straightened up.

"Wait! What? Just a few moments ago you said you didn't care if everyone knew about us."

"I've changed my mind. You were right; we should be discreet. Maybe even cool it for a while."

"Val —"

"I don't want this to be a problem for you, luv."

"So what? We were okay to fool around for the past year and now suddenly —"

"Now suddenly things have changed. I need you to be safe, and you need to spend time mourning the loss of your friend."

I was about to tell him that would be easier to do with him around, but he bent and gave me another kiss. "Don't worry," he said. "This is just for a few days. We'll meet again soon enough."

"You could have told me all this over the phone."

Val shook his head. "I didn't think it could wait." He reached out and brushed aside my hair, just like that first time in the library. "Besides, I wanted to see you. I wanted to make sure you were safe while I dealt with this problem."

He didn't give me the chance to say anything more. In a blur he was gone.

CHAPTER 6

NIGHT TREMORS

I hate funerals. But then again, I don't suppose anyone actually *likes* them.

I was glad when it was over, eager to get back to my flat. Before I left, Aunt Amelia gave me a small box of odds and ends that had belonged to Camille. "I thought you should have them," she said. "I think they'll mean more to you than to me."

There was a lot of stuff in there that brought tears to my eyes. Worthless little trinkets Camille and I had gathered together over the years. They were touchstones to the past. But the ratty hardcover wasn't one of them.

It was the book Camille had been talking about the day she died — *No Haven for Darkness*. There was a rubber band around it, and when I removed it, the book fell open to an envelope. At first I thought it was just something she'd been using as a bookmark, but when I picked it up I realized it wasn't empty.

I felt like I was trespassing as I dumped the contents of the envelope on my bed — two tickets, two visas, and some travel chits (like the sort you'd use for hotels) tumbled onto the sheets. The tickets were bookings for two first class cabins on a Lufthansa zeppelin to New York City. No date set.

All that talk about doing the tourist thing had been for real, I realized. I couldn't believe she'd been planning it without telling me. Heck, I couldn't believe she'd been planning it at all.

"What were you up to?" I wondered aloud. "Preparing some sort of a getaway with your latest boy toy?"

I picked up one of the visas and opened it. The black, stylized eagle of the Third Reich was emblazoned on the top of the page. Underneath was a bunch of German I could barely muddle through. Though it was a required language in school, it had never been my forte. But I didn't need to be fluent to read my own name — it was made out to me.

Camille had forged my signature, just as she must have done on the application form. But how had she gotten the visa without my ID?

I drew in a sharp breath as it dawned on me — she'd had my ID. A month ago, at the beach house, I'd been tearing the place apart looking from top to bottom for that damn card. Camille had left early in the morning for a wedding — some rich relative of hers. I hadn't thought anything of it; Aunt Amelia had always been making her attend those things. It would only have taken her an hour or two to get the visas.

When she'd returned to the beach house the next day she'd helped me find my ID card, supposedly stumbling upon it in the very same laundry hamper I'd dumped out and gone through at least a half dozen times the day before.

The night she'd died, the last thing Camille had said to me was, "I have a surprise for you."

I guess this was it.

I put everything back in the envelope and stuffed it into the top drawer of my dresser for safekeeping, not ready to deal with it at the moment. The funeral had left me tense and emotionally drained; this little bombshell just added fuel to the fire. I wanted to forget about it right now, so I drew a bath and lay back in it, letting the cool, sudsy water relax me as I read the book Camille had left behind, hoping it would take my mind off things.

No Haven for Darkness was an odd little fantasy, but it was easy enough to see why Camille had been so drawn to it. I knew she'd have imagined herself as the story's central character — Samantha Jarvis — who somehow had been transported from our world to one that resembled ours in many respects. But there was one dramatic difference — history had charted a different course from the early forties onward. The whole romantic angle was Camille's cup of tea; lovers torn apart by time and different worlds and all that. And if that hadn't satisfied, all the action and drama certainly would have, however improbable a lot of it seemed.

The thing that really stood out for me was what Camille had been talking about on the beach: the differences between our world and the one in which the central character found herself. I mean, who wouldn't want to live on an Earth that had never fallen victim to Gomorrah? I'd lived all my life in the shadow of that, in a world where the sovereignty of Haven was more illusion than reality.

In Samantha Jarvis's world, Haven didn't even exist. There were no vamps, because there'd been no virus. Hitler had died in '45, and the Allies had won the war. It was almost unimaginable. But even more incredible was picturing a planet full of *normal* people. Seven billion of them. It was mind-boggling. Billions of human beings living in thousands of cities in hundreds of countries.

Could our world really have been like that but for a single alteration to history?

It's just fantasy, I told myself. It was wild and outlandish and full of improbabilities. But it was also oddly seductive.

I'm not sure whether it was the story of Samantha Jarvis that was so compelling or all the implausible technologies and bizarre cultural affectations. In the real world, it could take you five days to get to New York City from Haven by zeppelin; in Samantha's alternate reality, people flew around the globe in enormous jet airplanes that could carry five hundred or more passengers at a time, crossing oceans in mere hours. The top speed of the electric along the Central Line was probably eighty miles an hour, but the trains in the book screamed along at a flabbergasting two or three hundred. The Nazis had had rockets dating back to the early years of the war, and they'd used them to devastate much of North America. But in the book, rockets had carried men to the moon! The moon, for Pete's sake.

The improbabilities were endless and ever more fantastical, until I couldn't help laughing at how ridiculous they were. Seriously? Computers small enough to fit in the palm of your hand that were hundreds of times more powerful than the machine in Haeden University that took up an entire floor! Did the author really think people would believe that? Or that people on his imaginary Earth would be linked to one another electronically? That they walked about the streets talking or texting (whatever that meant) on portable telephones that had no wire connections and were so tiny they could be carried in a pocket or purse? That you could go anywhere in the world and always be in touch with someone else? It not only sounded incredible, it was downright spooky.

In the fictional world of *No Haven for Darkness*, there were televisions as thin as glass and as big as small cinema screens. And they were in color! You could watch TV twenty-four hours a day on hundreds of channels. In Haven there was one channel, and the schedule started at six o'clock in the evening and finished at eleven; there was no TV on Sundays.

I kept reading, despite my disbelief, but in the end it all got rather boring. I wanted more story, and instead I had to wade through endless descriptions of technology and the effects it had on society and how it often bewildered Samantha. After a while it became almost incomprehensible.

I couldn't imagine living in such a place; it was so strange. It wasn't just that people spent inordinate amounts of time watching TV shows about people being stupid, or that their lives seemed increasingly absorbed with something called social media, or that a few thousand had so much while billions had so little. What really struck me was the assertion that this really was the way *our* world should have been, and that somehow something had happened that shouldn't have, making our world what it was today.

According to the author, that something was the Old Ones. *They* were behind Gomorrah, though to what extent was almost as much a mystery as the Old Ones themselves.

No one seemed to know much about them — not even the vamps, if Val was telling the truth. They seemed to have come from out of nowhere, though there were rumors they dated back millennia. Before the Roman Empire. Before Alexander the Great. Before the building of the pyramids.

"What are they like?" I'd once asked Val.

"Dangerous," he'd said. "Not something you ever want to tangle with. They're not like us . . . like vamps. They're older, stronger, faster. And if there was ever anything human about them, it vanished long ago."

He'd seemed almost frightened of them — as if a vamp could ever be frightened of anything.

But what really struck me now, as I thought back on that conversation and considered it in light of what I'd read in *No Haven for Darkness*, was when Val had asserted that the Old Ones were instrumental in the creation of Gomorrah.

It must have taken a particular kind of evil to have introduced to the world something as insidious as that, I thought.

I read the book well into the evening, lying curled up in bed in the negligée Camille had given me a few months back. By nine o'clock the wind was wailing, rustling the leaves of the trees that lined the street and peppered the Quad. The latter sat opposite my flat, bounded on three sides by Haeden University and usually full of students during the day. It stood empty at present, its unoccupied space an eerie counterpoint to the bells of Parliament's Peace Tower clock, which now peeled loudly in the distance, signaling the top of the hour.

It was still relatively early, but I could barely keep my eyes open. When I switched out the light and burrowed under the sheets, it didn't take me long to fall asleep. I drifted off listening to the wind in the trees and the distant boom of thunder. But an hour later, I was promptly roused by a loud crash and the sound of shattering glass.

Now wide awake, I lay perfectly still, barely breathing, trying to convince myself it had only been the storm. Maybe the wind had picked something up and thrown it against the window. But a moment later I heard the creak of floorboards and knew that wasn't the case. Someone was in the next room.

I fumbled for the phone on my nightstand but hit the alarm clock instead. It toppled over and went off, the mechanical clatter of its bells enough to wake the dead. In the room beyond I heard the thud of footsteps, louder than before.

I don't know what possessed me. I should have called the police and then locked myself in the bathroom. Instead I jumped out of bed and raced to the door, yanking it open with such force that I nearly tore it off its hinges. As I stood there on the threshold, lightning lit the sky. A searing white brilliance shone through the large open window and angled across the floor of my living room. Stark against this was the silhouette of a woman, her hair a wild cloud about her head.

"Hey!" I shouted — possibly the stupidest thing I could have done.

The intruder leapt to the window, a distance of no less than ten feet. Perched on the sill, she turned to me, masked in shadow and darkness, and hissed the way a cat might — more as a warning than a threat.

Although I couldn't see her face, I caught the glint of eyes and the gleam of fangs. And just as I was going to flick on the light for a better look, she sprang through the opening, disappearing out into the stormy night. I let out a cry, rushed to the window, and leaned out into the rain. It lashed at me as I stood there, dumbfounded, staring into emptiness.

The thief, or whatever she was, had vanished.

It was only once she was gone that I felt a shiver of fear race through me. With a trembling hand I reached out and pulled the window shut, noticing for the first time the pane that had been broken in order to access the latch. I looked down at my feet, saw blood, and realized too late that I was standing on shards of glass.

* * *

My landlady, Mrs. Del Flora, insisted on calling the police. I knew Inspector Havershaw would be keeping tabs on me, and something like this would be certain to draw his attention. Sure enough, not a half hour later he waltzed into my flat unannounced.

"Trouble has a way of finding you, Miss Harkness," he said.

"Yes, you do, don't you?"

Havershaw wasn't amused and strolled around my flat as though he owned the place. He made a perfunctory inspection, poking at things on the coffee table, picking up knickknacks and giving them a once-over, squinting at the books on the shelves and touching the spines of a few as though he'd a passing familiarity with them. I watched him pull one out and examine it, then put it back. He fingered another, and I caught my breath as he started to draw a well-worn leather volume from the shelf. My heartbeat quickened, and I wanted to rush forward and stop him. But I held myself in check, tense, relaxing only when he seemed to change his mind and shoved the book back amongst its neighbors.

"Quite a place for a high school student," Havershaw said, raising his eyebrows in my direction.

"I have a trust fund," I explained. "From the sale of my father's house."

Havershaw didn't bother to respond to that. Instead he moved on, his interest drawn to the large window the intruder had come through. Stepping toward it, he bent and examined the broken pane, then reached up, undid the latch, and pushed the window wide open against the wind and the rain. Leaning out, he looked down, turning his head left, then right to survey the ground in both directions.

"Quite a drop," he observed, straightening and closing the window. "What are we here?" He glanced back at me. "Third floor, isn't it?"

"Yes."

"How do you suppose your intruder managed to get up here in the first place?"

I crossed my arms and glowered at him defiantly. "You're the detective. You tell me."

He set his eyes on me. "There's nothing to climb out there. No real façade to gain a purchase on. No trellis. And the nearest tree is too far away for someone to have jumped across from." He pursed his lips, cocking an eyebrow shrewdly. "One might argue it would take *superhuman* strength."

I stood in silence, hugging closed the peignoir I'd thrown on over my negligée, hoping I didn't look as transparent as I felt.

"Did you see the intruder at all?" he asked.

"As I told the constable here," I said, jerking my head impatiently in the direction of the nearby policeman, "when I opened the door, the room was empty. I went to the window and looked out, but I didn't see anyone."

The last thing I wanted to tell him was that it might have been a vamp, because then it wouldn't be just a break-in. It would be a diplomatic incident, and that meant the PSS and a whole mess of trouble — and I kept thinking about Val and what he'd said on the streetcar about us lying low and me not getting involved. Besides, I told myself, it was only a little lie, and I couldn't have given Havershaw much of a description of the burglar, anyway.

"Too bad," the inspector said, but he didn't seem overly concerned. I suspected he had already deduced that it had been a vamp. Havershaw may have been many things, but stupid wasn't one of them.

"Ya should be takin' her to the hospital," Mrs. Del Flora interjected from where she stood off to the side.

"Oh?" Havershaw shot me a questioning look. "I thought you said the intruder was gone when you came into the room."

"Cut her feet, she did," said Mrs. Del Flora.

"I stepped on some of the broken glass." I gestured to the pieces still littering the floor.

Havershaw nudged a fragment with the toe of his shoe — a piece spotted with blood. "You're sure you're all right? You don't need stitches?"

"I'm a fast healer," I said, which was the truth.

He glanced down at my feet, and I blushed, suddenly self-conscious. I'd put on my slippers after dealing with the wounds, and while they were sturdy and comfortable footwear, they were probably about the least feminine thing I owned. Old leather moccasins, scuffed and faded, marred with shiny spots from years of shuffling about in them. Camille had tried to pitch them on more than one occasion, but I'd always retrieved them from the trash.

"I see you're the practical sort," Havershaw said, a hint of sarcasm in the words.

I just stared at him.

"If ya ain't goin' ta do nothin' more," said Mrs. Del Flora, "then ya best be leavin'." She gave Havershaw and the constable pointed looks. "The young lady has had more'n enough 'citement fer one day, what with that funeral an' all. Lost her best friend, she did. Now someone comes breakin' inta her home. Jus' ain't right. Best ya get busy findin' out who were responsible."

"You can go now," Havershaw said to the constable.

"Sir." The policeman nodded to the inspector, then tipped his hat to me. "Miss."

"And you, too," Havershaw added, staring bluntly at Mrs. Del Flora.

"I ain't leavin' this poor darlin' alone, I ain't!" my landlady proclaimed heatedly. "Not after the fright she were havin'."

"I'll be all right," I said, locking eyes with Havershaw. "Besides, the inspector will make certain nothing happens to me. Won't you, Inspector?"

"That's my job," Havershaw replied.

The old lady scowled at him before turning back to me. "Well, if ya says so," she grumbled. "But I'll be right downstairs if ya needs me, dearie."

"Thank you," I said as she shambled out of the room.

Once we were alone, Havershaw shut the door and turned to me. "I thought you might like to know the details of the autopsy on your friend."

"So you're really not here about my intruder."

"Two birds with one stone, as they say."

"Do tell."

"Your friend died from a broken neck. Fractured vertebrae and crushed larynx, to be exact. There was substantial bruising that came up postmortem. Doc says it's almost as if someone clamped her neck in a vice and squeezed until the bones gave. Odd thing is, the skin wasn't abraded, and there were no marks other than the severe bruising that came up sometime after she died."

"So what does that mean?" I asked.

Instead of answering, Havershaw said, "I understand you're quite the athlete, Miss Harkness."

I frowned, eyeing him warily. "I do okay."

"You're far too modest. You do more than okay. In fact, you have quite an extraordinary record of achievement at your school." He pulled out his notebook and consulted it. "You attend Humberton, don't you?" He glanced up at me for confirmation, though it was clear he'd known the answer before he'd asked the question.

"Yes. Humberton."

"I did a little checking there. You have the fastest sprint times. Longest jump. Farthest shot put. Highest high jump. The list goes on and on; it's an impressive one. You're a regular Olympian, I'd venture."

"So I excel in sports. So what? I also do pretty well in academics, thank you very much. I put a lot of effort into what I do. It's not a crime."

"No, it isn't."

"What has all that to do with Camille's murder?"

The corners of Havershaw's mouth turned up in a faint, cryptic smile. "Just being thorough."

"I hope you're not suggesting I could have —" I felt sick at the insinuation, and I wanted to slap him and kick him out.

"I'm not suggesting anything, Miss Harkness. Like I said, that's my job. I wouldn't be doing it properly if I didn't examine all possibilities."

I swallowed the bile in my throat and said, "It's a bit of a stretch, don't you think? I'm no scientist, but from what I remember of physics no one could do what you've described without some sort of mechanical aid." But it occurred to me as I said it that while no one *human* could do such a thing, it wasn't beyond the abilities of a vamp. Crushing the bones of someone's neck single-handedly wouldn't be much of a feat for the Undead.

In my mind's eye, I saw the photos of Val lurking in the background of the crime scene, and suddenly I was dizzy. He couldn't have been the one who had killed Camille. I refused to believe it.

"Are you feeling all right, Miss Harkness?" Inspector Havershaw asked.

"What do you think? I just buried my best friend, someone broke into my flat, and you keep trying to pin a murder on me. How am I supposed to feel?"

Havershaw studied his shoes, and when he looked up at me he actually appeared contrite. "Perhaps we should save this for another time. I'm sure it's been a trying day for you."

I didn't respond.

He moved to the door, started to open it, then paused, looking thoughtful as he rubbed the back of his neck with his free hand. "There's one thing," he said, looking across at me.

"Yes?"

"The other day, when you got back from Coral Beach . . ."

I stiffened, feeling my pulse hiccup. "What of it?"

"I'm just wondering what the vamp had to say."

"The vamp?" I repeated, feigning ignorance.

"Don't play coy with me, Miss Harkness. It's not every day one of them boards local transit. We received quite a few calls about it. People thinking there was a vamp on the loose or something, terrified we were being invaded — that sort of nonsense. And of course they didn't fail to mention the young lady he was talking to. They described you in remarkable detail."

"He knew my father," I said, which wasn't a lie.

"Yes, I know. But it's what he was doing with *you* I'm most curious about."

"Just asking how my father was faring."

"Interesting. I don't suppose you noticed he's the same vamp in the photos I had you look at. Quite a coincidence, wouldn't you say?"

I shrugged, trying to appear nonchalant. "The vamps do what they like, Inspector. Neither you nor I can change that, and maybe we shouldn't try. They've the advantage over us."

He heaved a breath and shook his head. "We can't think like that."

"Goodnight, Inspector Havershaw."

He nodded. "I'll have a squad car posted on the street for the rest of the night, but I don't expect you'll have any more trouble."

I locked the door behind him, then walked over to the bookshelf. With a shaking hand I pulled out the book he'd been about to examine before he'd turned his attention elsewhere. In all likelihood it would have meant nothing to him, and he wouldn't have realized it didn't belong. But I did. It hadn't been there earlier in the day, though it was a book with which I had some familiarity. I'd seen it once before, three years ago in a local chapter of the Caelo library.

It was my mother's journal.

CHAPTER 7
MARY WOLSTENCROFT

I saw my vampire when I was sixteen.

When I read those words from the opening entry of my mother's journal, it was as if a jolt of electricity had shot through me. I slammed the book shut and sat trembling as a lump rose in my throat.

My vampire.

What the hell? Was this for real? Could she really have . . . ? How?

I closed my eyes and took a breath. Could it be possible? Was this what my father had meant when he'd said I was just like my mother? Was this why he'd been so angry about my relationship with Val?

I was almost afraid to read on, afraid of what I was going to find. I wanted it to turn out to be nothing more than some girlish fantasy she'd had. I mean, I'd had those myself. Except mine had turned into a reality. Had hers?

I felt queasy, but in a strange sort of way I also felt a connection to my mother I'd never had before. Drawing in a deep breath, I opened the book again and started reading.

* * *

JOURNAL OF MARY WOLSTENCROFT — JULY 3, 1976

I call him "my vampire," though I don't really know him. And of course I wouldn't. Nobody in Haven ever really talks about them, though we all know they're there, up in that house overlooking the bay. A reminder, Mom says, that we're really not free.

Some of the girls and I decided to ride out there, though I don't think any of us really wanted to. But we backed ourselves into a corner, daring one another, until finally we just had to do it. It was as simple as that.

We were laughing and giggling all the way, but I think that was just to hide how nervous we were. I know I was scared, but I wasn't going to be the first to suggest we turn around.

We parked our bikes against some rocks and sat down on the grass where the long lane to the Embassy meets the main road that arcs around the bay. I think that was about as close as any of us wanted to be. I'd have been happy if we'd left right then, but somehow a game of Truth or Dare got started.

I thought Parma seemed far too eager when it came to my turn. She's always had it in for me. Maybe because I tend to stand up to her. She's sixteen like the rest of us, but the oldest by a few months, which she seems to believe makes her the leader — like we're her posse or something.

I wanted to choose truth, but I knew if I did she'd make it something I really didn't want anyone to know about. Like Bobby Chan kissing me. Lucy would go ballistic if she found out her boyfriend had planted one on me. So I ended up accepting the dare, even though I knew it was going to be something horrible.

I wasn't surprised when Parma dared me to go ring the bell at the Embassy gate. That was probably her intention right from the start. I mean, everyone knows the stories about the place. Of course people probably exaggerate that sort of stuff, it being vamps and all. But still . . .

Anyway, I tried to be cool about it. I think everyone was a little surprised, but I went through with it.

It was probably only a few hundred feet to that gate, but it felt like miles. The closer I rode, the more nervous I became. The only thing that kept me going was the sight of Parma standing at the bottom of the lane. That smug look on her face was all the motivation I needed. I just had to ring the stupid bell and scat. The vamps would never see me. Piece of cake.

Maybe it was the stories, but that place was seriously creepy. It was surrounded by a wall that must have been fifteen feet tall and was topped off with nasty spikes jutting from the top. I'd never seen anything like it, and I wondered why it was like that. To keep us out? I know people in Haven hate vamps, but I'm pretty sure no one would be stupid enough to try and break in there.

I knew that if I waited any longer I wouldn't be able to do it, so I just jabbed the button for the bell and tried to jump back on my bike as quick as I could. But by that point I was so nervous that my feet slipped on the pedals, and I lost my balance. It all happened so fast, and before I knew it, I was on the ground. My knee was bleeding and felt like it was on fire.

Then the wolf came.

I wanted to scream, but the noise seemed to catch in my throat. I ended up sitting there on the ground, scared out of my wits. That wolf was bigger than any dog I'd ever seen. Heck, it looked as big as a horse. Shaggy gray-black fur hung in thick strands from its belly, like bits of string or something. It glared at me, and I was afraid it would pounce on me and tear me apart if I so much as breathed.

The first wolf was joined by a second, and then I heard more of them on the other side of the gate. I felt like I was surrounded.

In my terror, I'd forgotten that I'd pushed the doorbell, so when I heard a man's voice coming from a speaker nearby I just lost it and screamed. I kept screaming, and those snarling wolves kept circling and pawing the ground and getting more and more agitated. They looked awfully hungry.

It was probably only a few minutes before someone came and rescued me, but it seemed like hours. By that time my leg had begun to really throb, and there seemed to be an awful lot of blood. I think I was probably close to fainting. Someone called out something in German, and just like that the wolves stopped pacing and sprawled on the ground, tongues hanging out, looking goofy and panting like a couple of friendly Great Danes.

It was all kind of surreal — especially when the vamp appeared. He was dressed so that barely an inch of his skin was visible. I couldn't even tell what he looked like until he knelt down at my side, and then all I saw was a young face cast in shadow, eyes concealed behind sunglasses. I don't think he could have been more than a year or two older than I was.

He asked if I was badly hurt, but I wasn't really thinking about how much my leg ached at that point. I was wondering what the sight of all that blood would do to him. It's really strange, but I think I was more curious than I was afraid.

He helped me to my feet, and when it was clear I couldn't walk, he swung me up into his arms. I don't know whether I was afraid or excited. Probably both. But I just held onto him. The weirdest thing is, a part of me never wanted to let go.

He carried me along the narrow road beyond the gate until we reached the broad steps of the Embassy a hundred yards or so beyond. Up close the latter looked like a giant concrete bunker. It had narrow windows that were all tinted dark so that in the daylight they looked black. There was a dome on the top with a flagpole sticking up, and a big swastika was flapping from it, just like the ones you see in pictures of the vamp cities. It was the color of blood.

The vamp set me down on the steps and told me to wait. Then he said something to the wolves, and they settled down on the ground at my feet, tucking their heads between their paws and looking at me kind of sheepishly. It was hard to believe they'd been so menacing just minutes before.

When the vamp reappeared, he carried a cloth and a basin of water and set about gently washing the blood from my leg. I just sat there while he worked, telling myself I should be nervous and afraid but feeling quite the opposite. The truth is, I kind of fancied myself as Marianne Dashwood in Sense and Sensibility, *rescued by the dashing John Willoughby after she sprains her ankle. And though I've no idea what the vamp might have been feeling, I felt there was some sort of bond between us. I bet Lucy would describe it as sexual tension. But it was more than that; I can't put it into words.*

Once he'd finished cleaning my wound, my leg didn't seem nearly so gruesome. The scrape had stopped bleeding, and I could see the injury was more of a bruise than anything else. Hardly the sort of thing that would warrant a trip to the hospital. Which was just as well. Ever since what happened to Izzy I've hated those places, and I certainly didn't want to spend the rest of the afternoon sitting around in one waiting for a doctor to look at me.

I was trying to think of something to say when a black limousine suddenly appeared in front of the steps. I was really surprised when the driver got out — he wasn't a vamp. I'd never figured an Immune would want to work for the vamps, but Mom says there are some people who'll do anything for money. I guess she was right.

The driver's name was Wilson, and the vamp told him to take me wherever I needed to go. Truthfully, I was a bit disappointed it was all over. I'm not sure why. Maybe I was thinking too much Jane Austen, which I suppose was a bit bizarre given that my rescuer was a vamp and all. I mean, it's not like, well, you know . . .

Anyway, just as we were driving away I yelled out the window and asked the vamp his name. When he told me, I thought it was perfect.

Valentine.

My vampire.

* * *

I sat there thunderstruck, my head spinning.

I looked at my mother's journal and wasn't sure what to feel. Reading her words — which could just as easily have been written by me — was eerie and strange and more than a little unnerving. There was a resonance there and an immediate bond with her that I'd never felt in all my years with my father. I understood her in this context, even though so much of her remained a mystery.

But I also felt confused and betrayed and angry.

Val had known her.

It really freaked me out. After all, here we were, more than a quarter of a century later, and he was still the same young man. It drove home the reality of what he was. And I realized, in that moment, that though the rational part of me had always known he was a vamp, emotionally I'd been continuously denying to myself that he was anything other than a man. A man for whom I harbored deep feelings.

I was shaky and unsettled as I set aside my mother's journal and looked toward the window. Driven by tropical gale-force winds, drops of rain clattered noisily against the glass. The broken pane had been covered over with plastic, and the taped piece alternately puffed inward and outward, as though the window were gasping for breath.

I got up from my reading chair and moved to look out at the landscape of sheeting rain and wind-whipped trees. It was pouring so hard you couldn't see across the Quad to the university; even the streetlights were little more than dim, disembodied fireballs.

I glanced back at the journal and wished fervently that I'd never found it.

Why hadn't Val ever said anything? Had he never made the connection? That seemed impossible. I had never spoken to him about my mother, mainly because there'd never been much to say. I'd never known her, except for the few things said by my father and Grace.

Still, when he had taken the journal from me, he must have known. And if not *then*, surely later.

So why didn't you tell me, Val? I thought.

Had he thought it wouldn't matter? Or maybe he seriously believed that garbage about how some truths were better left unsaid. I suppose all that would have been well and good if the journal hadn't found its way back to me. Which was a puzzle in and of itself. Why was it here? Why had that vamp broken in and left it?

I started thinking crazy thoughts: Maybe Val had a vamp lover, and she'd done it to get back at him. Maybe she was the problem from his past he'd spoken about. Except I couldn't believe that. He'd never do that to me — or so I told myself. But in reality, I wasn't so sure any longer. He had lied to me about Coral Beach. And in a way, he had lied to me about my mother. Omission was as a good as a lie in my mind.

But even so, I just couldn't imagine him with another vamp. And besides, if she'd been his jealous lover, it would have been a lot easier for her to have simply killed me.

No, there had to be more to it than that. It bothered me that there was. It bothered me a lot, but not as much as knowing that Val and my mother had known one another. I didn't know how to handle that, and I was already jumping to all sorts of conclusions about it — most of which I didn't like.

Of course, I was getting ahead of myself. I hadn't read the rest of the journal, and maybe that was the only time he and my mother had ever met. You could hardly blame him for not making a big deal about a minor event like that.

Even as I tried to convince myself of this, I felt my stomach knot. She must have seen him again. She wouldn't have left it at that.

I knew it to be true. I knew, because it had been the same for me. After the encounter in the library I'd been angry with him for taking my mother's journal, but eventually that had given way to something else. I'd started sending notes, addressed simply to "Valentine, Third Reich Embassy, Coast Road" in an effort to reach him. It had been a shot in the dark, but when the first hadn't come back stamped "Return to Sender" I'd figured it had gotten through, and so I'd written another.

At first the letters had simply been demands that he return the journal. For weeks there'd been no reply. Then I had changed tactics, striking a more conciliatory tone, telling him about myself and asking him things about vamps and the Third Reich. I'd implied I was strictly interested for the sake of a project I was working on at school. But he had remained reticent.

By then I'd invested so much time and effort into the endeavor that I'd been determined to continue. I had grown bolder and suggested that maybe he'd like a friend, since it must be quite lonely for a vamp living amidst so many people who didn't want to have anything to do with vampires. That had precipitated his first response.

When the letter had first arrived, I'd thought I'd broken the wall around him, but the note had simply informed me that he'd no need for friends and that I'd be wise to forget about him. "I'm not the sort of person you should get involved with," he'd written.

Of course, that had had exactly the opposite effect of what I'm sure he'd intended, and I had kept writing. More letters had gone unanswered, and I had started getting quite flippant. I'd even begun taunting him, challenging him. To say I'd been cheeky would have been an understatement.

And then one day I'd come home from school and there'd been another letter waiting for me. Like the first one, there'd been nothing on it to distinguish it as having come from the Embassy, but the moment I'd seen the handwriting I'd known its source.

Father had asked who it was from, and I had lied that it was just a letter from Camille. Given how he'd later reacted when he'd discovered my relationship with Val, I suspect he'd have gone ballistic if he'd known at the time what I'd been up to.

With that letter in hand, I'd rushed to my room, bolting the door and sitting on my bed for a good ten minutes just holding that envelope, staring at it, my heart thumping in my chest, my hands trembling.

When I'd finally gotten up the courage to open it, I'd found a rather disappointing formal note. But it had been a start, and gradually more casual ones had followed. The letters had led to a certain intimacy of shared thoughts and then to other things. And after that, well . . . after that we'd come to where we were now.

Had it gone that far with my mother and Val?

I didn't want to believe it, even though rationally I knew I had no right to be angry with him if it had. Val had never pretended to be anything other than what he was. He had even warned me on more than one occasion not to fall in love with him, and I think he'd done his best not to fall in love with me. If anything *had* happened between him and my mother in the years before I was born, wasn't it rather ridiculous to be jealous about it now?

But as logical as I tried to be, I didn't like the thought that his attraction to me might have had something to do with my mother. I'd always believed I was special to him. But maybe in the end I'd simply become a substitute for something he'd lost.

The journal begged further reading, but I was emotionally and physically drained. I couldn't bring myself to continue with it just yet. I wasn't ready for more revelations about a past I'd never been a part of. I'd tackle it again tomorrow morning before Grace arrived for lunch, a date that had been arranged some time ago and one I simply couldn't avoid. Now that I was on my own, my grandmother liked to check up on me. All of which meant that I'd better get some sleep — I'd have to be at the top of my game if I was going to make it through her visit. These days, all we seemed to do was argue.

CHAPTER 8
MORNING REVELATIONS

It took me a long time to muster the nerve to pick up my mother's journal the next morning. While there was definitely a part of me desperate to know more about her, I was also terrified of what I might find. There had to be a reason why my father and Grace never spoke about her much, and I wasn't sure I wanted to know what that reason was.

As I continued to read, I discovered a woman who resembled me in many respects but was quite unrecognizable in others. Sometimes it was difficult to believe we were even related. I had to keep reminding myself that I was seeing her through the lens of the present and without benefit of the context that would have come had she lived to raise me. At this point she hadn't been my mother; she was just a young woman trying to survive in a world I knew all too well was difficult to live in.

Val was a constant undercurrent in her writing. Even when she didn't speak of him directly, his presence was felt. You could tell she was comparing what she felt about the boys around her with what she felt for him. I experienced a chilling sense of recognition, realizing I'd done exactly the same thing.

It was that difference and maturity, which I, too, had seen in Val, that sent my mother back. Back to the Embassy and to a relationship that was in too many respects the mirror image of my own.

* * *

JOURNAL OF MARY WOLSTENCROFT — July 15, 1976

My brother Matt is always telling me these stories where the vampires are ugly and withered and rather sickly looking. According to him, they have cold eyes and sharp yellow teeth and lips that are red with blood. But Valentine isn't like that. He's not really handsome in a movie star sort of way, but his eyes are this wonderful brilliant green that sometimes seems almost incandescent, and he has this scar on his left cheek that sort of lends him character. Anyway, it's really not what he looks like that matters. There's just this aura about him, this genuine warmth. I can't think of him as being anything other than human.

So I couldn't help myself. I had to go back. I had to see him again. It's crazy, and it's really, really stupid, but I just had to do it. I rode my bike back to the Embassy, rehearsing what I was going to say, trying not to be too nervous. But the closer I got, the more anxious I felt.

I must have waited outside the gate for ages. I felt a bit foolish about it to be honest. The thing is, I just couldn't leave. I kept convincing myself he'd come. And finally he did, though at first I wasn't sure it was him; the car windows were tinted so dark that I couldn't see inside. I panicked because of that, suddenly struck by the realization I hadn't given much thought to the fact that he might not be the only vamp using that car.

I guess I was hoping he'd be happy to see me, but he didn't really react much at all. He just asked me if there was anything he could do for me, the way a salesman might inquire after a customer in a shoe store.

I was so nervous I could barely get the words out, lamely telling him I just wanted to thank him for what he'd done. I really put my foot in it when I said I hadn't expected a vamp to do something like what he'd done for me, even though I didn't mean it that way. He just laughed.

Maybe he took pity on me or something, because he was really nice about my showing up, acting as though it wasn't weird or anything. But he knew I hadn't biked all that way just to thank him, so I forced myself to tell him the real reason — I wanted to get to know him better, I thought there was something between us, and I didn't think I was the only one who thought it. I told him we should spend some time together, get to know one another. I'd devoted a lot of time to working out my arguments, and I laid them out, one after another, in a logical manner — even though of course the whole thing was utterly irrational.

It was hard judging his reaction. I think I kind of amused him. He said I made a good case, and that maybe one day I'd make a good lawyer, which made me laugh. Then I blushed, because he said he liked my laughter and that it had been a long time since he'd heard a woman laugh like that.

I'd never had anyone call me a woman before. I hoped that was an indication he didn't see me as just some silly schoolgirl, so I asked if we could at least talk. There couldn't be any harm in that, I told him.

I think I was kind of surprised that he agreed, and I was so happy I almost forgot to ask him when. He set a date for the next day, and then I rode off as fast as I could so he didn't have time to change his mind.

And that was that.

Lucy thinks I'm nuts. She says if anyone finds out . . . well, neither of us really knows what would happen. But she's certain it won't be good. Vamps just don't mix with Immunes, she says. Nobody likes them. She pretends she's scandalized, but I can tell she's envious.

JOURNAL OF MARY WOLSTENCROFT — July 16, 1976

When I went back to the Embassy today, Val took me for a walk in the gardens. The first time I saw them, after he rescued me from the wolves, I thought they were bleak looking. But when I was walking with him today, they were different. They were prettier than I remembered.

I felt so grown-up as we strolled along the path, my hand on his arm just like Elizabeth and Mr. Darcy. I felt as though I'd crossed some sort of threshold; any child that might have been in me was gone.

And now . . . I find I'm no longer interested in the things my other friends are interested in. I have what I want. A whole new world has opened up for me.

* * *

I told myself it was crazy to be so vexed by my mother's relationship with Val, but after reading her words it was hard not to be.

The deeper I got into the journal, the greater the gulf between the woman I'd always imagined my mother to be and the one I was beginning to discover she'd actually been.

The most distressing part of it all was the fact that Val seemed to have transferred his affection from her to me. Had there been something purposeful in that? I didn't want to think so. But if there was something behind it, some reason for him choosing me, I wanted to know what it was. If I was merely a substitute for her . . . well, I wasn't sure how I'd deal with *that*.

If only that damn book hadn't come into my possession again. I'd been perfectly happy in my ignorance. Now I kept thinking the whole thing was all so . . . so what? Awful? Sordid? Sick?

I was going to have it out with Val — and soon. Because now that I knew some of the truth, I wanted to know all of it.

But first things first. In a few short hours Grace would be here for lunch, and I'd a dozen things to do before my grandmother arrived.

I set my mother's journal aside, gathered my handbag and hat, and in minutes I was on a streetcar headed to the Bytown Market. New shipments had come in from South Island, and there was plenty of fresh produce; the vendors weren't having much trouble hawking the stuff. RB in hand, I went hunting, hoping I'd enough food coupons left from this month's allotment to really splurge.

Things were always tight these days in Haven. People were constantly moaning and bitching about the rationing and how, despite the government's promises of better days to come, things never really improved. If what Grace had told me was true, it had always been this way. Only the rich seemed to find a way to circumvent the severe rationing of all the goods and services on the islands. I was far from wealthy, and on more than one occasion I'd had to trade some of my old clothes and books on the black market for a few extra ration coupons to get me through the month. It was illegal, of course. But heck, a girl had to survive. And besides, everybody did it.

The market was a madhouse, and I had to fight with hundreds of others for some fresh fruit and the makings of a salad. There wasn't much haggling when practically everything was scarce. You paid or you went without.

"The trawlers came in this morning," said Luigi as I stopped by his stall. The merchant was an elderly man and one of a small group of the original settlers who'd actually made it out of Europe. He always seemed to have one foot planted firmly in the past and had never completely adapted to Haven. You could hear it in his voice and see it in his eyes; it made me wonder what it must be like to have known the world before the Fall.

"Did they bring back anything interesting?" I asked, picking through a crate of tomatoes that had already been thoroughly raided.

Luigi leaned toward me, whispering conspiratorially, "They got cod. *Atlantic* cod."

I stopped dead in my tracks and looked up at him in disbelief. "Are you for real? They actually went into the *Atlantic*? That's thousands of miles away. Even if they got through the Panama Canal, it would have taken weeks."

"No canal," Luigi snorted. "Nazis all over that place. Round the Horn they go." He made a dipping motion with one arm, then swung it upward, as if to mime the long passage through the South Pacific, around the southernmost tip of South America, and up into the North Atlantic.

"You're serious?"

He nodded, grinning like the cat that ate the canary.

"But the vamps *never* let us fish there," I said.

"That don't ever stop them scavies," said Luigi. "They know them vamps can't watch everything; there's a lot of ocean for little trawlers to hide in."

"Still . . . if they got caught or were spotted by one of the U-boats . . ."

Luigi shrugged and spread his hands. "Hey, cod is better than local fish we get, no? Something new."

"I guess," I said. "Must be terribly expensive, though."

He eyed my bags. "You cooking for your *nonnina*?"

I nodded. "But even for Grace —"

Luigi held up a finger. "*Un momento, mio caro.*" He ducked down behind the stacks of crates, reappearing a moment later with something wrapped in an old edition of the *Haven Chronicle*. Eyes darting left and right, he held it guardedly and peeled back a bit of the paper, revealing the scaly carcass of a large fish.

"For your *nonnina*," he said, presenting it to me with a beaming smile.

"I couldn't possibly," I said. "I wouldn't have nearly enough." It would cost me at least a few months' sugar allowance for a fish from half a world away.

"I give you cheap. Special for your *nonnina*." He held it closer to me, the reek of it more pronounced. My mouth was watering at the thought of it fried in butter with a little lemon. "Better than beef," Luigi added, sweetening the pot.

Beef and pork from the Third Reich constituted a substantial portion of our food trade with the vamps. They're big on that there. Not for the meat, of course, but for the blood. But beef and pork can get a little tiring, and everyone in Haven is always looking for something different. People will jump at the chance for even the most minor change.

"Sold," I said, realizing even then that I was being outrageously impulsive.

As I started back home, the scents of the market gave way to the aroma of baked goods, coffee, and the heavy undertones of industry. I popped into The Grind on the way and Pedro ground me a primo blend — the best beans from the plantations up on the Blue Mountains. Grace would think it terribly decadent, but it was a luxury she didn't often get, and I knew she'd appreciate it.

By the time I finished shopping it was almost eleven o'clock. I hurried back to my flat and rushed about straightening things up, trying to make the place look as presentable as possible before I got to work preparing lunch.

Grace considered domestic skills a necessity in any young woman, and whenever possible, she would trot out that old aphorism that the way to a man's heart was through his stomach. I often felt like arguing, but it wasn't worth it. Every time I did it spawned a debate about marriage, one of my grandmother's favorite topics.

At seventeen I was legally on the market, and the state required that all woman be married and producing children as soon as possible. Preferably by the time they were eighteen and *definitely* before they were twenty-five. Being single beyond that was unacceptable; there were few spinsters in Haven, and all of them were infertile. Even widows were expected to remarry if they were still of childbearing age. As far as the government was concerned, love didn't figure into the equation. All that mattered was increasing the population of the islands as quickly and as efficiently as possible — never mind that it was hard to sustain what we already had, even with all the rationing. Governments are seldom logical.

I gutted the fish, threw together a salad made from the fresh market greens, and popped some frozen bread dough into the tiny oven that was one of the luxuries of my flat. I set the timer and retreated to my bedroom to shower and get dressed.

I chose my outfit carefully. Grace had very particular ideas about what a proper young lady should wear. "Shorts," she always proclaimed, "are strictly for boys who have yet to become men and for girls who haven't yet grown old enough to realize they're women." As far as my grandmother was concerned, a young woman of my age, who should be doing everything she could to attract a mate, must always wear a dress and suitable shoes. Suitable shoes did not include sneakers or anything that didn't have at least a two-inch heel. So my shorts and blouse gave way to a sundress, while strappy high-heeled sandals replaced my comfortable canvas runners. I was afraid the cuts on my feet might show, but they'd well and truly healed, with barely a hint of scarring.

I'd just finished applying some makeup — another of Grace's musts for the civilized woman — and was primping my hair when there came a knock at the door. I made one last survey of the flat to ensure all was in good order, then drew a deep breath and girded myself for what was to come.

"Grandma," I started to say as I opened the door. But when I saw who was there, I stopped dead and stood for what seemed like minutes, my jaw ajar.

"May I come in?"

They have to ask. I don't understand why, but it's a thing about vamps. They have to be invited into your home, or they can't enter. I used to think it was just an old wives' tale — and I'm still not sure it isn't a bunch of malarkey — but Val had said it's true. Who knows? Maybe it's some effect of the virus on their brains or something. Anyway, after they've been invited in once, they can come and go as they please. But Val had never been here before. I'd always thought it too risky, what with all the students about, not to mention nosy Mrs. Del Flora. Now here he was, out of the blue, on today of all days.

"I heard about your intruder."

I blinked at him, my brain still not in gear. I gurgled some sort of response that was entirely unintelligible, while inside I was battling with myself, unable to reconcile my sudden physical desire with the newfound jealousy and hurt simmering just below the surface. Part of me wanted to kiss him; the other could just as easily have punched him in the nose.

"I was concerned you might have been hurt," Val said. He'd already removed his gloves and sunglasses and was starting to take off his hat and coat.

There were footsteps on the stairs behind him, attended by the steady clack of a cane — my grandmother.

"Get in here!" I hissed, yanking Val into the flat. Grace's stentorian tone was unmistakable in the cavernous hallways and stairwell as she chatted with Mrs. Del Flora.

I slammed the door and pressed my back against it, facing Val, my chest heaving as a flood of anxiety wiped away any other emotions. "You can't be here."

"But you just invited me in," he said, straightening his collar. "Though I confess it was a rather unorthodox invitation."

"My grandmother is coming up the stairs. In a few seconds she's going to be knocking on this door, and I can't have a *vamp* in my flat when she does."

"What would you suggest?" Val asked with irritating calm.

I looked around and spied the window, but he shook his head. "It's daylight," he said.

"You got here in it just fine, didn't you?"

"Do you really want people to see a vampire jumping out your window in the middle of the day?" he pointed out.

I chewed at my lower lip. "I don't suppose there's any truth to that turning into a bat business?"

Val laughed. "No, that's just something Bela Lugosi does for the movies. We get a good laugh out of it."

"Blast it," I muttered under my breath. I glanced to my bedroom door, grabbed his hand, and hauled him after me. "In here," I ordered, giving him a shove for good measure. "And don't make a sound."

Val made a flippant bow and tried to kiss me, but I darted out of reach.

"Not a peep," I said sternly, pointing a finger at him.

"On my word of honor."

I stood for a moment looking at him. My mother's words echoed in my mind, reminding me of what he'd meant to her — and possibly what she'd meant to him.

But there was no time to deal with that issue now. With a heavy sigh, I pulled the bedroom door shut behind me and went to greet Grace.

CHAPTER 9

FALL FROM GRACE

"You're awfully quiet, child," Grace said, regarding me curiously from across the table.

I looked up from my fish and forced a grin. "I've had a tough time of it lately," I said, which was putting it mildly.

"Ah. Yes, I was so sorry to hear about Camille. Such a pretty young thing." Grace shook her head. "A shameful business that was. Honestly, I just don't know what the world is coming to these days. People murdering one another, breaking into other people's homes. It never happened in my day," she proclaimed with an air of righteous indignation.

"What day was that, Grandma?" I asked.

She frowned at me. "Don't mock me, child."

"I'm not."

"Things were much different back in the beginning," Grace said. "We weren't so soft on crime. We couldn't afford to be. We had to —"

"Rebuild. Yes, I know. We all know. I know you don't think much of my generation, but we do understand."

"You could have fooled me," she muttered. "All you children seem to think about these days is yourselves. You just want to have fun and do things the way you want to do them. You forget what we went through to give you the lives you have today. You forget that

that horrid vamp Hitler and his hordes of bloodsucking Nazis are still sitting in Berlin, no doubt scheming of ways to get rid of us."

"I've heard rumors there are vamps rebelling against the Nazis."

Grace snorted. "We can only hope. But those rumors have come and gone many times over the years. Every now and then someone trots them out. There's no reason to believe anything has changed. On the other hand, perhaps we'll get lucky, and this time it won't just be a rumor. Maybe they'll finally kill each other off and free us of their scourge before they get rid of us."

"Don't you think they'd have done that by now if they really could? It's not like we could mount much of a defense against them."

"You're forgetting the truce, my dear. Honestly, what do they teach you in school these days?"

"It's really *their* truce, though, isn't it?" I said. "They were supposedly so bent on wiping us out, and then after the Battle of Cypress Hills they suddenly stopped and sued for peace. It doesn't make sense, if you ask me. Did we have some sort of secret weapon or something?"

Grace dabbed at her lips with her napkin. "I haven't the faintest. I spent the last few months of the war in a concentration camp in Alberta."

I had heard that particular story many times: the terrible hardship, the starvation, women giving birth in horrific conditions, the long ride through the Rocky Mountains to Vancouver, and the ships that had taken them to Haven. I didn't want her launching into it again, so I said, "But you were one of the first settlers — one of the Founders. You were part of the Forum; you helped write the first constitution."

"That was long after the truce was signed," she said. "And I'm sure they must have taught you that one of the terms agreed to by both sides —"

"Is that the contents remain secret to all but those in the highest office of the land," I interrupted, nodding. "Yeah, I know. And the president and his council are sworn under oath never to divulge anything. Some democracy."

"At least it is one," Grace said shortly. "And if you're so eager to know what's in the truce, then get yourself elected to the Council."

Which was pretty much the same thing Val always said — as if you simply went out and signed up or something. But politics in Haven was for the few, and mostly for the wealthy. People with money or people with ties to people who had money. Either way, there wasn't much chance of getting on the council if you didn't have connections.

"Why ever did you bring this up anyway?" Grace asked.

"Just thinking about relations between vamps and Immunes," I replied. "Just wondering if we'll ever really be able to live with one another."

She looked aghast. "Why would we want to, child? Mark my words, they're monsters. They were monsters sixty years ago, and they're monsters today. Nothing has changed."

"Maybe that's the problem," I said. "Maybe something needs to."

"Humph!" was all she said before going back to her fish. A few minutes later she was onto her favorite topic. "I suppose you're looking forward to your last year of school," she began, with deceptive earnestness.

I just shrugged in reply, not sure I was now that Camille would no longer be a part of it.

"A little education never hurt anyone, I always say," Grace continued, ignoring my indifference. "Mind you, too much and a young woman like yourself tends to get a bit pretentious. You don't want to scare the young men away by filling your head with too many facts. Men like to think they're smarter than we are. And why not let them? As long as they provide you with a good home and are a good father to your children, what more can you ask for?"

"Oh, I don't know," I said. "Maybe love."

"Love?" Grace made a fluttery gesture of dismissal. "What does love have to do with having children and raising them? That's what

Haven needs, my dear. And you have obligations — the same ones I had and the same ones your mother had. No woman has a right to shirk her duty to the Republic, child. It's been that way since the founding of our nation, and it will be that way until we take back what's rightfully ours. We can't save the world by being selfish."

"I know all about my obligations, Grandma. But I'm only seventeen. I have a few more years."

"Twenty-five is the deadline, my dear. That's not all that far off. And you know perfectly well that if you're fertile and haven't committed by then, the government will make the choice for you. They'll assign you someone, and then where will all your romantic notions of love be? Personally, I think you should try to get married next year. That gives you more time to have more children. Larger families get better ration quotas, you know."

If I hadn't known just how serious my grandmother was, I'd have laughed. There was no sense telling her there wasn't a chance in hell I was getting hitched next year; that was a bridge I didn't have to cross right now. Unfortunately, it was an issue that wouldn't go away, no matter how much wishing I did.

I thought of what Camille had said on the beach, how she had railed against it all. Certainly there were plenty of young women in Haven who were more than willing to fulfill their obligations by getting married young and bearing four or five children. But like Camille, I wasn't one of them. And that made the pressure on me all the worse. When you're in love with someone who simply can't help you achieve the state's expectations, it becomes somewhat problematic. I couldn't imagine being with anyone other than Val, but as far as having children, there was no getting around the fact that our relationship was a dead end in that respect.

After lunch we retired to the sitting area of my flat. I fussed with the radio, waiting impatiently for the tubes to warm up, and then tuning it to TIBS — Three Islands Broadcast Service. But I quickly abandoned the effort when the vamp Sinatra's voice came over the air. Grace loathed the fact that the government let any vamp culture invade our shores; she considered it an affront to our hard-won sovereignty.

Fortunately she didn't seem to notice Sinatra before I silenced the radio. Her attention was focused elsewhere. She was studying the patch of plastic that covered my broken window, giving it a penetrating look as she settled into her chair. I held my breath, expecting a long lecture, but she made no comment. I was thankful enough for that.

"My, it is warm today," she said, fanning herself with one hand as she glanced out the window. The wind had died down, and now even the leaves on the trees hung limp. Not a single cloud marred the brilliant blue sky.

"We live on the equator," I said. "When is it not warm?"

Grace sighed. "When I was a child in Saskatchewan we had seasons. Flowers in the spring, brightly colored leaves in the fall. Hot summers, cold winters. Snow."

"I wish I could see it," I said.

"See what? "

"Snow. It sounds wonderful." It certainly did, especially now. I pictured cold flakes drifting down, settling on my skin, melting. So deliciously cold.

Grace laughed. "It's not so wonderful when you're stuck on a farm miles from nowhere, and the roads are blocked because no one has been out to plow them. Still," she added wistfully, "there was always something beautiful about waking up to a fresh snowfall: the way it covered the branches of the trees and glistened and sparkled in the sunlight. Sometimes you would look at it and find yourself breathless with awe, realizing how extraordinary the world could be."

She fell silent, and there was sadness in her eyes. The same sort of sadness I'd sometimes seen in Val, and maybe for not so different reasons. My stomach clenched, thinking of him in the next room, so close to a woman who had lived in the same world of which he'd once been a part. A woman I was pretty sure would gladly drive a wooden stake through his heart. Grace was completely convinced all his kind were monsters and blamed them for the fact that she no longer lived in the world she was thinking about now.

Sweat dripped from my brow, so I got up and went over to where I kept my stash of Electric Allotment tokens. They had to last me until the government issued my next quarterly quota, so I was loath to use them. The constant shortage of hydro in Haven meant it was one of the most tightly controlled and rationed commodities on the islands. The windmills and the hydro-generating dams simply couldn't produce enough electrical output to fulfill the demands of two million people — especially in a country where oil and gasoline were almost as precious as gold. It was no wonder most homes still had wood-fueled cooking stoves and kerosene refrigerators.

But as precious as the tokens were, I hated to see Grace wilting, so I popped a couple into the regulator box connected to the overhead fan and watched the mechanical timer set itself for one hour. As it ticked away, the fan creaked to life. It started whirring faster and faster, sending down a wave of stale air that quickly became cooler and more pleasant.

"Better?" I asked.

"Much," Grace said, looking relieved. "I don't understand why you insist on living in this place when you could live with me. My house is much cooler, and I've plenty of room. You could save your father's money for when you get married."

"We've been over this before." Too many times, I thought. "You and I . . ." I spread my hands. "You know how it is with us. I love you, Grandma, but we're just . . . different."

"Is that the only reason?"

I frowned at her, puzzled, but said, "It's better this way. For both of us."

"Humph."

"Anyway, I won't need a place when I do the first tour of my M2S." If I had been from a wealthy family like Camille's, I probably could have escaped having to do the Mandatory Military Service. "Unless you're married, you have to live on base for the whole six months of your first tour. Something about learning discipline."

"A little discipline never hurt anyone," said Grace. "Sometimes I think you've not had nearly enough in your life."

"I don't really see the point of all that marching and firing guns and stuff."

"One day we'll take back this world, child, and we'll need an army to do it. Mandatory Military Service is important to achieving that goal. It's an honor to serve. Besides, we can never forget who the enemy is."

"The war was a long time ago," I said, perhaps a little wearily. "Why do you persist in hating them so?"

"You shouldn't even have to ask."

I sighed. "How about some coffee?" I suggested, trying to change the mood. "It's the Blue." Grace could never turn down a cup, no matter how hot the weather.

"Coffee would be delightful," she said.

I went to the kitchen and busied myself making the brew. Grace hated it if the coffee was burnt or boiled, so I was watching my cantankerous percolator religiously when she called out that she was going "to pay a penny." At first that slipped by me, but then it hit me like a smack to the forehead — Grace would have to go through my bedroom to get to the bathroom.

"Grandma!" I practically screamed.

The percolator was past sputtering, and the coffee was boiling as I dashed out of the kitchen and across the living room to my bedroom door. But it was too late. Grace stood just inside the threshold, her hand still on the doorknob. She was staring toward the bed, and when I came up behind her I could see the focus of her attention — Val sat there, looking sheepish as he stared back at her.

"Hello, Grace," he said. His eyes shifted to me, and he wrinkled his nose. "I think you've ruined the coffee."

CHAPTER 10
UNTURNED STONES

"This isn't what it looks like," I said.

Grace turned her head slightly and regarded me skeptically from the corner of her eye. "I see. So there isn't a vampire sitting on your bed?"

"Well, yes, but —"

"I had hoped you'd have come to your senses by now," she said, shaking her head.

I blinked at her and stood there, open-mouthed and confused.

Grace's regard was withering as she gave my leg a little poke with her cane. "Honestly, Sophie, did you take me for a fool? Did you think I didn't know about your little infatuation?"

I struggled to speak, but I was so flabbergasted that all I could do was splutter helplessly.

"Those times when you stayed with me, you always thought you were so clever when you went off to meet him," Grace went on. "Why do you think I didn't want you to have your own place? I knew the signs." She closed her eyes and hesitated. "I'd seen them before."

My eyes went wide. "You knew about Mom?"

She frowned, caught off guard. "I don't know how on earth you know about Mary" — she shot a dirty look at Val, as though to say he must have been the one who'd informed me — "but yes, I knew. I tried to stop it then, too."

I put out a hand to steady myself.

"How could you be so stupid, child?"

"I need to sit down," I said. I retreated into the other room and flopped into my reading chair, my right hand coming to rest on Mom's journal.

Grace walked over and sat down on the settee opposite me. As she settled in place, she raised her voice toward the bedroom and said, "You may as well join us, Val."

I stared at him as he entered the room, my thoughts in turmoil. He glanced at me and made a slight motion of resignation with his hands.

Grace looked from me to Val and back again. For a long time no one said anything. Finally, she let out a loud sigh and shook her head. "You're wasting your time," she said, fixing her eyes on me and pointedly ignoring Val. "You will *never* be anything more than a diversion to him." Her eyes darted to Val in a flickering glance of contempt. "He's incapable of love. Love is a *human* emotion, and he long ago ceased to be one of *us*." Her gaze intensified. "He's one of *them*, child. Do you understand that? One of the same lot who put us here. Never make the mistake of thinking you can trust them. You can't. They're the enemy. They have their own agenda, and it certainly doesn't fit with ours."

Val wasn't the sort to display a lot of emotion, so it was a shock to see him react so conspicuously to Grace's words. His entire body stiffened, and his face darkened, his eyes showing a flash of anger and resentment. "I'm not what you think I am, Grace," he said in a tightly controlled voice. "If anything I've done —"

"You corrupted my daughter!" Grace interrupted. She was livid and shakily pointed the tip of her cane at him. "You knew who she was, what she meant to me, but still you went after her."

Val didn't say anything at first. He turned to me, a look in his eyes that wasn't anything like what I'd anticipated. I had been expecting discomfort and perhaps contrition for having been found out — but instead there was pain. It reminded me of what I'd seen in the park that time he'd laid bare his soul and told me of his past. Or part of his past, I suppose. Clearly he'd left out some important details.

"Do you really want to be discussing this in front of her?" he said to Grace, his voice eerily calm.

"I want her to know the truth."

"*Your* truth?" he retorted. "Or the real truth?" There was bitterness, now.

Grace's face hardened. "There's only one truth. My daughter wouldn't have willingly become involved with you. You did to her whatever it is your kind do to make people think they need you. The same thing you've clearly done to my granddaughter."

"I didn't do anything to them," Val said. "I was only being me. You remember *me*, don't you, Grace?"

I sat bolt upright. "Wait! What? What the hell are you talking about?" I looked to Val, then Grace. "What's he talking about, Grandma?"

"Do you want to answer that?" Grace said to Val. "Or should I be the one to enlighten my granddaughter on the nature of the man she *thinks* she's in love with?"

Val clenched his jaw and turned to me. "You remember the girl I told you I went back for after I turned?" he said. "The one I was going to marry?"

I thought I would pass out as the truth hit me. "That . . . that was *you*?" I said to Grace. "You and Val —" I choked on the words.

"Vladimir Arghezi," she said, her eyes as hard as stones. "My first love. But Vladimir died in the war."

Val flinched, but he didn't voice an argument. He just stood there with that awful sorrow in his eyes.

"You never should have come back." Grace seemed to sag, looking small and frail.

"We made a promise," he said. "A promise to each other. I came here to keep that promise."

"There never could have been an *us*," she said.

"There was when it suited you. *You* were the one who came to *me* when Isa—"

"Stop!" Grace barked. She sat ramrod straight, shaking, a murderous look in her eyes. "I forbid it. I know what I owe you."

"What's between Sophie and me has nothing to do with *that*," said Val.

"What's between Sophie and you is nothing but a foolish little girl's romantic notion of love. And if I hadn't feared losing her completely by trying to stop it, I'd have intervened sooner."

"Grandma —" I started to say.

"I know you, child," she said to me. "You're so willful. If I had forbid you from seeing him it would only have made matters worse. You'd simply have become more determined and would have tried harder to do the exactly the opposite of what you were told. Just like when your father tried to make you see sense. But now you can see the truth. Now you can see what he truly is. You know as well as I do that the two of you can never be. You mean nothing to him. You never will. Enough is enough, and now it's time to end it."

Grace looked at me, and I was stung by the disdain I saw there. "I will not stand idly by and watch you ruin your life, child. I won't." She shook her head vehemently. "I won't go through that again."

I felt sick, once more recalling how my father had reacted when he'd found out. And I was again wracked by guilt, knowing that my actions had probably helped destroy him. I didn't want to go through the same thing with Grace. It was why I'd always been so careful about it with her — or so I had thought.

I shot a look at Val, wanting him to say something, to find some way of making this right, even though in my heart I knew that was impossible.

"I've said enough," Grace said, rising to her feet. She might have been diminutive and elderly, but at that moment, I felt cowed by her. She opened the door to let herself out. "You hurt your father with this, Sophie. You helped put him where he is. Thank goodness he can no longer be troubled by it."

I should have stopped her. I should have said something. But instead I just sat there and watched her go. I couldn't feel anything. There was just this odd emptiness inside me. It wasn't that I didn't care. I did — a lot. But I just didn't know how to feel. I'd been buried under a deluge of information, and I couldn't process it. I was numb.

The door to the flat stood open, and I heard Mrs. Del Flora down in the foyer, saying goodbye to Grace. There was still time to run after her. Still time to . . . to what?

I got up, moving mechanically, and shut the door. For a moment I just stood there, my hand on the doorknob, wondering if I'd just literally closed the door on one of the most important relationships in my life. When I finally turned around, Val was standing beside my reading chair, the journal in his hands.

I walked over and angrily snatched the book from his grasp. "What are you?" I said, my voice pitched high with emotion. I stepped back, putting distance between us. "I don't even think I know you anymore."

"I've never pretended to be anything other than what I am, Sophie," Val said. He looked at me with icy composure. "It's always been there for you to see."

"I'm not talking about that!" I said, almost shouting. "It's not about you being a vamp."

"Of course it is. How many times have I warned you that *this*" — he gestured to himself — "is not the truth. I'm not a boy, Sophie. I haven't been one for decades. I had a life before this happened. I had one before *you*."

"But you knew. You knew who I was, dammit! You should have told me."

"You yourself have often said the past is the past."

"Don't you dare try and twist this around! We're not talking about that. This is different. It's not about other women you may have loved before. It's about Grace and my mother, for pity's sake! What am I supposed to think, Val? You were engaged to my grandmother, for Christ's sake! You loved my mother. It's . . . it's . . . God, it's sick."

I could barely stand, and I wanted to throw up. My heart was thundering; my head was throbbing. When I tried to breathe, it was like sucking air through a straw. I didn't want to look at him, but I did. It hurt. It hurt so goddamn much. I wanted to hate him, but I couldn't stop loving him. I wanted to claw his eyes out, but I also wanted him to hold me and kiss me and make me forget.

I glanced down at the book in my hand and felt an uncontrollable urge to rip it to shreds. I wished I'd never seen it; I understood now that Val had been right all along, as far back as that day in the library when I'd first seen the cursed thing. I should have listened. I should have listened to everyone. But instead I had thought I'd known best. I had thought they were all wrong.

"Sophie —"

"No. Don't." I stumbled to the window, wanting air. "Just don't."

He stood silently watching me. I could feel it, the way I always could — as though we were somehow connected. It had been that way from the beginning, but now I wished it wasn't. Now I wished I could be done with him. I just wanted . . . I just wanted to be normal, but now I was thinking I wasn't, and that I never could be.

"This was not a plan," Val said.

I looked up, stared at him stone-faced.

"I never intended to fall in love with Mary. I tried hard not to. After . . ." He paused and ran a hand down his face. "When the truce came, I went to the camps, searching — looking for Grace. I'd heard rumors, and when the opportunity arose to come to Haven I thought maybe I was being given a chance to find what I'd lost. So I came. I came for Grace, hoping . . ."

"Hoping what, for God's sake?" I said. "That you could just somehow pick up where you'd left off?"

Why did I think it so incredible? Why was I so shocked that Val had thought he could have with Grace what I'd always wanted him to have with me? Maybe because I'd always known in my heart that it could never work. And now, when I looked at Grace as she was, in the waning years of her life, and looked at Val, so young and virile, I saw the future. I saw us, decades from now, split asunder by time.

He would leave me, I realized. How could he not? How could I not want him to? He would still be this young man, and it wouldn't be fair to either of us.

Except he isn't young, I thought. *He's lived so long, been through so much. And I've only just begun to have a life.*

Val lifted his head, focused on me, his face a chart of misery. "I wanted what I'd lost," he said. "I thought if she saw me, if she realized I was still the man she'd loved . . . that under all this I was . . ." He shrugged dejectedly.

"So Grace scorns you, and you go after my mother?" I said. I heard my words and felt the anger and the pain they encompassed. I heard them dropping into the space between us, one after another, meaningless and inert. They could have been pebbles falling into a pond — *plop, plop, plop.* Just sounds. Except they weren't. They were blows, full of cruelty and contempt, meant to strike and injure. "What was it, Val? Some sort of revenge? You knew Grace hated vamps so you thought you'd seduce her daughter?"

His jaw tightened. "Do you really think so little of me?"

I didn't answer. I just stood there waiting, revolted and wounded and wanting this to be over.

"It was an accident," he said quietly. "Literally an accident. She'd fallen off her bike near the Embassy, and I went to help her. And when I saw her . . ."

"I know what happened," I said. I didn't need to hear it repeated from his lips.

"No, you don't."

I'd never seen Val look so distraught, so utterly devastated. I thought to myself briefly that I should be comforting him, because that's what people do when they care about one another. But there was a wall between us now, and I couldn't see my way to breaking through it.

"I knew who she was the moment I saw her," he said. "The year before —" He stopped, shook his head, started again. "She looked so much like Grace, so much like —" He closed his eyes, waging some sort of internal struggle. "She looked the way Grace had looked before I left for the war. For a moment it was as if everything was the way it had been before . . ."

"But it wasn't," I said. "She wasn't Grace."

"No. No, she wasn't. She was something else. Her own person. I told myself that, and I didn't pursue it. I didn't encourage her. But she was persistent." His eyes locked with mine. "Like you."

"You could have told her no. You *should* have."

"I tried to. Just like I tried with you. But then . . . I just wanted . . ."

"Wanted what?"

Val clenched his fists. "To be normal. God, is that so hard for you to understand?"

"No," I whispered. And it wasn't. I was beginning to see him differently. Maybe I was even beginning to understand what I hadn't really understood before.

"For just a while it seemed possible," he said. "She didn't look at me as though I were a monster; she didn't treat me like some creature that deserved to die. She loved me in spite of what I was. Can you see that?"

Of course I could; he knew that.

"She made me feel what I'd felt before I was changed. Sometimes I could almost imagine I was human again. And it felt so good. It felt so wonderful to imagine I wasn't this . . . that I was what I was supposed to be. I convinced myself it wasn't wrong, that something that felt so good couldn't be a mistake. I told myself I deserved some happiness."

"Did you love her?" I asked. I wasn't sure I wanted him to answer, wasn't sure how I'd feel if he said yes. "I mean, did you *really* love her?"

Val shrugged again. "I don't know. Sometimes I think so. I told myself I did. But maybe it was just wanting to be human again." He looked at me, his eyes so full of despair. "Is that so wrong, Sophie? Does that make me a monster?"

"I don't know." The words sounded distant. "What about later, when my father came along?"

"I ended it. By then I'd realized . . ." He stopped, looking weary. Looking broken.

"She gave up, just like that? The two of you just walked away from one another?" I knew it couldn't have happened that easily. My mother wouldn't have given him up without a fight.

"No. But it was Haven. She had obligations. And I was what I was. Grace is right in that respect; there never could have been an us."

There was a long silence. The fan creaked overhead, and outside in the quad I could hear the leaves chatter in the trees as a faint breath of wind stirred them.

"So what am I to you?" I heard myself ask, hollow-voiced. "The next one? Just another escape from your vamp life? Another in the line of Wolstencroft women for you to conquer?"

"If you think that —"

"What should I think?"

"I warned you."

I wanted to shout at him, but I knew he was right. "Yes, you did," I said, the words almost lost in the space between us.

"You should have listened."

"Maybe I should have," I agreed. But I hadn't, and now here we were. My hand tightened on the journal. "Back at the library that day — what did it matter to you if I knew about you and my mother? There wasn't anything between us then."

"I didn't think you should find out that way."

"Are you sure you weren't just thinking ahead? You knew I was her daughter; maybe you had it all planned out."

"No. But I knew from the very first time I saw you that you were different."

"Different?"

"You're not like anyone I've ever met, Sophie. Not before I was changed, and certainly not after."

"I don't understand."

"I can't explain."

"Try. Be honest with me — for once."

"I just know we could be happy, Sophie. I was told about you. Told to wait for you."

"What the hell are you talking about?"

"It doesn't matter. It just matters that you and I, we were supposed to happen."

I shook my head ruefully. "I wish I could believe you." God, I wanted to. I wanted him to give me any excuse to forgive him, for things to go back to the way they'd been. But I wasn't there yet. There was too much to sort out, too much to try to make sense of.

"Maybe if you'd been honest with me from the start —" I began, but he cut me off.

"Honest with you?" In a blur of movement, Val was standing in front of me, clasping my arms, cold fingers digging into my warm flesh. "Look at me, Sophie."

"Val." I tried to squirm free of him. "Val, you're hurting me."

"Look at me!" he said, his voice commanding as he shook me.

I looked at him, stared into his eyes, and gasped as I watched them change color, turning from their familiar brilliant green to an inky black. The black spread to the whites, until his eyes were as empty and soulless as those of the Old Ones. The veins just beneath the surface of his skin became raised black cords that snaked up his neck and across his face.

There's that moment — that interlude between the start of something and your realization that it's happening — when you just seem caught. You're frozen in time, unable to react. And then instinct takes over. Fear rules. It's as if an explosion has gone off inside you. You think your heart is going to burst, and there's this flash through your body, like lava surging through your veins. It leaves you trembling and weak, your thoughts incoherent. You're not thinking; you're just afraid.

That's where I was, on the edge of hysteria. A scream bubbled up from inside me, but I couldn't get enough breath to give it life. In the back of my mind, there was the thought that this is what Grace had meant about them being monsters. It was the first time I'd ever seen Val like this. The first time I'd ever witnessed the *other* him.

My father had told me once we all have our dark sides, but I didn't think it could get much darker than this.

Val let go and staggered back, as though battling with himself. The black of his eyes faded; the green returned. In the space of a few breaths, he was as I'd always known him. Except, of course, he wasn't. I'd seen something he'd never shown me before, and I could never forget it. As I stood there, still trembling, still trying not to be afraid, I wondered if I'd ever truly known him. Maybe that *thing* was the real Valentine, and this was the illusion, the carefully crafted façade.

He didn't speak, just stood there, looking utterly desolate.

The silence between us stretched longer, until it seemed we'd been that way forever. Out on the Quad I heard voices: a boy and a girl talking, laughing, sounding intimate. Lovers.

"Say something," Val said at last.

"What?" I said, barely mouthing the word. "What should I say?"

"Anything. Say you forgive me. Say you hate me and never want to see me again. Just . . ."

"I can't."

"Sophie . . ."

I shook my head.

Val stepped toward me and reached for me gently. I backed away, but came up short against the windowsill.

"Don't," I said, my voice so faint. "Please, Val . . ." The words trailed off, but the feelings didn't. I was torn, conflicted, uncertain of which direction to turn. I wanted him to go; I wanted him to stay.

Val touched my cheek, but I brushed his hand aside. He caught mine in his, held it, brought it to his lips and kissed the palm. So softly. So passionately. I would never have thought such a simple act could be so powerfully evocative and penetrate so deeply into the core of me.

"I can't," I said again. "I can't." But I wanted to. I wanted to lose myself in him, to forget everything, to be submerged in the physical. It was so easy when it was like that. No complications. No worrying about what it meant and where it might lead; it was all instinct and sensation. I didn't have to face what he really was. I didn't have to deal with his past.

Val moved closer, and I shivered but didn't try to escape. I didn't want to now. I remembered what he'd said, and I told myself this couldn't be wrong. It couldn't be a mistake. We were too good together. We belonged with one another. I believed it. I knew it had to be true, that it couldn't be wrong.

I moved to him.

We didn't speak. Maybe we were afraid words would ruin everything again. He held me and ran his hands up my arms to my shoulders, to my face, his cool palms kissing my flesh. He leaned in, his lips brushing my forehead.

I was so hot, and he was the fresh breeze after a storm. I trembled as he kissed my earlobe. His hands drifted down my back, cool through the thin cotton of my dress, his fingers playing along my spine, easing the tension from me. My heart beat faster and faster;

my breathing escalated. The sounds of the Quad retreated, the girl's laughter fading into the distance. My whole world collapsed into this moment, the universe now just Val and me.

That was all I needed, all I wanted.

I felt his lips against my cheek, coming closer. "Don't," I breathed, and he hesitated. I sagged against him with a sigh. "Don't stop."

We kissed, and the journal fell from my hand, dropping to the floor with a soft thud. I lifted his shirt, ran my hands under it and over his chest. I drank in the feel of him, the taste, the smell. I couldn't stop myself and didn't want to. I wanted more and more of him, and I knew I could never get enough.

"It won't work," I whispered. "Us. Grace is right."

"You're not Grace. Or Mary," Val said softly. "And we can try, Sophie. Shouldn't we be happy? Don't we deserve it? How can that be wrong?"

He silenced any further debate, and I didn't fight it. I wanted there to be an *us*. It was the only thing that made this world bearable. And if I didn't have him, then what did I have?

He left in the night, slipping easily into the darkness, quickly lost in the shadows. I thought he'd take the journal with him, but later I found it on the floor where I'd dropped it. I thought it meant that something had changed, that we had passed another hurdle in our relationship. He was willing to let me discover the truth, no matter what that might be.

No matter what it might mean.

CHAPTER 11

TERROR IN THE MARGOLLIEAN

"Behold the potato," Camille says, holding it aloft in her soil-stained hand, poised as though playing Hamlet. "Fruit of the earth; food of the gods. Alas, how I hate thee, inglorious spud." She turns and grins at me, and even disheveled and dirty, she somehow manages to look amazing.

"You'll have them down on us again, if you don't stop fooling around," I say. I steal a look toward the far end of the field where the crew manager of our MLS shift is talking to the head farmer.

Camille snorts and tosses the potato into the basket at her feet. "What are they going to do? Throw me in the nick?" She bends and pulls up another plant, shaking it with exaggerated vigor to loosen clods of black earth. "Right now a jail cell is looking pretty good. This is slave labor, I tell you."

"You're such a rebel," I tease her.

"I just think they take advantage of us. I mean, can't somebody invent a machine to pull up these bloody things?" Camille pauses, studies her hands, and holds them out to me for inspection. "Look at my nails, for Pete's sake! I look like a scullery maid."

"We've only got another week."

"*This* year. Next year it'll be coffee or corn or some other wretched plant to harvest. All for the good of the state." She scowls. "What about the good of me?"

"You're making this far too personal," I tell her. "Everyone has to do it."

"Well, it sucks. This whole country sucks. I bet the vamps don't have to do stuff like this. And they sure as hell don't have to pop out babies like they're some sort of factory."

"Maybe there are some who wish they could," I point out.

Camille gives me an odd look. "You're strange, you know that? You have the weirdest ideas about vamps."

"I just think things might not be as simple as they teach us in school," I say.

"Now who's the rebel?" Camille says. "We're supposed to be working toward taking back the planet, aren't we? Remember that old hag we had first year at Humberton? What was her name?"

"Mrs. Bhutto?"

"Right." Camille straightens and takes on a sober mien. "'We're an island of humanity surrounded by an ocean of hostility,'" she says in a low, gravelly voice and lilting accent. "'We can't afford chaos in our society, girls. Everyone must know her place and fulfill the obligations bestowed upon her by the state.'"

I laugh at her impression. I can so clearly see our old teacher standing at the head of the class, pointing to a map of the world, and stabbing at the tiny little specks where the equator meets the antimeridian in the Pacific Ocean — Haven. All that remains of humanity.

"'One day, because of women like you and your proud contributions to the expansion of our society, we shall take back our world!'" Camille is in fine form now. She makes a fist and shakes it before her. "'We shall drive the scourge from the face of the earth until one day, girls, you will be able to live without ever having to fear seeing their like again.'"

"Hey! You two!" The manager is stomping across the field toward us, wagging a threatening finger. "Stop your lollygagging and get back to work."

"Yes, master," Camille mutters under her breath. She yanks out another plant, holds it up for him to see, and then shakes it so hard that one of the spuds breaks free, sails through the air, and nearly clobbers him. "Sorry," she calls, smiling innocently.

He starts to say something, but at that moment the lunch bell rings. It rings and rings and rings . . .

* * *

I awoke with a start, rolled over, and fumbled for the alarm clock. It took a few blows to silence it, and once I had, I lay there, staring up at the ceiling of my bedroom, listening to the faraway gong of the Peace Tower echo the morning hour. A crushing sense of disappointment engulfed me as I realized my moments with Camille had been nothing more than a dream. It had felt so real, and the awareness that it wasn't hurt so much. The deep ache inside of me was almost crippling; there was an emptiness in my heart where once she'd been.

Camille was still gone, and all I had left were my memories of her.

I rolled onto my side and stared out the window at the early morning light, not wanting to let that remembrance of her slip away.

God, how I missed her.

* * *

The first thing I did when I finally got out of bed was put my mother's journal away in a safe place. I was determined not to read any more of it. But that was easier said than done. As the final days of my vacation drifted away, I frequently found myself on the verge of surrendering to temptation, heedless of the awful things I might find, driven by a festering curiosity. The one thing that stayed my hand was the realization of how close that book had come to destroying what Val and I had.

It was amazing how damaging words could be. But the truth of the matter was, it wasn't really the words — only what they signified.

With September came the start of the new school year, and I fell back into my old routine. In a way it was a relief to be doing something so ordinary. But at Humberton it was hard to ignore the absence of Camille, and I was glad when classes were over for the day and I could immerse myself in my part-time job in the Margolliean Camera.

Occasionally Val snuck in, and we'd meet in the stacks for discussions that didn't involve a whole lot of talking. We were still a bit tentative with one another; for me there remained the issue of trust. I wanted him in my life so badly, yet I kept coming back to the whole issue of my mother and Grace. I didn't want it to bother me, but I couldn't deny it still did. How could it not?

And yet, for the second time, I had chosen Val over my family.

I was beginning to think I was really messed up and very much my mother's daughter.

A few weeks after the confrontation between Grace, Val, and I, things in my life began to take an even more dramatic turn. I was doing the night rounds in the library with the trolley, clearing up books left out by students, when I came across a cardboard box. Someone had left it in the Commerce section, tucked away amidst volumes on interisland trade statistics. I assumed it belonged to one of the students, and since they'd all left and it was near closing time, there was nothing for it but to turn it in at the lost and found.

In my rush to get down there before Mrs. M'domo, the head librarian, left, I tripped and spilled the contents of the box onto the floor. Notebooks, sheets of paper, photos, and several small containers scattered in all directions. Among the objects was a spool from a wire recorder that had fallen out of its Bakelite case and unraveled.

"Blast it!" I cursed under my breath. Getting down on my hands and knees, I set about gathering the items. When they were all packed away in the box once more, I took the loose wire and spool over to a dictation machine in one of the sound booths at the north end of the third floor to rewind it.

I wasn't very familiar with the bulky recorders and must have done something wrong when I was trying to get the machine to rewind, because suddenly there was a sharp crack of static, and a familiar voice boomed in the room.

"Uncle Matt?" I said aloud, my curiosity aroused.

I'd never had much of a relationship with any of my uncles or aunts; my father's entire family — mother, father, and sisters — had all died in a tragic accident when I was quite young, and the relatives on my mother's side seemed content to have nothing much to do with me. I'd asked Grace about it once, and she had been rather evasive, telling me simply that they were very busy people with important jobs in the government that took up a lot of time.

I'd often thought maybe it was because I was the reason their sister was dead. It couldn't be easy seeing a reminder of what they'd lost.

"If that's the case, then they're idiots," Camille had said when I'd confessed my suspicions to her. "You're better off without them. Besides, you don't need them; you've got me."

Only I don't have you anymore, I thought. *You left me.*

The recorder crackled, and I directed my attention to it again, listening to what seemed to be an interview of sorts — a pretty dull one at that. I was about to kill the volume and let the wire continue to spool in silence when there was an abrupt shift in my uncle's tone. He was discussing trade between Haven and the Third Reich, and I could hear him falter when the woman interviewing him implied there was something shady going on.

Woman interviewer: "There appears to be a substantial imbalance in our trade with the Nazis. They seem to be sending us far more in value than we're sending in return. That's difficult to understand."

Uncle Matt: "We're quite different cultures, with quite different needs."

Woman interviewer: "That doesn't address the issue of the imbalance, sir."

Uncle Matt: "These things aren't as simple as numbers on paper would make them appear to be."

My uncle was unquestionably nervous; I recognized that slight uncertainty people get when they're caught off guard and get flustered scrambling for an answer.

Woman interviewer: "Well then, let's talk about refrigeration units."

Uncle Matt: "Refrigeration units?"

I frowned. He didn't sound so much baffled as anxious.

Woman interviewer: "Yes. Can you explain why we'd be shipping technology like that to the vamps when it's clear they're more than capable of designing and manufacturing such things themselves?"

Uncle Matt: "I really couldn't comment on why the vamps do what they do."

Woman interviewer: "Doesn't it seem in the least bit strange to you? It's virtually the only technology of ours that they import. And considering their vast numbers, not a great deal of it at that."

I could picture my uncle trying to seem nonchalant and shrugging indifferently.

Uncle Matt: "I would never presume to understand the Nazi mind, Miss Donovan."

Donovan! I knew that name; she wrote for the *Haven Chronicle*. She'd done a piece on Camille's death. Was she conducting the interview for the newspaper?

Donovan: "So you don't see anything unusual about this?"

Uncle Matt: "The vamps do whatever they wish. You should know that by now. Be happy enough they supply us with the things we need to survive and only ask for a few refrigerators in return." He was trying to make light of it. *"Sounds like a bargain to me. Now if you'll excuse me, I've urgent matters to attend."*

After that it was only Donovan's voice on the wire. She made a few vocal notes to herself, including a reminder to check the manifests of cargo ships. It was the name of the company she mentioned that raised the hairs on the back of my neck — Island Transnational Shipping. That was John Westerly's company. *Uncle John.* And it sounded as though she suspected it of being involved in some sort of illicit transaction with the Nazis.

I didn't know what to make of the whole thing. The tone of the interview and the implication that Camille's father might be involved in criminal activities floored me. I sat there stunned for a moment or two before I realized the wire had finished spooling. I stared at it, watching it spin, the free end slapping against the magnetic heads of the machine with a metronomic regularity.

The bell rang to signal closing time for the Margollieian. I jumped at the sound of it, snatched the spool from the machine, and hurried back to where I'd left the box of research material. I had every intention of just tossing the spool in with the rest and being done with it. But of course I couldn't leave well enough alone.

I picked up one of the notebooks and flipped through it. There were reams of handwriting so illegible it might as well have been written in code. The others contained the same. I set the notebooks aside and went through the rest of the stuff, but most of it didn't make any sense to me. Then I found the shipping manifests with the Island Transnational Shipping logo at the top. Even a brief examination revealed that most of the freighters left Haven practically empty and came back with their hulls filled to the brim. And almost every outgoing ship carried cargo listed as "refrigerator units."

While I was still staring at the manifests, the lights dimmed. Ten minutes until the doors were locked. I started to cram the items back in the box, and I'd just about finished when I heard a faint sound filtering through the stacks.

Ca-klunk, hissssss, click. Ca-klunk, hissssss, click. Ca-klunk, hissssss, click.

The noise had a strange mechanical signature, spaced out every ten or fifteen seconds. *It must be one of the maintenance staff working on something*, I told myself. It wouldn't have been unusual. Almost everything in Haven was old and in constant need of repair.

Ca-klunk, hisssss, click.

A shiver ran through me, and I hastily threw the rest of the notebooks and papers into the box and secured the lid. Barely daring to breathe, I made my way toward the elevators, the eerie sound echoing around me. The library could be a very public place during peak hours, but by closing time it was as empty as a tomb — minus the dead bodies, of course. It put me on edge, and for some reason I couldn't stop thinking about the vamp who had left the journal in my flat. This was not the kind of place I wanted to meet someone like her again.

As I skirted the periodicals section, I realized the sound was getting louder; I was walking *toward* it. I slowed at the end of the aisle and crouched down behind an empty trolley, peering cautiously over the top toward the elevators. I could see the upper half of the doors on one of them. They were made of ornate panels salvaged from the *Mauritania*, one of the ships that had brought the refugees to Haven. As I watched, the doors slowly drew closed, then abruptly jolted to a stop a few inches apart. There was a fainter click, and then they opened. I waited, and the same thing happened again and again.

Ca-klunk, hisssss, click.

Something wasn't right.

I straightened up . . . and immediately wished I hadn't.

My heart seized, and the box slid from my grasp, dropping to the ground with a thump.

A woman lay on the elevator floor, her body inside, her head just over the threshold. When the doors closed, they rammed into her neck, pinching it between them before retracting. Each time this happened, her head jerked to one side, revealing eyes that were wide open and fixed.

I backpedaled, stumbling, trying to put distance between myself and the lifeless body. But before I knew what was happening, I was grabbed from behind and jerked off my feet. A beefy hand, reeking of sweat and tobacco, clamped over my mouth and nose. I thrashed wildly, and the man holding me hissed sharply in my ear, "I'll break yer ruddy neck like hers if ya don't stop."

I went as still as stone.

"Better. Now where is it, girly? She didn't have it with her. She saw I was followin' her, so she must have left it with ya."

I tried to shake my head.

"Don't give me none o' that. I saw ya with somethin', girly."

My eyes darted left, then right as I tried to get a glimpse of him. But he was all shadow, his head almost directly behind my own, so that all I caught was the barest peek of an unshaven chin.

"Answer me!" He shook me hard and tightened his grip, crushing my ribs.

I didn't know what he wanted until I spotted the cardboard box. It lay in the shadows, tilted on its side, the lid partially dislodged. Beyond it was the dead woman. It didn't take much to connect the two. I was pretty sure she was Donovan.

I tried to speak, and he said, "I'm goin' ta take me hand away. Mind ya don't scream none, or I'll do ya like I did her. Understand?"

I gulped and nodded meekly.

He lifted his hand slightly. "Now where is it?" he demanded.

"Down there," I said in a tiny voice. "Near the trolley."

The man shifted, and I knew he was searching for the box. When he spotted it, a triumphant chortle escaped him, and he relaxed his grip. At that moment the power went out, and without thinking, I reacted.

I threw my head back as hard as I could and felt the violent and painful collision of his face with the back of my skull. He howled bloody murder and crashed back into the shelves. Books tumbled down from above, a couple of them striking him on the head. I kicked back, wishing I was wearing heavy work boots instead of my school-issue Mary Janes. I must have struck him in the knee, because he howled in agony and collapsed to one side. I squirmed free as he fought to save himself from falling over.

And then I ran.

I fled into the stacks, fumbling my way through them as I heard him blundering about in pursuit. He was cursing and swearing. "I'll wring yer sweet little neck when I gits me hands on ya!" I heard him shout.

I tried not to panic, but I couldn't help it. I kept seeing the dead woman in my mind, and all I could think about was getting out of there. But I was so rattled I'd gotten turned around, and what should have been familiar suddenly wasn't. In the dark, the shelves of books had become a maze, and I groped through them, turning down one aisle and up the next. There was a loud report from a gun, and something exploded inches from my head.

I let out a shriek and ducked down another aisle. There was nowhere to go. All that laid ahead of me was the line of sound booths. I ran to the farthest one and slipped inside, pulling the door silently closed behind me and crawling under the table. I pressed up against the wall as far back as possible and sat there in the pitch black, hugging my knees to my chest, trying not to breathe as I listened to the thudding in my chest.

The killer was getting closer, muttering a string of profanity as he stumbled about in the dark, slamming the door of each booth as he checked them one by one. "I know yer in here," he called out. "Best make it easy on yerself."

His footsteps echoed close by. The doorknob of my booth turned, and the door swung open.

"Last chance, girly."

I stopped breathing and held my legs tighter, trying to make myself smaller. Outside the clouds parted, and a shaft of pale moonlight streamed down through the domed skylight high above. Now I could just make out the bottom half of the man at the end of the table, a faint silhouette in the ghostly light of the library. His knees bent as he slowly lowered himself and peered under the table.

"Ah, there you are. Too bad for you." He pointed the gun at me. "Sorry, girly, yer time's up."

He'd barely finished speaking when a low, animal-like hiss rose from out of the darkness behind him.

"What the —" The man whirled and tried to swing his gun around. "No. No! Git away!" he cried.

He never had a chance. I heard the crack of bones and a bloodcurdling scream. The gun tumbled to the floor. I could see no more than a shadow of his assailant, but the gunman's legs were in full view, kicking back and forth in a gruesome frenzy, several inches off the ground. For a few seconds he flailed about, making awful gurgling sounds. And then he stopped.

There was silence. I shivered and barely smothered a cry of fear as a deep, throaty growl filled the room. I had no idea what it was and no desire to find out.

The door closed, and I heard footsteps, followed by the sound of something heavy being dragged away, receding into the aisles between the stacks. I huddled there in the dark, scarcely breathing, trying not to make any noise, telling myself over and over again that everything was all right, that I was safe. How long I stayed like that, I've no idea. It might only have been seconds; it seemed like hours.

At length the door opened again.

"Sophie?"

That voice broke me from my spell. "Val?" I whispered, but I still didn't move. I'm not even sure I could have.

He lifted the table out of the way as though it were an empty box and swept me up in his arms. I buried my face in his neck, choking back sobs as terror ebbed and relief rushed in. I didn't want to be weak. I didn't want to be afraid. I didn't want to need him so badly.

But I was. And I did.

I clung to Val, eyes closed, and the world faded away.

CHAPTER 12
MRS. HARKNESS

Val waited with me until the police arrived, then dissolved into the shadows, vanishing before they had a chance to see him. He took the body of my assailant with him. He said he'd deal with it, that it was better that way. I didn't argue.

He'd have stayed if I'd asked him to, but I knew that would just complicate matters. I didn't want my relationship with him made any more public than it had already become. I was in enough trouble as it was.

Havershaw showed up and peppered me with questions, most of which I couldn't answer. No, I didn't know the reporter. No, I didn't know the assailant. No, I didn't know what he was after — which was only partly true. And no, I didn't know what had happened to him. As innocently as I could, I said he must have run off.

Of course they found the box with the notebooks and spools. I told Havershaw I'd found it in the stacks — which was the truth — and that I'd dropped the box and had been forced to gather everything up — also true. I thought I'd better tell him that so he'd know why my fingerprints were all over everything. I didn't see any reason to tell him what I'd seen or heard in Donovan's research material.

Eventually they let me go. I was grateful for the police escort across the Quad and not really unhappy to see a constable park himself by one of the lampposts where he could keep watch on my flat.

Unable to sleep, I made myself some tea. For the first time in weeks, I started thinking about my mother's journal again.

"Let sleeping dogs lie," Grace would have said.

But I couldn't. A few minutes later, I was sitting in my reading chair with the journal in my lap. It just didn't seem I could escape the past.

* * *

JOURNAL OF MARY WOLSTENCROFT — MARCH 10, 1981

Jonathan has asked me to marry him. He did it in fine style, taking me to Renoir's for an expensive meal, then getting down on one knee in front of a restaurant full of people and proposing. I didn't know what to say. How could I tell him I don't love him?

I wanted to say no, but then I remembered what Lucy told me when I mentioned that I thought it might happen soon. "You have to marry someone," she said, "and it can't be that ruddy vamp of yours. You're already well past when most get married. Better Jonathan than someone the government picks for you, which is going to happen if you reach twenty-five and you haven't committed. At least he *loves you — even if you don't love him."*

Lucy never uses Valentine's name. She always calls him "that ruddy vamp of yours" or "your bloody vamp," as though he were something contemptible. I suppose in her eyes he is. Everyone in Haven seems to feel the same way Lucy does. And she's right, of course; I can never marry Valentine. Not here. And there could never be a place for me on the mainland.

So what choice did I really have?

I wish Izzy were here. She'd understand. She always understood me in a way no one else ever could.

I know I'm being picky. Jonathan is sweet and kind and everything a woman could ask for. I probably could have loved him if I'd never met Valentine. But I don't feel anything more than friendship for Jonathan, and I'm not sure that's enough to sustain a marriage. There has to be something between the two of you that makes you certain there can never be anyone else. Jonathan will never be to me what Val is.

Mother just sees it all from a practical standpoint. She tells me I have to get married soon and that it might as well be to someone I like and someone who can take care of me. That just seems so cold. I can't believe she and Dad had only that to bind them to one another. But I could do a lot worse, I suppose. I think of all the other men I know, and I can't imagine marrying any of them and raising a family together.

I thought of all these things as Jonathan waited on his knee for my reply, and everyone in the restaurant seemed to hold their breath.

So I said yes.

I could barely speak, and there were tears in my eyes, which everyone, including Jonathan, assumed were tears of joy. But really, I was overcome by the realization that I'd just committed myself to a life I didn't want with someone I didn't love. And when Jonathan slipped that ring on my finger it was as though he'd put a chain around me and bound me to a rock.

* * *

As I flipped through the following entries, I could see that my mother kept putting off the wedding date. It was apparent she'd hoped something would happen, that the impossible would suddenly become possible. But it didn't.

Judging by the tone of her writing after the wedding, there was little doubt she was restless in married life. It seemed that was partly because Val, true to his word, had ended his relationship with her. That sent her into a spiral, and she began to live under a dark cloud. She was trapped in a job she didn't like and a marriage she felt was a sham.

It wasn't clear at what point she began trying to see Val again. She fooled herself into believing she could have it all, that she could fulfill her obligations to the state, have a secure home, build a family, and still keep her vampire. And when Val continued to rebuff her entreaties, it just seemed to increase her ardor.

I felt sorry for her, but also embarrassed. And it was impossible not to feel for my father, who at some point must have realized my mother didn't love him. I was pretty certain he had eventually discovered the truth about Mom and Val — especially considering what he'd said to me during our quarrel about my relationship with Val. That whole thing about me being like my mother was surely related to that. But whether he'd known about Mom and Val so soon into his marriage, I couldn't say. I was inclined to think not.

It all gave me pause to think, and I couldn't help wonder how it must have felt for my father to know his daughter was carrying on with the man who'd held his wife's heart captive. No wonder he'd started drinking so heavily.

I was reluctant to read on. Val's past warnings about some truths being better left unsaid rang in my head. The sensible thing would have been for me to have burned that bloody journal and been done with it. But I couldn't. Regardless of how much it might hurt and how horrible it might be, I had to know the truth. I justified continuing by telling myself it would be unfair to judge my mother without knowing all the facts. Besides, I'd come this far. How much worse could it get?

* * *

JOURNAL OF MARY WOLSTENCROFT — NOVEMBER 17, 1983

I woke up last night, thinking I heard him crying. But when I got up and went into the nursery, the crib was empty. It's been the same every night since I came home.

Why? Why did it happen to me? Why did it have to be my first one? Did I do something wrong? I was so careful. I did everything the doctors told me to do, because I really wanted him. I wanted him so much.

They told me everything was fine, that I was young and healthy and there weren't any problems with the pregnancy. They told me not to worry. Over and over they assured me that everything was going to be all right. But now my baby boy is gone.

The nurse said he died in the womb, but I swear I heard him. I know it. I heard him cry when he came into this world. I swear it. They told me it was my imagination, that I was too exhausted from the labor and the pain to make sense of anything. But I know what I heard. He was loud and healthy.

He was, wasn't he?

Why didn't they let me see him? I don't understand. What was so dangerous that his body had to be cremated right away? How could someone I carried inside of me for so many months be dangerous to me*? He was my son. He was part of me. How could any of that be wrong?*

I told Jonathan what I heard — our son. I told him about the young blond woman I saw. I think she was a doctor, and I know she was interested in my baby. I saw her talking to the nurses, giving them orders, just after my boy was born.

Jonathan thinks I'm just being emotional, that I'm not thinking straight. But I'm not crazy. I know what I heard. I know what I saw. I know my son was alive. The doctor and the nurses are lying. They took my son away somewhere, and I don't know why. But I know that woman had something to do with it.

I cry in bed at night, and Jonathan doesn't know what to do. Sometimes I wonder if I'll ever stop. The doctor told me it's postpartum depression and gave me drugs for it, but I don't want to take them. I'm afraid they'll make me forget. And I don't want to forget my son. If I do, it'll be as though he never existed at all.

Jonathan is trying hard to make things better, but when I look at him, I just keep thinking of my lost baby. He was the only thing we truly shared, the only thing that bound us together. Maybe I could have finally loved Jonathan. But my baby's death is a darkness between us, and all I want now is Valentine. Only he can make this pain go away.

* * *

A son?

I sat there, staring in shock at my mother's writing, the words swimming before my eyes. Neither Grace nor my father had ever mentioned there'd been a child before me. Until this moment I'd always believed I'd been my parents' first . . . and their last.

It was odd, but I felt a pang of sorrow for the brother I'd never known. And I felt an even greater heartache for my mother's loss. I couldn't even begin to fathom what it would be like to lose a child like that. In Haven, not surprisingly, everyone put a great deal of stock in having children. They were, as Mrs. Bhutto had told us, the future of our nation. It wasn't an exaggeration to say they were the future of humanity. Everything possible was done to make sure every child was brought safely into the world, and only in the most extreme situations would the government even consider allowing a pregnancy to be terminated.

But not all children conceived by Immunes were Immunes themselves. Of the four to six children a woman was expected to bear, she could anticipate that at least one of those would lack the gene that makes us invulnerable to Gomorrah. That was one of the finer points of detail in Mrs. Bhutto's health class. There was no hope for such children. They were always stillborn. And even if that hadn't been the case, if the virus somehow hadn't got them in the womb, it certainly would have infected them the moment they were out of it. After all, Gomorrah was everywhere, "drifting on the wind," as Mrs. Bhutto had so poetically put it. It was ruthless and brutal, relentless and uncompromising. There was no escaping it.

When the virus had first been unleashed, it had swiftly killed all non-Immune children throughout the world. And ever since the Fall, it had continued to work its horror on those with the misfortune of being conceived without the critical gene. It was as if Gomorrah was trying to remind us that it was never far away and that humanity's existence on this planet was fragile and precarious and subject to the whims of a genetic inheritance we had no control over.

Sadly, my brother had apparently been one of the unlucky ones in the gene lottery. When I thought of him and what his fate had been, I couldn't help but think of that old saying Grace often used: "There but for the grace of God go I."

But what kind of god made a world like this?

* * *

JOURNAL OF MARY WOLSTENCROFT — NOVEMBER 25, 1983

Jonathan says he's been investigating the death of our baby. He says it might get him into trouble doing an unauthorized check on the hospital, but he doesn't care.

JOURNAL OF MARY WOLSTENCROFT — NOVEMBER 29, 1983

Today Jonathan told me that he's found some other women with similar tales to mine. One said that when her third child was born, the doctor and nurses told her he was dead, but when she asked to see him, they refused. Another said she was sure she'd heard her baby crying, just like I heard mine, but the nurses took the child away, and when she asked about her daughter, they insisted the baby was stillborn. She wanted to see her, but they told her that wasn't allowed, that it was protocol to dispose of such cases immediately. There are dozens more stories like this, and a lot of them mention the blond woman. Jonathan calls her Lady X.

Jonathan doesn't see a pattern in any of it, and there doesn't seem to be any common denominator except Lady X. The women he's found have been different ages, different backgrounds, and different races. They don't all share the same religion. And Jonathan has found women who describe the same sort of thing happening decades ago.

I keep going over all the information, trying to piece it together, trying to build a picture of what's happening. But nothing works. Jonathan says that despite the number of women who claim their children were alive when born, there's never been an investigation, never been a single report issued. When he talked to doctors and nurses, they were very open about the situation, explaining that women are under a lot of stress during childbirth, even more so when a child is stillborn. He said he asked why they dispose of the bodies so quickly, and they told him that's been common medical practice since the beginning of Haven. None of them were quite sure why, but the suggestion was that it had started out as a precaution against Gomorrah, back in the days when they weren't quite sure what the virus was and how it worked. Now it's just policy, if for no other reason than the sanitary aspect.

I don't believe them.

Jonathan says he's gone as far as he can, that he can't do any more without making it official. He doesn't see the point in doing that because he doesn't think there's a problem. So he's done with it. He believes what the doctors and nurses told him and thinks that what I experienced is perfectly normal.

I know he's wrong. I didn't imagine hearing my baby.

I went through some of the cases he'd gathered, and there was one that caught my eye: a woman who actually got to see and hold her baby but later had him taken away. There wasn't a lot of detail, but there was an address and a phone number. I called and spoke to the woman, Fiona Richards. She confirmed that the birth of her last child was just like the first; everything seemed fine until the doctors did a routine blood test and informed her that her child was a non-Immune. A few hours later, a nurse came and took the baby away in some sort of incubator. Fiona demanded to know where she was taking him, but the nurse just told her that a doctor would be by later to explain everything.

When the doctor did come by, he told her that her baby had died of Gomorrah.

But did it? Did mine?

Even if Fiona's baby did eventually die of the virus, the fact that he lived for several hours outside the womb means they've been lying to us all along about how non-Immune babies are always stillborn.

But why would they lie? And if they've been lying about that, what else have they been lying about?

I told Fiona I wanted to talk with her in person and discuss the matter further. She was reluctant at first, but in the end she agreed to meet me tomorrow at the Calypso Café. It's a public enough place downtown, and out on the sidewalk terrace we should be able to talk without much fear of being overheard.

I haven't told Jonathan what I'm doing. I know he wouldn't approve. As far as he's concerned it's all water under the bridge; he wouldn't be happy if he knew I was still pursuing this. But what harm can there be? Fiona probably doesn't have any more information to give me, but I want to meet someone who went through the same sort of thing I did. I want to hear confirmation that I didn't imagine it all.

I want to know I'm not crazy.

JOURNAL OF MARY WOLSTENCROFT — NOVEMBER 30, 1983

I waited long past the agreed time for our meeting, but Fiona never showed. I felt like such a fool. She probably thought me mad and was just humoring me when she said she'd meet me.

Despite the crowd, I felt so alone as I sat there waiting. The worst part was the children — I can scarcely bear to watch them these days. It tears my heart out to see them. I think of all that could have been and feel emptiness because it wasn't.

I hadn't realized how badly I wanted to have children until I lost my baby. All those months of carrying him inside me, imagining what it would be like to finally hold him in my arms. And I never even got to see him. Never got to kiss him goodbye. I keep thinking of him dying, surrounded by strangers, the way I am now. And then I think of what they did to him after that.

How can that be right?

I don't think Jonathan really understands. And Mom just keeps telling me that it happens, that it's something we have to deal with. Lots of babies are stillborn because they don't have the gene, she says, and odds are the next one I have will be fine. She says it as though somehow that makes everything better.

I sat there at the café wishing Val would appear, thinking that everything would be all right if he did. He'd say the right things, the way he always used to. It's been so long since I've seen him, and I find myself wanting him so desperately. I want him to hold me and talk to me the way Jonathan never seems to do. I want him to make things right. I know that if Val had been there, he would have believed me. He wouldn't have dismissed me. He wouldn't have thought I was crazy.

Eventually I gave up on Fiona and left on my bike, heading down Queen to Republic and then on to Coast Road. I knew I shouldn't, but I couldn't stop myself. Thinking about Val had made me realize I had to talk to him.

When I reached the Embassy, the two wolves, Remus and Romulus, came out of the woods to greet me. Just like old times. It took me a while to get up the courage to call the house, and when I finally did, they said Val wasn't there.

I told myself I should go, that nothing good was going to come of waiting around for him. But I couldn't leave without at least catching a glimpse of him. It got quite late, and I began to think about Jonathan arriving home and not finding me there. He'd probably think I'd done something stupid. And I guess I had.

I was sitting by the wall when the Mercedes finally came up the lane. By the time it reached the gate, I'd gotten to my feet, waiting just where I used to. Except now I wasn't a girl; I was a married woman.

Val opened the door, and we talked in the back seat of the car, just outside the gate. I tried to explain why I had to see him. I told him everything: about the baby and what I'd heard, about my suspicions and Jonathan investigating them, about the other women and Fiona, about Lady X. I talked as fast as I could because I was afraid he'd stop listening like everyone else and just think me mad.

For a long time he was so quiet, and there was an unfathomable grief in his eyes. He said he was sorry about my son and wished he could help me, but there were some things beyond his control. And then he told me that I should listen to Jonathan and put it to rest.

That wasn't what I had expected him to say, and I let him know it.

But all he said was that there were terrible things in this world better left alone and that this was one of them. He told me to return to my husband, have more children, and forget about this.

I couldn't believe what I was hearing.

He told me to go. I waited, hoping he'd change his mind. But he didn't.

So I went, feeling devastated as the car rolled away. It felt like Valentine was gone forever.

I cried all the way home.

By the time I got back, I felt spent. I put on the news and waited for Jonathan to get home from work. I wasn't really listening until a reporter started talking about a body that had been fished out of the waters of Resolute Bay, not far from the commercial docks. He said the cause of death was suspected suicide. Then he said the victim was Fiona Richards of 16 Danbury Drive.

I couldn't believe it.

Surely it couldn't be a coincidence that she died the same day she was supposed to talk to me.

Could I have been responsible? If I'd never called her and badgered her, would she still be alive?

CHAPTER 13
BECOMING DARKNESS

Something broke in my mother after the death of Fiona Richards. On the surface you might think she'd finally been dragged back down to reality. Certainly her notions of what life *should be* seemed to become a shade more cynical, a touch less romantic.

But the biggest change was in the way she regarded my father. She seemed to grow closer to him, if only out of necessity. She needed to believe there was someone she could count on, someone who cared enough about her to protect her — because after Fiona's death she felt frightened and vulnerable.

She stopped poking around into the deaths of the babies at Mercy General Hospital. She returned to work, tried to assume some sort of normal life, and even made an effort to love my father. And for a couple of years it almost worked.

* * *

JOURNAL OF MARY WOLSTENCROFT — OCTOBER 21, 1985

Doctor C. says I'm doing fine. I want to believe him, but I can't rid myself of my doubts. I have these dreams — nightmares, really — where I'm hunting for something. There's this awful desire inside of me, a craving, an overpowering hunger for human blood. It's as though I'm not me anymore — as though I've become someone else. Something else. And when I wake up, I'm covered in sweat, exhausted and terrified.

I don't know what it means. Sometimes I think it must have something to do with Val. Something to do with what he is and how there was a time when I'd have done anything to be with him. Maybe in my dreams I'm becoming one of them.

JOURNAL OF MARY WOLSTENCROFT — NOVEMBER 14, 1985

I'm six months along now.

Jonathan gave me a beautiful crucifix. An unexpected gift to celebrate this new baby. When he put it on me I felt bad, because my first thought was of how Val, as a vamp, couldn't touch it. It was such a stupid and unexpected thought. Val is out of my life for good. Still, I can't help but wonder if driving that home wasn't Jonathan's motive.

My husband seems so happy these days. I want to be happy with him. I want to feel for him what I'm supposed to feel, so I try. Sometimes I think it's working. Sometimes I even think I'm beginning to love him.

I've made Jonathon promise to be there with me this time. I don't want to be alone. He says he will be, but his new job with the Presidential Security Service is demanding, and I worry he'll be away with the president somewhere when it happens.

I need him to be there in the hospital with me; I still don't trust them.

JOURNAL OF MARY WOLSTENCROFT — DECEMBER 18, 1985

I've been feeling awful today. Another one of those terrible headaches I've been getting lately. I can't even get out of bed.

Jonathan called Mom before he left for work and asked her to come over and look after me. She came in the morning and stayed all day. I actually found myself enjoying her company for a change. She fussed about and insisted on doing everything. When I did try to help, she made it clear that the only thing I should be doing is resting and keeping myself well.

Later, over brunch, I tried to share my fears about the hospital with her, but she said I'm being foolish, that everything is fine, and it's going to be all right. I didn't want to ruin the day by having it become another argument between us, so I just let it go.

JOURNAL OF MARY WOLSTENCROFT — DECEMBER 24, 1985

Jonathan wants to go to his parents' for the holidays, but I've been too ill. I've been worrying a lot about the pregnancy, afraid that maybe this baby will be another non-Immune. Mom and Jonathan tell me it's unlikely and so do the doctors. But still. I can't help but worry.

Doctor C. has been giving me a lot of vitamin shots lately, because he says I've been looking a little ragged. They've never done much good in the past, though, and now I'm running a fever and feeling sick as a dog. I have the chills, I'm tired, and my head is pounding. Sometimes I can't even think straight.

It's bad enough being ill, but my nightmares are just as exhausting. And they're more vivid than ever. Sometimes I can't tell the real from the imagined. I see things in my sleep I know can't be true, but then I wake up and can't believe they're not.

My friends are worried. I can see it in their faces. They know this isn't right. I think even Jonathan is beginning to get a bit concerned.

Am I going to lose this baby, too?

JOURNAL OF MARY WOLSTENCROFT — DECEMBER 25, 1985

Mom came by to make Christmas dinner at our place today. She's been coming around a lot these past few weeks since I'm still too sick to go anywhere. She even put up a tree and decorated the house. It looked nice. Reminded me of when I was a kid. Mom says it's important to keep traditions like Christmas alive to keep us rooted in the world we came from. But really, it's the world she *came from.*

After we opened presents, everyone sat around chatting. Jonathan did his best to be a gracious host, even though I know my three brothers get on his nerves. Especially Matthew, who's climbing his way up the ladder at External Affairs. He hounded Jonathan all night, wanting to talk about the Nazis and the president. He never seemed to be all that chummy back when Jonathan was just a police inspector.

I was glad when everyone left. They don't know there's something wrong in Haven; that something's going on. But I know. I know something's happening. I know someone is trying to keep me quiet.

They think Fiona Richards told me something, and now they're trying to kill me. Jonathan's past the point of even arguing with me about it. It's clear he thinks I'm going crazy. I hear him whispering to Mom, and I see the look on their faces.

I'll have to be careful. I can't let them take my baby.

JOURNAL OF MARY WOLSTENCROFT — JANUARY 5, 1986

Lucy came to visit today. I haven't seen her in so long. I could tell she was shocked by my appearance. She tried to hide it, but it was plain on her face.

She told me she and Hamoud are still trying hard to have their fourth baby, but I could tell she wants mine. I could see it in her eyes. But she's not going to get it. Nobody is.

I wanted her to go away, to leave me alone, but she stayed and had coffee. She'd brought a cake with her, but I didn't eat any. You never know what she might have put in it.

When she finally left, I felt like she'd abandoned and betrayed me.

I feel so confused. Sometimes I don't know what I want. I think I want this baby, but then there are moments when I hate it and just want to be done with it. I need this to end. I just don't understand. Why did it feel so right the last time? Why are there times now when it feels so terribly wrong?

This baby is killing me. She's always kicking and squirming inside me. I feel like she's sucking the life out of me. She's making me crazy. I just want her out of me. Everything will be all right then. I can hold her and love her and the nightmare will be over. I just have to hang on a little longer.

JOURNAL OF MARY WOLSTENCROFT — JANUARY 6, 1986

This morning I woke up with another pounding headache and didn't have a clue where I was. It took me several minutes to orient myself. I was sick and confused, but I knew something had happened.

There was blood on my clothes. I thought I'd had a miscarriage. I thought maybe I was hemorrhaging. My hands were sticky with blood, and I could taste it on my lips. I managed to make it to the bathroom, but when I saw myself in the mirror I almost passed out.

There was blood all over me.

I vomited into the sink. On the third go it was just horrid burning bile, and it hurt so much I had tears in my eyes. I could barely catch my breath.

Jonathan found me lying on the bathroom floor. I was afraid of what he'd say. But he just cleaned me up, changed my clothes, and carried me back to bed.

I didn't want him to let go of me, so he stayed and held me until I stopped weeping. But then I started wondering if he'd done this to me.

Maybe he doesn't want me to have this baby. Maybe none of them do. Maybe they're trying to stop me because they know I know.

I'm different now. I see things differently. The whole world seems sharper, more in focus. I can feel things I've never felt before, things I was never even aware of. Everything tastes different. Sounds hurt, and my skin is sensitive; my sense of smell is more acute.

It's all for my baby, so I can protect her.

Jonathan tried to convince me to let him call the doctors. I refused. I don't trust them.

I told Jonathan about my last dream. Lucy was in it, and she wanted my baby. I told him I wasn't going to let her have it, and that I'd kill her if she tried to take it from me. He looked strange after that and went off into the next room.

When he came back, he was staring at me like he didn't know me. He said he'd just called, and Lucy was dead; she'd been attacked by some sort of animal.

That was good. I have to protect my baby.

* * *

I slowly closed Mom's journal, laboring to breathe, feeling lightheaded. It was no wonder Val hadn't wanted me to read this stuff.

My head was full of all sorts of horrible thoughts. I couldn't imagine how my father had dealt with all of this. His wife going over the edge while pregnant with his daughter.

I knew a little about what it was like to watch someone you love slowly disintegrate before your eyes. But I'd always managed to compartmentalize my father's deterioration, to avoid it to a certain extent. He was under the care of others, and the only time his illness impinged upon my life was on those occasions when I went to visit him.

I couldn't think of anything more terrifying than losing your mind. There are a lot of unpleasant diseases, but the ones that drive a person to madness have got to be among the worst. And here I was, with parents who'd both lost touch with reality.

I'd always felt terrible about my father, but now I also felt responsible for what had happened to my mother. The closer she'd gotten to giving birth to me, the more insane she'd become. It was hard not to feel like I was part of the reason.

The remainder of her journal entries became increasingly erratic, degrading to the point of incoherence. The graceful hand in which my mother started the book had begun to devolve shortly after she'd become pregnant with me, and by the end of her pregnancy, it was a sloppy, manic scrawl. It looked primitive and childlike; blots of ink, smudges, and fingerprints were scattered everywhere. Then it became even wilder, almost savage, the nib of the pen cutting through the paper in places, the characters rendered like vicious scratches across the page.

As I flipped forward, I saw that on February 5, the day before I was born, the journal stopped. There was just one final sentence, a crude, barely decipherable submission:

"Now I am eternal, becoming darkness."

I stared at those words for a long time, wondering what it could possibly mean. It sounded like something a vamp would say.

I could only think that my mother had somehow guessed that she would die in childbirth. Even in her madness she must have realized how ill she was. My father and Grace had told me she'd been in a terrible physical state the day I was born.

The journal told me a lot, but it didn't tell me everything. Not least being what had happened when I'd been born. And there was nothing about what had happened after. Grace would know, but I couldn't go to her.

There was only one other person who could tell me what I wanted to know. But the last *real* conversation we'd had had descended into an ugly shouting match.

I didn't want to go see him, but I knew I had to.

Whether my father would tell me anything was another question altogether.

CHAPTER 14

THE MAN WITH HOLES IN HIS HEAD

The following day the weather was spectacular and perfect for a drive along the coast. Still, I put off leaving my flat for as long as possible, not yet recovered from the revelations of the night before and, in all honesty, not eager for what lay ahead. I never liked these visits with my father, and this one wouldn't be made any easier by the questions I wanted answered.

I kept my father's Stormway Athena in storage, paying a small fee each month for the privilege. It was the electric he'd taught me to drive in, and whenever I used it, I recalled those moments with him. Sometimes I would think of how Mom must have sat in that car, and I would convince myself I could feel something of her in the worn leather and fabric.

By no stretch of the imagination was it a luxury vehicle. Very few in Haven were. They were generally all very basic. "Tin boxes with wheels," as Camille had often described them. They were a far cry from the gas-powered behemoths imported from Germany — of which there could only have been a couple of hundred on the islands.

"Ugly as sin but functional," my father used to say of the Stormway, though I'd always been inclined to think it rather cute — in a dilapidated sort of way. I'd even taken to calling it "Peppy."

After handing over a few Electric Allotment transportation coupons from my Ration Book to cover the hydro for the battery charge, I drove off down Harvard. The tall palm trees that flanked the road flickered past like the pickets of a fence, and the bright face of the sun darted through the thick fronds that crowned them.

As I made my way along Coast Road and approached the promontory where the Third Reich Embassy was situated, I felt a little off-kilter. In the past I'd always had a heightened sense of excitement and expectation when I'd gone there, knowing I'd be with Val. But now I couldn't help but think about the times my mother had been in that place, and an uncomfortable feeling crept over me.

I slowed near the lane leading up to the Embassy, thinking about how easy it would be to drop in on him. But I forced myself to keep going. We weren't yet back to where we'd been in our relationship, and I was still trying to sort out all this business about my mother and Grace and where it was that I fit in when it came to Val.

Leaving the Embassy, the road curved south, following the shoreline of Resolute Bay, the glitter of the sea never far from view. I tried to lose myself in the drive, hoping to put troubled thoughts behind me.

To my right were the houses of West Borough; opposite them stood the stately manors of Cliffside, including the Westerly estate. The latter crouched along the bank of the bay, the expansive grounds dropping precipitously to the narrow white beach far below. Camille and I had walked those sands on many occasions, gathering shells and building sand castles as kids, and later just using the quiet and isolation to confide in one another. It was still difficult for me to accept that I'd never get an opportunity to do that again.

Aunt Amelia had extended me an open invitation to come visit whenever I wished to drop in at their mansion. But there were too many memories of Camille caught up in that place, of weekends and sleepovers, birthday parties and Christmases. Even now I was haunted by recollections of us running through the halls as children, squealing with laughter as Aunt Amelia pretended to be a monster chasing us. At night she would read to us, stories from books that had been written before the Fall, and we would ask her questions about that time. She would tell us that one day it would be like that again. That one day the world would be ours, that we would beat the vamps and take back what rightly belonged to us.

I'd learned a lot about being strong from Aunt Amelia, but maybe not enough. I knew I wouldn't be able to stand in that house for more than five minutes before I'd be bawling.

I floored the accelerator, and Peppy whined in protest, shaking vigorously and rattling as the needle on the speedometer valiantly tried to climb past sixty. Only once the Westerly estate was well behind me and out of view did I let up.

It seemed that in no time at all I arrived at the Clarkson facility, where my father lived these days. It was an isolated place, right on the coast, with a great view of the bay. Unfortunately, that was about the best one could say of it.

I parked the electric in the visitor lot and plugged it into the hitch. After dropping some tokens in the charge meter, I girded myself for what was to come and went inside.

"I think he's having a good day," the receptionist said as she buzzed me through the locked doors. "He'll be pleased to see you."

I didn't think that was likely, but I smiled and thanked her all the same.

Clarkson was a grim place, but at least my father's room had a window that overlooked the sea. I would sometimes find him sitting in a chair, staring out at the far horizon, his eyes fixed on nothing I could fathom. I often wondered if he was thinking of better times — or if he was thinking at all. Unfortunately, those were usually the bad days, when he never spoke or reacted to anything.

My anxiety built as I approached his room. I had convinced myself that some secret would be revealed today. But even though I'd come forearmed with news of Camille's murder, Donovan's information, and what I'd read in my mother's journal, the idea that my father would actually tell me anything of consequence was pretty ludicrous. Still, I wanted to believe that if anything could cut through the fog of his dementia, it would be the mystery they presented. After all, he'd been a detective at one time — solving puzzles had been his bread and butter.

As I reached the door to my father's room, it swung open abruptly, and I jumped back with a start.

"Miss Harkness," Inspector Havershaw said from just inside the room, "I hadn't expected to see you here."

I stared at him, speechless for a moment. "What the hell are you doing here?" I demanded. I must have looked quite furious, standing there with my brows knit and my hands balled into tight fists. "You don't have any right harassing a man who can't even defend himself."

A knot had formed in my gut. I couldn't imagine what Havershaw was up to, but I was certain that whatever it was, it couldn't be good.

"Your father and I are old friends," said Havershaw.

I snorted. "Funny, he never mentioned you."

He spread his hands. "We were partners on the force. Before he joined the PSS."

"Partners? Then how come you didn't know he was here until I told you?"

The inspector's face colored. "We didn't really keep in touch. I'd heard he'd retired and always meant to stop by and see him. Still, better late than never."

"No, it isn't." I gave him a cold look. "A few months ago he might have recognized you. Now you're just a strange face."

I knew I shouldn't be so hard on him. There'd been plenty of others like him — friends of Father's who'd made promises to come see him and never had. People could be such cowards.

I looked past Havershaw to where Father was seated in a chair, staring out the window. My spirits sank. This didn't appear to be one of his good days.

"I take it you're leaving," I said, hoping to encourage Havershaw on his way.

"Yes. Quite." He fidgeted, glanced back over his shoulder into the room, then focused on me and tendered a wan grin. "Your father and I had an interesting conversation."

I regarded him coolly. "Really. I find that hard to believe."

"We discussed an old case."

A chill ran through me.

"You don't look so well, Miss Harkness," Havershaw said.

"You seem to have that effect on me," I said coldly.

He smiled again, though this time it was more a smirk. "Just doing my job."

"So you always say. And you think badgering a man with holes in his head can help you how?"

"It's the parts of his head that don't have holes I'm interested in," Havershaw replied. "Your father was a fine detective. It was a sorry day when he left the force, but the President's office was adamant. Didn't even want him to finish up the cases he was working on."

That was the first I'd heard of it, but it wasn't all that surprising. My father had never been very forthcoming about his past. Even on the occasions when he had told me stories, there'd always been something vague and nebulous about them.

"So," I said, "did he solve the case for you?"

Havershaw shook his head. "No. No, I'm afraid not. Still, he had some interesting things to say."

I looked at my father. "When he's like this he never talks to anyone. Not even me." I shifted my gaze back to Havershaw. "Not *anyone*. Ever."

"There are more ways to answer questions than with words, Miss Harkness."

"So you're a mind reader now?" I said sarcastically.

"When you've been a detective as long as I have, you get to know people. There are things you pick up on."

A sour laugh escaped me. "That must be quite the trick with an Alzheimer's patient."

Havershaw glanced back at my father, then eyed me, sober-faced. "There's still a lot of the man he used to be somewhere inside him. He's still your father."

For some reason those words were like a slap on the face. I looked at the inspector for a long time, then pushed my way past him and into the room. How dare he presume to know my father better than I did.

"Miss Harkness —" he started to say.

I cut him off. "Please leave us alone."

"I didn't —"

"Please!" I said it sharply, the word shaped by tears that were poised to fall.

Havershaw stood in the doorway for a long moment, grim-faced and silent. Then he turned and left. I heard his footsteps retreating down the hall, and a sense of loneliness encompassed me. It was just my father and me in the room, and it seemed to me that really meant there was only me.

My father was so old now — far older than his years. His eyes were rheumy, his hair gray and thinning, his flesh pasty and drooping. The disease was eating his mind, but it had taken a terrible toll on the rest of him as well. He was physically diminished.

For a few minutes I knelt by his chair and held his hand, which lay limp and unresponsive in mine. I wanted him to say something, anything. I wanted him to utter a few words or a sentence or two. I wanted him to come back from wherever it was he'd gone — if there was, in fact, anywhere to which he withdrew in that wreckage of his consciousness.

I bowed my head to our clasped hands, closed my eyes, and held back the tears. I missed my father terribly. I missed hearing his voice and his laughter. I even missed the times when he'd argued with me.

And then the most incredible thing happened. I felt a hand on my head, gentle and soothing, conveying compassion in its simple touch. When I looked up I saw my father turned in his seat, his hand stroking my hair, his eyes fixed on me.

"Don't cry, little angel," Father said, his voice a rusty hinge. "Don't cry."

"Dad," I whispered. I lifted my head, leaned closer, and put my arms around him, hugging him tightly.

"I must follow them," he said. "I must follow the innocents. It's all about them."

I pulled away a bit and frowned at him. "The innocents? What are you talking about?"

For a moment, it was as though my father had awoken from a drug-induced stupor. He clutched at my arms, surprisingly strong, and said, "I thought I knew." He gave his head a palsied shake. "I thought I knew the truth. But I wasn't careful." His stare bored into me, but I wasn't sure he was conscious of who he was looking at.

"What about the innocents?" I asked.

"I wasn't careful enough. And they got you." His face crumbled. "Oh, Mary, I should have stopped. I lied to you. I should have stopped. It wouldn't have happened if I'd stopped. They wouldn't have hurt you."

"I'm not —" I began to say before restraining myself. My father was clearly somewhere else, lost in a memory that was more real to him than I was. But whatever memory it was, it still might lead to answers. I bit my lip and fought for patience, even though I had a million questions to ask.

"You were right," he muttered. "You were right. It took me years. Years. But I found it. I found the truth. Yes. I found the truth."

"Tell me what you found, Jonathan," I said.

Father's eyelids fluttered, and he stared at me vacantly. "I told you — the innocents."

In the months since he had been here, my father had rarely been as lucid as this. This was probably the best chance I'd ever have of getting any answers. "Tell me about my . . . about Sophie's birth," I said. "What happened? Can you tell me that, Jonathan?"

He didn't answer. Quite suddenly he shot up and stood there shaking. I rose beside him, clinging to his hand. "What is it?" I asked. "What's wrong?"

"They're here," he whispered, eyes widening.

"What?" I stared at him, bewildered. "Who's here?"

He didn't answer, but instead pulled free of me, roughly pushing me aside and shuffling over to the battered bureau that stood against the wall opposite his bed. He yanked open a drawer and began plucking clothes from it, dumping them on the floor, all the while mumbling to himself about something I couldn't quite make out.

I started picking up shirts and socks and trying to put them back in the drawer, but he shoved me out of the way. "No, no, no, no, no, no," he said.

On he went, wrenching open the next drawer once he'd emptied the first, becoming more and more agitated, his face creasing with lines of frustration. "Here, here, here," he said, knotting his fists and grinding his teeth.

"Dad!" I exclaimed. I tried to stop him, but he shrugged out of my grasp and heaved more clothes out of the drawers, pitching armfuls of them onto the threadbare carpet.

"Here, here, here," he chanted again. "Know it. Know the truth. They've come to stop me."

He was on the third drawer when he suddenly stopped. It was as though someone had simply switched him off. I stood to one side, breathless, hoping he'd say something that would make sense.

I put the clothes on the bed, stepped over to my father, and gently put a hand on his shoulder. It startled him, and he peered at me with wild eyes, looking as though he were on the verge of tears. He wore the terrified look of a lost child confronting a stranger. "Have you come to take me away?" he asked.

"No, Dad."

His expression turned blank. "Do you have it, Mary?"

"Have what?" I asked, trying to control my frustration, to keep it from my voice.

"I gave it to you this morning."

I almost corrected him, but it would have been wasted breath. He was obviously living in some past event, and nothing I could say was going to change that.

"It was the one you left," he went on. "The one you wanted me to find, so I'd know it was you who did it."

"Did what?"

"Do you have it?" He said it loudly.

"Yeah," I said, humoring him. "Sure, Da—" I winced. "Sure, Jonathan, I have it." I'd no idea what he was talking about.

"You look different from this morning," he went on. "Your hair. Your hair is a different color."

"No —" I caught myself again and forced a smile. "Yeah, I changed the color. You like it?"

My father shook his head. "No, no, no," he said emphatically, pouting like a child. "It's wrong. All wrong." He smiled, a strange, unsettling mien, like something you might imagine from an automaton. "I lifted your hair when I put it on you. It was like gold silk."

I figured he must have been reliving an old memory, some moment in the past that he'd shared with my mother. She'd had blond hair, a sharp contrast to my own raven locks.

"Come and sit down," I said, gently guiding my father back to the chair. When he sat, it was with a thump. He simply relaxed all his muscles at once and collapsed into the seat.

While my father gave the bay his undivided attention, I folded his clothes and put them back in the drawers. I used to do the same thing for him at home; it had been one of the things I'd done to seek his approval. I had wanted him to see that it wasn't such a bad thing that I'd lived and Mom had died. But I guess deep down I'd always known nothing could ever make up for that.

Once I'd tidied up, I sat with him again, pulling up a chair beside his and settling in to watch the ships and the waves. It was a beautiful view of paradise, the sort of scene that might have appeared on postcards back in the days before the Fall, when the wealthy, fortunate few in northern countries like Canada had ventured to more southerly climes during the winter to bask in the warmth and glow of the tropics.

Father never said another word for the hour or so I stayed. Not even the gibberish that was his usual output.

I thought about what he'd said earlier and tried to connect it to my mother and the things she'd written in her journal. It was like having the pieces of a puzzle before you and not having a clue what the final image was supposed to be. I thought of Val's words of caution and wondered again whether I should even try making sense of this. What did it matter, anyway? My mother was long dead, and my father . . . well, my father would be better off if he were. What could I possibly stand to gain poking my nose around into God only knew what?

"I have to go now, Dad," I said. I stood up and put the chair back, then went over to my father and leaned over to kiss him. He sat stiff, like a piece of waxwork or a mannequin, unresponsive to my touch. I felt despair but smothered it, refusing to let it drag me down into the depression that too often took hold after my visits.

"You take care of yourself," I whispered in his ear. When I pulled away, I squeezed his hand and felt something in it. "What have you got there?"

My father's fingers were tightly clenched, and he resisted my efforts to pry them apart. With a little coaxing, I managed to free the object from his grasp. All the while he remained motionless, eyes still fixed on nothing in particular.

I looked at what I held in my hand — a bundle of keys, which glinted gold and silver in the light shining through the window. Recalling my father's habit of walking into our house in North

Borough and dropping those same keys onto the telephone table, I felt a stab of melancholy. That distinctive clinking and clattering had summoned me to his side as a child — and later served as a warning when things got bad. I had looked high and low for them when I'd cleared out the house earlier in the year. How he'd kept them from me I didn't know.

I thought to leave them with him, believing that perhaps there was some sentimental value to them that even his ruined brain could fathom. But when I tried to give them back, he just pushed my hand away. I relented and slipped them into my pocket, kissed him on the forehead again, and left.

Outside, I walked distractedly to my car, barely aware of my surroundings. There were only two other vehicles in the lot, one a service truck and the other a black Universal electric. A tall man stood lounging against the latter, puffing on a cigarette. I thought about saying, "Those things'll kill you," as I went past, but I just smiled at him instead. He nodded indifferently, staring at me with hooded eyes.

I unplugged Peppy and climbed inside. It was hellishly hot, and I had a brief thought of snow as I rolled down the windows and sat for a moment composing myself. Usually I needed to decompress after each visit, and this time was no exception.

I tried to tell myself that today's rants were nothing, just a further progression of my father's disease, but I knew there was more to it than that. He'd been trying to tell me something. I was sure of it. But I was still stumbling about in the dark. Somehow I had to figure out what it was he'd been talking about and how it connected to what was in the journal.

I pressed the start button, and Peppy hummed to life. As I drove off, Clarkson dwindled in the rearview mirror, shrinking against the backdrop of a vivid blue sky. In moments it was lost to view behind rows of palms and acacia.

I looked ahead to the road, feeling incredibly alone and empty inside.

CHAPTER 15
BLOWOUT

With the windows down, the warm air tousled my hair, and I knew that by the time I got home it would be a tangled mess. I didn't care. I liked the illusion of freedom it gave me. For just a while, out there on the open road, far from the city, it was possible to imagine myself somewhere else.

I thought of *No Haven for Darkness* and the rich tapestry of that world. I imagined myself there, in a place so remarkably different from the real world. A place where there were literally billions of people. A place where the overarching fear wasn't that there'd be too *small* a population to sustain humanity, but rather one too *large* to keep it viable. A place where people could dream incredible dreams and actually have them come true.

I remembered Camille and how she had chafed at our confinement and the limitations of the world in which we lived. That book had changed her life. It had made her see things differently. When I thought of my own situation, I began to understand what she'd felt. In another world, Val might be an ordinary man, and we could actually hope to have a life together.

Except it would never have worked out like that, I realized. If there'd never been a virus, Val would have returned home and married Grace. And everything else would have been different. I never would have existed.

In school they were always saying that one day things would be the way they were supposed to be. But what if they were supposed to be like this? Was this all we could ever hope for?

Just then Peppy jounced over a rock, and the keys in my pocket jabbed me, jolting me out of my reverie. I fumbled for them, and for a moment I considered tossing them. They were pretty much worthless; I had no idea what half of them were even for.

But as I held them, the metal warm in my hand, I was struck by the thought that it may have been no accident my father had given them to me. Some part of his brain had been working when I'd been with him today.

But if he'd meant them for me, I had no idea why.

I was mulling that over as I came around a sharp bend and saw Inspector Havershaw standing by the roadside with his car pulled onto the shoulder. My first inclination was to drive on past, but the Good Samaritan in me couldn't ignore him. I screeched to a stop, a cloud of dust rolling over him. Havershaw leaned down and looked at me through the open window on the passenger's side.

"Having a spot of trouble?" I asked, slightly amused.

"Battery's dead."

"Dear me," I said in mock dismay. "And such a long way from town. I do hope you wore some decent walking shoes, Inspector. It's a good twenty miles back to the city."

His face fell.

I pressed on the accelerator and started off. In the rearview mirror I could see him standing by the road, a hangdog look on his face. Of course, I had no intention of leaving him in the lurch. Traffic was infrequent, and the nearest phone was probably back at Clarkson, ten miles up the road. He could be waiting for hours in the hot sun, so a couple of hundred feet along I stopped and leaned out the window. "Well, you'd better hurry!" I half shouted. "I haven't got all day."

Havershaw hesitated, as though doubting me, then jogged up and got in. "Thanks," he grunted, sweaty and dusty and looking a shade sheepish. I wondered if he was uncomfortable hitching a ride with one of his suspects. "I'd just about given up hope that someone would come along."

"It's always a pleasure to help one of the city's finest," I said, trying hard not to sound too sardonic. I glanced at him out the corner of my eye, and for a moment I wondered if he'd really had car trouble. Despite what he'd just said, he had to have known I'd be along at some point — it was the only route back to Caelo. Maybe this was just a ploy to get me alone and ask me more questions I didn't want to answer.

"You sure this thing is safe?" Havershaw asked as we rattled along.

I patted the dash affectionately. "There, there, Peppy, don't you mind the mean old inspector."

Havershaw gave me a wry grin, and for the next few minutes we drove in relative silence. "So how was your visit with your father?" he asked at length.

"The usual," I lied, shooting him a cold look. "I told you he never talks when he's in that state."

"Too bad."

"Yes. It is."

"He's rather young for it, don't you think?"

"People can get it in their thirties and forties," I said.

Havershaw raised his eyebrows. "Really? I didn't know."

"It's worse, then. It usually progresses faster. Although some might argue it's better that way. Have it over sooner, I suppose."

"Yes, I suppose," he said. The wind was whipping at his hair and making a thorough mess of it, but he seemed determined not to roll up the window.

"I often find myself wishing it would be over for him," I said casually, my eyes focused on the road ahead. I could feel Havershaw appraising me. "He never did anything to deserve this kind of slow death."

"No, I don't imagine he did. He was a good man. Still is."

"Yes."

"I think it would be better to die quickly."

That wasn't what I'd expected from him. A lot of people don't get it. So many think it's some sort of moral obligation to keep a loved one alive at all costs, hooked up to machines, tubes running in and out of them. I just think they're selfish.

"It must be difficult," Havershaw continued.

"At least he doesn't know," I said. "I take comfort in that." At least I *hoped* my father didn't know, but I'd often wondered if there was some residual part of people with dementia — even the very advanced cases — that was aware they were diminished.

"Were the two of you close?" Havershaw asked.

"That's a rather personal question, Inspector." My hands tightened on the wheel, and I didn't dare look at him. "I don't see what that has to do with my friend's murder."

"This isn't an interrogation, Miss Harkness."

"If you say so."

He sighed. "Just trying to make conversation."

"And maybe find out a little about your prime suspect?" I said, a little short-tempered.

"It's nothing personal."

"Of course it is."

Havershaw made no comment, and we rode in silence, except for Peppy and the hum of the wheels on the road.

"We had our moments," I said abruptly.

"I beg your pardon?" He gave me a bewildered look.

"My father and I. You asked me if we were close. I like to think we were. But sometimes . . ." I shrugged. "I don't think it was easy for him to raise a daughter alone. And I always thought he blamed me for my mother's death."

"I doubt that," Havershaw said.

"How would you know?" There was an edge to my voice that I made no effort to bury.

"I was your father's partner for a few years."

"So you said. So what?"

"You get to know a lot about a man when you rely on him to guard your back on a daily basis."

"If you were such good pals, how come you didn't cut me any slack in Coral Beach?" I countered.

"I didn't book you, Miss Harkness. Others would have."

"You want me to believe that was because of my father?"

Havershaw chuckled. "I told you he had influence."

"That's not why you showed up at my flat," I said.

"I just happened to hear that on the police band. I was close, so I thought I'd look in and make sure everything was all right."

"It didn't seem like a courtesy call."

He shrugged slightly. "As I said before, trouble seems to follow you. Murder. Robbery. Vampires. Who knows what else?"

"I don't make a habit of it, Inspector."

He laughed. "Are you sure? After last night . . ."

"Last night I just happened to be in the wrong place at the wrong time," I said. "I didn't know Donovan."

"But she seemed to know you."

I was so taken aback that I swerved onto the dusty shoulder, the right wheel bumping loudly over stones and potholes before I managed to wrestle the little electric back onto the tarmac. Havershaw let out a sigh of relief and relaxed.

"What do you mean she seemed to know me?" I asked when I'd regained my composure.

"Your name and address were in one of her notebooks."

"That doesn't make any sense," I said. And it didn't. "It must have been a mistake."

He shrugged. "Just one of many mysteries surrounding this case."

"And what case is that? You seem to have a rather full plate, Inspector."

"I'm still investigating Camille Westerly's death. It all leads back to that."

"You think the reporter's death is connected?"

"Yes."

"How?" I asked. I could feel his eyes on me, and a shiver ran up my spine.

"You're the only common denominator," Havershaw replied.

"That's not true. Donovan was looking into Island Transnational Shipping."

His eyes narrowed. "I thought you didn't know her."

"I don't. I told you I dropped the box with her research in it. When I was picking up all the stuff I happened to notice the manifests."

"Just happened to, eh?"

"Yes," I said sharply. "I'm not blind, Inspector."

He laughed. "I hope not; you're the one driving. And you'll forgive me for saying so, but you need all the advantage you can get in that department."

I stuck my tongue out at him. It was a childish thing to do, but it was more impulse than anything else.

He laughed again. "My daughters would like you," he said.

"Your daughters sound like intelligent young women of discerning tastes," I said primly. "They must take after their mother."

"Ouch."

I glanced over at Havershaw and grinned. He grinned back, and for the first time, I actually found myself feeling less hostile toward him.

"They'd probably say you remind them of Samantha Jarvis," he said. "Feisty. Determined. Confident. And not shy to put a man in his place."

"Samantha Jarvis?" I repeated, surprised.

"She's a character in a book called *No Haven for Darkness.*"

"Yes. I know. But why Samantha Jarvis? I don't really fit the description."

"More than you think, Miss Harkness. Besides, her adventures began with a murder."

"But she fancied herself a bit of a detective. I don't have any such delusions."

"I hope not. Best to leave that sort of thing to the professionals."

I was on the verge of saying something rather witty in response when there was a loud bang, and the car suddenly spun out of control. The steering wheel twisted in my grip even as I took my foot off the accelerator and tried to brake.

What happened next was over so quickly that there was really no time to react. And yet, it was almost as though time had also slowed, and everything around me was moving at a glacial pace.

The car leapt from the tarmac and onto the soft shoulder, the wheels digging in and yanking the steering wheel farther around. We crashed through the safety railing, smashing through the wood planks and sending splinters and rocks flying through the air. The windshield had become a web of cracks, and beside me I heard Havershaw cry out. I gripped the steering wheel and pushed back against it, as if by doing so I could somehow avoid the inevitable.

Peppy became airborne in a cloud of dust and debris. For a brief moment, there was a sense of weightlessness, rather akin to that feeling you sometimes get in the pit of your stomach as an elevator starts moving. Over the screech of metal and the fierce whine of the electric motor, I heard myself scream.

And then we plunged into the sea.

CHAPTER 16

BLOOD AND BULLETS

They say that when you're on the precipice of death, your entire life flashes before your eyes. In an instant, you relive all the choices you made, both good and bad — all the moments you went right instead of left or wished you'd gone up instead of down.

None of that happened to me — maybe there just wasn't time. In the seconds before the electric struck the water, I didn't see anything of my past; there was just the turmoil of the moment. And then the warm, salty water was around me, and I was fighting a surge of panic as I held my breath and freed myself from the sinking car. Moments later I burst through the surface of the bay and gasped for air.

I looked around, still in shock. Bubbles boiled up from below and agitated the sea, marking where the car was sinking toward the silt bottom.

"Inspector!" I cried out. I treaded water and turned about, scanning the nearby waters of the bay, fear mounting in me. "Havershaw!"

But there was no sign of him anywhere. I took a deep breath and dove beneath the surface once more, pulling fiercely with my arms and kicking furiously with my legs. The water was as clear as glass, and just a few feet below I could see the Stormway, its front bumper embedded in the rippled ocean floor, its stubby rear pointing straight toward the surface of the sea. Trails of bubbles streamed from the vehicle, jiggling and writhing as they expanded upward.

I swam around to the passenger side and saw Havershaw, seemingly unconscious and bobbing against the seat. I tried to pull him out through the open window, but it was impossible. Frantic, I struggled with the door, bracing my feet against the side of the car as I hauled on the handle. My arms and legs strained, some distant inner voice telling me I couldn't possibly succeed.

But a moment later there was a sharp crack and a muffled creak as the door abruptly came open, slowly flopping downward as I reached in and grabbed hold of the inspector. He was limp in my arms as I dragged him toward the surface, and even as I sought open air, I feared he was dead.

Somehow I managed to get him ashore and out of the water. Although I was breathless and still in a bit of a daze, I cleared most of the fluid from his lungs and started CPR. Moments later his body abruptly seized with a spasm, after which he spat up seawater and began coughing and gasping all at once.

I sat back on my heels, exhausted, water dripping down my face, the salt stinging my eyes. I was trembling, though not from cold.

Havershaw slowly came back to life, his breathing growing steadier and the color returning to his flesh. A couple of minutes later his eyelids fluttered, and he looked up, trying to focus. It took him a moment or two, then with a grunt of effort he slowly propped himself up on his elbows and peered silently across the water before turning to me. "What happened?" he asked.

I shook my head, water flying from the wet strands of my hair. "I . . . I don't know," I said, trying to replay the crash in my mind. "A tire blowout, I guess. It all happened so fast." I took a breath. "I heard a loud bang, and then I guess I lost control."

Havershaw gave me an ironic look. "Apparently," he said. He swept his damp hair off his forehead with one hand. "It's just one thing after another with you, isn't it, Miss Harkness?"

"I'm sorry," I blurted out.

He shrugged. "No harm done, I guess. Except maybe to your car." He looked back at the water, where a few lonely bubbles still stirred the surface, the only indication of Peppy's location. "You brought me ashore?"

I nodded. "You must have been knocked unconscious when we hit the water."

"And you weren't?"

I didn't reply. I was too busy thinking to myself that this was the fourth time in a matter of weeks I'd had a close call. Camille's murder, the break-in at my flat, the killer in the library, and now this. Was it really just coincidence?

"We need to get you to a doctor," said Havershaw.

"I'm fine," I said.

"I don't think so."

"What?" I frowned at him in confusion. He was staring at my stomach in alarm, and when I glanced down, I noticed for the first time the pinkish-red stain spreading across my white cotton blouse. At the center of it there was a hole in the cloth. I gaped at it, dumbfounded.

Havershaw leaned toward me, reached out, and gently lifted the material, exposing my midriff. There, on the right-hand side, was a wound about the diameter of my forefinger. Blood was oozing from it.

"I don't think the crash was an accident," the inspector said. He looked up at me, his expression grave. "You've been shot."

"Oh," I said, wide-eyed. And then I fainted.

* * *

I don't know how long I was out. When I awoke, I was in Mercy General Hospital, flat on my back in bed in a ward with a half dozen other patients. It took me a few moments to orient myself, but when I did, I remembered the crash and Havershaw's assertion I'd been shot.

It had to have been an accident. A farmer trying to shoot some pest or a kid out playing with a gun he shouldn't have had.

"You gave us quite the scare," a familiar voice said.

I turned my head and was surprised to see Grace sitting in a chair next to my bed. She got to her feet, came to my side, and forced a grin.

"I thought you'd washed your hands of me," I said.

"Don't be more of a fool than you are, child." Her voice crackled with emotion.

I struggled to say something, but suddenly I didn't care why she was there; I only cared that she was. "Thank you," I whispered.

She patted my hand.

"How did I get here?" I asked.

"Apparently your friend Inspector Havershaw carried you up to the road after the crash and managed to flag down a farmer who was on his way to Caelo. They drove here as fast as they could. You lost a lot of blood. By most counts you should have died. It's a miracle you didn't. When the doctors operated to remove the bullet, they weren't very optimistic, but you surprised them. From what they've told me, you're making a remarkable recovery."

"How long have I been here, then?" I asked.

"Almost two days."

I gasped and tried to sit up. "Two days! But I have classes and —"

"You're not going anywhere," Grace announced, pushing me back with a surprisingly strong thrust. "You have to rest up until you're properly healed."

"I feel fine," I insisted, but it wasn't entirely true. My head ached, and when I peeked under my hospital gown, I could see a wicked bruise on the right-hand side of my belly. I ran a hand gingerly across my stomach, wincing as my fingers traced out the circumference of the bandaged wound.

"You were shot, young lady," Grace reminded me. "Be thankful you're even alive."

She was right, of course, but that did nothing to lessen my impatience and the anxiety that was jangling my nerves. I didn't like doctors, and I hated hospitals — especially *this* one. This was where my mother had died after giving birth to me. Every time I passed the place I thought about that and was filled with dread. And now on top of that I had all those images painted by the words my mother had written in her journal: losing her son, her descent into madness, Lady X.

"Why can't I recover in my flat?" I asked Grace. "I can lie there in bed just as well as here."

"You'll be safer here," my grandmother replied.

I knew there'd be no arguing with her. I was going to be stuck here until the doctors said it was okay for me to leave.

Soon after that, a nurse came around and checked my blood pressure. She was an overly cheery, matronly sort. It was all, "How are we this morning, dearie?" and, "Are we hungry?" and, "Do we need to use the potty?" She wrote something on a chart at the end of the bed and then left, informing me a doctor would be by to see me soon. I was more than glad to see her go; I'd been on the verge of telling her just what she could do with her "potty."

Grace prattled on for hours after that. And just when I thought I couldn't take another minute of it, Havershaw showed up. I was actually happy to see him — a sure indication of how desperate I was beginning to feel.

"Inspector," Grace said, her face lighting up when she saw him. "How good of you to come."

"Mrs. Wolstencroft," Havershaw said, inclining his head in her direction. "Miss Harkness."

"It seems I owe you my life," I said.

"I didn't have much choice."

"Oh?" I said.

"Had to even the score," he said. "You saved me first."

"I was afraid you might have thought the whole thing some diabolical scheme of mine to get rid of you," I told him.

"The thought had crossed my mind," the inspector said, allowing himself a grin. "But the bullet they took out of you was pretty convincing. And then there's the fact that someone shot out the front tire of your electric."

Grace gasped. "Who on earth would do such a thing?"

"I'm afraid I don't have any answers yet," said Havershaw.

On one hand, I was gratified to know it wasn't my driving that had sent Peppy over the cliff. But on the other, the thought that someone had actually targeted me was more than a little disconcerting. One shot might have been an accident, but two . . . two was no mistake.

"Any clues?" I asked.

Havershaw shook his head. "Unfortunately about all we know so far is that you were shot from some distance by a high-powered rifle."

"You mean by someone like a sniper?" There was no hiding my shock.

"Isn't that a rather specialized field?" said Grace.

Havershaw shook his head. "It's part of everyone's military service, ma'am. There're probably a good many in Haven — both male and female — who'd be capable of pulling off a shot like that."

"A lot of suspects," I said. "You'll have your work cut out for you, Inspector."

"So it would seem. But we may be able to narrow it down if there's anything you can remember from that day that may have struck you as unusual."

I shook my head. "Sorry. I drove up to Clarkson, saw my father, and —" I stopped and blinked.

"What is it?" asked Havershaw.

"Just something I remembered. Probably nothing."

"It's the 'nothings' detectives thrive on," he said.

"It's just that I'm pretty familiar with the people who visit there, but when I came out there was a man I'd never seen before waiting by a Universal."

"There's no law against that."

"No, there's not. But it just seemed odd. He didn't appear to . . ." I paused, feeling awkward.

"Didn't appear to what?" Grace prodded, a stern look on her face.

"Belong," I finished. "Honestly, he looked like something out of one of those old gangster movies." The moment the words were out I realized how ridiculous it sounded. "Never mind. He was probably just some poor bloke working up the courage to go in. It's not the easiest thing to see someone you love living like that."

Havershaw dug out his notebook and pen and scribbled something down. "I'll check it out anyway," he said as he wrote. "Maybe make another visit out there myself. Someone else might have seen something out of the ordinary."

I've no idea why, but the moment he said that, I had a sudden premonition there was something terribly wrong at Clarkson. It was irrational, of course, but then most intuitions initially seem that way.

"Has anyone from Clarkson called?" I asked Grace.

"I don't know," she said. "I've been here at the hospital since they brought you in."

I looked to Havershaw, but he shook his head and said, "I've been busy with retrieving your electric and having forensics give it the once over."

"I need to use a phone," I said, fighting the anxiety mounting inside me. There was dread and urgency in my voice, and both my grandmother and Havershaw looked at me with concern.

"Is something wrong?" Grace asked.

"I hope not," I said. "I just want to make sure Dad's all right. I mean, if they were after me —"

"They?" Havershaw and Grace said together.

"Whoever it was who took a shot at me."

"We don't know there was more than one person involved," the inspector pointed out. "It could have been someone with a grudge against you. Some old enemy."

"I'm seventeen years old, Inspector. How many old enemies do you think I could possibly have? And even if I had any, they certainly wouldn't be the sort who'd pick up a gun and try to shoot me."

"How do you know my granddaughter was the target?" Grace asked. "In your profession, I'm sure there are likely a number of individuals who might wish to see you dead, Inspector."

"I wasn't the one they were shooting at, Mrs. Wolstencroft."

"I don't know how you can be so sure," she said.

"Because it was *my* electric," I said, meeting Havershaw's gaze. "Whoever took that shot couldn't have possibly known I'd give the inspector a lift. But that doesn't matter right now. I want to know if Dad's all right."

"I still don't —"

"Grandma!"

"I'll see what I can find out," said Havershaw.

He left the room, and once he was gone Grace turned to me. "Whatever happened out there?" she asked.

"The inspector's electric broke down," I explained. "I picked him up. A few minutes later someone shot at us."

"I told you he was a curse," said Grace.

"What? Who?" I frowned at her.

"You know very well who."

I shook my head, partly in astonishment and partly in frustration. "What are you talking about? Val didn't have anything to do with this."

Havershaw returned before we could get into an argument. When we saw the inspector's face, Grace put one hand to her mouth and grasped mine with the other.

"How?" I whispered.

"There was a fire," he said. "They say your father fell asleep smoking. The bed caught fire, and by the time they got to the room and doused the flames, it was too late. He was burnt beyond recognition."

Beside me Grace was weeping openly. Havershaw helped her into the chair by the bed. I barely noticed.

"I think you have a problem, Inspector," I said in a faint voice.

He looked at me, puzzled.

"My father didn't smoke."

* * *

I was inconsolable.

Maybe it seems strange that I should break down and cry after everything I'd said about wishing my father dead. But however much you may think you've prepared yourself for something, the reality is always quite different. When it's the death of someone you know and love, the impact can catch you completely off guard. Rationality is lost; emotion reigns.

I couldn't believe my father was truly gone. I couldn't believe I'd never see him again, never hear him, never touch him. All I had left were memories.

It was an odd thought to have in that moment of utter devastation, but it struck me that I was now an orphan.

A nurse came in and shooed the inspector out of my room. I felt her fussing over me, and then there was a pinprick in my arm. The world rushed away, and an ocean of despair faded quickly into the geography of blissful numbness.

For a while I was at peace.

CHAPTER 17
LADY X

I heard a baby's cry, and then someone said, "I'm sorry, Sophie, but he's dead."

I screamed, and I yelled at them to let me see my baby. But I couldn't get up, and the nurses and doctor just walked away, leaving me in my bed while I held out my hands, desperate for the child they'd stolen.

Then a blond woman appeared in the door, face hidden in shadow, and said, "I'm sorry, Sophie, but you know too much. That just won't do." She raised her hand, and there was a flash of light followed by a deafening boom. I felt a pain in my side and blacked out.

* * *

I sat up with a jerk, my chest heaving as I gasped for breath, a cold sweat covering my body. It took me a moment to realize I'd been dreaming, longer still to realize where I was. Slowly the details of the past few hours reassembled themselves, and the tide of emotion rose in me again. I bit back a sob and buried my face in my hands.

The chair Grace had been sitting in was empty, and Havershaw was nowhere to be seen. I felt painfully alone in the dimly lit ward, even though there were patients in some of the other beds.

Throat dry and sore, I fumbled for the pitcher of water on the table by my bed and groaned when I found it empty. There wasn't a nurse in sight, and ten minutes after I'd pushed the call button, there was still no response.

Thirsty and growing impatient, I climbed out of bed. The polished concrete floor felt refreshingly cool under my bare feet, and I closed my eyes, savoring the sensation. It wasn't until I took a step forward that a shock of pain lanced through my side where the bullet had entered. Instinctively I reached out and grabbed hold of the nearest available object — the metal stand holding my IV bottle. I stared at it dumbly, and for the first time, I noticed the tube extending from the bottle to a point on my forearm where a needle was taped in place.

Using the stand as a crutch, I limped slowly between the beds on a quest for water. I couldn't see any other pitchers on the other nightstands, but that might have had a lot to do with the patients in the other beds looking suspiciously comatose. They were hooked up to machines that made rhythmic mechanical sounds and beeped with an irritating regularity.

I made it to the doors at the end of the ward and peered through the windows, trying to see to the left and right down the hallway. There didn't appear to be anyone in sight, which puzzled me. Even though I was a bit fuzzy on the details, I was certain I'd heard Havershaw say he'd be posting a guard.

"Hello," I called out in a hoarse voice as I stepped out into the hall. "Is anyone there?" No one replied.

I set off in the direction of the nursing station, but I'd gone only a step or two when I heard someone cry out. The outburst was short and sharp, and when I turned back, I heard faltering footsteps. A moment later, a policeman stumbled around the corner where the hallway was bisected by another corridor. He lunged toward me, clutching at his throat, and leaving a trail of blood on the floor. There was a wild, desperate look in his eyes as he mouthed something and stretched out an arm in my direction.

I walked toward him, and in one last rush he threw himself against me, taking us both down to the ground. The IV needle ripped free from my arm as the stand toppled over with us. The bottle shattered against the hard concrete, splattering the clear liquid in all directions and mixing with the puddle of blood spreading from the wounded man.

"Run!" he wheezed in a watery breath.

I lay there for a brief moment, dazed, and then instinct took over. Oblivious to the searing pain in my side, I struggled to my feet and staggered to the iron handrail that ran along the length of wall. Using the rail as support, I made my way down the hallway toward the nearest set of doors. Behind me, the rhythmic tap of approaching footsteps grew louder, emanating from the corridor where the policeman had just appeared.

I pushed through the first set of windowed doors. They swung wide and banged loudly against the stops. Fifty feet onward, I forced my way through a second set, and as the latter closed behind me, I heard a faint *pop* and *hiss*. Almost in the same instant, one of the glass panels in the first set of doors shattered explosively, showering the floor in an avalanche of shards.

I stifled a squeal of terror and nearly fell to my knees, but somehow I managed to carry on and made it to the next corridor just as the windows in the second set of doors exploded. When I glanced back, I saw a man running in my direction, arm outstretched, a strange long-barreled gun aimed directly at me.

There was a flash and then that faint *pop* and *hiss* again. As I ducked around the corner, a bullet struck the wall and sent a spray of concrete fragments and dust in all directions.

I spied a bank of elevators up ahead and pushed off from the wall, launching myself toward them, running awkwardly, clutching at my side. When I got there I stabbed at the call button, pressing it again and again, as though somehow that would make the elevator arrive faster.

The footsteps behind me drew closer. I turned and pressed myself back against the nearest set of elevator doors, staring toward the corridor entrance. The man stalking me came around the corner just as the doors opened behind me. The next thing I knew, I was falling backward into the elevator, a bullet slicing through the space my head had occupied mere seconds before.

I screamed, reached up, and jabbed blindly at the panel of floor buttons. The doors *whooshed* closed, and I slumped back against the wall, my entire body shuddering as the elevator began its ascent.

A few floors later, the car came to a jarring halt, and the doors slid open once again. I peered out cautiously and found myself staring at the large curved counter of a reception room. From where I was sitting, I couldn't see anyone behind it, so I hauled myself to my feet and limped out into the open space to have a look around. No one appeared to be on duty, but down the hallway to the left, I saw several closed doors that offered the promise of assistance.

Clutching my side, I started off in that direction, but I hadn't taken more than a step or two when I heard the approach of the second elevator. I jumped at the sound and frantically looked around for a place to hide. Across from me, the door to a storeroom stood open. Ignoring the agony of my wound, I dashed over to it and quickly slipped inside, closing it almost entirely behind me.

When I looked out through the narrow open crack between the door and the frame, I saw a nurse in white surgical garb backing out of the elevator. She was pulling a large, box-like piece of equipment on a cart. Another nurse followed, pushing the apparatus from the rear.

I was about to call out when the gunman who'd taken a shot at me walked out from behind them. He was wearing a lab coat and moved with an easy familiarity that suggested he knew the hospital and was well acquainted with the staff. If he still had the gun, it was well concealed.

A security guard and another nurse exited a room down the hallway and joined the three, and a moment later, a well-dressed woman stepped into view. Her stride was purposeful, her deportment commanding. The moment I saw her it was all I could do not to gasp. I recognized her. I should have after all; I'd known her a good part of my life.

It was Aunt Amelia.

I didn't know what to think. For just a moment, I had the overwhelming compulsion to run to her and ask her to protect me. But gut instinct held me back. I watched, confused, scarcely breathing as she spoke to the gunman, addressing him like she knew him. Whatever she was saying wasn't making him happy, and from where I stood, it sure looked like he was getting a dressing down.

The gunman grew agitated and argumentative, then reached under his white coat and withdrew his gun. Nobody gave it so much as a second glance. Aunt Amelia just shoved it back at him angrily. She glared at him, said something, and he nodded. Then he put the weapon away, and he and the security guard promptly went off down the hallway.

Aunt Amelia turned to the two nurses who were herding the bulky piece of equipment and spoke to them in a calmer, more conversational tone. I stood there, spying through the crack in the doorway, still in shock, still not quite sure what I was seeing.

I told myself I was jumping to conclusions, that it wasn't what it looked like. I knew Aunt Amelia. I'd practically been a second daughter to her. She had treated me like one of the family. Hell, she'd even accompanied me to the doctor's when I'd had to go for the first of my mandatory gynecological examinations.

She was Camille's mother, for heaven's sake!

And yet here she was, apparently in cahoots with the man who'd just tried to put another bullet in me.

I felt ill, terrified, and utterly distraught.

The nurses parted company with Aunt Amelia, veering to the right and heading toward a large door that was unlike any of the others on the floor. This one was a large sheet of glass set in a polished steel frame. There was a metal box attached to the frame, and as I watched, one of the nurses took out a metal punch card and inserted it into a narrow slot on the front. A loud click ensued, and a light above the door turned green.

The door opened with a hiss of vented air, and the nurses marshaled the equipment into the room beyond, one pushing and the other pulling as they guided it over the threshold. As the machine passed my view I got a better look at it. There were gauges and blinking lights, assorted black knobs and switches, and a large glass cylinder that was frosted over. Wisps of chilled air rose off the device, like the breath of cold that sometimes comes out of a freezer when you open it on a hot day.

The nurses and the machine disappeared into the room beyond, and the door sealed behind them. I shifted positions and could just barely see into the chamber. As I watched, the two women donned rubber suits, rubber gloves, and boots, then secured glass fishbowl-like helmets over their heads. Now fully entombed, they resumed command of the equipment they were ferrying and proceeded beyond another airtight door, quickly vanishing from view.

With the nurses gone, I turned my attention to the exit. Aunt Amelia was berating the reception nurse; the security guard and the gunman were still nowhere to be seen. Finally Aunt Amelia stalked off down the hallway and disappeared into one of the rooms, her long blond hair swinging behind her.

CHAPTER 18

SAFE HAVEN

The moment the opportunity arose, I made my escape. I swapped my hospital johnny for a pair of grungy coveralls I found in the storeroom, slipped my feet into a pair of ill-fitting rubber boots, and hightailed it out of there when the receptionist wasn't looking. I took the stairs down to the basement, sticking to the shadows and keeping a watchful eye out for the gunman. It was a maze of tunnels down there, but eventually I found one that took me outside. From there I wasted no time flagging down a cab.

It wasn't until I'd jumped into the backseat that I realized I had no idea where to go. I thought of the police station, but I wasn't sure I could trust them. Not if Aunt Amelia was involved in this. And it would be idiotic to go home to my flat. I considered Grace's, but I was afraid that was one of the first places they'd look for me.

There was only one option that seemed even remotely safe, only one person I wanted to be with. It bordered on ironic — especially considering what had happened between us recently — that I should now see him as the only person I could trust in a situation like this.

I gave the driver the address. He glanced over his shoulder at me, an odd look on his face. "You sure about this, miss?" he asked.

I nodded. "Yes. As fast as you can."

By the time the cab pulled up outside the gate, I was nearly hysterical. The adrenaline and the events of the past few hours had finally caught up with me, and I was starting to crash. I kept thinking about what I'd seen at Mercy, shattered by the realization that someone I thought I knew, someone I loved, might have betrayed me. Lately it seemed I was surrounded by people with dark secrets.

"You okay, miss?" the driver asked.

"Just wait here," I said, my voice quavering.

He didn't look pleased by the prospect. "I ain't sure it's safe for you to be here," he said.

I laughed nervously and hopped out of the cab, crossing quickly to the brass plate at the side of the gate. The oversized boots I wore knocked and thumped against my shins with each hurried step. A sob caught in my throat, and I gulped hard to keep it down.

Just hold it together a while longer, I told myself. *Then you'll be with him, and everything will be all right.*

I pushed the button on the plate and waited. I knew from previous visits that the Embassy was equipped with something they called closed-circuit television — a sort of spy camera hidden somewhere so they could see who was at the gate. But dressed as I was, I didn't blame the guards for not recognizing me right off the bat. Besides, in the past I'd always come through in the limousine.

A voice rang out from the darkness, German and displaying no hint of emotion. I turned in the direction of it and said in a tiny voice, "Val, I need help. Someone just tried to kill me, and I'm scared, and I don't know what to do, and I didn't know where to go, so I came here in a zebra, but I haven't any money or coupons to pay the fare, and you're the only person I could think of, and I didn't know where else to go —"

The words poured out of me in an unbroken string, my hands shaking as I pushed strands of hair behind my ears. The tears came faster than I could blink them away.

There was a long silence. The night was eerily still. And then, without warning, the gates shook, rattling loudly, then slowly retracting. From the corner of my eye, I saw the cabbie tighten his grip on the steering wheel and peer guardedly into the Embassy compound. Out of the shroud of dark, two wolves loped through the open gate, making a beeline for me. The cabbie yelped in alarm, rolling up the window as quickly as he could manage.

Tristan and Isolde circled me, bumping their heads against my thighs, soliciting a few friendly pats. I put out a hand and touched their soft fur, feeling a bit of my fear melt away at their contact.

I went back to the cab and got in behind the driver. He was sitting rigidly behind the steering wheel, eyes round with disbelief. "Are . . . are you . . . are you one of them?" he stammered.

On any other occasion I probably would have laughed and rolled my eyes at how absurd that was, but now all I did was shake my head. "Just drive to the house," I said.

"In *there*?"

"You'll get your money there," I promised.

"Okay," he said, looking none too pleased.

Tristan and Isolde kept pace with us as we drove up the stretch of crushed coral and cobblestones to the manor. Val's tall, wiry physique appeared before us, looking otherworldly in the conflicting play of light and darkness. The cabbie braked a couple of meters from him, but even before the electric stopped, I was fumbling with the door handle. I scrambled out and raced to Val, throwing myself at him, pressing my head to his chest and sobbing.

"Sophie," he said, putting his arms around me. In that moment I knew I was safe, that he'd never let anything happen to me.

A few moments later we were inside the Embassy, and Val was pouring me tea. He kept encouraging me to drink it down and told me everything was going to be all right. But I was trembling violently, and every time I started to tell him what had happened, a little sob would hiccup from me, and tears would start in my eyes again.

I don't know whether I'd just finally hit bottom, or whether there had been something in that tea, because the next thing I knew, Val was carrying me down a long hallway.

A good ten or twelve hours must have passed before I awoke. Mrs. Barker, one of the Immunes who worked for the Embassy, blew into the room and threw aside the heavy blackout drapes, opening the windows and letting in sunlight that was bright enough to signal midmorning. She set out a basin of water and some toiletries before hastening out. A few minutes later she returned with some clothing, which she carefully laid out for me on a chair while I busied myself washing.

Once I was cleaned up, Mrs. Barker fretted over my wound, insisting on redressing it. "Are you sure you was shot, ducky?" she asked in surprise when she removed the bloodied bandages. "There ain't much here but a bit of a scar and some bruising."

After that she helped me get dressed, though I kept insisting I was fine and could manage perfectly well myself. I wasn't the sort of person used to having someone help me put on my clothes, and all her fussing made me uncomfortable and reminded me far too much of Grace.

I didn't bother asking where the gorgeous layered white linen sundress or the strappy sandals and intimates had come from. Val had clearly sent her out to pick them up early in the morning, and from the labels I knew he'd spared no expense. They were from a shop Camille had often frequented and would have cost me a month's pay and more ration coupons than I ever could have afforded to give up.

When I was done getting ready, Mrs. Barker led me to the dining hall, a large room that faced north. There was a wall of windows letting in the warm glow of day but no direct sunlight. It was like being in an entirely different part of the world in this place, but even so, it was impossible to forget that not far away lay the rest of Haven, where the night before someone had done his level best to put an end to my life.

Gerald, the Embassy butler, drew out a chair for me near the end of the table. While he poured me a cup of coffee, Val entered the room. I got up and rushed to him.

In the past when staff members had been around Val had always been a bit aloof, but now he didn't hesitate in taking me in his arms. I savored the feel of him as I leaned into his body. "Feeling better?"

"Much."

"I'm glad you're safe. I've been worried about you." He uttered a faint, nervous chuckle. "You seem to have a penchant for getting yourself into all sorts of trouble."

I lifted my head from his chest and looked up into the warmth of his eyes. Concern shadowed his features. "I've been minding my own business," I insisted.

"Yes, well, whether you like it or not, you seem to have become someone else's," he said, leading me back to the table.

I took my seat, and Val settled in the chair across from mine. Gerald brought him a wineglass that wasn't filled with wine, carefully setting it on the table in easy reach. Val thanked him, and the butler bowed a retreat.

I purposefully turned my attention to the plate of food that had appeared in front of me — eggs and bacon. Vamps don't eat, but the Embassy had a kitchen of some sort for the times when the ambassador entertained Immune guests, and there was always food on hand for the Immune staff who worked here.

"If you're feeling up to it —" Val began.

Before he could finish I launched into my story, telling him everything I could remember. When I'd finished, we sat in silence, Val staring into his glass, pensive, and me waiting impatiently for him to speak.

"You should have called me after you got shot," he said at length.

"I didn't get the chance. Grace was there and so was Havershaw, and then when I found out about Dad —" My throat tightened, and I closed my eyes, heaving a shuddering breath.

Val put a hand on mine, his cool touch sweeping through me, soothing the sting of my grief. "I'm so sorry, Sophie. I know what he meant to you."

"What's going on, Val? First Camille, then the break-in, and then some reporter I've never met is murdered and the guy who did it tries to kill me. Then I'm shot, and while I'm in the hospital trying to recover, someone almost finishes the job. On top of that I find out that Aunt Amelia might be mixed up in whatever it is that's going on."

"I can't answer your questions," Val said.

"Can't?" I said. "Or won't? I almost got killed last night! The only reason I'm alive —" I gulped a few quick breaths, my chest heaving as I tried to control a sudden wave of apprehension.

He looked at me sternly. "Let it be, Sophie. Trust me on this one. Sometimes there are things we're better off not knowing. This is definitely one of them. Just forget it."

"Isn't it a bit late for that? People are trying to kill me!"

Val almost seemed to sigh, and he looked away for a moment, staring out the window. "Loving you can be so exasperating."

"Why?" I pressed. "Because I want to know the truth?"

"Because you're never satisfied." His voice was rough, almost harsh. "I showed you the truth once. I don't think you liked what you saw." There was conflict in his expression, making it difficult to read. In a softer tone he added, "I too often forget how young you are."

"What's that supposed to mean?" I glared at him, annoyed.

"Only that I've lived nearly eight decades, while you've not even finished two. You haven't seen the things I've seen," Val told me. "You haven't experienced enough to understand just how complicated the world is. The problem with you, Sophie, is that you think in terms of black and white. As far as you're concerned, there's right and there's wrong and there's nothing in between. But it isn't like that, luv. It's not that simple."

"Then explain it to me, Val."

He looked at me, his eyes intense, and I felt my pulse quicken. "There are forces at work here that profit from a situation that has existed since the signing of the truce. They've no desire to see that change. That's all I can tell you."

"Okay, you're right. I don't understand. Why can't you just give me a straight answer?"

"Because I don't want you getting hurt," Val said forcefully, his voice rising, colored by anguish. "Look at what knowing just a little bit has done. If I could, I'd watch over you twenty-four hours a day, but unfortunately . . ." He lifted his shoulders in a modest shrug. "Even taking precautions, I can only risk brief periods in sunlight. I've tried to protect you, but you certainly don't make it easy."

"Well, I'm not going to just sit in my flat all day!" I glared at him, bristling with defiance.

"Exactly my point!" he said. "If I thought I could get away with it, I'd have you stay here. But the ambassador will be returning from Berlin tomorrow . . ."

"I have a life, Val. School. My job." *You,* I suddenly wanted to say but didn't. That part of my life was just too damn complicated at the moment.

"And I want you to keep that life. Which is why you're better off knowing as little as possible. I may be able to stop them from making more attempts on you if I can persuade them you don't know anything."

"*Them?* Who are they, Val, and how do you know them?"

His face hardened. "We're not going there," he said in an even tone. "You need to forget this."

"Forget it? What about Camille? And my mother? And everything else? I'm just supposed to pretend none of that happened?"

"You're talking about separate things," Val said. "Your friend wasn't killed by the people trying to kill you. She was mistaken for someone else."

"Mistaken?" I bit at my lip, trying to make sense of that. Camille had been *mistaken* for someone else. But who? Not me; I didn't look anything like her. But it struck me that she had looked like someone else I knew — her mother.

Jesus!

I slowly pieced it together. Camille had been wearing Amelia's dress and jewelry the night she was murdered. In the dark, someone easily could have mistaken her for Aunt Amelia, especially given how much they resembled one another.

"Her mother," I finally said aloud. I turned to Val, staring at him in shock. "Do you think someone mistook her for Amelia?"

He shook his head. "Don't do this to yourself, Sophie."

But I ignored him, the gears in my head turning faster now. I was thinking about Amelia's past, about how she'd been a doctor when she was younger. And then I thought about what my mother had written in her journal, about the young blond woman who'd been present at several of those incidents with the babies. And then I thought about last night; Amelia had been at Mercy, even though she didn't practice medicine anymore.

I drummed my fingers on the table, feeling the pieces of the puzzle coming together to form a horrifying picture. "No," I whispered, shaking my head. "It can't be. It just can't."

"Sophie . . ."

I blinked and looked at Val as though just realizing he was there. "Amelia must be Lady X," I said. If he had read that journal, as I was sure he had, he knew exactly what I meant.

But he didn't react. Not a single muscle twitched. I could see something in his eyes, though, something that hinted at things he knew. Things he maybe wanted to say but for some reason simply couldn't.

I should have left it at that, but I couldn't. "So whoever killed Camille thought he was killing Aunt Amelia? But why? Was that why you were really in Coral Beach? You tracked the killer there and you were going to try to stop him?" I looked at him, brimming with expectation.

Val remained stubbornly silent.

"Who is he?" I asked.

"No," he said.

"No, what?"

"No, I won't help you. This has to stop. *You* have to stop. Just walk away from it. Please. Do it for me if you won't do it for yourself."

He might as well have been whistling into the wind for all that I heard him. "It was a vamp," I mused. "I know that much. That's the only way her neck could have been broken like that."

Val's fist came down hard on the table, making me jump. "That's more than enough," he said. His voice was like ice, and anger flared in his eyes. "It'll only hurt you to know more."

I hesitated a moment, but then heard myself say, "It's all related, isn't it? My mother's death, Camille's murder, the dead reporter, the people trying to kill me?"

He sat still, then slowly picked up his glass and finished his drink. There was no mistaking his barely restrained rage as he set the empty glass down with force and briskly wiped his lips with a napkin. He tossed the crumpled cloth on the table and stood up. As he rose, the chair made a noisy screech, like fingernails on a blackboard. "Come on," he said, holding out a hand.

I looked up at him, conscious of his ire. "Where are we going?" I asked warily.

"Just come."

He waited for me to take his hand. Eventually I did, and he led me away, his strides brisk, bordering on impatient.

"Where are we going?" I asked again as I hurried along with him.

"To your flat so you can pick up some things, then to Grace's."

"Wait! What? How am I going to be safe *there*?"

"I've already talked to Havershaw, and he's going to assign someone to keep an eye on you."

"You already —" I scowled at him and pulled back, breaking free of his grasp and backpedalling. "You planned this behind my back without even asking me what *I* want?"

"Someone has to look out for you," Val replied, as though it were a simple fact.

"Well, if I'm going anywhere, I'm going back to my flat." I faced him defiantly, hands on my hips.

He shook his head. "Grace lives in a safe neighborhood, and it'll be easier to watch over the two of you."

"You think Grace may be in danger?" I felt my insides twist at the thought.

"You don't?" Val asked incredulously. "After your father —" He caught himself, but it was too late.

A wave of despair crashed into me. My legs went weak, and without warning I was on my knees, my face in my hands.

Val knelt beside me, put his hands on my shoulders, and drew me to him. "You shouldn't be alone at the moment," he said. "Not after all that's happened. For pity's sake, Sophie, you were shot. And you've suffered a terrible loss. Let Grace take care of you. Maybe the two of you . . ." He didn't finish.

"You know how I hate her fussing," I said through tears.

"It's just for a few days."

"And then what? All this magically goes away?"

"I told you, I'm going to try and fix it."

"How?" I asked.

"I don't know yet. But I have some connections."

"More secrets, Val?"

He gave a slight shake of his head. "We all have them, Sophie."

I sighed. "I wish you would trust me. I wish you felt you could tell me."

"It's not that I don't want to," Val said, "but there's a whole other world outside Haven, and I don't want you caught up in it."

"Does it have anything to do with all those refrigerators being shipped from Haven to the Third Reich?" I asked. I don't know where that question came from. It just slipped out, though I suppose I'd been planning to confront him about it at some point.

Val immediately stiffened. "I wouldn't know anything about that," he said. "I'm not the trade attaché."

He helped me to my feet, and we stood for a moment facing one another, Val holding my hands. He raised them to his lips and gently kissed them. "I'm going to try and set this right, Sophie. I'm going to try to put a stop to it. I promise."

An ugly thought was beginning to insinuate itself in my mind. "Are you part of it, Val?" I heard myself ask in a faint whisper.

It was a moment before he shook his head. "My world is a lot more complex than you can imagine. You people think you know us, that we're all of a kind. But it's just not that simple. Before there was the Fall, there was a war, Sophie. A lot of us haven't forgotten that."

I wondered what he meant by that, but before I could pursue the matter, he stepped closer, swept me into his arms, and bent his head to mine.

"Please," Val said. "Just for once in your life do what I ask. Don't be like her."

"Like who?" I asked.

"Mary. You're —" He stopped and shook his head. "Never mind. Just let me take you to Grace's."

I hesitated. If Val thought I should forget all of this, then maybe I should. But I really didn't see how I could. Not when people were shooting at me.

"Okay," I said at last. "You win." *For now.*

"Thank you." He kissed me, and I kissed him back. It almost made up for his reticence.

Almost.

CHAPTER 19

THE GIRL IN THE PHOTOGRAPH

I got an earful from Grace when I arrived. She ragged me for not calling her and told me I was insensitive to her feelings. But Val had already informed me that he'd sent a message to my grandmother the night before to bring her up to date on what had happened, so I didn't feel too guilty.

She was happy to see the police electric parked out on the street "in light of the circumstances," as she said. But, of course, she'd have preferred that it wasn't necessary.

Join the club, I thought. I wasn't enamored of the thought of being watched all day, either.

Grace's home was typical of most Haven residences. "Mediterranean" was how she described it. It was small and white, the walls made of concrete and stone with a stucco overlay, and the roof a peaked expanse of terra cotta tiles on a wood beam frame. The windows were deep set and positioned so that the rooms were generally reasonably free of sunlight during the hottest part of the day. Nobody but those living in Cliffside had air conditioners — which was another reason I'd always enjoyed going to Camille's house.

There wasn't a lot of space inside Grace's home, which meant that about the only way I could get any privacy was to keep to my room. I did this a lot over the next few days, trying to avoid my grandmother as much as possible.

After less than a week at Grace's I was beginning to go a bit stir crazy. About the only thing keeping me from going completely round-the-bend was schoolwork. And I was immersed in one of the assignments a classmate had dropped off for me when Grace came to my room and knocked lightly on the door.

"Can you spare a moment?" she asked. She had a large leather-bound book in her arms and came over and stood near the footboard.

I was sitting cross-legged on the bed, industriously pecking away at the keys on my portable typewriter, laboring over an essay about the division of power between the office of the president and Parliament. It was heavy stuff, and I was glad to take a break. I paused, fingers resting on the keys, and looked up at her. Grace came closer and handed me the book.

"What is this?" I asked.

"Pictures of your mother."

I sat up straighter and gaped at her. "I thought —"

"Your father didn't want you seeing them," Grace explained. "I think he believed it would just make matters more . . . *difficult*." She sighed regretfully. "I never saw eye to eye with him on that, but so long as he was alive, I honored his request. He said he wouldn't let me see you if I didn't. But now —" She hesitated, bowed her head a moment, then focused on me again. "I think you should see them."

I set the book in my lap and opened it, handling it like a delicate treasure. The first page had a black-and-white picture of a baby, head peeping out from beneath a blanket, one tiny hand curled against its cheek. The words *Mary — age two weeks* were written just beneath in a long, looping cursive. The date in the corner was 1960.

"Mom," I whispered. I gently touched the picture with my fingertips, as though I could connect with the person in that image, could somehow reach back in time to know someone I'd never met.

"I thought I'd never have any more children after Matthew," said Grace. "I thought I might be too old. But then . . ." She smiled sadly.

"Why?" I looked up at her, the beginnings of tears in my eyes.

"It was my duty," she said.

I shook my head. "No, not that. I mean why did she die? Was it me? Did I —"

Grace sat down and reached out, putting a gnarled hand on my knee. "Oh, my dear child, you can't think like that. You can't ever believe *that.* What happened to your mother . . ." She faltered, a pained expression on her face. "It had nothing to do with you."

"But she died when I was born," I said. I almost added that Mom had gone mad because of me, but Grace didn't know about the journal, and I wasn't sure I wanted to tell her.

My grandmother looked away, and I had the feeling she was avoiding direct eye contact, as though she were afraid I'd see something she didn't want me to see. "Your mother was dead long before that," she said in a low, broken voice. "It's not something . . ." She stopped and seemed to wrestle with herself, engaged in some inner conflict.

"Grandma, please. Please tell me what happened."

Grace's gaze dropped to the photo album, then she got up and walked out.

"Grandma!" I called after her, thinking she was gone. But a moment later she returned, came straight to me, and took up one of my hands. She pressed something into it and said, "Maybe these can give you some answers."

When she took her hand away I looked down at a bundle of keys, the same ones my father had given me. I'd forgotten about them in the commotion of recent events. "Where did these come from?" I asked.

"I took your clothes home from the hospital," Grace explained. "The shirt was ruined — such an unfortunate waste — but the shorts were salvageable. I found those" — she nodded to the keys — "when I was going through your pockets."

"How are *these* going to tell me anything?" I dangled the keys before me, looking past them to her. "I don't even know what most of them are for."

"When you've finished with the pictures I'll show you."

"Show me now," I pleaded.

Grace shook her head. "You're always so impatient, Sophie. It'll be your undoing if you don't watch out." She left the room again, and this time she didn't come back.

I stared at the keys in my hand again, thinking of my father, and closed my fist around them. The photo album still lay open in my lap. I looked down at it and slowly turned the page.

* * *

There are probably very few people who ever truly know their parents. They may think they do, may have seen pictures and read letters and listened to stories about the lives of the people to whom they owe their existence. But the truth is, none of that is anything more than window dressing.

Mostly, I think, we can never really know our parents, because we simply can't imagine them ever having been like us.

I'd read my mother's journal, beginning in her teens and ending shortly before she died, and I was now seeing pictures of her throughout her childhood and youth. And yet still she remained elusive.

The photos in the album meant little to me. I couldn't tell what they were about, because I had no real context. I couldn't get inside them and experience the mood of the moment and determine the minds of the subjects. They were all about strangers in distant times.

I saw pictures of my mother at Christmas, playing at the beach, riding a horse, climbing a tree. Pictures of her at church, at school, at a birthday party. With each page she got a little older — one, two, three, and on.

There she was at fifteen, and suddenly I could see she was different. I could see it in her face. Something had happened. There was a haunted look in her eyes. She stood staring at the camera, but it was as though she wanted to flee.

What had happened to change that girl? I wondered.

I flipped back through the book, examining the pictures again, and it was then that I noticed something about the pages of the album. There were faded spots on most of them, places where other pictures had been. Someone had removed several of them and rearranged the others in a feeble attempt to camouflage the empty spaces.

I studied the picture of my mother at fifteen, took in the forlorn expression on her face, and realized I recognized it. I'd seen it reflected in the mirror in the days since my father's death. It was the look of loss. But who had Mom lost?

I tried to do the math. The picture of my mother at fifteen had been taken before she'd met Val and several years before her father had died. Her brothers were currently all alive and well, to the best of my knowledge, so it couldn't have been one of them. And yet there was no mistaking her despair.

Still puzzling over it, I turned the page. There were no more faded spots now, and there seemed to be more pictures on each sheet.

On these subsequent pages my mother's melancholy waned. The photo of her sixteenth birthday showed a livelier young woman, though there was still sorrow in her eyes. Whatever had been troubling her abruptly vanished in the next few snapshots. I didn't have to guess at why — that's when she'd met Val. You could see there was something different about her. She positively radiated in the succeeding images.

I paused at a picture of my mother proudly holding up her diploma at her high school graduation. She'd been only a bit older then than I was now. I stared at that image and felt like I was beginning to understand her. The world she had lived in wasn't so different from mine, and when that picture had been taken we'd been at similar milestones in our lives.

And then there was Val. He linked us. It was eerie and unsettling, but it gave me an insight into her I might not otherwise have had.

I turned the page, and my breath caught — my father stared back at me. Younger than I'd ever known him, with his arm around my mother. He was beaming broadly, and though she smiled beside him, it wasn't quite real.

After that there were wedding pictures. My mother looked exquisite in them. She'd always been beautiful; the record of that was in the photos. But in the white, strapless wedding gown, she was a fairy-tale princess. To say she was gorgeous would not have done her justice. She was like something Hollywood might have produced when it had existed.

The remaining pictures were of my mother when she was pregnant. At first I thought they were all the same pregnancy, but then I realized they were from two separate occasions. In the second it was me inside her, probably sometime in the second trimester — before everything had fallen apart. It was strange to look at that photograph of her with her hands on her growing belly and know I was the one she was smiling about.

That was the last picture ever taken of her.

I stared at that image for a long time, feeling so resentful that I'd never gotten to know her.

When I finally closed the book, something fluttered to the floor. A picture had come unstuck and fallen out — a photograph of my mother when she was about ten. I found the page it belonged to and was about to replace it when something on the back of the picture caught my eye.

Izzy, age ten, 1970.

I flipped the photo over again and stared at it, frowning. The girl in the picture was my mother. She had the same hair, the same face, the same eyes.

I looked at the back of the photograph again and read it once more, thinking it must be a mistake. Who the heck was Izzy?

I knew I'd seen that name before, not too long ago, but it took me a moment to place it. Then it came to me — my mother had mentioned it in her journal. At the time I had just assumed Izzy was a friend of hers. Apparently not.

I sat there, puzzling over the image, peering out the window at the sun-dappled street. White-stucco terrace homes brooded on the edge of the curb, their front gardens tiny oases of green against the cracked and faded tarmac of the road. An electric hummed by, its motor barely audible even through the open windows. A breeze rustled the leaves of the magnolia trees, and the scent of the flowers wafted over me.

Haven wore the patina of paradise, but I could see it crumbling before me. Bit by bit, piece by piece, the world I knew was changing in front of my eyes. Everything I thought I knew was being challenged.

I put the photo album aside, and as I stood up, I noticed the keys resting where I'd dropped them. I stared at them a moment, then looked at the photo still in my hand. Grace had suggested the keys might hold some clues. I snatched them up and went in search of her, hoping for answers. Not that I was expecting much. These days it seemed that the more I learned, the less I found I knew.

* * *

Grace was drinking coffee in the drawing room when I entered. She smiled faintly and gestured to the chair opposite her. I flopped down in it, feeling irritable.

"Who's Izzy?" I demanded.

Grace froze, the cup of steaming coffee halfway to her lips. "Wherever did you hear that name?" she asked in a tremulous voice. She placed the cup on the saucer in her other hand, the two pieces of china chattering against one another as her hands shook. Black coffee spilt over the lip of the cup and pooled in the saucer. She set it down quickly on the table between us.

I tossed the photo down beside the cup. "I found this in the album," I said. "I thought it was Mom."

"It is," Grace said.

"No. It says *Izzy* on the back."

"That's a mistake."

I glowered at her, the way I used to when I was a little kid. "I just wish someone would tell me the whole truth for a change," I said.

Grace inhaled a breath and regarded me with rheumy eyes. "The things you want to know have no simple answers," she said.

"You gave me the keys. You must want me to find out the truth."

"Yes. But this . . ." Her voice faded, and she looked so old and small and beaten.

"Was it really so terrible?" I asked.

There was a long silence.

"It was a long time ago," Grace said finally. "Before you were born. It doesn't concern you." She leaned forward and picked up the picture on the table. For several long seconds, she sat staring at it.

"That *is* Izzy, isn't it?"

Grace nodded. "Isabelle. Yes." She touched the photo lovingly with the tips of her fingers, and I saw tears glittering in her eyes.

"Was she my aunt?" I asked.

"Yes." My grandmother's voice crackled with emotion as she confirmed my suspicions. "Your mother's identical twin, though they were really nothing alike."

"What happened to her? How did she die?"

"Die?" Grace shook herself and looked up at me, her pain almost palpable. "Yes. Yes, I suppose she died."

"Suppose?" I said. "What does that mean?"

But my grandmother ignored me. "She'd just turned fifteen," she went on. "She and your mother. We'd had a beautiful party, and everything seemed so perfect. But then Isabelle got sick. We thought it was just a cold at first. But it didn't go away, and she just kept getting worse. Over the course of the following weeks she got weaker and weaker. We took her to the hospital, and they ran some tests."

Grace looked away, and I could see she didn't want to talk about it, didn't want to remember it. But I couldn't stop myself from prodding her further. "What did they find?" I asked.

"After several weeks they determined it was some sort of autoimmune disease," she said. "Though they couldn't be certain. Whatever it was, it weakened her system, leaving her susceptible to a host of infections."

"Oh, my God," I said, putting a hand to my mouth. *Susceptible to a host of infections.* I knew what that had to mean; as a child, that phrase had haunted me for years.

Immunes are not invulnerable; we can catch other diseases. When I'd been in grade one, there'd been an outbreak of measles. People had panicked, and I hadn't understood why until much later, when Mrs. Bhutto had explained how in some rare cases, one infection could leave a person compromised and subsequently open to infections of another sort — one in particular. One with implications far more serious and terrifying than those of the average disease.

"You understand?" said Grace.

I nodded, subdued. "Gomorrah," I whispered. I fought for breath. "Jesus . . ."

I ran my fingers through my hair and found that I was shaking. No one ever really talked about that sort of thing, of course, but there'd always been rumors it could happen . . . that it *had* happened.

"That must have been terrible for all of you," I said at last. "I can't imagine watching someone I love die like that."

There were tears in Grace's eyes, and I wasn't sure she'd even heard me. "We have rules." She looked at me stiffly. "When she was transformed . . ." She stopped, holding trembling fingers to her lips.

"Wait! Hold on a minute." I sat up straighter. "Are you telling me Gomorrah didn't kill her?"

The look Grace gave me was answer enough. "In the early stages she begged us to end it. She wanted to die. She was so afraid of what she would become. Some of the doctors tried to persuade me to let them do it. It was the only compassionate thing to do, they said. It would have to be done eventually. That was the law. But I couldn't."

Grace looked at me, her eyes beseeching me to understand. Isabelle had been her daughter, her child, her flesh and blood. She had carried her for nine months, nurtured her and cared for her over the next fifteen years. I couldn't pretend to understand a bond like that, but it was impossible not to have some inkling of just how devastating it would have been to lose her daughter in such a manner.

People died all the time from accidents and other diseases. Some of them young people. But to have your child *put down* like an animal . . .

I didn't even want to think about.

"So the government —" I began but couldn't bring myself to say it.

"They would have."

I blinked, frowned, and gave her a bewildered look. "What do you mean they *would* have?"

"Whatever she had become, she was still my daughter." Grace spoke sharply, defiantly. "At least, when it happened I thought she was."

I struggled with the meaning of those words. "Are you telling me she's . . . that she's *alive*?"

"Alive?" Grace stared at me, horrorstruck. "To be a vamp is not living, child. When it happened to her, she was no longer one of us. I realized that soon enough."

"But you didn't let the government kill her."

She lowered her eyes. "I should have. And as far as they know, Isabelle *is* dead."

I put a hand to my forehead, trying to make sense of that. "So what, then? I mean, what happened to her?"

"She was one of *them*; there was no question of keeping her around. She had to go."

"Had to go?" My voice rose in pitch. "Had to go where?"

Grace shook her head. "It doesn't matter. Just away."

"Doesn't matter, Grandma? She's your daughter!"

"Was. She *was* my daughter. That thing she became . . ." Grace looked stricken. "If you'd seen her . . ."

"Did Mom know?" I asked.

She shot me a scornful look. "Of course not. It was all kept quiet. It always is. As far as your mother knew, her sister simply got sick and died in the hospital. The only time she saw Isabelle before the . . . the transformation, was when the doctors did tests on Mary to try and figure out why she hadn't been affected like her twin. After Isabelle changed and had been dealt with, we had a funeral and a coffin. For all intents and purposes, Isabelle was gone and buried. It was better that way."

"So Isabelle . . ." I fumbled for words. "Where . . . where is she now? What did you do with her?"

Grace gave me a stern look. "I told you it doesn't matter. It's all in the past, and that's where it should stay."

"I'm a part of this family!" I protested. "I have a right to know."

She lifted her eyes to mine, and the look she gave me was hollow. "If you're so determined to have the truth, ask your vampire," she said. "He took care of it."

"Val?" I said. Another secret he was keeping from me?

"He's very good at that," Grace said in a flat tone. "Taking care of things."

"So then it's true what he said? *You* went to him? After what you said about him?"

"I couldn't just let her . . ." She choked back the words. "As much as I despised the thing Isabelle had become, I couldn't bring myself to do it, to . . ." She fell silent for a moment, then said, "I thought maybe there might still be some part of the man I'd known inside of

Val, and that if there was, he'd take care of her. He'd take her to *their* world and look out for her and make sure she was safe."

"And is she?" I asked.

"I don't know," Grace said, barely more than a whisper. "I never asked him, and I've never heard from her since . . ." She didn't finish. She didn't need to.

In the back of my mind, I found myself wondering how Val had reacted when he'd seen Isabelle. Had it been the same as when he'd first encountered my mother? Except Isabelle would have been a vamp by then. Changed. Maybe he couldn't feel for his own kind what he felt for us.

I put my hands to my head and closed my eyes a moment, feeling completely overwhelmed. It was all so damn complicated; it was such a nightmare.

"It's ironic," Grace was saying. "The virus saved Isabelle in a way. The doctors said that when her immune system crashed, she should have died. Her body was prey to any number of pathogens. Instead, she became one of them . . . one of those . . . those monsters."

"But you saved her."

"Saved her?" Grace stared at me as though I'd said something truly odious. "Oh, child, you've no idea what you're saying. There isn't a day that goes by that I don't wish I'd had the courage to listen to the doctors. I wish I hadn't broken the law, because it would have been better if we'd done it the government's way, rather than have her be a part of *their* world. What I did was treason and far from kind."

On the surface there was something horribly cold in her remarks, but I remembered how I'd felt about Father, and in a way I could understand some of it. In her eyes I could see the depths of her despair and tried to imagine what it would have been like to make such a choice — dead for good or Undead forever. Most Immunes would probably say it was better to be the former than the latter.

Grace and I sat cocooned in silence for quite some time, and I kept wondering about the girl in the photograph. I tried to picture

Isabelle suddenly torn from Haven at fifteen years old, thrust into a totally alien environment. For years she'd been brought up knowing the vamps as the enemy, as something unconscionable that must be eradicated. And then in a matter of weeks she'd become one of them — one of those things that practically everyone in Haven feels should be hunted down and destroyed. Wiped from the face of the earth.

I felt the keys in my hand, squeezed them until their rough teeth bit into my palm. At last I said, "I think it's time we talked about these."

Grace nodded wordlessly. She put down the picture of Isabelle and rose to her feet. "You've come this far," she said. "But don't blame me if you don't like what you find. And whatever you do find, child, for God's sake, keep it to yourself. Don't get some foolish notion in your head that you've got to do something about it. You can't change the world."

CHAPTER 20

THE CABINET OF SECRETS AND CURIOSITIES

My father and I had lived in the same house for more than sixteen years, but in so many ways he and I had been strangers. We'd kept secrets from each other, though I'd always thought that was more on my side than his. Now I knew otherwise.

His effects were in boxes in Grace's basement, along with some pieces of furniture from our house that I'd wanted to keep but hadn't had room for in my flat. Among these was a black lacquered wood cabinet that had always fascinated me as a child. My father had told me it had originally come from China and was several hundred years old. It was one of the few things his father had brought with him from America after the Fall, and it was in this that Grace told me to search. Somewhere within it were buried secrets.

The paintings that covered the cabinet doors seemed to be alive: long-legged birds taking flight, red on the right, white on the left; a lake overlooked by two palaces, one small and on an island, the other large with snow-capped mountains in the background; a man and woman rendered in such a way that they seemed to be kissing when the doors where closed and reaching longingly for one another when the doors were open.

For a while I just sat there staring at that picture, recalling a past that was beginning to seem more and more like a work of fiction. Knowing what it might contain, I should have been eager to open the cabinet as quickly as possible. But I held back, wondering if I was wrong. Maybe I should just leave it be. Let Val fix things. As Grace had said, he was good at that.

But I couldn't. I had to know.

Best get it over with, I told myself. I put aside my flashlight and fished the keys from my pocket, selecting the appropriate one and inserting it into the lock. The mechanism was stiff and resisted my efforts to work it, but with a little pressure it gave, and I was able to turn the key until I heard a faint click. My heart leapt, and it was an effort to breathe.

I forced a calm on myself and pulled open the doors. The lovers parted, the birds sailed off in different directions, and the palaces drifted apart. Inside the black interior there were two shelves of file folders. I reached for one and examined it in the dim light. The words *TAX RETURNS* were written on the front. I dropped it on the floor and pulled out another. The next was simply marked *BANK*. There were more of the same, and my spirits flagged as the pile at my feet mounted.

Just when I was beginning to think Grace had been wrong about this, I came across a file labeled *MARY — MEDICAL*. I held it before me, hand shaking just a little, filled with dread and expectation.

I sat down on a nearby box and opened the folder. It contained records of two separate pregnancies. The first wasn't extensive, amounting to only a few pages, most of which were things like admission papers, blood tests, release forms and the like. The last page set my skin crawling — the death certificate of my mother's first child.

I was sobered by the brutally clinical nature of the content. It recorded time of birth, noted the child was male, stated it was stillborn "most probably due to infection from Gormorrah" and stipulated that, "pursuant to government regulations, the baby was immediately removed and cremated." There were a few other stats, a brief report indicating that all protocols had been adhered to, and the signature of one Dr. Cherkov — likely the "Doctor C." mentioned in several of my mother's later journal entries.

There didn't appear to be anything unusual about the death certificate, so I tucked it behind the other papers in the file and moved on to the hospital record for the second pregnancy. This was much larger and started far earlier, recording physiological conditions that seemed to echo what my mother had written about in her journal.

I had limited medical knowledge, but I could see that contrary to what "Doctor C." had been telling her, my mother had been far from well. There were pages of notes detailing what appeared to be a deterioration of her immune system.

For several seconds I stared at that entry, growing cold inside. I looked at the records of my mother's initial visits and saw something circled in red pencil and annotated. I couldn't read it in the dim light, so I picked up the flashlight and shone it on the paper, illuminating what looked like my father's handwriting. He seemed to be questioning the "vitamin" injections Dr. Cherkov had been administering. There was an arrow drawn from the entry for them to the one detailing my mother's immune system failure.

I sat there, rigid, trying to breathe. I glanced down at the paper again, hands trembling, and tried to continue. But I couldn't. Isabelle flashed into my mind.

Immune system failure.

The notes my father had scrawled in the margins had a sense of urgency about them. They all seemed focused on pointing out seeming correlations between the injections and my mother's deteriorating health. I flipped to another sheet and found more of the same. There were vague references to other women with difficult pregnancies, and it was evident my father had been trying to establish a link between them.

Eventually I came upon a copy of my own birth record, with the basic details: weight, gender, general state of health, time of birth, etc. Nothing out of the ordinary that I could see.

But then, in a box labeled *Clinical Observations*, I saw the words, "No signs infant has been affected by Gomorrah, despite infection of mother."

I reeled backward as though someone had hit me, falling off the box and onto the floor, the papers littered about me. The oddest sensation seized hold; it was more than just terror and panic. It was more than that awful sense of being empty and overcome at the same time. It actually felt worse than when the police had told me Camille was dead, worse than what I'd felt when I'd heard the news about my father. It was like what I imagined you might feel if someone had given you a drink and then, after you'd drunk it, they'd told you it was deadly poison.

One thought kept reverberating in my head — *She was infected when she was pregnant with me.*

Infected with the virus. *The* virus.

I started to shake, my head started to throb, and quite unexpectedly, I threw up. On hands and knees, I heaved and gasped, moaning and retching in the dim light. It was several long minutes before I found the strength to rise and climb back upstairs to the kitchen.

Once there, I cleaned myself up, took a few sips of water to get the vile taste out of my mouth, and then just stood leaning on the counter for support, staring out the window and not really seeing anything.

What am I worried about? I asked myself. *I'm fine. I've always been fine. If Gomorrah were going to have an effect on me, it would have been in the womb.*

But I had the gene. I had to have it. I was an Immune. And that had saved me, spared me from being one of the stillborn.

So why the hell did I feel so terrified?

Grace came in and made tea, and we sat at the little table. I didn't say anything, and she didn't push me. There was so much I wanted to ask, but I knew it was too early. I looked at the door to the basement and felt my stomach churn again, but I knew I had to go back down there and finish what I'd started.

* * *

There was another report from Cherkov, this time suggesting that my mother's immune system collapse and subsequent infection were related to those of Isabelle. He implied there was a genetic component to it.

But scrawled on this same page, in my father's handwriting, was the word "misdirection" with an arrow pointing to the margin. In tinier, barely legible script, he'd written:

"No material evidence yet but remain convinced C. had something to do with it. Possibly same thing that happened to Isabelle. Doctor evasive regarding injections. Insists were nothing more than vitamins.

"Disconcerting similarities in Isabelle's records. Also 'vitamin' injections. Also suggestions Cherkov doing research on twins. Other incidents like case of Isabelle.

"Asked Val. Said it was something I should keep my nose out of. Best for my daughter. Knows more than he's telling? Need to check out a few leads."

I looked through the next few papers, searching for my mother's death certificate. I wanted to see whether Cherkov's name was on it. But the certificate wasn't there. I rifled through the papers again but couldn't find it anywhere in the file.

I felt woozy again and bowed my head to my knees. I sat bent over for a long time, willing myself not to be sick.

Why hadn't my father told me my mother had died of Gomorrah? How could he let me go through life thinking I'd been responsible?

Maybe because she hadn't *died.*

At first I thought it ludicrous. Of course she had died; I'd seen her grave enough times to know that. I'd watched father put flowers on it. But then I thought of Isabelle and how she *hadn't* died of Gomorrah. Presumably there was a grave for her, but she sure as hell wasn't in it. She and my mother had been twins, so maybe the virus had affected them in the same way. Maybe . . .

But that was all a lot of supposition. There wasn't any solid evidence. Just the fact that both of them had gotten sick and both had subsequently become infected with Gomorrah.

And Cherkov had been involved in both cases.

I gathered myself, forced myself to sit up, and went through the other files in the cabinet. It didn't take long to spot one that looked promising. *INFANT MORTALITY RECORDS*, my father had written on it.

Inside were smudged carbon copies of hospital records dating back decades. There were dozens of them, but one stood out — Fiona Richards. The woman my mother had gone to meet. The one who had been found dead in the harbor.

I pulled out her sheet. Father had circled the reference to the death of Fiona's child. And in bold strokes he'd underlined the name of the doctor who had signed off on the report — Cherkov.

They were all like that. All the reports Father had gathered concerning stillborn births had been signed by Cherkov. It didn't matter which hospital. It didn't matter which year. The good doctor had had a hand in *all* of them. And in every single case, the bodies were listed as having been cremated according to government protocol.

That might not have seemed strange if Cherkov had been Haven's Chief Medical Officer, but Father's notes stated otherwise. The doctor had been a fully certified obstetrician and gynecologist, but it didn't appear he'd practiced on a regular basis. The information Father had gathered seemed to suggest a man more engaged in research, though the nature of that research wasn't actually defined. Father had wondered if it'd had anything to do with the babies but hadn't been able to find solid evidence to support that conclusion.

One thing was clear, however — whatever it was Cherkov had been up to, Father's notes implied that the man had been getting a lot of backing for it. Backing that couldn't be easily traced. The notes mentioned a succession of shell companies — from which one could infer that someone was trying to hide something. It all seemed rather fishy.

"These are only a handful of known cases," Father's notes said with regard to the stillborn babies. *"Source suggests thousands more."*

I gulped back bile as I read that notation.

Thousands? Thousands of stillborn births Cherkov had had a hand in?

Maybe it was all innocent enough, but the hidden finances, the subterfuge, and the fact that Cherkov was involved in medical matters that seemed beyond his purview said otherwise — and so did my gut.

"Have examined cremation records," Father had scribbled. *"Do not correlate with supposed disposal of dead babies. Cherkov blames poor record keeping."*

I sat there mulling this over, my imagination running wild. What if all those babies hadn't been cremated? What if Cherkov had been using them in his research? It was a repugnant thought, and I couldn't imagine he'd ever have been granted government approval for something like *that.* Although I suppose if they were dead . . . how was that any worse than medical students carving up a cadaver?

If they were dead.

I thought of my mother's claim that she'd heard her son after giving birth. What some other women had said had echoed that. But how was that possible? Gomorrah killed non-Immunes in the womb. Everyone knew that.

This just didn't add up.

I shivered and felt goose bumps.

Cherkov taking non-Immune babies and experimenting on them was one thing, but what I needed to figure out was what he'd done to my mother. Were my father's suspicions correct? Had that cocktail of "vitamins" he'd claimed to be administering been something else entirely? And if so, what had that stuff done to me while I was inside her? I couldn't recall having suffered an illness of any sort in my entire life, but maybe something like that would take years to show up.

I feel fine, I reminded myself. But maybe I wouldn't in a year or two or ten. Who knew? Maybe it would just strike at me suddenly. And then . . .

And then what?

You can't worry about that now.

I took out more of the folders and started rifling through their contents. There were newspaper clippings dating back to the early eighties, all of them about unsolved murders. Mixed in with these I found copies of police cold case files, and as I looked through them, I could see a pattern developing. My father's notes made it clear he had seen it as well:

"Victims all women with stillborn babies who continued to challenge hospitals on matter or have been individuals independently looking into situation. Also two reporters: Haven Chronicle*, Island TV. According to records and coworkers interviewed, both were investigating claims surrounding stillborn babies crying after birth. Sounds like Mary's story.*

"Have found other instances of individuals who may have been murdered to silence them. No material evidence to sustain suppositions, however. Seems clear further investigation would be unsafe. Wife may already have been victim. Have since been more discreet.

"Cherkov clearly involved. Isn't acting alone. Funding and secrecy of research speak of high-placed individuals. Difficult to believe president unaware of what's going on.

"Don't know who to trust. Better for all concerned I remain quiet. Need solid evidence. Then consider approaching president with findings. Can only hope I won't regret it. If this goes right to the top, then everyone I care about may become a target.

"Discussed matter with Val, but his reaction not what I expected. Again had feeling he was hiding something. Can't see how or why. Seems to be locally run operation. But maybe there's more to it than I think.

"Val urged me to give up. Again said he believes my life and my daughter's are in serious jeopardy if I continue. My fears, too. But don't like the idea of these people getting away with something.

"He may be a vamp, but I've grown to trust him ever since dealing with Mary. Has always seemed honest. Not what I'd anticipated. Have to admit it's difficult to put aside prejudices. But he helped Mary. Don't know what I'd have done without his assistance. If he feels I should drop this, then maybe I should. He knows things I don't. Desire for justice isn't worth the life of my daughter."

* * *

Beneath the folders on the bottom shelf of the cabinet I found a soiled and beaten notebook. In an entry near the back, my father had written about the Westerlys. His notes implied that John Westerly's company was linked to what was going on in the hospitals and that there was a connection between Dr. Cherkov and whatever was being shipped to the Third Reich.

As I flipped through the remainder of the notebook, I came across a folded piece of paper attached by a paperclip to a sheet at the back. I pulled it free, unfolding it and smoothing it out, and recognized what it was immediately — an Island Transnational Shipping manifest similar the one I'd seen back in the library among Donovan's research materials. On it, my father had written "New York City" in bold letters and underlined it several times.

I thumbed back through the notebook to the period between my mother's death and the end of the millennium. The entries were few and far between and often cryptically referred to files that didn't appear to be among those in the cabinet. I breezed through them all, until I came to one marked "December 31, 1999."

I had an unsettled feeling when I read that date. That was the night of the alleyway murder. The first time I'd seen Val. I could never forget it; it seemed a turning point in so many ways. Maybe in ways I wasn't even aware of yet.

* * *

Dec/31/1999 — J. Harkness, Chief Officer PSS

Arrived at scene. Sizable police presence. Nothing like dozens of cops and emergency response personnel to attract attention of reporters and gawkers.

Homicide squad waiting inside entrance to alley. Recognized Havershaw. Didn't look too happy to see me. Can't blame him. Never much cared for interference from PSS when I was on the force, but back then there'd never been anything like this.

Havershaw looked as miserable as I felt.

Examined crime scene. Decapitated head, covered with police tarp. Empty syringe with residue of what may have been blood. Immune blood? Looked like vic had to be a vamp.

About to examine head, but Val arrived. Havershaw even unhappier. Told him I called Val in because I thought it best to keep vamps in the loop. Don't want any nasty surprises.

Val examined body. Dropped bombshell: vic wasn't vamp after all. Said that all Embassy staff accounted for. I suggested it could be zeppelin crew member, but he pointed out they're not permitted to leave the aerodrome grounds. And since there are no vamp tourists . . .

At Val's insistence we examined ironwood knife, sort used to kill vamps during War. "Now, I am become Death" scratched into hilt. Seemed to support vic being vamp, but Val said was a plant. Was still examining knife while Val went and examined head, came back and showed me something — set of fake fangs. Just stuff you buy for Halloween. Wondered why anyone would go to the trouble of making it look like guy was vamp.

Val suggested could have been done to make statement and arouse our attention. Had the feeling that by "our" he meant him and me specifically. Whoever did this went to a lot of trouble to stage it like this. Knew was only way Val and I would be called to a local murder. Anything involving a vamp comes under PSS purview. And the killing of a vamp would have to be brought to Embassy's attention.

Saw Val eyeing knife again. Told me it should disappear. Then said I should move carefully on this one. Asked why and he told me to take another careful look at body. Saw it instantly, hidden under the lapel of jacket.

Crucifix.

I understood what Val was getting at. Knew it didn't belong to this poor sod. Someone planted it. I know who. I took damned thing and pocketed it. No way it was going to sit in police lockup.

I was furious. Told Val he was supposed to have taken care of this, was supposed to have made sure nothing like this ever happened.

Asked him what it meant. Why this guy? He told me to go look at head. Didn't want to, but he told me I'd seen face before, thirteen years ago.

Went over to where head was, lifted tarp, and had shock of my life. Face is older and more drawn than I remember, but I recognized him. Could never forget that face. After that clues fell in place. I understood what it meant. Knew I couldn't let this get out into open.

The killer's message is clear: "They took something, and they have to pay."

God help us all.

* * *

In the cool silence of the basement I sat staring ahead, unfocused. My gut was telling me something my mind didn't want to believe. But the clues were beginning to mount toward an unavoidable conclusion.

Stuck between the pages of Father's notebook was a clipping from a newspaper — an obituary for Dr. Cherkov. It was dated only a few days after the alleyway murder. Was it possible the body in the alley had been Cherkov? Why else would my father have kept it with these notes?

But if Cherkov was the victim, who was the killer?

I set this aside and reached for the last item in the cabinet. It was a solitary envelope that had been glued to the shelf by age. I carefully pried it loose and studied it, turning it over, noting the broken red-wax seal on the back. It looked like one of those expensive linen envelopes Aunt Amelia always used for all her correspondence, and the thought turned me cold. But closer examination revealed the presidential emblem embossed on the front. Inside was a single sheet of paper bearing script written in a fine, bold hand:

Jonathan,

In light of our conversation regarding the incident of Dec/31, I have taken it upon myself to act posthaste to address your concerns. I do not think it necessary to advise you that this matter must be dealt with in the most discreet manner possible. It is no small exaggeration to say that the very future of our great nation could be at stake should details become known to the public.

Knowing you to be loyal and faithful to this office and to the people of Haven, I call upon your full cooperation in containing this unfortunate turn of events. You will, of course, have complete authority to act as you see fit in dealing with the local constabulary.

I have known you to be a most trustworthy and able officer of the PSS and count you as both friend and ally. Therefore, it is with greatest respect that I beseech you for the sake of your family and all of Haven that the truths you have laid bare before me go no further than our counsel.

Your most humble servant, the Right Honorable President of the Republic of Haven,

Quinton Mallory

I folded the paper and returned it to the envelope. If the president was involved, whatever was going on was big indeed.

I gathered all the papers and was in the process of putting them back in the cabinet when something caught my eye. In the far corner, where the shelf abutted the back of the cabinet interior, was a slip of brown paper. I reached in, snagged it with my fingertips, and coaxed it free. Under the light I could see it was a receipt from a jewelry store on Wellington, dated November 13, 1985. In an unfamiliar hand was written:

One silver crucifix — $100

One silver chain — $50

Engraving at $5/letter — $80

"Our Love is Eternal"

At the bottom was my father's signature.

I recalled the entry in my mother's diary for November 14, when she had mentioned receiving this from my father. He had intended it to be an expression of how much he loved her. Knowing what I now knew, I'm not sure she'd ever loved him.

I put the receipt with the rest of the papers and closed the cabinet doors. The two lovers kissed, and the kingdoms came together.

CHAPTER 21
GOODBYE

I found Grace in the drawing room, watching TV. Or at least pretending she was. The news was on, and when I glanced at the grainy black-and-white image on the Telefunken, I realized it was Hitler engaged in one of his latest rants outside the Volkshalle.

I stood in the doorway, watching for a moment, then went over and turned it off. Arms crossed, I faced my grandmother. "Is Mom alive? Is she a vamp?"

Grace looked up at me, and it was difficult to read her.

"Well?" I eyed her expectantly.

Her shoulders sagged. "I let your father deal with it. After Isabelle . . . after that I just couldn't go through anything like that again. So I told your father to take care of it."

"So for all you know she could be out there somewhere," I said, making a sweeping gesture with one arm. "Maybe in New York with Izzy."

"Your father told me she was dead, and I believed him."

"But you never saw the body."

"She was cremated," Grace said. "I saw the ashes." She stared up at me and added in a low voice, "And you've seen the grave."

She was right — I had. Many times. But now I wondered if I'd been paying my respects to a lie.

"Did Father ever talk to you about that murder?" I asked.

"Murder?" She looked bewildered.

"The one you got all angry about when you heard he'd taken me to it. Remember? New Year's Eve a few years ago? You guys got into a hellish fight over it."

"Your father never discussed his work," Grace said. "You know that as well as I do."

"I just thought . . ." I sighed, letting my hands fall to my sides, and slumped into a nearby chair.

"We should discuss the funeral," Grace said after a few moments of silence.

I didn't want to. I wanted to talk about my mother, about the possibility that she might be alive. If she was, then maybe she'd been the intruder who'd broken into my flat — her or Izzy.

The more I considered it, the more it seemed to be the only thing that made sense. Of course, that led to other things I didn't want to consider. Like the possibility that my mother had been Val's "problem," the one he'd taken off to New York for. The one that had brought him to Coral Beach that night.

And if my mother had been at Coral Beach, that meant there was a chance she'd killed Camille. Why else would Val have been loitering around the crime scene? The thought of my mother as a murderer was such a devastating one, however, that I told myself it couldn't possibly be true. There had to be another explanation. Yet as I went over what I knew, I couldn't say for certain it was impossible. I didn't know my mother much beyond what I'd read in her journals and the things I'd heard third hand, and all of that was from before she'd become a vamp. Even supposing she was responsible for Camille's death, it left the question of why? Was it because she'd thought Camille was Aunt Amelia? Because she blamed Amelia for her son being taken from her?

I didn't seem to be getting any closer to the answers; just digging up more questions. The sort of questions that didn't necessarily have pleasant resolutions.

"The president's office has informed me that he and some of the council members will be attending," Grace said, her words breaking through my thoughts.

I looked up at her and blinked, almost grateful to be distracted by talk of the funeral. But as her words sank in, I recalled the letter I'd just read in the basement. My father had been a middle-class guy, yet as chief of the PSS, he'd moved among the biggest movers and shakers in the republic. Powerful people. *Rich* and powerful people.

Like Amelia Westerly, I thought, clenching my teeth.

"I was thinking it might be best if you didn't go," said Grace.

I sat bolt upright. "What are you talking about?"

"If there are people trying to . . ." Her hand shook as she wiped at her brow. "I don't want to lose you, child."

"I'm not going to miss my own father's funeral," I said, outraged by the very thought.

"I'm sure inspector Havershaw would say —"

"To hell with him!"

"Sophie!" Grace looked at me sharply. "I'll not have you speaking like that in this house."

I scowled, fuming. "If the president is going to be there, then the place will be swarming with PSS and police," I said. "No one is going to get anywhere near there with a gun. Besides, they wouldn't try it in public. They haven't so far."

I wasn't about to let anyone keep me from seeing my father into his grave. Grace and Havershaw would have to chain me up to stop me.

* * *

It rained the day of the funeral.

At St. Paul's the pews were full. I suspect it had more to do with the presence of the president than with people wanting to pay their respects to my father. The president gave a eulogy that was quite touching and sincere. There was no doubting he'd thought highly of my father.

When it was my turn to speak, I found it difficult to get the words out. More than once I had to stop and take a few breaths as I fought back the tears. I was glad when it was over.

After the service we drove out of the city to Beechwood Cemetery, a long line of cars moving in a solemn procession. I stood beside the grave with Grace, surrounded by hundreds of people, and watched as my father's coffin was lowered into the ground. One by one people passed by, dropping in flowers or handfuls of earth.

There was an awful finality about it. I watched and thought of all the grief I'd brought him in those last years and all the things I should have done to try and make it better. But it was too late.

It's always too late when someone you love dies. You think of all the things you should have said, all the little kindnesses you could have done. But it's too late. You missed your chance, and you'll never get another. You have to live the rest of your life with that regret.

I stared into the grave and wished I could have said "I love you" to him one last time. More than that, I wished he could have understood it.

Before long there was only me, Grace, Havershaw, and a few dozen policemen scattered about the grounds. I could tell the inspector wanted to talk to me, so I told Grace I'd get a cab and catch up with her later. She wasn't keen on leaving me and argued that it wasn't safe, but I pointed out that there was a lot of security around and insisted I'd be fine.

My grandmother left in the limo the funeral home had provided, and I found myself facing Havershaw in the rain, the steady patter of it against the umbrella the only sound in the sepulchral quiet of that graveyard.

"I'm sorry about your father," the inspector said, looking respectably sympathetic.

"You've nothing to be sorry about." *The people who killed him do*, I wanted to say.

"Perhaps if I —" Havershaw began.

"If you'd what? Stayed? Been more observant?" I shook my head. "I've been over that with myself for days now. Even if someone had been watching him every minute of the hour, I think they'd have gotten to him eventually."

"They," Havershaw said, as though he still wasn't sure about it.

"Yes. *They*. Or do you honestly think all those deaths and the attempts to kill me were just coincidences?" My tone was cutting, and I knew my face was flushed. "I'm probably risking my life right now, standing here talking to you."

"I didn't want you to come," he said. "I told your grandmother —"

"Did you really think I could stay away?"

The inspector looked at me without saying anything for a long time. When he did speak, it was with some hesitation. "I interviewed the hospital staff," he said.

"Why do I get the feeling you're going to tell me something I don't want to hear?"

Havershaw sighed. "No one knows anything about an attempt on your life."

"There was no one around, except the ones who were clearly in on it."

"The hospital says otherwise. They say they were fully staffed and that there were several personnel on your floor."

I scowled at him. "They're lying. And what about the cop?"

Havershaw studied the tips of his shoes.

"Inspector!"

"There was no body. Nor any evidence of a shooting."

"Then where is he?" I asked.

"It's been brought to my attention that Officer Ishiro had some gambling debts. The phone records at the hospital show he received a call around eleven o'clock at night. We traced it to a local bookie."

"And let me guess," I said. "When you went to check out the bookie he gave you a long spiel about how Ishiro had owed certain people a lot of money, and they were going to collect. So you figure they paid him a visit, and he fled rather than have his knees capped or whatever it is they do." I shook my head. "How convenient that it should all happen on the very night you chose to have him watch over me."

"There were witnesses."

I scoffed at that. "Of course there were. I'm sure they were well paid for their services."

Thunder boomed out at sea, fast approaching the islands.

"Did you talk to Aunt —" I caught myself. "What about Amelia Westerly?"

"The hospital administration admits she has visited Mercy on occasion in her capacity as a member of the President's Council, but no one saw her on the night in question."

"I did," I insisted.

"Miss Harkness, you'd been sedated. Sometimes —"

"I wasn't hallucinating!"

"Her alibi checks out." Havershaw had raised his voice now, too, and stood with his jaw set, hands in the pockets of his trench coat, a combative expression on his face. Rain streamed off the broad brim of his fedora, reminding me of the night of the alleyway murder back in '99.

"You were there that night, four years ago," I said.

"I beg your pardon?" he said.

"The murder. The one that was made to look like the killing of a vamp."

His eyes widened. "How do you know about that?"

"I was there."

"You?"

"New Year's Eve, 1999. They called my father. We were supposed to go see the fireworks at the Parliament Buildings."

"It was raining. They'd have called them off."

"It didn't matter. We never got there."

"And your father told you about the murder?" Havershaw looked incredulous.

"No, of course not. I was thirteen. I read about it in the papers and in some notes he left."

"Notes?"

"A notebook I found. He was investigating claims by women that there was something unusual about their pregnancies. Some of them insisted the non-Immune babies they gave birth to weren't dead, even though the hospitals maintained they were."

"And you think that has something to do with what you say you saw at the hospital?"

"I didn't imagine it, Inspector."

"I don't see the connections you're claiming. What would that have to do with what your father was investigating? The sixth floor of the hospital is just a research facility, Miss Harkness. There's equipment going in and out of there all the time. And the reason part of it is kept under quarantine is because they're dealing with contagious specimens. It's kept off limits to everybody but authorized personnel. You can't get in there without special access."

"A perfect cover," I said.

"For what?"

"For whatever it is this is all about! Can't you get a warrant or something? That's what cops do, isn't it?"

"And what am I going to tell the judge?"

"The truth!"

"And what is that, exactly?" Havershaw sounded exasperated. "You say you saw a cop killed, but there's no body and no evidence of a killing. You say you were chased by a gunman to the sixth floor, but the hospital says that's not possible, that there's a guard at the elevator on the sixth floor —"

"He wasn't at his post," I half shouted. "And before you tell me there's also a nurse on duty all the time — she wasn't there either."

"All right. But even if I take your word for it, it's not enough. The hospital has countless witnesses who will attest to there having been nothing unusual about the night."

"How do they explain that there's no record of me signing out?" I asked.

Havershaw chewed at his lower lip, shook his head, and gave me a temperate look. "I saw your release," he said. "You signed yourself out. Your signature is on the paper."

"That's ridiculous," I said, eyeing him with contempt. "Obviously someone forged it."

The inspector hunched his shoulders and said nothing.

"What about the reporter's research stuff?"

"You mean the box," he said.

"Yeah. It had all sorts of stuff in it. Stuff about Island Transnational, the hospitals, and that guy Cherkov."

"The box has gone missing from the police evidence lockup." Havershaw was at least honest enough to look guilty.

The tattoo of rain on the fabric of the umbrella was like cannon fire in my head. "Gone missing," I said slowly. "Just like that?"

He looked away, avoiding eye contact.

"My father was afraid for my life," I said, my voice thin, charged with emotion. I faced Havershaw, grateful for the rain so he couldn't see my tears. "He was afraid they might use me to send a message to him."

"A message to your father?" He frowned. "About what?"

"To stop."

"Stop?" He stared at me blankly.

I tilted my head slightly as I looked back at him through the rain. Val had almost convinced me I should just let this be; maybe a few days ago I would have. But after what I'd read in my father's files and now knowing what had been done to my mother, I couldn't just sweep it under the rug and forget about it. It had changed my life. And I had a feeling it wasn't going to stop until someone did something about it.

"My father was looking for the truth," I said. "It's what every *good* cop is supposed to do. Maybe you should try it."

The wind blew stronger, making the umbrella shudder in my grasp. There was a flash of lightning that lit up the sky. I could smell electricity in the air, and beneath it, the undertones of the sea. All around the islands, I imagined people closing windows and shutting doors, battening down for the gathering storm.

"I should take you home," said Havershaw.

I didn't want him to. When I'd spotted him earlier, I had hoped for more. Hoped he'd be able to help. But I had wanted too much, and I couldn't help wondering if someone had already gotten to him. He had a family. A wife. Kids. Maybe it was foolish to expect he'd put their lives in jeopardy. After all, what would he be risking them for? A stranger? Some unexpressed ideal? Was that worth giving up so much?

"I'm going to take a taxi," I said.

"I'd rather you didn't."

"Why? What's the danger? According to you I've imagined all this."

"Miss Harkness —"

I cut him off. "You can follow in your car, if you're so concerned about my safety."

There was a long silence, broken only by the sound of the rain on the umbrella.

"I'm sorry," Havershaw said at last, looking unsettled and embarrassed.

I regarded him with cold indifference. "You already said that."

"I don't mean about your father."

I raised an eyebrow.

"There are people in high places with things to hide," Havershaw said. He wiped his face with one hand, pulling at the sun-weathered flesh, cupping his jaw for a moment and appearing beleaguered. He looked like a man who wanted to do the right thing but couldn't. A man held back by things even more important to a husband and father than principles. "Even if I wanted to," he went on, "I don't know how much further I could go. If there really is something going on —"

"There is," I said firmly.

"Yes. Well, then it goes way up the political ladder."

I thought of the president and his letter to my father. "Maybe all the way to the top," I said.

Havershaw shifted uneasily. "Maybe," he echoed. He fixed his eyes on mine. "And maybe there's a reason for that. A *good* one."

"Then find out what it is."

He opened his mouth, then closed it without saying a word. If it was possible, he actually looked more miserable than before.

"Do your job, Inspector." With that, I turned and walked away.

Tall kapok trees lined both sides of the crushed coral road that ran down the center of the cemetery, thick-trunked monoliths that towered above me, their outspread foliage sheltering me from the worst of the rain. At the far end of this corridor stood two massive iron gates, reminiscent of those at the entrance to the Third Reich Embassy.

I felt vulnerable walking out in the open like that. I could see policemen positioned all around, huddled against the rain in oiled-canvas ponchos, but they didn't really make me feel any safer. The sooner I got back to Grace's place the better.

I heard a car coming up the avenue behind me from the direction of President Margolliean's tomb, its wheels crunching on the coral.

At first I assumed it was Havershaw, but then I recognized the soft rumble of a gasoline engine. I stopped, turned, and found myself caught in the headlights of the limousine.

The Mercedes rolled abreast of me, Wilson at the wheel. He glanced at me, gave a slight nod to the back. The car inched forward, and the tinted rear passenger window rolled down with a smooth, electric whine. Val leaned his face close to the opening and looked out at me.

"I didn't expect you to be here," I said.

"I wanted to pay my respects."

"Dad would have appreciated that," I said, but I appreciated it even more.

Val studied me, warmth in his eyes. "Are you going to get in, or do you plan on walking all the way home?" He looked down at my shoes, a pair of black, narrow-toed leather pumps I'd purchased for Camille's funeral. They were hellishly uncomfortable. "It's a long way back to Grace's for such pretty feet," he observed.

"What makes you so sure I want a lift from *you*?" I asked. "I'm still mad at you."

"For trying to protect you?"

"Do you have any idea what it's like being stuck in that house all day with Grace?"

Val laughed and gave his head a little shake. "I can't say that I do. But it's for your own good."

I rolled my eyes. "I keep hearing that."

"We just want you safe."

I looked at him sharply. "Yes, but safe from what?"

"Where should I start? You and trouble seem to have a distinct affinity for one another."

I stuck my tongue out at him; he laughed again.

"Look, why don't you get in, and we can discuss it in more detail." He waggled his eyebrows, giving me a provocative look. "Unless of course you're afraid someone might see us."

"I think that train has left the station. Besides, I don't care what people think anymore. Not when it comes to us. They can go to hell, for all I care."

Val smiled warmly. "Well, come on then, before you completely ruin those very stylish shoes." He opened the door and scooted aside.

I glanced back the way I'd come and saw Havershaw standing beside his car, watching me.

"All right," I said as I closed my umbrella and shook it out. I climbed in beside Val. "It'll save me on Electric Allotment. The way I've been using my hydro rations lately I'll be spending the last few days of the month sitting in the dark."

The air-conditioning in the limo, a luxury unheard of in most Haven automobiles, kept the steamy heat of outdoors at bay. I slipped off my shoes, glad to be free of them as I wiggled my toes. Val poured me a drink — tonic water and a twist of lime in a fancy stemmed glass. For himself he chose red wine — alcohol being about the only things vamps could consume other than blood.

"So what now?" he asked, regarding me with a level eye.

I shrugged and sipped at my drink, peering at him inquisitively over the rim of the glass. "You tell me," I mumbled into the tonic water. "You said you were going to do something about it."

"I'm working on it."

"Well, work faster, dammit."

"It would be easier if you promised to keep your nose out of things."

"You mean like uncovering the fact that my mother's alive?" I waited, expecting him to deny it. Of course, I still wasn't one hundred percent sure she actually *was* alive, but if anyone knew for certain, Val would be the one.

"Wow," he said, rubbing the back of his neck.

"So you don't deny it?" It felt like my entire body was a bundle of nerves as I awaited his answer.

“You think you’ve got it all figured out, don’t you?” Val said by way of reply. “But the more you dig, darling, the more you’re not going to like what you find.”

I shot him a withering look. “And you actually think telling me that is going to make me just drop everything?”

“I was hoping you’d have the sense to see what’s best for us all.”

“For us all, Val? Or for *you*?” I watched him for a reaction. When a moment or two had passed with no response, I finally burst out: “Jesus, why didn’t you just tell me from the start what happened to her?”

Val cupped his glass with both hands, studying the wine speculatively. “It wasn’t my place to do so. Your father made me promise —”

“Don’t use a dead man as an excuse. You had a chance to say something after he died.”

“I didn’t see much point in it,” Val said, his voice oddly flat. “It’s not like it would have made your life better. For all intents and purposes she *is* dead. You should leave it at that.”

I looked at him in disbelief. “Are you kidding? She’s my mother, for pity’s sake! I’ve lived my whole life thinking she’s buried in a grave back there.”

It was hard to keep my emotions in check. My heart felt like it was going full gallop, and my head was awhirl with the reality of something I think I’d been hoping wouldn’t be true.

“Sophie . . .” Val reached out for my hand, but I pulled it back.

“You can’t even begin to imagine how it feels to know she’s still alive,” I said.

He shook his head. “She’s not your mother anymore. Mary ceased to exist even before you were born. Your father understood that.” He glanced at me, no sign of contrition in his eyes. “Why do you think he didn’t tell you? He didn’t want you to know about her madness, about the thing she’d become.”

"He made me think I was responsible."

"Are you sure about that?"

I started to argue, but then realized that maybe he was right. Maybe part of the problem between my father and me had been more a result of what I'd believed, rather than what he had. Maybe I'd just assumed he blamed me for what had happened to my mother, when in reality I was the one blaming myself.

I had made a mess of everything.

"You've had a hard day," Val said. He set his glass down, took mine, and placed it beside his own. Then he turned to face me. "You shouldn't be thinking about any of that stuff."

"I want to see her, Val. I *have* to."

He gave one short, firm shake of his head. "That's out of the question."

"Why? Because she's in New York?"

"No. Because I don't know where she is." His lips became a tight line.

"But she was here, wasn't she? And this wasn't the first time, was it?"

"Yes, she was. And no, it wasn't. She's incredibly intelligent. And determined."

"About what?" I asked.

Val shrugged. "Revenge. Protecting you. Perhaps, in some bizarre way, trying to get back what she once had. Who knows? Maybe in that addled mind of hers she does some of these things to spite me. And then there's the whole issue of your father. Even before she descended into madness, I knew she felt guilty about not being able to love him the way he loved her."

I tried to digest all this and heard myself say, "What happened to Camille . . . it was her, wasn't it?"

"I think so."

"And that guy in the library? You weren't the one who saved me, were you?"

"No, it wasn't me."

"It sounded like an animal."

"I suppose in many respects that's what she's become."

My stomach clenched, and a lump formed in my throat. "And she left the journal?"

"Yes."

"And you really don't know where she is?"

"I wouldn't lie to you."

"I wish I could believe that."

"I always have to keep proving myself to you, don't I?" Val said. He leaned toward me, kissed me.

I wanted to pull back. I wanted to ask more questions, even though I knew I probably wouldn't get any answers. But it was so easy to let Val take control, to just get lost in the moment and feel something besides the heartache and confusion that had dominated my life the past few weeks.

The limo drove through the gates of the cemetery and turned east on Republic Avenue, heading toward the city. Val was working on my ear, navigating his way down toward my neck. I wanted to turn up the air-conditioning because I was getting really hot. I couldn't help but think that I'd just buried my father, and I sure as hell shouldn't be making out with my boyfriend in the backseat of his limo. It was insane.

Val was following the line of my neck, back toward my mouth, his lips soft, caressing. His hand was on my thigh, and I felt myself responding, my body doing all the thinking as I sank deeper into the soft leather seat, stretching my legs out before me, and remembering how it had been so many times in the past.

Val's lips were on mine, and right then, I'd have forgiven him anything. Right then, the only answers I needed were the ones he was giving me.

CHAPTER 22
TRUSTING DARKNESS

I had just surfaced for a much needed breath of air when Wilson's voice came over the intercom. "Spot of trouble ahead, sir. Looks like a serious accident."

Val and I disentangled ourselves and sat up straighter. I smoothed my skirt, buttoned my blouse, and brushed back my hair, then leaned forward a bit and squinted through the tinted privacy shield.

Val pressed a button on a panel beside him, and the shield dropped down, giving us a clear view through the front windscreen. The wipers were doing double time against the downpour, but beyond the rain I could see the amorphous flashing lights of police cars, fire trucks, and probably an ambulance or two.

I looked anxiously at Val.

"It's a busy road," he said. "It's probably nothing. A minor fender bender."

I wanted to believe him, but I knew minor fender-benders didn't require fire trucks, police cars, and ambulances. I had a terrible feeling in my gut.

Wilson slowed the car to a crawl as we approached the accident. Blue and red lights flashed everywhere, and through the sheeting rain I could see people across the road in silhouette, dashing to and fro. It looked frantic and chaotic.

Just ahead a policeman in a rain slicker and safety vest was waving a lighted baton, directing everyone to stop and pull over. There were several cars already parked on the soft shoulder ahead of us.

Wilson did likewise, steering the Mercedes onto the broad expanse of crushed coral and gliding up behind a small electric. "Should I go see how long it'll be, sir?"

"I don't think that'll be necessary," Val said, lifting a hand slightly to indicate the policeman approaching us.

I saw the constable hesitate when he saw the stylized eagle of the Third Reich emblem on the front grill of the car; for a moment, I thought he might turn away. But he stepped up to the driver's side and rapped on the tinted glass.

Wilson responded by opening his window, but Val quickly lowered his own and leaned out. "Officer," he said in a friendly manner.

The policeman turned away from Wilson and took a step closer to the rear of the car. "I'm sorry, sir," he said to Val, face rigid. "There'll be some delay, I'm afraid. There's been a bit of a nasty bingle."

"An accident?" said Val. "Nothing serious I hope."

"'Fraid so, sir. A funeral home limousine and a truck collided. Doesn't look good."

My reaction was instinctive. I was out the door and into the rain before he'd even finished speaking. Barefoot, I skirted between the parked electrics and dashed out onto the slick tarmac, heading straight for the knot of emergency vehicles.

"Hey!" the constable shouted after me. "Stop! You can't go there!"

But I wasn't listening to him. By now I'd gone far enough to see the wreck sprawled across the road, the limousine about half the length it had been, crushed against the side of a truck now parked on the wrong side of the road. There was smoke and steam, and a group of men swarmed over the smashup, swinging axes and hauling on ropes, bending crowbars to the task.

Men in uniforms turned and started to run toward me, aiming to cut me off, but I dodged them, slipping past the fire trucks. I was only thirty or forty feet from the wreckage when Val caught up to me.

"Sophie! Stop!" he commanded, grabbing me around the waist from behind.

I thrashed and kicked in his grasp, trying to tear myself free, yelling at him to let me go. But he held on, pulling me close against him, lifting me off the ground and pinning my arms. Slowly the fight went out of me, and I collapsed, staring dully at the nightmare of broken machinery.

"Sophie. Let them do their job."

I started sobbing, gut-wrenching sobs that shook my entire body. Val stood there, arms encompassing me as the rain came down and the lights flashed and men and women shouted in the dark.

The activity around the accident shifted abruptly. The men on the limousine leapt off and started sprinting away, waving their arms and hollering for everyone to get clear. Flames erupted where the car had intersected the truck, bright yellow and orange tongues of fire that soared upward, insensible to the rain.

Val hoisted me up and turned to run, but before he'd taken more than three or four strides, the car and truck exploded in a fireball that lit up the sky. We went down hard, Val shielding me as the shockwave hammered us, and debris rained in all directions.

"Grace!" I screamed as we fell.

I have absolutely no recollection of what happened after that. All I know is that I became conscious of where I was when someone thrust a cup of tea into my hands. I held it and stared at it dumbly, then looked up and around, reality rushing back in. It was still raining, and I was sitting in the open back of an ambulance with a blanket wrapped around me and a medic applying a bandage to my forehead. Somebody was talking to me, but I wasn't making any sense of what he was saying.

"What?" I said. I turned to the speaker and realized he was a cop.

"You knew one of the victims, miss?" he asked.

"Victims?"

"Her grandmother," said Val.

I recognized the look in the constable's eyes, the one I'd seen far too often when people spotted Val. The look people in Haven reserve for when they're talking about vamps.

"Grandmother?" the constable said, addressing me. "Then you're not —"

"No, she isn't," said Val. He said it tersely, though you had to know him to realize there was an undercurrent of antagonism there. "I should think it obvious."

"It's just that you were together . . . in the limo —" The constable was visibly flustered. "I mean, it's from the Embassy, so I assumed . . ." The glance he shot my way sent a chill through me.

Assumed what? I wondered. *That I was a vamp?*

I thought of the taxi driver the night I'd fled the hospital; he'd made the same ridiculous assumption. People on the islands were so blinded by their prejudice that they couldn't bring themselves to even contemplate the possibility of an Immune and a vamp together. Not in an intimate way, at least. Not ever.

Havershaw showed up at that moment, sparing the constable further discomfort. The inspector flashed his badge, made his way through the cordon, and came straight to me.

"Are you all right?" he asked. When I didn't answer he looked to Val.

"Her grandmother," Val explained. He pointed with his chin toward the smoldering wreck, which the emergency crews were once again crawling all over.

"I know," Havershaw said, staring through the downpour at the crash site. He wasn't wearing his hat, and his hair was wet; he ran a hand over it, sweeping it back. His eyes darted to me again, then to Val, and finally back to the wreck. I thought I heard him swear.

"You were supposed to protect us," I whispered hoarsely. I didn't have the strength to scream at him, otherwise I would have. I didn't have the strength for anything.

"I —" Havershaw started, then faltered and went silent.

"She's dead because of you." It was an unfair thing for me to say, and the dismay in the inspector's eyes spoke of how those words cut to the bone.

"I'll be back in a moment," he said, walking off to consult with one of the constables.

"It was an accident, Sophie," Val said.

"Please don't. Don't pretend. The driver of the truck has vanished, and I think we both know why." I didn't continue; it hurt too much to say any more.

The rain kept coming down, dripping off the edge of the ambulance and running in tiny rivers across the pavement. The flashing lights were reflected in the puddles and the sheen of water, and there was an eerie beauty to it that stood in stark contrast to the nightmare only feet away.

Val stepped up into the ambulance and out of the rain. He sat down beside me, wrapped an arm around me, and drew me close. I rested my head against his shoulder, shut my eyes, and felt a sudden wave of exhaustion.

"You can stay at the Embassy tonight," he said, stroking my hair. "The ambassador has been delayed in Berlin for a few days."

I sighed. "Let's go."

"The inspector —"

"Please. Now."

I was still barefoot, so Val carried me. As we left, I glanced back over his shoulder at the crash scene. In the watery light, I could see the scarred and twisted ruin of the truck. It was just possible to make out the words painted on its side — Island Transnational Shipping.

Wilson met us with an umbrella and dutifully held it aloft as we made our way past gawking firemen and constables and the line of curious drivers who stood by their electrics waiting and watching. By the time we reached the limousine, I was crashing. Val laid me out in the backseat, then climbed in the front beside Wilson. I heard the murmur of their voices and tried to follow what they were saying, but within moments I was dead to the world.

I vaguely recall waking momentarily to find a concerned Mrs. Barker fretting over me, getting me out of my wet clothes and into a silk nightgown that must have been purchased since my last visit. And then I was gone again.

The next time I awoke, I was in the four-poster bed. Val was sitting in a chair by the open window, staring out at the stars. He had changed out of his soaked suit and was wearing black denims, a linen button-down shirt, and polished black oxfords. Even casually dressed he looked dapper.

I pushed aside the sheets and padded barefoot across the old Persian carpet, the silk of my nightgown making soft shushing sounds. Val turned to look at me, then held out a hand. I went to him, climbed into his lap, curled up like a little child in the crook of his arm, my hands together against his chest. We stared out at the stars, the Milky Way a spray of shining silver dust that arched from one horizon to the other, bisecting the heavens.

I saw a point of light moving amidst the stars, and at first I thought it was a meteor. But it was too slow and constant for that. Then I realized it must be one of those new artificial moons the Nazis had recently lofted into orbit. What had the writer in *No Haven for Darkness* called them? Satellites?

Mrs. Bhutto had told us that Nazi technology like that was another direct threat to our freedom, something the vamps intended to use to spy on us from space and know our every move. According to her, it was just one more reason why we had to continue the struggle and couldn't afford to waver.

After a moment, the satellite disappeared beyond the horizon. I let out a breath and closed my eyes a moment, savoring the evening breeze that came in from the sea.

"Are you all right now?" Val asked after a time.

"No," I said, hearing the tears in my voice. "I don't know whether I ever shall be." I snuggled closer, trying to burrow inside him. I slipped a hand under his shirt, felt the cool hard muscles of his chest, and shivered despite the tropical air. "What's happening?"

He didn't answer immediately, then said, "What always happens when people try to keep secrets — eventually it all unravels, and they do whatever they can to stop it."

"Isn't it better that people know?" I asked.

"Do you feel better having discovered the things you have?" Val shot me a pointed look.

He knew I couldn't say yes. And he knew I understood the unspoken part of what he meant — that people had died because of what I'd uncovered.

"You're not going to help me get to the bottom of this, are you?" I said.

Val shook his head. "I don't want to be going to your funeral."

"I can't leave it, Val. Not after all they've done. I have to know."

"We'll talk about it later." He kissed my forehead and held me closer. I knew what "later" meant. He'd keep at me until eventually he wore me down and I gave in.

Outside, the wolves howled, and I thought of the first time I'd seen them, of how they'd terrified me the same way they'd terrified my mother. I was afraid of other things now.

"Tell me about your home," I said sleepily. "Tell me about New York City."

I listened as Val spoke and realized he was the only one I could turn to in Haven. Camille had been my only real friend, and now she was gone. Besides, even if there were others I'd trusted as much, I wouldn't have been willing to draw them into this nightmare.

I was a hostage to truths I didn't yet know.

The only way I was going to be free was to find out what those truths were. But because of the very fact that he loved me, I knew Val wasn't going to help me. Far away, across an ocean and a continent, I thought there might be someone who would. It was crazy and a long shot, but I was in just as much danger here in Haven. And if I stayed, I'd never know what had happened to my mother and what it was our own government was keeping from us.

People had died because of secrets. Didn't I owe it to them to find out why?

"Does it have to be you?" Camille would have asked.

"There's no one else," I'd have answered.

But if I was going to do anything, I knew I had better do it soon. Who knew what might happen if I waited any longer?

What was it my philosophy teacher was always saying? *Carpe Diem.* Seize the day. In this case, in more ways than one.

In the back of my mind Camille whispered, "I hope you know what you're doing."

So do I, I thought.

The truth was, I was about to do one of the stupidest things I'd ever done. But sometimes you just have no choice. Sometimes you have to leap without looking.

PART TWO:
THE THIRD REICH

CHAPTER 23
JOURNEY INTO DARKNESS

The world fell away.

It was the day following the crash that had killed Grace, and I stood in the starboard observation lounge of the *Eva Braun,* pride of the Lufthansa fleet. It probably bordered on insane to be aboard a vamp ship, leaving the islands — the only home I'd ever known — behind me. And yet here I was.

For the next few days I'd be a captive in this tiny world. It would be just me, a few dozen other passengers, and a crew that was equally split between Immunes and vamps. And though technically we were all protected under the provisions of a travel agreement between the governments of Haven and Berlin that had been worked out many years before, from here on out we were essentially under the jurisdiction of the Third Reich. Aboard the ship, Nazi law prevailed, and I don't think anyone imagined for a single moment that if something went seriously wrong, the Haven government would be able to do much more than lodge a formal protest.

Most of the passengers were tourists, but there were also some businessmen and temporary workers. A few decades ago, the Third Reich had requested the opening of a temporary foreign-worker program that would allow vamp businesses to hire Immunes for jobs vamps could not or would not do. Most of these involved industries where working outside in daylight was a requirement. Vamps could do that sort of thing, of course, but not without restrictive protective gear and considerable risk.

For those Immunes daring enough to brave living among millions of vamps for several months at a time, the foreign-worker program was a boon. One month in New York City could earn a man almost as much money as he'd make in a year on the islands. Despite that, only the most adventurous signed on for work visas — probably because few could get past their fear and loathing of vamps or their contempt for the Nazi regime long enough to commit themselves for a lengthy stay. It was one thing to be there for a week or two as a tourist; it was quite another to remain for six months to a year. After all, the Third Reich wasn't exactly friendly territory.

With that in mind, I watched Kensington Aerodrome drop from under me as the ship lifted off. There was an unsettled sensation in my gut that had nothing to do with becoming airborne. My muscles tensed, and I kept telling myself this wasn't crazy, that everything was going to be okay. I was just off to New York; people did it all the time. Except, of course, they didn't. Not really, and certainly never with the intentions I had in mind.

The aerodrome shrank steadily, and eventually all of Haven was swallowed up by the vastness of the Pacific until it was like that point on the map Mrs. Bhutto had jabbed at. I felt suddenly alone, despite all the people around me.

Looking back toward the archipelago, I was reminded of how constricting Camille had found the islands, of how Grace had called them our prison. But despite the hardships, I had never truly felt that way — until now.

Only a few hours ago, I had persuaded Val to let me visit my flat. "I just need to pick up some clothes and a few essentials, and then I'll come right back," I had assured him. "Nobody is going to attack a car belonging to the Embassy. And besides, Wilson will be there to make sure nothing happens."

That had probably been the clincher, because I knew that above all else, Val trusted Wilson. They'd been together a long time, and Wilson was guardian to many of Val's secrets. Probably a great many I didn't know.

What I'd told Val hadn't been a total lie. I had packed a few things and picked up some necessities; I just hadn't returned to the Embassy when I'd finished. After Wilson had checked the apartment to make sure it was safe, I'd sent him back to the limo with a suitcase of clothes. Meanwhile, I'd quickly packed another bag, retrieved the ticket and visa Camille had left me, and snuck out the back way. I felt bad knowing that Val would certainly be furious with Wilson for having been duped. But I'd had more important things to consider than bruised feelings. Val might think he could make things right, but I had my doubts. If he wasn't going to help me get what I wanted, and if Haven was no longer safe for me, then I'd do what no one would ever expect of me. I doubted the people trying to silence me would ever think I'd literally take off for the Third Reich.

It was all a gamble, of course, and maybe nothing would come of it. Maybe I was jumping from the frying pan into the fire. But at least I was doing something.

* * *

"It really is quite remarkable," said Mrs. Worthing, a fellow passenger who had taken it upon herself to be my unofficial chaperone for the duration of the trip.

It was the second morning out, and we were seated in one of the airship's observation lounges, watching the ocean drift by below. The Pacific spread far and wide, its deep, mercurial waters meeting brilliant blue skies at the razor edge of the horizon. Looking at it, you had the sense of a world without end, stretching infinitely in all directions. It almost made it possible to temporarily forget the reality of where we lived.

"One never truly has much of a sense of just how big the world is until one is in the air and looking down upon it," Mrs. Worthing continued, staring through the large square window to where bits of cloud scudded by between us and the rolling whitecaps. "Wouldn't you agree, dear?"

"Yes, ma'am," I said. "It does sort of put things in perspective, doesn't it?"

We sat quietly for a moment, admiring the view. I glanced at Mrs. Worthing out the corner of my eye and allowed myself a smile. She was of the notion that I was a tourist like all the other passengers, and I couldn't help wondering what she'd think if she knew the truth. No doubt she'd be horrified and caution me that I was taking a terrible risk — which was probably a lot closer to the truth than I cared to admit.

"You're very much the talk of the ship, you know," Mrs. Worthing said abruptly.

"Me? Really?" My eyes widened in disbelief. "I can't imagine why." But a spike of apprehension shot through me. Maybe someone knew why I was here. That would be disastrous. It would be very easy to go missing from an airship high over the ocean.

"Oh, come, come, child, you can't be that insensible to your attractions," she said. "That Haeden group are beside themselves about you. Surely it hasn't escaped your notice how those boys have been falling over one another to get seated at your table." She chuckled. "It's like watching musical chairs."

I felt my cheeks go hot at that.

Mrs. Worthing looked at me, and her face crinkled with laughter. "My, you are ever so enchanting," she said. "There's something about you I can't quite put my finger on. You're a bit exotic, which makes your natural beauty all the more extraordinary. I suspect that by the end of the voyage you'll have most of the males on this ship thoroughly besotted." She sat back and nodded sagely to herself. "Yes, I imagine there'll be a few marriage proposals."

I laughed a little nervously.

"I must say, though, I'm surprised your parents would let a young lady like you travel to New York on her own."

"I was supposed to go with a friend," I said with a shrug. "Things didn't work out." I left it at that.

"Well, you must be on your guard, darling. You're the youngest aboard and the only unattached woman to boot. You wouldn't want to be taken advantage of."

"I don't think there's any chance of that," I assured her. "I'm already committed."

"Good. He's a very lucky man. I'm sure you'll have a long and happy life together."

I smiled anemically, but didn't say anything.

A few hours later, I was playing cards with some of the boys from Haeden University. I'd met them all briefly for the first time the day before, but none of them had made much of an impression on me. But in light of my conversation with Mrs. Worthing, I found myself watching them guardedly, wondering if they regarded me as some sort of potential mate. They were all in their early twenties, after all, and must be feeling the pressure to get hitched and have a family.

Whatever the case, as I sat there playing, I couldn't help but feel I was some sort of prize to be won. It was only when the game ended that I realized just how close to the truth that was.

"Well, boys," said Harry Trager, one of the brashest of the lot, "read 'em and weep." He spread his last hand on the table and leaned back, cracking his knuckles and grinning triumphantly from ear to ear. The others gave him sullen looks, but that only served to fuel his glee at having emerged the victor. "Don't worry, lads. There'll be further opportunities."

The other boys left, and I found myself alone with Harry. He reminded me of Camille's brothers: raised in wealth and privilege and with the mind-set that they were a gift to the world and should be regarded accordingly.

"I should be going," I said, starting to rise.

Harry caught my wrist. "Not yet," he said. "We've only just begun to have fun."

I looked down at the scattered cards on the table. "The game's over. You won."

He smiled in an odd way. "Yes, I did."

I just stood there, frowning at him.

"Oh, come, Sophie. We're not little children." Harry got up and moved closer, still holding my wrist. "I thought we might get to know one another a bit better. I'm told the observation bubbles are an excellent place to talk."

I knew exactly what sort of *talking* he wanted to do. "I think I need to go wash my hair," I said, pulling away from him and starting toward the passenger quarters.

Harry stepped in front of me, blocking my path. "Let's not fight it," he said. "Surely you've felt it."

I furrowed my brow. "Felt it?"

"You're a girl, I'm a guy." He grinned and put his hands on my arms. "We were meant for one another."

"Wow," I said. "You must have the girls swooning with lines like that."

His hands tightened, fingers digging into my flesh. "I'm sure a girl like you knows how to have all sorts of fun," he said.

My eyebrows shot up. "I beg your pardon?"

"I've seen the way they look at you."

"*They?*" I repeated.

"The vamp crew," Harry said pointedly.

"I'm sure I don't know what you're talking about." I twisted in his grip. "I really must go."

"Don't be such a tease."

"Is there a problem, miss?" a voice interrupted.

Harry and I both started. Neither of us had heard the steward approach. Now he stood a couple of meters away, eerily silent as he stared intently at Harry.

"This isn't any of your concern," Harry snarled, his eyes ablaze with that familiar Haven contempt.

The vamp didn't even flinch. "I think perhaps you'd best leave, sir. It doesn't appear the young lady appreciates your company." He spoke in a measured tone and a refined British accent, but his eyes were cold and dark. There was a hint of what Val had shown me in them — that hidden part of them, the scary part.

Harry let go of me and stepped back. "The captain will be hearing about this," he said, glaring at the vamp.

"Yes, sir, he will."

Harry opened his mouth but shut it again, looking like a fish. Without another word, he turned and stormed out of the lounge.

"Thank you," I said to the steward.

"My pleasure, miss," he said with a courtly bow. "If you should need anything, the crew will be more than pleased to assist."

I watched him go, thinking it rather odd that I'd felt safer in his presence than in Harry's.

* * *

Life aboard the *Eva Braun* was one of luxury. No ration coupons, no having to produce my ID at every turn, no hydro blackouts or water shortages. It was like being on another planet and served as an eye-opener when it came to the wealth of the Third Reich.

I had a cabin all to myself. It was nothing more than a small aluminum box with basic amenities, but it had a wonderfully large window that looked out and down onto the port side of the airship, allowing me to watch the clouds and the ocean and whatever else might come into view. It was the perfect place to sit and read a book. If only I'd brought one. There wasn't exactly a variety to choose from onboard; Nazi propaganda made up the bulk of the library's content, with at least a dozen copies of *Mein Kampf* gracing the shelves.

"Truly wretched," said Mr. Chen, a fellow passenger, as we sat eating lunch on the third day. "That book makes me shudder every time I see it."

"I'd get used to it, if I were you," said Mr. James. "You're going to work for them, and believe me, there are plenty of them who buy into that garbage. It'll be a long six months if you work yourself into a lather about it."

"I don't know how you can do it," Mrs. Hassan said from her seat one table over. She was with her husband and another couple who were playing tourist.

"Do what?" asked Mr. James.

"Work for them, my good man. It just seems —"

"Disloyal?" Mr. James laughed. "No more so than playing tourist, ma'am."

She harrumphed. "It's not the same at all."

"We make good money," Mr. James said. "Which helps the economy back home. And it's not like we're building bombs or anything. Just doing the things the vamps can't or won't do themselves."

"You must get terribly lonely," said Mrs. Worthing.

"Homesick sometimes. But there are at least a thousand of us working in New York. More in the other cities. And not all the vamps are bad. It's not like they're going to bite us and suck our blood, now is it? Not unless they're suicidal." He laughed, and several others joined in.

"I think it's shameful," said Mrs. Hassan. "They're still monsters."

He shrugged. "We share a world, and they're not going away, so I figure we've got to learn to live with them. Doesn't mean we have to like them or what they are. Besides, you don't seem to have a problem being served by them on this ship."

"I only deal with the Immune crew," Mrs. Hassan said, sniffing her disapproval. "I'd not deign to have anything to do with those vamps."

"Then why on earth are you going to New York?" Mr. James asked.

She didn't answer him. Instead she turned to me and said, "You're very friendly with the vamp crew, child. Do you think that's wise?" By the way she raised her voice, I got the feeling she wanted everyone — the vamps included — to hear her.

"Oh, but surely you've noticed that vamps are positively infatuated with Sophie," said Harry, who to my dismay had somehow managed to get himself seated at my table. He leered at me, a hardness in his eyes. "They just want to eat her up." He said it in such a way as to make it sound literal.

Mrs. Hassan was scandalized. "My word," she said, placing a hand on her ample and heaving bosom. "Whatever can you mean, young man?"

"I'm afraid Harry thinks he's being funny," I said to her in my sweetest, most endearing tone. Under the table I gave Harry a swift kick in the shin, hoping I'd crippled him for life.

"You must be careful, my dear," Mrs. Hassan said, ignoring Harry's strangled grunt of pain. "You can't trust them, you know."

"Oh, but they absolutely adore Sophie," Harry purred, shifting his legs out of my reach. "Haven't you noticed how they watch her?"

"Young man, you can't possibly be suggesting that any of these vamps would have feelings for one of our pure Haven girls." Mrs. Hassan held her head high, radiating indignation. The way she said *feelings* clearly implied she didn't think vamps had any.

"But how can they avoid it, ma'am? One look at her and they must think they've found their queen."

"My word!" She lifted her spectacles, which hung on a gold chain around her roly-poly neck, and squinted at me through half-moon lenses with her little piggy eyes. It was as though she were seeing me for the first time. "Well, you are rather pale, my dear."

"Positively vampish," Harry agreed.

I glared at him. Since the kick hadn't done the trick, I picked up my drinking glass and dashed the contents in his face. As he sat there, dazed and dripping tonic water, I stood, smoothed my dress, and casually walked away.

Every eye in the dining lounge followed me as I left. I caught Mrs. Worthing smiling approvingly and thought of how delighted Camille would have been. "Just like in the movies," she'd have said.

"My word," I heard Mrs. Hassan say again, and I couldn't help but grin.

* * *

By late afternoon the Pacific was behind us, and we'd begun crossing what had once been the continental United States. There was an observation room in the prow of the *Eva Braun*'s main hull, and I was up there alone, standing at the rail, when the captain appeared at my side. It was unusual to see him in daylight hours, but the sun was on the aft quarter of the airship, so there was no risk to him of direct exposure.

Captain Clauswitz wasn't a man of imposing stature, but in his uniform he exuded an air of quiet authority. He was a gracious and charming gentleman of the old school, who just happened to be a vamp. In his company, it was easy to forget our respective places in this world.

"Fräulein Harkness," said the captain. He assumed a post beside me, standing with his hands behind his back.

"Captain," I said, straightening and facing him. "I'm honored, sir."

"The honor is all mine," he assured me. He looked out over the wrinkled mass of the Sierra Nevada directly ahead of us. Clouds hovered over distant snow-capped peaks. Caught by the dying sunlight, they almost resembled the Japanese lanterns strung up in Caelo for the Founding Day celebrations.

"Impressive, isn't it?" he said.

"Yes, very," I agreed.

I found myself fidgeting a little as I glanced back at the view. Earlier we'd passed over the ruins of San Francisco, long ago abandoned, just like practically every other city in the world. It had been a bleak expanse of weathered and broken concrete spires, now overrun by flora and fauna. I had seen it in films made before the Fall, and it was hard to believe it was the same place. Gone was the city bustling with life and filled to bursting with the dynamic energy of an America arising from the Great Depression. Now it was a graveyard, a reminder of the billions who had died and of how the human world had shrunk to Haven. The same was true of Los Angeles and Chicago, Vancouver and Toronto, Sydney and Tokyo. Across the globe, east and west, north and south, they were now crumpling into dust, soon to vanish back into the landscape from whence they'd sprung.

"I traveled here often — *before* the Fall," Captain Clauswitz said, staring regretfully at the world that passed below. "Not so many great ships like these back then. But I remember the first *Hindenburg*." He shook his head in a wistful manner. "There were so many people then; it was a great country with so much promise. Now all that's left is New York. In all the Americas, just that one city — and even it is a shadow of what it once was."

He made it all sound so stark and desolate, his tone speaking to the sorrow that was the plague and to what little remained of the world it had left in its wake.

"I trust you've been enjoying the comforts of our fine ship," said Clauswitz, changing the subject. His face brightened noticeably.

"Very much," I said. "I've never flown before."

"Ah." He smiled. "Then I envy you."

I looked at him with surprise. "Why?"

"It's new. It's all fresh to you. When you've lived —" The captain stopped and chuckled dryly. "When you've been *around* as long as I have, sometimes it all just seems . . ." He made a slight motion with his shoulders. "You understand?"

I must have looked confused, because when Clauswitz glanced at me, he shook his head. "No, I don't suppose you do. You're not old enough to have wearied of anything."

"It must be strange," I said.

"To exist for so long?" He made a face.

"Yes."

"It's not without its benefits. If you've found someone to love, as I have, then eternity hardly seems enough. But eternity under tyranny, well, sometimes even love isn't enough to tolerate *that.*"

It surprised me to hear the captain speak of such things so frankly, though I suppose it shouldn't have. I knew Val had no love for Hitler's regime, and he'd always hinted that there were others of the same opinion. I guess I just never expected to run into any.

I waited for the captain to continue, but it was a long time before he did.

"There's a small matter I wish to discuss with you," he said at last.

Here it comes, I thought. *He's going to tell me I've been found out and they're not going to let me get off in New York.*

"I've some concern you may not understand what you're getting yourself into, Fräulein," the captain went on.

"Sir?" I said. My mind was racing; by now Val knew for certain I was gone, and he might have figured out I'd left on the *Eva Braun*. The airship had a shortwave radio, so it was possible he could have contacted the captain and told him I wasn't to get off the ship under any circumstances.

"Captain Miller of the day watch has informed me that some of the other passengers are quite concerned about you traveling into the Third Reich on your own without benefit of a guardian or chaperone," Clauswitz said. "They feel a young woman such as yourself may not be aware of the dangers in New York."

I felt a flood of relief and struggled to hide it. "I'm just doing the tourist thing," I said, trying to make it sound like the truth. My pulse quickened, and I was well aware from my experiences with Val that vamps could detect that sort of thing. "My best friend arranged all of this. We were to go together, but she was killed. I just wanted to honor her by going through with it. I knew it was what she would have wanted." I could only hope that maybe he'd think that was why I was so anxious.

The captain gave me a severe look. "I sincerely hope that's the case, Fräulein. Now wouldn't be a good time to be seeking adventure."

That sounded suspiciously like what Val had said when he'd refused to answer my questions.

"The thing is," Clauswitz continued, "the crew and I are also concerned."

"You needn't be," I insisted. "I'm not planning on doing anything stupid." Well, not anything more stupid than what I'd already done. "I've a room booked at the Grand, and I'm not going to go into any of the proscribed areas of the city."

"I pray not, Fräulein. My men are inclined to think of you as someone special."

"Special?" I cocked a curious eye at him.

Clauswitz nodded. "Indeed. When it comes to our kind, most Immunes are scarcely civil. One can always sense their uneasiness and fear and the undercurrent of their loathing. But there is none of that with you. It would be fair to say we've never had anyone quite like you aboard this ship. Some of my men believe you represent the future. They think you are an indication that change is in the offing."

I laughed. "I'm just a seventeen-year-old girl who wants to see a bit of the world, Captain. I don't think that's going to do much to change it."

"Well, I hope you find what you're looking for, Fräulein Harkness. And should you ever require assistance, don't hesitate to call on me." With that, the captain gave a courteous bow and left.

I stared after him, wondering what all that had really been about. After a moment, I looked back out the window. Behind me, the ashes of a world that no longer existed spread as far as the horizon. Down there, on those vast plains, there wasn't a single human being — or vamp, for that matter. Not that anyone knew of, at least. Outside of New York, the Americas were wild and barren and might never be home to anyone again.

I thought of what I'd read in my father's notebook, recalling the quote he'd seen inscribed on the ironwood knife they'd found at the alleyway crime scene. For some reason those words resonated within me as I looked out on the desolation that mirrored so much of the world in which we lived. A shiver ran up my spine, and I hugged myself.

Now, I am become death.

CHAPTER 24
NEW YORK CITY

In the evening light of a fading sun, the *Eva Braun* came in from the seaward side. Everyone stood crowded about the windows of the lounge and looked out upon what had long been emblematic of the United States — Lady Liberty, they'd once called her. Now she was broken and corroded; parts of her had fallen away, but enough of her remained to remind of what had once been.

It was a sad, pathetic sight.

Close by, Mr. Chen murmured, "'Give me your tired, your poor, your huddled masses yearning to breathe free.'"

They were words that had once meant something. Now, in the context of this city and the world in which it existed, they were nothing more than a grim reminder of all that had been lost.

Watching the Statue of Liberty drift past, I thought of home, of sailing with Camille and her parents around the turquoise seas of Resolute Bay in their private yacht, *Nemesis*. I thought of *Salvation and Hope,* the statue in the waters at the entrance to the harbor, which we would circle about almost every time we went out. The statue — raised to celebrate the tenth anniversary of Haven's founding — was a giant bronze sculpture of stylized male and female figures who stood back to back, one facing east, the other west, her left hand entwined with his right, their free hands raised. And on the stone plinth upon which they stood, a bronze plaque bore the simple inscription: "If we be but two, it be enough."

Was that true? I shuddered, and I looked toward New York City.

As the *Eva Braun* sailed in over Manhattan, the evidence of all the destruction the city had witnessed during the war was clear. Even in the waning light I could see there were craters here and there; and the rubble of fallen buildings, spotted with green, rose in heaps that resembled ancient burial mounds and pyramids.

How many people had died under those collapsed structures? I wondered. *Thousands? Millions?*

We all watched, somewhat subdued, as the city passed by beneath us. Everyone seemed in awe of the forest of skyscrapers that rose in the declining light, each casting long shadows that smothered the streets in darkness. Many were in a state of disrepair, and there was no evidence the vamps had added anything new since the end of the war. But even so, it overwhelmed.

"It's so much larger than I ever imagined," said Mrs. Worthing.

"And I thought Caelo was big," Mr. Chen added, shaking his head in wonderment.

"It's still not the New York you see in those old movies and magazines," said Mr. James, his words a melancholy note that resonated with truth.

I half listened to the other passengers, more interested in seeing the city than in hearing their comments. To the west I spotted a chain of piers. There were large seagoing behemoths tied up there, the majority of them warships flying the flag of the Third Reich. But not far from them, the hulk of the *Normandie* lay rusting on its side at Pier 88, unmoved since the day fire and the efforts of the US Navy had ended her career in 1942.

Before the war, she had been a magnificent ocean liner, ferrying people across the Atlantic — some to start new lives in America.

She'd been the pride of France until the country had fallen to the Nazis. After that, the US government had appropriated her, renamed her *Lafayette*, and converted her into a troop ship. But there'd been a welding accident, and she'd caught fire. The weight of all the water used to fight the flames had set her on her side, and there she'd lain all these decades, rusting away, forgotten, a physical metaphor for the city that was her grave. Perhaps a metaphor for the world as a whole.

We docked at the Empire State Building and disembarked from the *Eva Braun* through a partially enclosed gangway that creaked and shifted as we descended. "I feel rather like Fay Wray in *King Kong*," said one of the women, glancing through an opening at the city that sprawled so far below.

"It's perfectly safe," Mr. James assured her, just as a gust of wind shook and rattled everything, eliciting a few squeals of fright from some of the passengers.

I breathed a sigh of relief once we were inside the building. It was only as we rode the elevators down that it hit me — I was finally standing on Nazi soil. By the looks on the faces of the Havenites around me, it was evident the same thought had just occurred to them.

We were on our own now, far from the world we knew, amidst people who had long ago ceased to be human. It had been one thing to be on the airship with a few dozen vamps, but it was quite another to be in the heart of a city full of them. There were many times more of them here than the entire population of Haven.

At a desk on the ground floor, an officious looking customs officer thrust his hand at me, a note of impatience in his expression. "Papers!" he barked.

I handed over my travel documents, and he carefully examined my stamps from the Embassy, studied the signatures, and compared it all to something on the screen of a bulky TV that sat on his desk. Even as he was doing this, he started to type on an odd keyboard that resembled some sort of electromechanical typewriter.

At other desks, vamps were stamping the visas of my fellow passengers and sending them on their way with terse exclamations of, "Enjoy your stay in New York."

I broke out in a cold sweat as the officer dealing with me picked up a phone and started jabbering into it, his clipped German too fast for me to follow. When he finished, he gestured to one of the guards standing off to the side. The man approached, and the officer muttered something to him.

"Is anything wrong?" I asked, growing steadily more anxious.

"Please wait over there, Fräulein," the officer instructed me, pointing to a wooden bench by the wall.

The other passengers from the *Eva Braun* had stopped to watch, curious about what was taking me so long, but the armed guards were having none of that and urged them on their way. Mrs. Worthing tried to resist and called out to me that she would contact the Haven Embassy, but then she and the rest were gone. I was left to sit alone, sick with fear and wishing I hadn't been so stubborn and persistent and stupidly impetuous.

After an hour had passed, I was getting really jittery. I could feel the vamps watching me, staring at me oddly, their lingering looks leaving me increasingly uncomfortable. I tried not to look as scared as I felt, but it was hard to pretend I wasn't in serious trouble. My one feeble hope was that maybe Val was behind this. Maybe he'd told them to detain me. Maybe they'd just bundle me up and put me back on the next flight home.

One of the entrance doors opened, and I looked hopefully in that direction. But the sight of a Gestapo officer marching into the foyer made my heart stop. He halted and stared at me, then went over to the customs officer who'd been dealing with me and spoke to him at length. The latter produced the punch card I was certain held my data. The Gestapo officer gestured to the teleputing machine, and the customs officer dutifully inserted the card in a slot, typed something, and stared expectantly at the TV screen.

From where I sat, I couldn't see what they saw, but it seemed to have the Gestapo officer excited. He gave a nod of satisfaction, then marched straight over to me.

"Fräulein Harkness," the Gestapo agent said, clicking his heels together and making a perfunctory bow. "My name is Colonel Müller. I'm here to escort you."

"Escort me?" The words came out in a quavering voice.

"There has been a change of plans," Müller said. He wore a malignant grin as he gestured toward the entrance. "If you'll come with me, please."

"Have I done something wrong?" I asked, anxiety throttling my voice. "Is there a problem with my papers? "

"Just come with me, please." There was something feral in the way he looked at me, like a cat cornering its prey. "There would appear to have been a mix-up with your —" He hesitated for a moment, glanced toward the front entrance, then focused his hard eyes on me again. "Reservations," he finished. "I will be taking you to suitable accommodations."

I felt the hairs on the back of my neck stand on end. I wanted to run. I thought of what Captain Clauswitz had said and wished I could get back to the ship. "I'd rather stay with the other tourists," I said.

"I'm afraid that's not possible," Müller said in an oily tone. "I have a car waiting outside."

He crooked his arm and snapped his fingers in the direction of one of the SS troopers and barked an order in German. The trooper hurried forward and took my bags, then followed in our wake as Müller, with a firm hand on my elbow, steered me through the doors and out onto the street.

My heart was thumping in my chest. I felt like the silly girl I knew I was — the idiot who thought she knew better, who thought she was being so smart sneaking off right under the noses of the people trying to kill her in Haven. I really had jumped from the frying pan into the fire.

A guard opened the back door of the Mercedes sedan parked by the curb, and I slid in. I didn't have a choice. Müller got in on the other side and spoke to the driver. A moment later we were on our way, headed out into the night, down the glittering canyons of the streets. Headlights flared as cars and trucks rushed toward us, large gasoline-powered vehicles that made the electrics in Haven look like tin toys. I stared at the city as it slid by, barely registering it.

"You are nervous, Fräulein," said Müller.

"I don't know what's happening," I said, keeping my eyes focused straight ahead. "I'm just here to see New York. I don't know why there's a problem. My government isn't going to be happy about this."

Müller cackled. "You Havenites, always making your threats. Always thinking you can somehow bargain your way out of anything. But here, Fräulein, you are just a girl. Here, there is nothing your government can do for you."

I could feel his cold gaze on me. I could barely breathe, and I just wanted this to be over. I wanted Val to rescue me, but I'd left him thousands of miles away, out in the middle of the Pacific.

I needed a miracle.

And then, as if on cue, there was an explosion just ahead. A brilliant fireball erupted from one of the buildings on our left, spewing volcanically into the street and mushrooming into something vast and amorphous and blindingly bright. Flames roared in all directions, engulfing cars and pedestrians alike, instantly turning dozens of vamps into blazing funeral pyres and heaps of ash.

The sound of the explosion was deafening, and up and down the street, hundreds of windows disintegrated into millions of shards of glass. The glass and bits of concrete fell in an avalanche around us, clattering against the roof of the car, driving like a heavy rain against the street. The Mercedes shook violently and seemed to lift off the ground. Suddenly we were careening to the right, crashing between two sedans, and bouncing up onto the sidewalk as the driver fought for control.

Before I had time to brace myself, we smashed into a lamppost and jolted to a halt. I was flung forward and banged my head against the glass partition. The pain was incredible, and I thought I was going to black out. I heard Müller swearing in German; in the front seat, the driver sat slumped over the wheel.

Disoriented, I struggled to sit up, a wave of nausea washing over me. On the streets there was pandemonium. Vamps — out in droves now that the sun was below the horizon — were running and screaming in all directions. Flames were rolling up the side of the building where the explosion had originated, and smoke billowed into the night, blotting out the moon, turning the evening autumnal light shades darker. Dust filled the air.

Somewhere alarms sounded, and within minutes a Gestapo car with lights flashing and sirens wailing screeched to a halt a few feet from the perimeter of the blast. Behind it came a troop carrier with several dozen SS soldiers in the back. They jumped out and took up positions along the street, machine guns at the ready, as though anticipating trouble.

"What's happening?" I asked, my thoughts still dulled by the blow.

"Terrorists," Müller growled.

I was sure I must have misheard him. Terrorists? Here? They were all vamps, for pity's sake. But I recalled the rumors I'd mentioned to Grace, the suggestion that there were growing divisions among the vamps and talk of open rebellion. Val had laughed it off when I'd brought it up, but that didn't mean it wasn't true.

"Stay here," Müller ordered as he pushed open the door. He got out of the Mercedes and hurried off toward the knot of SS soldiers, pulling his sidearm from its holster.

I was sitting there, still dazed, when a blond girl wearing a black bandanna over the lower half of her face ran up to the driver's side of the car and smashed her gloved fist through the window. In a blur of motion almost too quick for the eye, she impaled the driver through the heart with a wooden stake.

I screamed and tried to push myself as far away as possible. But in a flash, the girl leapt over the car and shattered the window next to me. Bits of glass flew everywhere. There was a horrendous shriek as she ripped the door off its hinges and tossed it aside as though it were a scrap of paper.

I screamed again and shouted for help, scrambling across the backseat as I tried to get out the other side. But the vamp grabbed me and wrenched me out the car, half dragging me down the street as I yelled and fought her.

I must have had a good twenty pounds on her and was nearly a head taller, but she was more than a match for me. As I called for help again, she turned on me, her hand nearly crushing my arm, and said, "Shut up, you silly twit! If you've got even an ounce of sense in that pathetic little brain of yours you'll let me rescue you."

I gawked at her. "Who are you?" I blurted out.

"Like we've got time for that," the girl snapped. She gave me a sharp jerk. "Come on. Now!"

I stumbled after her, tottering in my heels as I struggled to keep pace with her.

She looked down at my feet and swore. "Bugger all! Take those ridiculous things off," she said. "We've got seconds before the next blast. And we have to be out of here before Müller notices you're gone."

I hopped on one foot, slipped off a shoe, then did the same with the other, wishing I'd opted for comfort over style as I ran barefoot with her along the pavement. Behind us I thought I heard Müller shouting, but his voice vanished in the thunder of the second explosion.

I glanced back, and a hot gale scorched my face and tore at my hair, nearly bowling me over. It was as if I were looking straight into the mouth of Hell.

When I'd left Haven I'd expected to find the Third Reich a much different place from home. I just hadn't imagined anything quite like this.

CHAPTER 25
ISABELLE

A few blocks from the explosion, we veered down a side street that was littered with trash. The girl stopped next to a Mercedes, jimmied open the door, and jumped in behind the steering wheel. I got in on the passenger side and sat, watching numbly, as she hot-wired the ignition. With a squeal of wheels we were off. I held on tightly as we tore down the road and quickly merged with the night traffic, weaving in and out of lanes in a reckless manner.

"What's going on?" I demanded.

"What's going on?" She stole a look in my direction, then focused forward again. "You're kidding, right?"

"No. What happened back there?" I glanced over my shoulder.

"What happened is that I was saving your ruddy neck."

"I don't understand. That explosion was set off so you could get to me?"

"We had to act fast."

I stared at her in disbelief.

She glanced at me, laughing sardonically. "Not the world you're used to is it, honey?"

"No," I said, hesitating. "And not exactly what I expected either."

"Really?" She seemed surprised at that. "I'd have thought Valentine would have told you."

"Valentine?" I sat with my mouth ajar. "Val sent you?"

"Of course. I wouldn't be risking my arse if he hadn't."

A shroud of confusion blanketed me. "Who the hell are you?" I asked again.

The girl pulled down the bandanna, and in the dim light of streetlights I found myself looking at my mother's face as I'd seen it in those photos Grace had let me see. She had the same flaxen hair, the same brilliant blue eyes — but this wasn't my mother. This girl looked no more than fifteen, though I knew it had been nearly three decades since she'd left Haven. Three decades in which she had lived as a vamp.

"Isabelle," I gasped. It was more than I'd imagined possible when I'd decided to come here.

"What's the matter, girl?" She laughed. "Didn't expect to find your dear old Aunt Isabelle undead and living in New York?"

I didn't know what to say. Of course I'd hoped. I just hadn't imagined I'd find her like this. And though I'd sort of mentally prepared myself for what she'd look like, it was still a bit of a shock to see her as a teenager rather than as a woman in her forties.

"You've really got Val pissed, gal. He's not too happy you decided to take off on your own. Can't say I blame him." Isabelle shot me a reproachful look and shook her head. "What on earth were you thinking? Do you have any idea how much danger you're in? Do you know what trouble you've caused? I had to pull in a fistful of favors to rig that little escape back there."

"Müller said it was the work of terrorists."

She snorted in disdain. "Everything's terrorists to that Nazi bastard."

"I don't understand."

"Of course you don't. You thought you'd just come here and snoop around and the Nazis would just turn a blind eye to it." Isabelle's disapproval filled the car. "Girl, are you freakin' out of your mind? Do you have any idea what the Gestapo would do to you? If I hadn't rescued you, there's a good chance that would have been the last anyone ever saw or heard of you."

"What's going to happen now?" I asked. "Surely they'll be hunting for me?"

"There are places we can go and stay safe awhile."

"And then what?"

She flashed an unsettling grin. "Then we try to get you out of this mess."

I studied her for a long moment. "Val never mentioned you."

Isabelle shrugged and said, "Probably worried you'd come looking for me if he did."

I couldn't argue with that. After all, it was pretty close to the truth. "The people who set off that explosion —" I began.

"Fellow believers," she said.

"Believers?"

"Rebels, if you like."

"Then the rumors are true?"

Isabelle laughed, an outburst tinged with bitterness. "You didn't think that just because we're vamps we're all Nazis, did you?"

"No." I thought of Val but then realized that even though he'd intimated there were vamps who weren't adherents to the Nazi ideology, I'd always thought of him as being the exception rather than the rule.

"Does that mean Val is one of you?" I asked.

"One of us?" She sounded incredulous. "Hell, girl, he helped start the rebellion. We sure wouldn't have risked bringing the Gestapo down on us if he were just some bureaucrat asking a favor."

"How long has this been going on?"

"Almost since the end of the war."

"Seriously? So the rumors are actually true?" I wrinkled my brow. "But why hasn't anything happened? I mean —" Her look cut me short.

"You expected revolution overnight?"

"No, but . . ." I finished with a shrug.

"It takes a long time to build a following, especially under a tyranny like this one," Isabelle said by way of explanation. "Hitler has never been the trusting sort, and it's literally taken us decades to get our people into high-level positions in preparation for when we decide to bring the house down. We're fighting for a different world, and we want to make sure we win when we go to war."

"What sort of different world?" I asked guardedly. The fact that the rebelling vamps hated the Nazis didn't mean they'd end up loving us if they were victorious. And God only knew, Isabelle probably had plenty of reasons for hating Haven.

She must have realized what I was thinking, because she glanced at me and laughed again. "I know that look," she said as she swerved around a truck and practically rear-ended a van. "You're wondering if we're just interested in getting rid of the Nazis and taking over the world for ourselves. No Hitler. No Old Ones. And no Immunes."

"Aren't you?" I asked.

"Don't fret, kid. Do you honestly believe your beloved Valentine would be involved in plotting the extinction of humankind?"

"Of course not."

Isabelle's smirk made it clear she'd seen the doubt in my eyes. "You're going to have to learn to lie better than that," she said. "I know the way you think. I was a Havenite once, remember? It took me years to get all that propaganda out of my system. But I haven't forgotten what it was like to be human."

"Other vamps have."

"I'm not like them." There was something hard and terrible in her voice — anger and rejection and more emotion than I could imagine anyone bottling up.

I thought of Isabelle as a fifteen-year-old girl suddenly dumped in New York City, smack in the middle of a world she'd been taught to fear and abhor. I was admittedly terrified at the moment, but it must have been far worse for her. It was incredible that she'd survived at all, and she probably had Val to thank for that.

I slumped in my seat, massaged a sore foot, and sighed.

"What's the matter, kid? This all too much for you?" Isabelle asked.

I nodded feebly — though she couldn't begin to imagine just how much and why.

"I guess you've had a lot on your plate lately," she allowed. "Val mentioned you'd had a few problems."

"A few?" That was an understatement if ever there was one. "You don't know the half of it. Everything's changing." I shot her a sidelong long. "And then there's you."

"Me?" Isabelle raised her thin eyebrows, looking puzzled. "You have a problem with me? It's the whole vamp thing, isn't it?"

"No. I don't have a problem with vamps. I mean, not ones like you and Val. It's just that until a few days ago I didn't even know you existed."

Isabelle was silent a moment, then said, "Does that really surprise you? Grace never could get past her hate."

"She managed to get past it long enough to ask Val to help you."

Her expression soured, her eyes growing cold and dark. "It wasn't compassion that drove her to do that," she said.

"What do you mean?"

"Your grandmother has a few dark secrets of her own, kid. Did she ever mention the fact that she was among the founding members of Haven?"

I shrugged one shoulder. "I've heard all about her being a part of the Forum. What's so shameful about that?"

"Nothing. It's what she agreed to once the government was formed that's the problem. She consented to the terms of the truce and to Cherkov's plan."

"Cherkov's plan?"

Isabelle grinned, but there wasn't a shred of mirth in it. "He claimed he could defeat Gomorrah and prevent stillborn births caused by the virus — or at least some of them. After all, almost every childbearing woman in Haven can expect to have at least one. Cherkov insisted that with enough resources he could figure out a way to somehow protect some of the non-Immune babies from the virus and bring them to maturity." She paused and shook her head. "You can imagine how the government would have responded to that. They'd always believed that if they could beat Gomorrah it would only be a matter of time before they could beat the vamps. I'm sure they thought stopping even a few babies from being stillborn would be a step in the right direction. At the very least, the population would grow faster."

"The government?" I frowned, recalling something in my father's notes about uncovering shell companies. "When I was going through some of my father's old stuff I found notes about Cherkov. He suspected the doctor was conducting unorthodox experiments on Haven women and that the government might be involved somehow. But if it was, it hid its tracks well. I don't think my father was ever able to find enough evidence to prove anything conclusively."

"That's not hard to believe," said Isabelle. "The good doctor didn't exactly have a sterling reputation. He'd been a researcher for the Nazis before the Fall; even after most of them had been transformed, he continued to work for them. The bastard did some pretty nasty things from what I understand, so it's easy to see why the Haven government would want to maintain some distance between themselves and what Cherkov was doing on the islands. There were some things he did while conducting his research . . ." She visibly shuddered. "Let's just say the less said the better."

"If he was such a monster, how on earth did he get into Haven in the first place?" I was incredulous.

She shrugged. "I don't think they turned away any Immunes back then. You've got to remember they were desperate for people — still are. From what I gather, he was somehow part of the truce. Not sure exactly how all that worked, but apparently the Nazis handed him over, and the Haven government agreed to take him in."

"And they just let him go to work again?" I asked, horrified.

"I guess."

"But that's —" I stopped and averted my gaze, feeling sick.

"What?" Isabelle looked amused. "You thought they'd put him on trial for crimes against humanity?" She made a sort of chortling sound. "Kid, if they'd done that there'd have been no end to it. Back in the early days, Haven was full of all sorts of unsavory characters who probably should have ended their days locked away forever. But as far as the government of Haven was concerned, vamps were the only enemy."

"So where do you come into it? I don't understand that part."

"The good doctor convinced everyone it was all part of his experiments to rid us of Gomorrah's curse. But he had another agenda, and as part of that he started experimenting on live subjects. Twins were his favorites."

"You and Mom," I said, my stomach knotting.

"Yeah. You might say I was the guinea pig; Mary was supposed to be the control."

"I can't believe Grace would ever have consented to that," I said in disbelief.

"I guess she didn't really have much of a choice since she'd agreed to the protocols — though I don't imagine for a moment she ever thought one of her own children would eventually fit them."

"The protocols?" I had no clue what she was talking about.

Isabelle's jaw tightened. "I got sick."

I stared at her, still confused. "I don't get it."

"The government had a list of symptoms. If you fell within those parameters, then you became part of the experiments. It was all for the good of Haven, of course. After all, what could be nobler than ending the tyranny of the virus and saving non-Immune babies from becoming infected by Gomorrah? But they didn't know it was all a lie; Cherkov was looking for something else. Either that or they chose to turn a willfully blind eye to the truth."

"You really think Grace could have known —"

"If she didn't, she should have," Isabelle said heatedly. "They were playing with fire. It was Gomorrah, for Christ's sake! They all should have foreseen it ending like this." She gestured angrily to herself, a circular, sweeping motion that encompassed her face.

"But still, she did ask Val to take care of you."

She laughed bitterly. "I told you, that wasn't because she cared about me after I'd changed. Grace hated vamps and detested what I'd become. If she hadn't been such a coward she'd have let the government deal with me the way they'd dealt with Cherkov's other rejects."

I opened my mouth to protest but then thought better of it. Given what had happened to Isabelle, maybe Grace didn't deserve defending. "What about the others?" I asked.

"Over the four decades Cherkov ran his evil little lab, he stole the lives of hundreds like me. And that doesn't include all those babies that just disappeared."

I shivered, recalling my father's suspicions and wondering how deep that secret went in the Haven government. And what had the government done with all the others Isabelle claimed had been part of Cherkov's experiments? Some might have died from whatever it was the doctor had been doing to them, but surely there'd been many who'd —

Who'd what? I realized. *Become vamps?*

And what happened after that? I remembered what Grace had said to me after she'd told me about Isabelle — there were rules. The government couldn't have a bunch of vamps running around the islands, and they certainly didn't want to contribute to Hitler's forces. Given that, there was really only one logical conclusion, however repulsive it might be.

It shouldn't have bothered me. After all, they were just vamps; the world certainly didn't need more of them. But I liked to think I'd never really thought like that — certainly not since I'd known Val.

And now there was Isabelle. I looked at her and saw the girl from Grace's photo album. That girl hadn't been a monster, and I couldn't bring myself to think of her as one now.

"Val saved you," I said, studying her.

"Yes," Isabelle agreed, although she didn't seem particularly happy about it. "If you want to call it that."

"And the others?"

"He managed to help a few. Not as many as he wished. Smuggling people out of Haven isn't as easy as you might think. Not even for someone as well connected as Val is."

"But he got Mom out."

Isabelle nodded. "Yeah. But . . ."

"But what?" I asked.

"After she changed, Mary didn't belong in either world. Val thought we could look after her, that we could help her. But we couldn't. She's something else now. She's in her own space, sometimes filled with unspeakable hate and violence. When she's in that state, she's like a wild animal hunting for blood and vengeance."

"I read some of my father's notes," I said. "He seemed to point the finger at Cherkov, suggesting he made her sick."

"I don't doubt that's true. From what I've been able to piece together over the years, Cherkov was getting desperate in his research and wanted to experiment on a pregnant woman. I suspect the people overseeing him suggested Mary and arranged to have him assigned as her obstetrician. Haven medical care is all government run, so it would have been easy enough to do."

"And it was an easy way to keep her quiet," I guessed.

Isabelle nodded. "Mary's attempts at playing detective a few years earlier must have rattled more than a few of the higher-ups, and they might have been concerned about your father getting curious again. I'm guessing they would have thought it was a way of silencing them both. A win-win as far as Cherkov and his overseers went. They'd get rid of a problem without sullying their hands, and the doctor got to take his research a step further. Whether Mary died outright or was transformed, no one would ever be the wiser. Either way, she'd be gone. It would all seem so natural."

"Except my father had his suspicions."

Isabelle made another of her shrugs. "And did he ever act upon them?"

I felt a flicker of shame, recalling my father's notes, his allusions to warnings from Val to stop poking around for my sake. "No," I admitted. "He gave up."

"Well, there you have it." She grimaced. "I guess the people behind old Cherkov got their way."

"I don't understand why they didn't just kill Mom after her first pregnancy. That's when she was nosing around. That's when she was a threat." I thought of Fiona Richards, the woman my mother had tried to talk to when she'd been investigating what had happened to her son. That death had almost certainly been foul play.

"I suspect Val played a role in keeping her safe. For a while, anyway."

"Val?"

"Like I said, he has connections. And a lot of influence in and out of the Haven government."

"And yet in the end they still got to her," I said angrily.

Isabelle looked away. "I don't think he realized what was happening until it was too late. He hadn't really been in contact with Mary for some time."

"And then he helped my father because of what? Guilt?"

She shook her head. "I can't answer that. I don't know if even he can. I do know he was pretty torn up about it. And Mary would have simply been another statistic if he hadn't taken her away from Haven."

"Maybe he shouldn't have," I said. "Maybe he should have just let the government . . ."

"Yeah. Maybe."

If my father and Grace had simply stood aside and followed the rules of Haven, everything would be different, I realized. Camille would never have been murdered, and none of this would have happened. I'd be back in Haven right now, going to school, living my life the way I always had, merrily ignorant of the darkness that littered my past as well as Haven's.

Isabelle gave me a sympathetic look. "I know how you feel," she said. "I've often fantasized about how my life would have been if I hadn't gotten sick."

I winced, feeling wretched, and said, "In my father's notes he suggested there was a connection between what happened to you and what happened to Mom. Something about vitamin injections."

Isabelle nodded. "That's how we think Cherkov did it. When I got sick he began administering his special vitamin cocktail. It was supposed to make me better, but the more I had, the worse I got. It was the same for the others. It was almost certainly the same for Mary."

That brought to mind something else that puzzled me. "If the same thing was done to both of you, then why was the result so different?"

"Val said it was because her chemistry was altered as a result of the pregnancy. That changed the outcome. The virus did something else to her, something beyond just transforming her. Mary's stuck halfway between being a vamp and being human. She has none of our weaknesses and all of our strengths. But it came at a terrible price — it messed up her head."

"So it really wasn't me who drove her mad," I said, feeling relieved.

"You?" Isabelle snorted. "That's all on Cherkov, kid."

"And you're certain Val didn't know about any of this when it was being done to her?" I asked. I waited on pins and needles for her reply, desperately wanting her to say what I wanted to hear.

"Are you kidding? Do you seriously think he'd have just stood aside and let them have at it? There was a time when he loved Mary; even after she was no longer a part of his life, he'd have done anything to protect her. But he didn't find out what was going on until your father went begging for help. By then, of course, it was far too late. She was already transformed, and all Val could do was what he'd done for me and for the others. He got Mary out of Haven and shipped her to New York."

I looked out the window of the car, staring at the landscape of an alien city. My head was spinning with all these revelations. I felt like I needed a scorecard to keep track of it all, and I couldn't shake the feeling I was still missing a lot. Cherkov's experiments, the stillborn babies, the 'refrigerators,' Mary, Isabelle, Val, my father, the Westerlys — the list went on and on. And they were all connected.

"It's still hard to believe the government would be party to any of this," I said, shaking my head. But Father had thought it might have gone as far as the top, right to the president.

"Cherkov fooled a lot of people," Isabelle said. "And the thing is, it looks like he actually may have been working on some sort of solution to Gomorrah. It just wasn't the only thing he was working on. He was a mad scientist, in a literal sense of the word. I know, because I witnessed it firsthand. I was a part of it."

I waited for her to elaborate, but she didn't. "I wonder what else the Haven government is hiding," I finally said.

"I suspect if you dig deep enough you'll find plenty of skeletons in its closet. The details of the truce, for one." Isabelle made a face. "The world isn't what you think it is, kid. There are a lot of bad people in it, and not all of them are vamps."

I was beginning to realize just how true that was.

We drove on in silence. I sat mulling over what she had told me, trying to make sense of it, trying to accept it, even though every fiber of my being wanted to reject it. I needed time to think, but I didn't have that luxury. Things were happening fast. A lot faster than I had anticipated, and not at all in the way I'd imagined.

A few minutes later, Isabelle turned the Mercedes sharply into a side street, the back end of the car fishtailing. "The first thing we have to do is get you some suitable clothing," she said. "Got to make you look like one of the tribe."

"The tribe?"

"Vamps, babe." She made a noise through her nose and shook her head as she appraised my outfit. "Is that really what they're wearing in Haven these days? It almost makes me glad I had to leave."

I looked down at the knee-length skirt, pastel-yellow midthigh cloth jacket, and white peplum blouse I was wearing. The outfit was modern and stylish Haven attire, but based on the brief glimpses I'd had of the vamps on the streets of New York, I was positively dowdy by comparison. Their clothing was avant-garde and provocative. The women wore bold splashes of color in outfits that shaped and revealed. Tight pencil skirts or pants that looked like they'd been painted on; jackets with broad collars and wide belts; heavy jewelry and other accessories. The men dressed predominately in silver, gray, and black in cuts that were spare and tailored. It was a more muted statement but no less theatrical. It was as though their clothing was a defiant declaration of their existence. They seemed to be pushing back against the weight of the oppression that hung over the city.

"I'll never pass for a vamp," I said, puzzled by how Isabelle could even think it possible.

She just looked out the corner of her eye at me and said, "We'll see."

CHAPTER 26
TRANSFORMATION

Vampires are generally creatures of shade and darkness, and Isabelle and I were making our way through the city at the peak of nighttime activity. Everywhere I looked there were people and machines moving in chaotic synchronicity.

On the surface it didn't appear much different from Haven. People went to work, doing the things that must be done, the things that allowed a city to function. But looking at those faces I had the sense that there was a weariness to it all. Was that what happened when you didn't age, when life didn't slow down? You went on, day after day, one day the same as the next, doing whatever it was you did because the state demanded it of you?

Nothing is free, I realized. Not even for vamps.

It seemed like we'd been driving for hours, but when I looked at my watch I saw it had been mere minutes. "Are we going to Val's?" I asked.

"What? Hell, no," Isabelle said. "His penthouse is in Nazi central. There're guards crawling all over that place. Besides, we can't risk causing him any more problems. If we got caught . . ."

I was disappointed. Ever since that night when Val had told me about New York, I'd yearned to see his home. I had thought maybe it'd help me understand him better. And if I was being honest, I hoped that by being there I'd feel something of him, the way I could in Caelo when I passed by spots where we'd had our little trysts. I missed him; it was as plain and as simple as that.

It must have shown on my face, because Isabelle chuckled and gave me a pitying look. "Oh, kid, you've got it bad."

I blushed, annoyed that I was so transparent.

"I was wondering," I said slowly. "I mean, what with you and Mom being twins . . . was there ever anything —" I paused, felt the awkwardness of what I was trying to say. "You know? You and Val . . . you never . . ."

"Him and me?" Isabelle feigned shock, then laughed and shook her head — though in her eyes there were hints of something else. "When I first came here I was in a bad way. Val took care of me and genuinely cared about me. But he never felt *that* way about me. Maybe I was too young. I mean, look at me; I'm trapped in a fifteen-year-old body."

"But still," I said, "he told me when he first saw Mary . . ."

"Yeah, I know. I wondered about that when I first found out, too. Why her and not me? What was different? It took me a long time to realize he just didn't see us the same way, and a lot of that had to do with the fact that I was a vamp. But also that I was nothing like my mother, whereas Mary had been. He saw Grace in her — or Grace as she had been, back when they'd both been young. He saw something he'd lost, and I guess he thought he could maybe get it back through Mary." Isabelle looked resigned. "I think we both know how that worked out."

I don't know why, but I said, "I'm sorry."

She shrugged. "Don't be. It's no big deal. You can't force people to love you. And Val . . . well, he's complicated. Sometimes I don't think he even understands himself. And sometimes I think he's the biggest fool I've ever met. A man with dreams too big to ever be fulfilled."

I was beginning to see that.

"He's kind of a Pinocchio, I sometimes think — if you get what I mean." Isabelle grinned sardonically. "A vamp wanting to be human. Or at least wanting to be human *again*."

I didn't know what to say to that, so I changed the subject. "If we're not going to his place, then where are we going?"

"I have a pad," Isabelle replied.

"Pad?"

"You know? A flat. An apartment. Nothing luxurious, mind you. There's not much that's luxurious in this hellhole unless you're one of the bigwigs. Anyway, it'll do for the moment. We have to keep you safe. Until Val arrives, if necessary."

"He's coming here?" I couldn't stop my heart rate from jumping at that news.

"Trying to. But don't get your hopes up; we're not going to wait for him. Right now the most important thing is keeping you out of Müller's clutches."

That sounded easier said than done.

* * *

"Nothing luxurious" was a gross understatement when it came to describing Isabelle's pad. It was a dump. Even in Haven it would have been condemned and burned to the ground — and we don't like wasting anything. It was an old brownstone located in someplace called Park Slope. Isabelle insisted it had once been a ritzy area, but it was clear those days were long past. The whole area looked like a ghetto.

"Put these on," Isabelle commanded.

We were standing in a bedroom, which I assumed was hers, a shabby little space with a large four-poster bed, a battered bureau, and a rubbishy dresser that looked as though it had been salvaged from the trash. I kept expecting to see rats scurry across the floorboards and spiders crawl up the walls.

I couldn't for the life of me imagine falling asleep in a place like this. Of course, vamps don't really sleep, but that was beside the point.

"Val gave me a vague idea of your size." Isabelle held out a pile of clothing. "You know men." She flashed a blindingly white grin. "Anyway, I did the best I could. I hope they fit."

I took the clothes and inspected them with a dubious eye. They were of the same vein as hers and quite unlike anything I'd ever worn in my life. Holding the pants at arm's length, I regarded them in disbelief. I'm slim, but they looked as though they were made for a stick. "You can't be serious," I said.

"They'll be looking for an Immune," she said. "We need you to blend in."

"Clothes aren't going to make me a vamp. I don't see how dressing up will fool anyone. Least of all that Müller chap."

"You let me worry about that." Isabelle sounded so confident that it was easy to be seduced into believing she knew what she was doing.

"Why can't I just stay here until Val arrives?" I sounded whiney.

"Because we can't remain in one place. Besides, Val can't come *here* to pick you up. It's too risky with Müller on the prowl. We may have to keep on the move until we can get you out of the city and back to Haven without the Gestapo catching wind of it."

"Get me out of the city?" I said. "And how do you propose to do that? They'll surely be watching the airships like hawks."

Isabelle's lips twitched in a lopsided grin. "Island Transnational Shipping has cargo ships coming and going on a weekly basis. We're thinking of smuggling you aboard one of those."

"As a stowaway?"

"You're an Immune." She sniffed dismissively. "They'd hardly toss you overboard."

She had a point. And the mention of Island Transnational Shipping brought to mind the whole business with the refrigerators

that had been in the reporter Donovan's notes. S aboard one of the ITS ships might allow me to g cargo and solve part of the mystery that had brought n York City in the first place.

I was pretty sure it was more than refrigerator units those ships were ferrying from Haven. But what could that cargo be? What was it Haven had that the vamps would want so badly? And how was all that connected to Cherkov and the non-Immune babies?

Maybe it was the setting or the conversation Isabelle and I had had coming here, but a rather wild idea suddenly popped in my head — blood. The non-Immune babies were the only source of normal human blood in existence. What if someone had created some sort of black market for the product as a specialty item? Could someone be draining the blood, bottling it, and shipping it to the vamps?

Admittedly, it was a bit of a stretch. Maybe even more than a bit. Vamps seemed to survive perfectly fine drinking animal blood. But maybe it was like wine or something, and human blood just tasted better. People would pay a lot of money for good wine in Haven. Maybe vamps would pay a lot of money for human blood of the non-Immune variety — the kind that wouldn't turn them into a pile of ash.

I was about to ask Isabelle, but before I could open my mouth she said, "I've got to go make some calls." And with that she left.

I stood in her bedroom, feeling very alone and alienated. None of this was familiar. I was in a world I didn't understand, amidst people who on so many levels were the antithesis of everything I knew.

There was a book on the nightstand. I went over and picked it up, surprised to find it was a tattered, well-read copy of *No Haven for Darkness* with several pages bookmarked. I stared at it, thinking how odd it was to see it here. I wondered if the author had any idea how truly bizarre his world was when compared with reality.

"Hurry up!" Isabelle called from downstairs.

I dropped the book and turned to the clothes, reluctantly attempting to put them on. It was like trying to don rubber. They were skintight and uncomfortable, and it took me a little while to figure out how some of them were supposed to be worn.

By the time I had finished and surveyed the results in the mirror, I wasn't sure what to think. I looked at my bosom, thinking of what Mrs. Hassan would say. Even in a bathing suit I didn't show this much cleavage. I'll admit, though, I looked a lot more like a vamp than I had a few minutes before.

When Isabelle returned, she inspected me up and down, nodding approvingly. "Just a few finishing touches and you'll even fool Müller," she said. She went into the grotty bathroom, rummaged around, and resurfaced moments later with a makeup kit and some scissors.

"What are those for?" I asked, eyes widening in alarm as she held up the shears and worked them so they made metallic *snick-snick* sounds.

"They'll be looking for someone with long hair," she said. "The easiest way to change your look is to cut it. You're far too Haven like that. We'll give you something more New York."

Isabelle pulled out a chair and made me sit in it, then draped a sheet around my neck and went to town on my hair, cropping my wonderfully long black tresses into a boyish bob. I stared at the locks on the floor and felt like crying.

"That's better," she said, stepping back to admire her work. "Now for the finishing touches." She brushed away the loose hairs around my face and neck, then picked up the makeup kit and set about transforming me.

While she worked on me, I thought of Camille, who had never gone anywhere without spending at least half an hour in front of a mirror dolling herself up. She'd been almost religious about it, and she had never ceased trying to convert me to the wonders of cosmetics.

"Not that you really need it," she used to tell me. "You have such gorgeous lips and lashes. But still, guys expect it." And she would wink, as though it were a great trade secret. Whenever we'd gone out for the evening, she'd insisted on doing my makeup for me. I'd always relented, even though I'd never really felt like me under all that stuff. It had seemed like a mask, a disguise, hiding me from the world around me. Now, of course, that was exactly the effect Isabelle was shooting for.

"All done," Isabelle said at last. She beamed appreciatively, and I got the impression, however fleeting, that she was actually enjoying herself. For a moment or two I experienced a sense of closeness to her, as though we were sisters doing the girly thing. Just like it had been with Camille and me.

"Take a look," she urged, moving aside so I could see in the mirror again.

I sat there speechless, not sure what to think. Even I would have had a hard time recognizing the girl who looked back at me. I now had scarlet lips, black eyelids, even longer and darker lashes, and porcelain skin. Whatever Haven coloring I'd had was buried under a layer of foundation. I actually might pass as a vamp, which was rather disturbing the more I thought about it.

"So what do you think?" Isabelle asked.

I didn't say anything as I studied the new me again, touching my hair and turning my head from side to side. I was already missing my sundresses and shorts, my sneakers and sandals. I told myself this was temporary, that soon it would be over and — and what? How could I go back to Haven without the answers I'd come here for?

"We need to talk," I finally said.

"Later," she said. "Right now we have to get going."

"Going? Already? I thought we'd be hiding out here awhile."

Isabelle shook her head. "I made a few calls while you were dressing. There are some people we have to meet right away. If we're going to get you out of here, we're going to need a lot of help. I can't do it alone."

"I think we should wait for Val," I protested.

She shook her head again. "Better if we do this without him."

It was the strangest thing, but listening to Isabelle made me realize how I must have sounded to Val — for the first time I understood some of his exasperation.

"It must be genetic," I said under my breath.

"What must be?" she asked.

"Pigheadedness."

CHAPTER 27

THE CLUB SCENE

"Just let me do all the talking," Isabelle said. We were out on the streets, walking in the dark, the car abandoned behind us.

"Fine," I said. "But who are these people?"

"They're my contacts in the underground."

"The subway?"

"Well, actually, sort of. I'm talking about the underground in the political sense, but to get to them we'll have to go down into some of the old Interborough Rapid Transit tunnels. That's where La Sang Rouge is."

"La Sang Rouge?"

"It's a club. Mostly for vamps of my kind."

"*Your* kind?" I raised an eyebrow.

"Vamps who weren't turned during the Fall."

More of Cherkov's failed experiments? I wondered. *The "others" she had mentioned earlier?* I heaved a breath. Things in the Third Reich weren't at all what they seemed. It was an entirely different world I was being introduced to at a whirlwind pace.

"I hope you don't mind rats," said Isabelle.

My eyes went round. "Rats? Real live rats?"

"Well, there's no reason to be afraid of the dead ones."

"You're serious?" I said.

She nodded. "The tunnels are crawling with the blighters."

I shuddered. "How lovely."

Isabelle grinned. "Don't worry, they don't usually bite — much."

* * *

Eventually we came to a set of stairs that descended into darkness. Isabelle paused and slipped off the knapsack she'd brought with her. As I waited, hugging myself against the chill, she rummaged inside it and produced a large and very lethal-looking pistol.

"For the rats?" I asked hopefully.

She gave a dry chuckle. "The two-legged variety."

"Are you kidding?"

"No."

"But I thought bullets were useless against vamps."

"These aren't ordinary bullets," she explained. "They're infused with highly concentrated Immune blood." She hefted the pistol, which looked enormous in her tiny hand. "Don't even have to hit the heart with these babies. Just a nick will eventually snuff out a vamp. That's the way Immunes did it back in the war."

"Where on earth do you get Immune blood?" I asked.

"On the black market. These weapons are Nazi stuff."

"Why would the Nazis want something that can kill vamps?" I asked. And where were *they* getting the blood? Was that another of the Haven government's dirty little secrets?

Isabelle looked at me as though I were stupid. "Hitler needs to arm his troops with something powerful enough to keep the masses in check," she said.

"You don't have any problem using it?" I asked, gesturing to the gun.

"On a vamp?" She wrinkled her nose in distaste. "There's no love lost between me and most of them, especially not the Gestapo and the SS."

Isabelle rummaged in her bag again and pulled out some flashlights. They were likely more for my benefit than hers; as a vamp she could see far better in the dark than I could. I suspected a flashlight was pretty superfluous as far as she was concerned.

Shouldering the knapsack, she led the way, descending the stairs to the cavernous space at the bottom. It was knee-deep in garbage, but a path cut through the piled litter, opening into a place that had clearly been abandoned decades before. I imagined this was what it might be like to enter an Egyptian tomb, and I half expected to find the mummified remains of those who had died from the virus during the Fall. There were no mummies, but I did see plenty of bones scattered about. "Are they —" I started to ask.

"Human?" Isabelle gave one an indecorous kick, sending it skittering beyond the circle of light. "Probably."

"From the Fall?"

She gave a shrug that indicated the answer was yes. "There was mass panic when the plague hit New York. Immunes herded tens of thousands of infected into the subways and firebombed the places. Improvised crematoria, I guess."

"They burned them alive," I said. Val had mentioned something about that, but seeing it for myself was something else entirely. I swallowed back my horror, feeling more than a little peaked — maybe even a little ashamed.

"Don't get all choked up about it. They were infected, kid. They were either going to die a painful death or be transformed." Isabelle toed another bone, knocking it toward some rats. They scattered when it fell in their midst, disappearing into the shadows. "There was a lot of fear going through the minds of people back then; they were fighting a disease they didn't understand without a single useful weapon in their entire medical arsenal. The only way they could think of to stop the spread of the plague was to eliminate any sources. Immolation is one of the few ways you can kill a vamp and hopefully destroy any remnants of Gomorrah."

I didn't say anything, but I knew she was right. In school we'd learned about the panic that had engulfed the world as the plague had spread. The history books were full of anecdotes from survivors, but most had been about the heroism and courage of the Immunes. Details were scarce when it came to the vamp side of things. I looked around the tunnel and imagined the screaming and the smell as the flames had swept through the bodies that had been packed in here. It made my skin crawl.

"You know, they razed entire towns and villages," Isabelle continued. She spoke conversationally, as if she were talking about the weather. "Burnt them right into the ground till there wasn't a single blade of grass left. It was literally a scorched-earth policy."

I shuddered. "And it still didn't work."

She shrugged. "Depends on how you look at it, I guess. Prevented hundreds of millions of vamps from being spawned." She grinned at me. "That was a good thing."

I stared at the bones littering the ruin of the subway station and realized how lucky I was not to have lived through those times. I couldn't begin to imagine what it must have been like to watch the world descend into darkness. How had people kept sane in the midst of that terror and chaos? How had they lived with the things they'd been forced to do in order to survive? How had they even done them in the first place?

Isabelle seemed to read my mind. "I wouldn't be too hard on them, kid. You wouldn't even exist if those people hadn't done the things they did to save what little of humanity they could."

"I guess."

She eyed me curiously. "You're an odd one, you know that? I never knew anyone back in Haven who gave a hoot about vamps."

Your sister, I thought to say to her. *My mother.* But I didn't. Instead, I just walked on in silence.

Isabelle hadn't being kidding about the rats, I soon realized. As we jumped down onto the tracks, I could hear what sounded like thousands of them scurrying away. And when I directed the beam of my flashlight around the tunnel, I wished I hadn't. I caught glimpses of them, and they were enormous — all the more so thanks to the way the light made their shadows expand and leap up the walls.

"They helped, you know," Isabelle said abruptly, aiming her light at a group of the vermin. "Gomorrah was initially an airborne disease, but the rats helped spread it. They brought it here. The rats and the bloody fleas. Dispersed it everywhere in the world: Australia, Africa, Asia, the Americas, Iceland, you name it. Just weeks after the outbreak in Europe. No justice either. Stupid virus doesn't affect rodents."

"You think they still have it?"

"Of course they do. It's everywhere. But what are you worried about? You're an Immune."

"So were you, once," I pointed out.

Isabelle shook her head. "There's no chance of you being like me, kid. Cherkov made me what I am, and there was nothing natural about that. As long as you're healthy, they could pump you full of Gomorrah, and it wouldn't make one bit of difference."

We were silent a moment or two after that, moving steadily forward through the tunnel until finally I had to ask. "What was it like?"

"What was what like?"

"You know. Becoming —" I felt myself flush and realized that maybe I shouldn't have brought it up; maybe I was overstepping my bounds. How could it not be a sensitive topic with her?

"You mean changing? Becoming a vamp?"

I nodded.

Isabelle didn't say anything for a long time. Finally she spoke: "Painful. Terrifying. And then there were the dreams . . ."

"Dreams?" I said. "About what?"

"Ever read a book called *No Haven for Darkness*?"

"Yes." I eyed her curiously, recalling the copy on her nightstand and wondering what the hell that had to do with the whole transformation thing.

"That's what I saw in my dreams," she explained.

"Seriously?"

"Well, that or something like it. But here's the kicker — that damn book wasn't written until years *after* I'd changed. I'll tell you, old Cherkov was really interested in what I saw. And I wasn't the only one. There was this other boy, Jason, who experienced the same thing. *Exactly* the same thing. We talked about it a lot while we were in the hospital."

"You both had the same dreams?"

She nodded. "Yeah, I know. Weird, huh? I mean, what the hell was that all about?"

I didn't answer.

"It was bizarre, but it felt so damn real." Isabelle was quiet for a moment. "And I'll tell you, I wish I'd never woken up from it."

"What happened to him? The boy, I mean."

"Jason?" She shrugged indifferently. "He's around. Val managed to save him, but he never . . ." She grimaced. "Jason just never really accepted the whole vampire thing. He's obsessed with the place we saw in our dreams and some girl he saw in them."

"But it was just a dream," I said.

"That's what I tell myself. But maybe it wasn't. It was so real . . ." Isabelle paused, smiled grimly, and glanced at me. "When I woke up from it, I thought this was the nightmare. Sometimes I'm not sure it isn't."

She was tight-lipped from then on, marching purposefully forward while I struggled to keep up. The rats scampered away from us, the furry little beasts retreating into the shadows or bolting down their holes whenever our lights swept over them.

It was sometime later that I heard the music. At first it was so faint that I thought I was imagining it. As we neared a sharp bend in the tunnel, however, it grew louder and louder until at last we stepped around the corner, and the noise became distinguishable as some sort of primal beat. Like African drums or something.

"La Sang Rouge," said Isabelle.

Up ahead I could see a station platform lit up like a Christmas tree, some of the lights pulsing to the sound of the music. The silhouettes of vamps were visible, moving against the bright spots, the dance of shadows indicating still others farther back. There must have been at least two or three hundred, possibly more. Although Isabelle was beside me and showed no hint of trepidation, I found myself on edge.

"Who are they?" I asked in a low voice.

"Friends," she replied. "And you needn't be so frightened — they're not Nazis."

"They're going to help us?"

"Them?" She laughed. "Most of them are just here for a good time. But you can usually count on a few rebels being about."

I glanced at her but couldn't see the expression on her face.

"Switch off your light," she commanded, turning off her own.

"But —" I started to protest

Isabelle grabbed the flashlight, extinguishing the beam. I stumbled almost immediately and reached out reflexively, my hand falling onto her shoulder.

"Sorry," I said.

She grunted and shook her head. "You're such a human," she muttered as she stuffed the flashlights back into her pack. "It's going to get rougher ahead, and if you're not careful you're going to get yourself killed."

I felt my cheeks burn. She really did make me feel like a kid.

"Come on," Isabelle said. She grabbed my hand and pulled me after her, heading at a brisk pace toward the platform. Above it, painted on the moldy crumbling wall of the tunnel in thick red paint, were the words *La Sang Rouge.* The paint itself had dripped in long streaks so that it resembled blood weeping from a wound.

We climbed up onto the platform and entered the jostling crowd of vamps. They were all writhing and twisting, men and women gyrating wildly, as though possessed. Their hands roamed over one another, caressing and stroking; they appeared to be making as much physical contact as possible. I gaped, feeling almost as strangely excited as I was shocked and disgusted.

A vamp carrying a silver tray with what looked like hors d'oeuvres on it wove a path toward us. She paused a meter away, proffered the tray, and smiled encouragingly. Isabelle held up a hand, palm out, and shook it in time with a similar motion of her head. The vamp lifted her brows, gave a little shrug, and moved on.

As she passed I studied the contents of the tray. "Cheese and crackers?" I said to Isabelle, bewildered. I had to shout to be heard above the music. "I thought vamps couldn't eat."

"These ones can," Isabelle said as others gladly took up what the vamp with the tray was offering. "They're like me. Cherkov's failures. But we —" She seemed to stop herself.

"Yes?" I prodded her with a look.

"It's like booze for us." She was clearly trying hard to be blasé, but if she could have blushed, I think she would have.

I blinked.

Isabelle averted her eyes and hemmed and hawed before finally blurting out, "We get a buzz eating food, okay? As long as it's only a little. A lot would kill us. Satisfied?"

I was still trying to process the idea of vamps getting as high as a kite on cheese and crackers when she pulled me deeper into the crowd. I staggered after her, thinking to myself that there was a lot more to vamps than I'd ever imagined.

"Yellow Hair!" someone hollered from the vicinity of what I took to be a bar. Isabelle's head immediately swiveled, and we started moving in that direction.

"Yellow Hair?" I looked to Isabelle, my faint smile a question mark.

"We don't use our real names," Isabelle said, as though it were obvious. "It's one of the rules, just in case one of us gets picked up by Müller and company."

"They do that?"

"Honestly, you've got to stop thinking like a Havenite. The Gestapo is the final authority on *everything* here. Even the Nazi governor appointed by Berlin is subservient to the chief of the Gestapo in New York."

As we approached the bar, a large vampire with a shock of silver hair painting a line through his dark mane rose from his stool and held wide his arms in greeting. "Welcome," he said.

Isabelle went to him, and I watched as the two embraced, the bear of a man engulfing her and raising her off her feet as though she were a small child.

"Silver Lock," she said, smiling warmly as he put her down. "How are things?"

He made a face and shook his head. "Rotten as ever," he replied in a thick Slavic accent. English was clearly not his native tongue. "Damned Gestapo and SS is making life difficult."

"Tell me about it."

He looked past her to me, and I shrank slightly from his scrutiny. "Is this the one, then?" he asked, lifting a hand in my direction. "The human? Valentine's pet?"

"Yeah," Isabelle said, pivoting to face me.

Silver Lock approached, eyeballing me as though I were some sort of sculpture. I tensed as he leaned closer, grateful that the pounding beat of the music masked the equally booming beats of my heart. Who knew how the other vamps might react if they heard that and twigged to my true identity?

Towering over me, Silver Lock closed his eyes and seemed to inhale, nostrils flaring. After he'd repeated this, he stepped back abruptly, a frown beetling his brow. He glanced at Isabelle and quirked an eyebrow. She spread her hands, as though to say, "Don't ask me."

"What was that all about?" I asked, stepping closer to her. I wanted to put as much distance between me and the other vamps as possible.

"Nothing," said Isabelle, but the way she said it implied otherwise.

"Drink?" Silver Lock offered, holding up his glass. In the flashing light it was impossible to tell what was in it, but I was pretty sure I knew.

Isabelle nodded, and the big vamp turned to the bartender, yelling something I couldn't hear over the pulsating music. I glanced back at the crowd on the platform, rather embarrassed that I found them so fascinating. I'd never seen anything so uninhibited in my life; there was certainly nothing in Haven that even remotely compared. The Mrs. Hassans of our world would make sure there never was.

"You are still wanting to smuggle cargo?" Silver Lock asked as he handed Isabelle and me each a tall glass of something.

I raised my drink toward my nose to sniff it; I was positive I'd know what it was just by the scent. But Isabelle discreetly put her hand on my arm and pushed it down, giving me a sidelong look and an almost imperceptible shake of her head. That answered that. When Silver Lock wasn't looking, I gave the drink to a passing vamp, who glanced at me, puzzled, then smiled and lifted the glass in a salute as she flounced her way into the crowd.

"We're still interested," Isabelle said in answer to Silver Lock's question.

He chugged his drink and swept the back of his hand across his lips. "Is dangerous," he said. "Why you want to do it this way? Airship is easier."

"It's Valentine's idea," she said, which was only partially true. "And anyway, airships will have far too many Nazis watching them.

Not to mention they're technically Third Reich territory. That's not the case with Haven ships, and there's little chance of the Gestapo being on one of those."

He eyed her warily.

"So can you get us in?"

"Surely," he said, nodding.

While Isabelle was sipping at her drink, I jumped in, driven by the same impetuosity that had got me into this mess in the first place. "Do you know anything about the cargo that comes off the ships from Haven?" I asked.

Silver Lock leapt back as a mouthful of drink spewed from Isabelle's mouth. She shot me a dirty look as she wiped at her lips and chin, but I ignored her, eyes fixed on the big vamp who was now staring at me, bemused.

"Why you interested in that?" he asked.

I shrugged, trying to seem nonchalant. "I'd like to know what the cargo is."

"This is very dangerous thing you are wanting. Whatever cargo is, is big secret. The Nazis are — how you say? — guarding like crown jewels, no?" He grinned.

"Most of what comes into New York on Haven cargo ships is listed as refrigerator units," I told him.

"Refrigerator units?" Silver Lock scratched his head. "How you know this?"

"I've seen manifests," I replied. Isabelle elbowed me in the ribs before I could elaborate.

"Is strange. Why would Nazis need these things? Can make in Berlin, surely."

"I don't know. That's what I ne—" I broke off, thought better of what I was going to say, and started again. "That's what I want to find out."

"Why?" He gave me a probing look.

I glanced at Isabelle.

"Valentine thinks the information may be useful for the rebellion," she lied.

"I'm wondering if maybe they contain blood," I added quickly. "Human blood — the normal kind. Not Immune."

Silver Lock looked surprised for a moment. "Hmmm." He stroked his chin pensively, then shook his head. "Does not make sense. Is not enough."

"What?" I frowned. "What do you mean? If it's just a luxury item —"

"Luxury?" He stared at me bewildered, then turned to Isabelle, frowning at her.

Isabelle tried to intervene, but Silver Lock swept La Sang Rouge with his large dark eyes, then fixed them on me again. "But is not luxury. All are dependent upon it."

My mouth dropped open. I wasn't sure I'd understood him, but before I could say anything else, Isabelle thrust her glass at him and said, "How about another?"

He shifted his attention from me to her, his face breaking into a broad grin. "For you, anything, darling." He pronounced it "dahlink."

As he turned back to the bar and engaged the bartender, Isabelle grabbed me by the arm and hauled me over to a concrete column where we were somewhat shielded from the music's rumbling bass.

"What the devil are you playing at?" she yelled in my ear. Her face was livid.

"I came here for answers."

"Are you looking to get yourself killed?"

"If they can smuggle me onto a ship surely they can get me in to see the cargo."

"That's not what we're here for. Valentine —"

"Val's not here!" I glared at her. "And I have to find out what's going on. The people behind this killed my father. They killed

Grace. And they were trying to kill me. If I can find out why, maybe I can stop them."

Isabelle shook her head. "You don't know what you're doing." But I could see her resolve breaking down.

"Why would vamps need human blood?" I asked. "Val never said anything about it."

"Oh, for crying out loud! Of course he wouldn't, you ninny." She looked heavenward, closed her eyes for a moment, and seemed to struggle to restrain herself.

When she finally turned back to me she said, "Look, mostly we drink animal blood, but it's not enough. There's something in human blood . . . it's like an essential vitamin or whatever. You know? Like vitamin C for you Immunes. If you didn't get enough you'd get scurvy and eventually you'd die. It's the same with vamps and human blood. They — *we* — don't need much, a thimbleful every now and then. But if we don't get it . . ." Isabelle went silent, bit at her lip, and dropped her gaze.

I waited, watching her, noting the play of emotions across her face.

"If we don't get it," she said at last, "we just sort of start shutting down. If we go too long without it, then we sort of die. The vamp equivalent of dying, anyway."

"All of you?" I said.

"Yes. *All* of us, Sophie. Even Val."

I staggered back a pace, reeling. I could barely contain my revulsion. I kept thinking of all those occasions I'd sat with Val when he'd been drinking blood. Those times when he'd knocked back a shot glass of the stuff, like it was some sort of after-dinner liqueur. How often had that been human blood? I was dizzy and confused and had to lean against the column for support. All around me the world seemed to be whirling about, faster and faster.

Concentrate, I told myself. I had to focus on why I was here and what I needed to know.

"So what, then?" I said, voice trembling. "The Nazis dole the stuff out like some sort of monthly allotment?"

"Sort of," Isabelle admitted. "It's another way of controlling the population."

"But . . ." I thought of the theory I'd concocted about the stillborn babies, about how blood might be coming from them. But that didn't add up. Even if there were thousands of babies a year to draw from and you drained every last drop from their bodies, it would be nowhere near enough to supply two hundred million vamps.

"They can't be getting it all in shipments from Haven," I said aloud, more to myself than Isabelle. She looked at me as though she didn't really understand what I was talking about. "Silver Lock's right about that. You'd have to fill the hold of every cargo ship in Haven practically every trip to feed two hundred million vamps, even if it was just a sip or two a month. But where would the Nazis be getting the blood if they don't get it from us?"

"I have no idea," said Isabelle. "They told us they'd found a way of synthesizing it."

"And you believed them?" I asked in astonishment.

She stared at the ground for a moment. "I wanted to." She looked up, visibly conflicted. "I just tried not to think about it."

"But . . . I mean, coming from where you came from . . ." I hesitated, not sure what to feel. Contempt? Disgust? Sympathy? "You had to wonder."

"You don't understand!" Isabelle looked distraught. "It's like being a junkie who needs a fix. You don't ask, and they don't tell. All that matters is that you get it."

"But you had to wonder," I said again, thrusting the words at her like an accusation.

Isabelle's jaw clenched, and she studied the floor. "Yes! Of course I did!" She lifted her eyes and glared up at me again. "Satisfied?"

I didn't answer.

"I didn't care," she went on. "Without it . . ." She struggled for words. "It's not like we have a choice, Sophie."

I stood there speechless for a minute or two, struggling with what I knew, realizing that being upset with Isabelle wouldn't get me anywhere. I needed her, and I told myself that if I'd been in her shoes, I'd probably have done the same.

"I have to see that cargo," I said at last, pleading with her. "Now, more than ever. I have to, Izzy."

Her eyes widened, and her face rippled with emotion, sadness passing across it like a shadow. I saw her lips moving but could barely make out more than a syllable or two over the thumping music.

I kept watching her, a sinking feeling in my gut. I must have offended her, I realized, wondering if I'd well and truly put my foot in it now. "What did you say?" I shouted.

She looked straight at me, and if vamps could cry, I'm sure she would have. "No one has called me Izzy since I left Haven," she said, loud enough for me to make out the words this time.

I waited, nerves beginning to fray, anticipating some sort of explosion.

"Okay," she finally said, lifting her head. A lopsided grin turned up the corners of her lips. "Val will kill me if he finds out, but to hell with him. I'll help you."

I reacted instinctively, throwing my arms around her and hugging her tightly. For a moment she was stiff, resistant, but then she relaxed and put her arms around me, squeezing me back. Suddenly it was as though the wall that had been between us just fell away.

When Silver Lock came back, Isabelle took him aside. There was a lot of gesturing and his eyebrows climbed higher and higher on his forehead, like two furry caterpillars inching up a tree. He kept looking my way, more and more incredulous, until finally they finished, and the two of them came over.

"I have contact," he said. "Girl in train station. That is where Nazis are taking cargo from ships. Is best place to see cargo before they are shipping it. Contact is knowing station and trains."

"How long?" asked Isabelle.

"You are in hurry?"

She gave him a pointed look. "Müller is looking for her."

The two caterpillars shot up again. "Really?" Silver Lock spat in disgust and grunted what I was sure was a swear word in another language. "Is bad news, Yellow Hair. Much trouble. Much trouble."

"Yeah, tell me about it. He seems to have a particular interest in her," she added, eyes darting in my direction.

I thought of Havershaw and Val and how they'd both remarked that trouble had a way of finding me. It certainly did.

CHAPTER 28
GRAND CENTRAL

Although I had seen Grand Central Terminal in the movies, I never thought I'd see it in real life. But the following afternoon, late in the day, the three of us made our way over to the station. The shadows were deep in the city, the sun long since lost behind the thicket of concrete spires surrounding us. The traffic was beginning to increase as vamps took to the streets to begin their nightly routines, and we were largely lost in the anonymity of the masses.

We headed along 42nd Street, crossed Park Avenue, and stopped in front of the train terminal. It was an ornate building, dating back to before World War I. Statues of Mercury, Minerva, and Hercules adorned the exterior pediment, surrounding a large clock with a Tiffany glass face which showed the time as 6:45 p.m.

"This is where we go our separate ways," Isabelle said. She clasped hands with Silver Lock, who grinned broadly.

"Good luck," he said. "We keep eye on you. If trouble —" He held up a battered leather case which I knew contained several pounds of explosive. Enough to do some nasty damage — which he seemed inordinately pleased about.

"Hopefully it won't come to that," said Isabelle. "But if it does," she added, with a look of stern reproach, "try not to blow up the whole bloody station. Please."

She took my hand and led me inside. I gasped as I saw the interior for the first time. It was larger than I'd ever imagined it — larger than anything in Haven. I looked up, stunned by the ceiling high overhead, a representation of the constellations as they'd normally be seen in the night sky. The stars and figures were done in gilt, making them stand out against the darker background. The effect was riveting, and I felt myself swallowed up by the vast volume of literal and figurative space.

"Don't gawk," Isabelle hissed, tugging on my hand and pulling me after her. "You're a vamp now; you don't want to look like a ruddy tourist."

"Right, sorry," I said. And I hustled to match her pace, even though I sorely wished I had more time to absorb it all.

We started across the concourse, and it was then I spied them — the student group from Haeden. I recognized Harry Trager front and center. I swore under my breath, and Isabelle glanced at me, eyebrows pinched together in a tight frown.

"I know them," I whispered, pointing with my chin.

She looked toward Harry and his friends. "The Immunes?"

"Yes." I ducked behind Isabelle, trying to make myself small.

Harry and the guys were ogling the vamp women, most of whom ignored them. A few seemed mildly amused and actually reached out as they walked past, touching the young men's faces, stroking their cheeks, trailing long-nailed fingers along clean-shaven chins, and giggling seductively as they strode off in a rhythm of tightly clad hips. The students' minder, a dour-faced Nazi, didn't even crack a smile. He appeared bored, as though he'd seen it all a thousand times before. He probably had.

"Just act natural," Isabelle said as Harry and his posse approached.

I wanted to ask her what "natural" was since I wasn't a vamp, but it was too late — Harry and the other Haeden students were striding past us in the opposite direction. As we came abreast of one another, Harry's eyes met mine, initially with the same leer he'd used on the vamp women. But rather than moving on, he kept staring at me, looking puzzled, and nudged one of the other men.

I quickly turned away, facing forward, and walked beside Isabelle as casually as I could. Twenty pairs of eyes were focused on my back, and I was sure that at any moment Harry or one of the others was going to shout out my name.

We were moving faster now, headed toward a structure in the center of the concourse. It was some sort of information booth surrounding a pagoda-like tower, the latter crowned by a four-faced brass clock. The entire arrangement was dwarfed by the immensity of the building in which it resided. I glanced at the time as we approached and noted it was closing in on seven o'clock. According to what Isabelle had told me earlier, that was when the station began to reach its peak traffic cycle.

I had the sense she was a lot more anxious about this whole affair than she'd let on, which did nothing to ease my feelings of insecurity. But as fearful and self-conscious as I was, none of the vamps seemed to pay us any attention. My only immediate concern was the Haeden group. I glanced quickly back over my shoulder; they were still watching us.

We were close to the information booth, on our way to the lower levels where the train platforms were, when a shrill whistle cut through the hubbub of the crowd. Beside me Isabelle froze.

"What is it?" I asked.

"Gestapo," she said through her teeth.

I glanced around, back toward the entrance, and spotted a group of men in black uniforms — Colonel Müller in the lead. Harry and the rest of the Haeden gang, having been led aside by their minder, gaped at the Gestapo goons as though this were all a thrilling sideshow put on for their benefit.

"What do we do?" I hissed at Isabelle, wishing I could disappear.

"Just stay calm. They may not be looking for us. They're always conducting searches, just to stir up fear in the population. Lets everyone know who's in charge. As long as we don't panic we should be fine. Nobody else has picked up on you."

"What about Harry?" I asked, darting a look in his direction.

"Those kids?" Isabelle glanced their way.

I nodded anxiously.

"If they've got any sense they'll keep their traps shut."

"What about Müller?" I said. "He'll recognize me."

"You're a vamp, remember? He's looking for a young Haven woman. You're not her. Not anymore."

I gulped, more than a little unnerved and completely lacking the confidence Isabelle seemed to have in my masquerade. "What are the wolves for?" I asked in a strained voice as more men appeared, this time led by a half dozen of the beasts.

"Uh-oh," Isabelle said as she caught sight of them.

I looked at her wildly. "What?"

"That's not their usual procedure," she explained. "The Nazis generally reserve the wolves for hunting."

"Hunting?" A lump formed in my throat. "Hunting what?"

"Vamps, of course. You really can't beat wolves when it comes to that. They track you by smell, then take you down. Fast. Efficient. Lethal."

"But I should be all right," I said. "I mean, if they're not tracking humans . . ."

Isabelle gave me an odd look. "He didn't tell you?"

I frowned at her. "Who didn't tell me what?"

"Val. He didn't tell you that you smell kind of like us?"

I blinked at her, dumbfounded.

"You don't smell *human*, Sophie."

My whole body went cold as I thought of that conversation, now so long ago, when Val had told me my scent was intoxicating. Was this what he'd actually meant? I almost swore, but bit back the word.

"Honestly, I thought you must have known," she said. "It's so obvious to us."

"He said I was *different*; he didn't say I smelt like a vamp!"

Isabelle just shrugged.

"That's crazy," I said. But I thought of the night before at La Sang Rouge, of Silver Lock sniffing me and clearly not knowing what to make of me. And then there was Clauswitz telling me I was special, and the vamp crew of the *Eva Braun* acting as though I were. Had that all been connected to the way . . . to the way I smelt?

Jesus! I thought.

My stomach knotted. This had to have something to do with my mother's pregnancy. It hadn't only changed *her*. Just as I'd feared, it had somehow changed me as well. All my earlier concerns reared their ugly heads. Until now, I'd consciously been avoiding the subject, but now there was undeniable evidence I wasn't what I'd always believed myself to be. It was hard to just shrug it off and carry on as though it were incidental.

Glancing over at Harry, I recalled the remarks he'd made during that infamous dinner on the airship, describing me as "positively vampish." Had he been subconsciously picking up on ways in which I was different? Things about me that set me apart, which I had simply ignored or brushed off in the past — or hadn't even been conscious of myself?

But I wasn't a vamp. I didn't have vamp traits. I had a beating heart. I was aging. I needed to breathe air. I needed to eat. I didn't bubble up and turn to ash in sunlight. A crucifix wasn't going to send me into paroxysms of terror and burn me if I touched it. And if I got hurt, I didn't heal in a matter of seconds.

My heart skipped a beat. Maybe I didn't heal in *seconds*, but I had always healed quickly. I thought back to the cuts on my feet from the glass of my broken flat window; they'd mended overnight. And the bullet wound I'd suffered while driving on Coast Road with Havershaw had taken no more than a couple of days.

And then there was what Havershaw had said about my athletic record. I'd never given it much thought before because I'd always been stronger and faster than all the girls I'd ever known — most of the boys, too. Natural talent, I'd assumed. Using the gifts nature had given me. Except maybe that wasn't the case at all. Maybe it had all come from somewhere else.

I reeled back, struck by an overpowering dread. It was a sick feeling that started in the pit of my stomach and crawled up into my chest. I was finding it difficult to breathe. *What the hell am I?* I wondered. Then it dawned on me. *Oh, God! Jesus . . . Val must have known all along.* Could that have been what had attracted him to me in the first place? *You should have told me, Val. God damn you! You should have told me*, I thought. But then I realized something. *He didn't tell you because he didn't want you to know the truth.*

But was that to protect me?

I felt Isabelle's reassuring hand on my arm. "Take it easy," she said gently — though I don't think she had any idea what was going on inside my head. Regardless, she was right. This was no time for hysterics.

I took a breath, then another, and forced a calm, trying to focus on the here and now. That was all that mattered at the moment. The rest could wait. "What about Müller?" I asked. "Wouldn't he have picked up on my scent? On the fact that I'm . . . *different*."

Isabelle nodded. "No question. Maybe that's why they're so interested in you."

I ignored what that implied. "But if I don't smell human, how can he be tracking just me? Shouldn't I just blend in with the crowd?"

"They must have your specific scent. Probably from your luggage. Anything you'd worn would be enough."

"Oh, that's just swell! Anything else you want to dump on me, Izzy?"

"We'll get out of this," she promised.

"How?"

"We still have Silver Lock."

Müller and his entourage of soldiers and wolves were moving deeper into the concourse now. Vampires hurried away in all directions, creating a chaotic frenzy into which the colonel and his party waded. I felt Isabelle's hand tighten around mine and knew she'd seen it, too. I expected a change of plans, but instead we kept pushing through the crowd.

By the time we reached the information booth, we could scarcely maneuver because of the mob around us. I was afraid I was going to become separated from Isabelle as the vamps nearby grew more and more agitated and pressed in around me.

"We have to get out of here," Isabelle whispered in my ear.

"No kidding," I muttered. But I couldn't see any means of escape. We were pressed right up against the wall of the booth, wood and glass panels preventing further retreat. Everyone in the terminal had stopped moving, a low murmur rising as Müller and his terror squad thrust deeper into the masses. I looked at Isabelle and saw her eyes darting in all directions, seeking a getaway route.

Beyond the closest vamps, I could see Müller heading almost straight for us. It was only a matter of time before he spotted and recognized me.

Vamps parted in front of me, drawing back as a wolf padded into the newly cleared space. It sniffed the air in a predatory manner, turning its head this way and that, ears twitching, teeth bared. There was nothing I could do. The animal kept probing the air with its snout, edging closer and closer to me with each noisy snort. Thirty or forty feet back, a soldier stepped in its wake, a formidable looking weapon in his hands.

If Isabelle hadn't been a vamp I'd likely have crushed her fingers as my grasp on her hand tightened. My heart was throbbing, and I could hear the blood rushing in my head. I was afraid I was going to shake myself to pieces.

The wolf came to a standstill right in front of me and nudged its wet nose against my knee, sniffing loudly. I felt its hot wet breath and stopped breathing.

This is it, I thought. I tried not to look at it, tried not to think about it. But the pounding ache in my chest was unbearable, and the air around me seemed to have grown too thin to breathe. I felt faint and wanted to lie down before I fell.

I looked ahead and saw Müller. He still hadn't seen me. I closed my eyes for a moment and held my breath, waiting for the inevitable.

"Sophie!" Harry shouted.

Müller went ramrod straight. He was looking at Harry, and Harry was looking at me, and I was trying to pretend I didn't see either of them. Müller turned slowly, his hand going to the gun in the black leather holster at his waist. His eyes met mine and went from icy blue to black as a triumphant grin spread across his face. He started to shout something to the soldiers beside him, and then in an instant, the world disintegrated into madness.

KA-BOOM!

The blast hit me like a sledgehammer and knocked me off my feet. People were tossed through the air like dolls. Isabelle fell to the floor beside me, and to the left I saw a flash and a ball of flame opening out into the concourse, an enormous flower unfolding to sunlight.

Around us, the windows erupted in geysers of glass, hurling inward to the vast hollow of the terminal. One of the enormous chandeliers was torn loose by the shockwave and plunged earthward, crashing to the marble floor and shattering, filling the air with a fountain of debris. Suddenly the whole place was a riot as thousands of vamps scrambled for the exits.

I lay there stunned, covered in bits of rubble, my ears ringing. It took a few seconds for my hearing to clear enough for me to make sense of the panic that boomed in the cavernous interior of Grand Central. When I sat up I caught sight of a bloodied Müller picking himself off the ground and shouting orders. The wolves — those that weren't lying on the floor in broken heaps — were howling and snapping. The armed soldiers were trying to hold their ground as the station descended into utter mayhem.

"This way!" someone shouted from nearby.

I looked up and saw a vamp on the other side of the information booth counter. She gestured with urgency, and the next thing I knew Isabelle was climbing up over the counter and dragging me after her. I fell inside the booth and sat there, dazed, as concrete dust drifted down around us. Something trickled down the side of my face. I reached up and touched my forehead tentatively, wincing at the pain. When I drew my hand back, my trembling fingertips came away covered in blood. Carefully exploring the rest of my face, I realized I hadn't escaped the flying glass and other debris. Across from me, Isabelle sat with a long shard of metal sticking out her left forearm.

"Are . . . are you okay?" I asked.

She looked down, seemed to notice the shrapnel in her arm for the first time, and swore. "Dammit, Silver Lock," she said under her breath. "I just wanted a small diversion, not half the goddamn station blown up."

Without so much as an exclamation of pain, Isabelle grasped the offending shard in her right hand and pulled it out, chucking it aside with an air of mild irritation. It was an unsettling sight: thick, gooey blood oozed out from a large hole at least the diameter of my thumb. But even as I watched, the flow was stanched, diminishing to a trickle as the wound began to heal.

"Come on," said the young vamp who had offered us shelter. As shouts and screams continued to echo in the terminal, she led us to a hidden door in the pagoda beneath the clock. We went through it and climbed down a spiral staircase that led into another information booth serving the lower level concourse. The turmoil above was mirrored below, but our guide managed to steer us clear of the worst of it, leading us effortlessly to the lower level tracks.

"Who are you?" Isabelle demanded.

"Ticket," the young vamp replied.

"What?"

"My nickname," she said in a lilting, little-girl voice that carried the trace of a German accent. She looked to be about sixteen, but for all I knew, she could have been eighty. "They call me Ticket because I used to work the ticket booths before they moved me to information."

"Who are you with?" Isabelle asked, eyeing the vamp suspiciously.

"Hell's Kitchen. Silver Lock sent word."

Isabelle seemed to relax a bit, but a hint of wariness still remained in her eyes. "You know what we want?" she asked.

The girl shot us a vaporous grin, practically gone before it even registered. "The cargo from Haven, right? We were told you wanted to see what they're shipping north." Ticket looked the two of us up and down, and added, "What's so important about it, anyway?"

"That's what we're here to find out," Isabelle said.

"The Jacks sure seem bent on making sure no one does."

"The Jacks?" I shot a query Isabelle's way.

"The Gestapo," she explained. "Because of the jackboots they wear."

I grabbed her arm and pulled her close to me. "Can we trust her?" I whispered.

"Hell if I know. But Silver Lock does, so that's good enough for me."

Ticket glanced back at us, poker-faced. "You don't have to worry about me," she said, rolling up the sleeve of her jacket to expose her left forearm. A line of numbers was tattooed on her white skin. "There's no love lost between me and Hitler's thugs."

I puzzled over the tattoo and swapped looks with Isabelle. "Auschwitz," she said, visibly subdued.

My eyes nearly popped out of my head. "You're a Jew?" I said to Ticket.

"Yes."

"But how? I thought the Nazis hunted you all down." Except for the handful who'd made it to Haven.

"They did their best, but some of us got lucky — if you can call it that." Ticket's expression sobered, and she chuckled sardonically. "The plague swept through the inmates at Auschwitz faster than the Nazis guarding the place because our immune systems were already compromised. Of course, many died of the virus outright, but those of us who became vampires easily overwhelmed the guards."

"And you managed to stay hidden all these years," I said, astonished.

"With help."

"What does this all mean for you?" I asked. "Are you just in it for revenge?"

"Isn't that enough?" Ticket tilted her head to one side, eyeing me curiously. "Wouldn't you do the same if you'd seen your entire family gassed to death?"

There was a look in her eyes I'd never seen before, so haunted and full of guilt and sorrow and every conceivable measure of despair. But more than that, there was an unrestrained hatred that made me recoil. Not even Havenites despised the Nazis *that* much.

"We need to find where they store the cargo going out of the city on a train," Isabelle told Ticket as we trotted after her.

"Well, you're in luck. The Nazis have just restarted shipping cargo from here. Freighters from Haven come into New York six months a year, and there's only one train that ever carries their cargo."

"Where do they go the other six months?" I asked.

Ticket shrugged. "I don't know. Heard rumors of someplace down in the Antarctic where they send the stuff from April through September."

"The Antarctic? Why?"

Ticket lifted her hands. "I've no idea."

"What about the train?" Isabelle said.

"It leaves on a regular schedule every week — always loaded up with shipments and always on time," Ticket replied. "The Nazis built a track that runs straight out of the city. The train must be going quite a ways, too. The engine is always fully fueled, and it doesn't return until the day before it's due to depart again. And it's always carrying the same thing: a few large metal containers with some sort of machinery attached to them and a small number of boxes and crates."

"What's in them?" I asked.

Ticket shook her head and rolled her shoulders. "I don't have a clue, but it must be valuable, because the Nazis guard it like it was gold or something. That has to be what you're looking for."

"Sounds like it," Isabelle agreed.

"You'll never get near that train, though," Ticket said. "Probably the only thing with more protection is Hitler himself."

"We just need to see the cargo," I said.

"They keep that locked up and guarded until they load it. It won't be easy."

"But you have a way."

"If you don't mind getting a little dirty," Ticket said with a laugh. "I know this place better than almost anyone."

"Then let's go."

She led us to a door that opened onto a labyrinth of maintenance corridors and access tunnels and forged ahead, never hesitating. A few minutes later, we were climbing through an air duct barely large enough for us to slither through.

"How long have the Nazis been doing this?" Isabelle asked.

"Shipping cargo north?"

"Yeah."

"Decades," Ticket said in a quiet voice as we squirmed our way through what seemed like a century of dust. "It's always been the same routine — ships from Haven dock at the pier, offload their cargo, and a while later it appears here. Like clockwork."

"For decades?" I whispered. "So this has been going on ever since the truce was signed?"

"Pretty much," she said.

Why on earth were the Nazis shipping stuff up north? I wondered. I had to be missing something here. The odd thing was, in the back of my mind, I was certain I had the vital clue, that it was something I'd seen or read or heard. I just had to think. I just had to lay out all the evidence, and then I'd be able to assemble a picture of the sort of transaction taking place between Haven and the Third Reich.

One thing I was pretty certain about — I wasn't going to like what I found. Nobody buried secrets this deep unless what they had to hide wasn't something they wanted the public to know.

The air duct terminated in a mesh grille. Ticket halted, and behind her I waited. I could hear Isabelle behind me, impatient and edgy, clearly wanting to get on with this and get back to safety as soon as possible.

"The coast is clear," Ticket said, her words shaking me out of my reverie. There was a rattling of metal, and the next thing I knew, she was gone. Isabelle gave me a nudge from behind, and I scrambled out the duct on my hands and knees, crawling into the room beyond.

I got to my feet and stood, dusting myself off as I looked around. We were in a large, dimly lit storage bay that smelt strongly of oil, metal, and engine exhaust. I coughed once or twice. The air was vaguely suffocating — even worse than the fume-choked streets of New York.

Isabelle joined me and gave the room a once-over, her razor-sharp gaze locking on the half dozen pea-green metal containers sitting on the floor. Each one was about fifteen feet high, ten feet wide, and thirty feet long. They were all covered in dents and scratches, as though they'd seen a lot of travel over many years. On top of each was some type of machinery, which emitted a low, steady thrum and filled the entire bay with its mechanical rhythm. It reminded me of the noise made by the compressor on my old refrigerator back home.

Isabelle knelt down and replaced the mesh grille, covering our tracks. As she was doing so, I heard something deep inside the air duct, the sound of movement and maybe even a distant cry. It made me shudder, and I was about to ask her what it was, but Ticket grabbed my hand and pulled me away.

"Come on," she said. "The guards are on the outside. The Jacks are too pinheaded to think anyone would use the air ducts to get in." She looked at us expectantly. "It's perfectly safe. I've been here many times before."

"Why?" Isabelle asked, a thread of distrust filtering into her voice.

"This isn't all they put in here," said Ticket. "Sometimes there's other stuff."

"Other stuff? Like what?"

"Let's just say that whoever is on the receiving end is being well looked after," Ticket told us. "You'd think the Nazis were supplying a town or something with all those little luxuries they ship out of here. Makes for good trade on the black market if you can get your hands on any of it."

Isabelle eyes met mine. "Anything else they store here?" she asked.

Ticket gave another of her patented shrugs. "Sure. All sorts of things. Equipment, mostly."

"What sort of equipment?"

"I don't know. Metal boxes with dials and switches. Lots of glass stuff, like you might see in a lab or something. Some sort of liquid. At least, that's what the containers say."

I locked eyes with Isabelle again and said, "All this security, the secretiveness . . . this has to be big. Really big. Whatever is going on between Haven and the Third Reich, someone is going to a lot of trouble to make sure nobody knows about it."

"Yeah," said Isabelle. "But what could it be? What are they hiding?"

I couldn't answer that. There was definitely more to it than a few gallons of blood. But beyond the blood that might be coming from stillborn babies, I couldn't think of anything produced in Haven that would warrant this level of security.

And then there remained the even bigger unanswered question — where on earth were the Nazis getting the kind of human blood supplies they'd need to provide two hundred million vamps with a regular fix?

I looked toward the green containers. Was it possible the answer was inside those?

As if reading my thoughts, Isabelle wandered deeper into the storage bay, stepping closer to the containers. "What are they?" she wondered aloud, running her hand along the outside of one. She paused, pressed her ear against it, and closed her eyes as she listened.

I followed suit and tried to make sense of what I heard, but it just sounded mechanical to me. There was a lot of chugging and gurgling, as though fluid was being pumped through pipes or something. It could have been just about anything.

Isabelle stepped away from the container and walked slowly around it, surveying it up and down. She paused at one end and said, "It opens here."

I joined her, with Ticket trailing disinterestedly behind me. "They're always locked tighter than a drum," she said.

"Maybe," Isabelle allowed. She stepped back and looked up. "Hold this." She handed me her knapsack.

"What are you going to do?"

"See if I can find another way in." She crouched slightly, and then sprang upwards, leaping easily to the top of the container. It was hard not to be impressed. Isabelle seemed such a slip of a thing, but then I recalled how effortlessly she'd ripped off the door of Müller's limousine. The strongest man in Haven would be a weakling compared to her.

Ticket followed her, leaving me alone on the storage bay floor. "Coming?" she called down, eyeing me expectantly.

"Toss me the bag," said Isabelle.

I threw her the knapsack, and she caught it deftly.

"Can you make it?" she asked.

"I'll need help."

Ticket looked at me oddly, and I wondered for a moment if maybe she hadn't yet twigged to the fact that I was an Immune. There was probably enough noise around to mask my heartbeat, and if I smelled like a vamp and now kind of even resembled one . . . well . . .

No way, I told myself. *I don't have that aura about me.*

Or did I? Somewhere in the back of my mind, I rebelled at the notion. It was just so wrong; it gave me the creeps. I didn't want to think about my mother and Gomorrah and what it all might have done to me . . . what it meant I might be.

I looked up at Ticket again, and her eyes narrowed. If she didn't know now, she'd figure it out soon enough. How would she react when she did? I wasn't sure she cared for humans any more than she did the Jacks. After all, she'd have lived through all the unspeakable horrors Immunes had inflicted on vamps during the war and the spread of the plague.

"Come on," Isabelle said, sounding impatient.

I blew out a breath, closed my eyes, and shook out my hands in preparation.

"What on earth are you doing?" she demanded. "Just jump, for crying out loud."

"Okay. Okay. Give me a break."

"Wait." Isabelle dropped the knapsack, stretched out on top of the container, and extended her arm. "Okay. Try now."

I took a deep breath. Even with help, it was still a fairly big jump. I inhaled deeply again, bent my knees, and uncoiled upward, reaching for Isabelle's open hand. I jumped with far more force than

I'd expected, and she easily grabbed hold of me, taking my weight without so much as a grunt. She swung me up onto the container, and I landed feet first on the cold steel, grimacing from the impact.

Ticket stared at me inquisitively, then looked to Isabelle, who simply ignored her and busied herself inspecting the top of the container. At least a quarter of it was bulky machinery, which, on closer examination, did in fact resemble some sort of refrigeration unit. The whole thing was powered by a small gas engine. That was the source of the exhaust fumes, and standing this close to them, the choking stench was intolerable. Instinctively I cupped a hand over my nose in a futile attempt to filter the air I was breathing.

Ticket studied me again and cocked her head inquisitively. By now she had surely drawn the only logical conclusion. As vamps, she and Isabelle weren't bothered by the fumes. They didn't need to breathe; they only took in air to smell and to fill their lungs so they could speak. You couldn't get much sound out of vocal cords if you're weren't pushing air past them.

Aside from the puttering motors, there was a raised vent atop the container, just large enough for someone to squeeze through it if it were opened. Isabelle knelt next to it and ran her fingers around the edge, then stopped, an elfin grin turning up the corners of her mouth.

"Found something?" I asked.

"It's hinged."

"Can you open it?"

"Does the sun rise?" she retorted. With that, she braced herself, grasped the vent lid with both hands, and tugged hard. A grunt escaped her as she strained against the resistance.

A few seconds later, there was a shriek of tearing metal, and the lid lifted open. A dense white fog fountained upward from the gaping hole, dissipating slowly as it billowed about our feet. Isabelle didn't wait for it to clear; she jumped down through the opening and vanished inside.

I moved to the edge of the hole and looked down. A blast of frigid air hit me, and through the thinning mist, I could see the glow of lights. They were too faint and insubstantial to serve as any sort of illumination. "What can you see?" I called down.

She was slow to respond. "I think you should come look for yourself."

Clinging to the rim of the opening, I swung my legs over and eased myself down into the interior, then let go and dropped. I hit the metal floor with a thump. When I stood up, I found myself surrounded by dozens of electromechanical units identical to the one I'd seen the nurses pushing into the quarantine ward of Mercy General back in Caelo. They were stacked several high and ran in rows down the length of the container. Red and amber lights winked on and off on the control panels affixed to each, casting a spectral glow that shifted and danced in the billowing mist.

"Over here," Isabelle said, a wispy cloud puffing from her mouth as she spoke. She raised a hand to one of the units, pointing to where she'd cleared away the frost that encrusted its glass.

"What is it?" I asked. I flicked on my flashlight and stepped closer, feeling equal measures of curiosity and fear rising within me.

Isabelle's face spoke volumes as she moved aside for me to see. She held the light, and I leaned toward the cleared patch on the glass, cupped my hands and peered inside. And then I just stood there, staring — so stunned I forgot to breathe. The world came crashing to a halt.

Lying unconscious within the glass cylinder was a tiny baby no more than a couple of months old. Its eyes were closed and its chest rose and fell in a glacial motion.

I didn't know what to think. I didn't want to believe what I was seeing, because to believe that was to understand something I didn't want to accept. To believe it was to acknowledge something truly heinous. All sorts of terrible things happened in the war, some of them beyond description. Some of them so appalling that even from the distance of decades they still had the power to shock and shame. But what I was looking at now seemed the most abominable crime of all.

"Do you know what it means?" Isabelle asked in a timid voice.

"Yes," I said, barely able to speak. "I think so. But I wish I didn't."

I moved to another of the cylinders, rubbing at the surface and trying to remove the frost. Eventually I cleared a large enough circle to see within. It was another baby, resting just like the first, with a tube inserted in one nostril and intravenous lines in both arms. It wasn't moving and it scarcely breathed, but it was clearly alive — the dials and lights of the device seemed to bleat and flash confirmation. Heart rate. Respiration. Brain activity.

Brain activity. I stared at it, at the nearly flat lines on the green oscilloscope-like screen. It didn't look right. I recalled the comatose patients in the ward at Mercy. Even their cerebral activity had seemed more substantial than this.

Vegetative. The word popped into my head, and I knew that was what I was looking at. It was the same for all the others I checked as I moved frantically down the line. Finally I stopped, realizing it was fruitless to examine any more. I knew they'd all be the same; they all served the same purpose.

"Does this mean what I think it means?" Isabelle asked. She sounded almost frightened — as if fearful of what I was going to tell her.

I blinked and looked at her. "I think this is the source of all the blood."

"You mean these are non-Immunes?" she said. "How is that possible? Non-Immune babies are always stillborn. These are all clearly alive."

"They've been lying to us," I said. "Right from the beginning." I thought of my mother hearing her son cry. I thought of Fiona Richards and all the other stories my father had gathered.

"Somehow some of the non-Immunes are born alive. This must be what Cherkov created. These machines. They put them in these to keep them from being infected by Gomorrah."

Isabelle looked around, staring at the stacked units, as much horror written on her face as I felt inside of me.

The two of us remained silent, unmoving.

"What do you want to do?" she said at length in a tiny voice.

I stood in the narrow space between the stacks and rows and stared at her. For the first time since I'd met her, Isabelle seemed every bit the fifteen-year-old girl she appeared to be. She sounded lost and afraid and maybe a lot more than that.

"What do I want to do?" I said dully. I shook my head. "I don't know."

What could I do? Someone in Haven was trafficking human beings — and not just any human beings. These were non-Immunes. They were supposed to be dead. They were supposed to have been cremated. That was the way it was *supposed* to work.

This had to be about more than *selling* blood to the Nazis and making a profit. An operation of this magnitude couldn't have gone unnoticed by the Haven government. I was certain the government not only knew about it but was intimately involved. That was what Donovan had been close to discovering when she'd interviewed Uncle Matt. That's what Father must have uncovered — and maybe that had something to do with the letter President Mallory had sent him. It might also explain why Amelia Westerly had been at so many of those births and why she'd been at the hospital the night I'd seen her.

I thought about the truce, about how the Nazis had suddenly capitulated in 1948 and offered up peace, even though they'd had the upper hand — they could've easily wiped out every last one of the Immunes. It made sense, now. They'd needed a source of non-Immune human blood, and they must have known from the concentration camp births in Alberta that Immunes sometimes gave birth to non-Immunes — and that sometimes those non-Immunes weren't stillborn.

Every one of the babies inside this container was a factory producing nontoxic blood. As long as they were kept alive and kept free of the virus, they'd go on producing the stuff until they died a natural death. They were the price we paid for peace.

"So this is it," I said in a low voice. "This is the source of the human blood you all need."

Isabelle said nothing, just stood there, perhaps not able to come to grips with the truth herself. Or maybe she simply refused to believe it. It might be one thing for the vamps who traced their origins back to the Fall to accept this, but Isabelle had been born in Haven. She had a connection to these babies. How must it feel for her to know her continued existence came at such a dreadful cost?

I turned slowly, surveying the nightmare of machinery. How could anyone have ever agreed to this? How could they go on doing it and live with themselves, knowing that peace between Haven and the Third Reich was literally paid in blood?

Anger welled up in me, and tears sprang from my eyes. I wanted to get out of here, out of New York, away from these hordes of Undead. I hated them. They had shattered the beliefs I had in my own people. It was hard not to look at these units with their fragile, innocent contents and not wonder just who the real monsters were — the vamps for taking this blood or the government of Haven for giving it to them?

"Oh, God," I said. I repeated it again and again, shaking and clutching at my head as I stared at the machines.

"Sophie," Isabelle started to say. She stepped toward me, but I quickly backed away.

"Don't," I said. "Don't touch me."

The look in her eyes was heartrending, and I wondered if that's what she'd looked like when she'd been exiled from the world she'd been born into. I hated myself for hurting her, but I just couldn't get past what I knew.

But there was no time for grief or recriminations. Just then a loud clanging rang outside the container, and a second later Ticket lowered herself through the open vent.

"We've got company," she said in a tight voice as she dangled from one arm. She reached up with her free hand and pulled the vent cover back in place, then dropped down between us. With the opening sealed it was darker inside, but the flashlight glow provided enough light to see the worried look in her eyes.

"I think they're going to load the containers on the train," she said in a harsh whisper.

"We've got to get out of here!" I said, my voice pitched high. But the words had barely escaped me when something heavy crashed into the container, sending us sprawling.

"Too late," said Isabelle.

As though to emphasize her words, the container shuddered, then shifted, forcing me to clutch at the nearest support. As I held on tightly to metal piping, the container seemed to rise into the air, then swiveled and jerked forward. Above the constant thrum of the units I could hear an exterior mechanical whine.

"Forklift," Ticket said as she braced against one stack of units.

"We'll have to wait until they load this container on the train," Isabelle said in a hushed tone.

"Are you crazy?" I said, louder than I'd intended. "If we don't get out of here right now we could be trapped."

"We already are," she hissed. "There are almost certainly soldiers out there."

"Then what do we do?"

Isabelle sat down on the floor and leaned back against the machinery. "We wait," she said. "Once they've loaded the containers we can slip out and escape."

I closed my eyes as the metal beneath my feet vibrated, and I imagined myself back home in my comfy bed, safe in my flat. I pictured myself the way I'd been only weeks before, happy and ignorant. How could my life have been turned upside down so quickly?

"They're putting us on the train," Ticket announced. She'd been sitting and listening carefully to the noises outside and now shot a look heavenward as a deafening rattle made me clamp my hands over my ears. It sounded like heavy chains being dragged across the outside of the container.

"They're securing us to one of the cars," Ticket said.

There was a metallic sliding noise, then an earsplitting bang.

"That would be the door on the railcar."

Silence followed, shortly interrupted by a soft pattering overhead — like muffled footsteps.

"What's that?" I asked in a thready whisper, staring at the ceiling.

Ticket shook her head. "Rats, maybe? They're all over the place."

"Awfully big rats," Isabelle said.

A chill ran through me that had nothing to do with the icy temperatures inside. I had a feeling we were being followed — by whom or by what I'd no idea, but I didn't think it was the SS or Gestapo.

"We have to get out of here," I said, stating the obvious again. "Before the train gets underway."

Just then there was a clang of metal on metal that echoed in the distance, and the container was jarred violently. Through the soles of my boots I could feel a steady sequence of vibrations, a rumbling that could mean only one thing — the train was moving.

"Hang on," said Ticket. "We're on our way."

CHAPTER 29

THE TRAIN

There's something to be said for limited horizons.

I don't think I really began to understand the world I lived in until I was five or six years old. Before that time, Haven had been everything — nothing had existed beyond. I'd had no idea there was another, entirely different, world far from the shores of the islands. As a child, the Pacific Ocean, stretching as far as the eye could see, had represented the boundaries of the universe.

I'd never paid any attention to the news back then, so I hadn't really been conscious of the vamps. Hitler and his Nazis were something I'd occasionally picked up on here and there, perhaps in an overheard conversation between my father and Grace or as something mentioned on the television. Vamps, for the most part, were a nebulous notion, generally conjured up around the time of Halloween.

I don't recall how I felt when I first discovered there was more to the world than Haven. It wasn't an epiphany but rather a slow awakening. Eventually that had led to an awareness that there was "us," and there was "them," and we had very little to do with one another.

But despite everything I had been taught about vamps, I'd always been more fascinated by them than I was afraid. I'd never developed the enmity for them that so many in Haven seemed to have. I'm not sure why. Maybe it was just an acceptance of the fact that that was the way the world was. For all the propaganda in our schools and the realities of the Third Reich, I simply couldn't bring myself to view vamps the same way people like Grace — who'd lived through the Fall and had fought against them — did.

And when I fell in love with Val, any fears I might still have had about the world we lived in mostly melted away. I refused to believe that anyplace in which he existed could be bad.

Now I didn't know what to think. Now I was at sea, rudderless and hopelessly lost. My universe had become too big, and what I knew of it too overwhelming. I wanted to be back in those days when I'd been innocent and ignorant, when the dark underbelly of the world had lain unexposed to me. Years ago, when I'd first come upon my mother's journal, Val had warned me that there were some truths better left unknown. Now I understood what he meant. But I wasn't sure I understood much else.

The only thing I knew for certain was that there were monsters in this world. I just didn't know whether it was us or them.

* * *

"It's no use," said Isabelle, dropping back down to the floor of the container. "It won't budge. There's something holding it shut."

She'd been trying for the better part of an hour to pry the cover off the vent, but it was jammed shut. Despite her best efforts, she hadn't been able to budge it. Ticket had tried as well, but to no avail. I hadn't bothered; if neither of them could get it open, I knew I didn't have the slightest hope in hell.

"So we're trapped," I said, trying not to sound as alarmed by the prospect as I felt.

"I suppose so. At least until they offload this stuff."

"And then what?"

Isabelle motioned indifferently. "We'll cross that bridge when we come to it."

"And when will that be?" I asked, annoyed by her cavalier attitude. "In case you've forgotten, I'm not like you. I can't go days without food and water."

Isabelle hefted her knapsack. "In case *you've* forgotten, you were going to be holed up for a few days anyway. I packed some stuff for you — water, some food. There's enough to last you a week if you ration it."

Ticket was looking at the two of us while we talked, her eyebrows knit together in a deepening frown. I knew what was coming next. "What are you?" she demanded, eyeing me warily from the other side of the container. "You mentioned Haven, but you don't seem like one of *them*."

"And yet she is," said Isabelle with casual disregard. "Born and bred on the islands, under the light of a tropical sun." She made it sound like the blurb on one of those posters advertising Coral Beach.

"An Immune!" Ticket's eyes grew huge, and a raft of emotions played across her face. "But she —" She stopped, gaze fixed on me, and studied me even more intently.

"Her mother's like me," Isabelle explained. "At least, like me as far as being born an Immune and changed."

Now Ticket gaped at her. "How is that possible? If you were Immune —"

"I can't tell you the science behind it," Isabelle said. "It's way over my head. Something about critically suppressed immune systems and the like. I got sick, and my illness made me vulnerable to Gomorrah. There were certain protocols in place for when that sort of thing happened. No one had a choice in the matter, so I became part of an experiment. But the result wasn't supposed to be this." She gestured to herself with what bordered on disdain. "At least, not as far as the people who supported the research were led to believe. They thought it was all about finding a cure for Gomorrah. I was supposed to get better . . ." She laughed, though it was bitter and filled with sadness.

I tensed, watching Ticket's reaction. "I've heard of your kind," she said to Isabelle. "I always thought you were a myth."

"Very real, unfortunately."

"And her?" Ticket pointed to me with her chin. "If her mother was changed, then what is she?"

Isabelle's eyes locked with mine, and there was almost a hint of amusement in them. "We're not sure," she said. "But she's not like other Immunes. Maybe something between what I am and what they are. Or maybe something else altogether. Who knows?"

"Something *else*?" The word caught in my throat, and my earlier fears, the same ones I'd been hit with when Isabelle pointed out my abnormal scent, came rushing back.

"I'll bet you've never been sick a day in your life," she continued, her words directed at me. "You've probably never had measles or chicken pox or even a cold."

My mouth went dry, and I sketched a nod.

"Yeah, I thought so. You probably heal really fast, too."

"That doesn't make me —"

"A monster?" Isabelle laughed, though it was heavyhearted, and she shook her head. "No. But it doesn't make you human, either. Or maybe I should say it makes you *more* than human. Who knows? Maybe you're some sort of human-vampire hybrid."

I felt woozy. Despite the bitter cold of the container, I was suddenly very hot. I tried to calm myself, to rationalize and ignore the emotional impact of what she'd just said. But even though I'd had the same thoughts myself earlier, having her confirm my suspicions didn't make them any easier to reconcile.

"Don't take it so hard," Isabelle said. "Look at this way, kid — if it's true, then maybe you got the best of both worlds. All the perks without any of the hassles. You're not dependent on human blood. You're not a prisoner of the darkness like the rest of us. You're Mary without the madness. Hell, maybe you're even immortal." She laughed, though there was no mirth in it. When I looked in her eyes, all I saw was honest pity.

Ticket regarded me in awe, as though she'd never seen anything like me. I suppose she hadn't. No one had. And just what did that mean? What was to become of me? Could I go home? When I left Haven, I'd never imagined I might not be able to return. But knowing what I now did, could I really believe I belonged there? And if I didn't belong there, where did I belong?

The train picked up speed, the *click-clack*, *click-clack* of the wheels on the track rising to a steady staccato. It reminded me of the electric back home, which only made me feel worse. I wanted to be there, sitting in one of those coaches, staring out the window as sunlit fields swept by and familiar landscapes unfolded ahead.

Instead, I was stuck here in this cramped, cold container. Being vamps, Ticket and Isabelle were impervious to temperature extremes. We could be in the high Arctic or in the middle of the Sahara desert; it made no difference to them. But for all that Isabelle might think I wasn't human — or that I was *more* than human — I was shivering uncontrollably, my teeth chattering.

I tried not to think about it, tried to focus on other things, but it didn't help. My thoughts were firmly centered on things I didn't want filling my head. *You can't go there right now*, I told myself. All that mattered at the moment was staying alive and getting out of this mess.

"How long do you think before we reach the end of the line?" I asked, my voice wavering as my teeth clicked against one another.

"It's a fast train," said Ticket. "But the round-trip cycle is a week, so we figure it still takes at least two or three days to get to wherever it's going."

"I can't last that long in here," I said, hugging myself and uttering a moan.

"Then that settles it," said Isabelle. "We're going to have to find a way out before you freeze to death."

Ticket and I looked at her curiously, but she was busy studying the floor of the container with a calculating eye. She dropped to her hands and knees and began examining the metal plating, then turned her attention to the ceiling. Finally she rose to her feet and regarded the two of us. "How high do you think the roof of the container is from the floor?" she asked.

Ticket and I looked up and down in unison. I stood and lifted an arm, reaching as high as I could, recalling how far away the top had seemed when I'd been trying to get there from the outside. Judging by the current distance between the ceiling and my outstretched fingertips, there was a clear discrepancy.

"It's not the same inside as outside," I said.

"A good three feet, I reckon," Isabelle said.

"So there's something underneath us?" said Ticket.

Isabelle shrugged. "Maybe."

"It's probably just more machinery," I said.

"I imagine so," Isabelle agreed. "But it might also be a way out." With that, she reached down and pulled out a small but lethal-looking knife that was secreted in the top of her boot. She flipped it in her hand and caught it expertly by the hilt.

"You can't be serious," I said, eyeing the knife. "You can't cut your way through steel with *that*."

Isabelle shot me a withering look. "I don't intend to." She sank to the floor again, this time sweeping her hand back and forth over it while edging forward.

"What the hell are you doing?" I asked.

"Looking for some sort of access port."

"Over here," said Ticket, who had mimicked Isabelle's actions. "There are some screws here."

Isabelle joined her and set to work, using the blade as a screwdriver to loosen the screws that secured a two-foot-by-two-foot metal plate to the ground. In a matter of minutes, she had removed it and was worming her way into a dark crawl space below.

I stretched out on the floor and poked my head down through the opening, aiming the light in the direction Isabelle had gone. "Well?" I called after her. "Can we get out?"

She grunted something unintelligible, and I heard banging, followed by what sounded like the screech of metal being bent aside. I shone the light through a maze of hardware: pipes, valves, wires, etc. Beyond that, at the far end of the container, Isabelle was struggling to haul herself out through an opening she'd made by forcing back the external skin of the container. As I watched, she disappeared from view.

I entered the crawl space headfirst, pulling the knapsack after me. "Come on," I called up to Ticket.

Not waiting to see if she was following, I made my way to the egress Isabelle had created. I felt like a contortionist as I maneuvered through the disorder of the apparatus, and more than once I was afraid I was stuck. Eventually I reached the hole and squirmed my way out into the darkness beyond.

I'm not sure what I'd expected, but it certainly wasn't to find myself on some sort of semi-enclosed railcar with little room to maneuver. I panned my flashlight up and down, the beam revealing a cage-like structure that enclosed the cargo. We were standing in a narrow space between two of the Haven containers, the wind howling fiercely, clawing at us. Overhead I could see steel paneling that barely cleared the cargo. I moved to the corner and flashed the light down the narrow space on the side. Long lengths of chain glinted in the beam, strung over the container to hold it securely in place.

"What now?" I asked. But Isabelle had vanished. Ticket stood alone with me in the narrow space, shielding her eyes from the bright light I turned on her. "Where'd she go?" I asked, hollering to be heard above the wind.

"Over here!" Isabelle shouted, her words muffled and distorted by the rush of air around us. She'd squeezed between the container and the railcar and was working on the door latch. Within moments she had it open, and with one quick shove, she slid the door aside.

The cold night air tore at us viciously, but after prolonged exposure to the container's frosty interior, it was welcome warmth. Beyond the opening, moon-spun shadows stretched across the open plains of the fields around us. Here and there, the silvery light of the moon created stark silhouettes out of what might have been the remains of buildings, while the wild, expansive countryside rushed by at a dizzying pace. The train must have been moving at more than a hundred miles an hour.

I gasped at the speed, and instinctively grabbed for a handhold. Beside me Ticket did the same. Isabelle perched precariously on the edge of the opening, a hand wrapped casually about one of the chains that held the container in place. The wind rifled her hair, twisting and tossing it about her face.

"Now what?" I shouted. I had thought maybe we'd be able to jump off, but I knew now there was no way I could survive something like that. I might be more than human, but I wasn't a vamp. At this speed, I wasn't even sure a vamp could make it; judging by the look on Ticket's face, she had no desire to find out.

Isabelle leaned out farther, ignoring the danger at hand. She looked up, then glanced at me and pointed to the roof of the railcar. I understood what she meant, but I thought she was insane. Before I could voice an objection, however, she stepped out and to the side and started climbing the exterior, using the steel slats like the rungs of a ladder. In seconds, she was out of sight.

I held my breath, waiting, and suddenly Isabelle reappeared, hanging half upside down, her face visible at the top of the doorway. "Come on!" she shouted against the wind.

"Are you out of your mind?" I screamed.

Ticket, despite any reservations she might have harbored, moved with alacrity and quickly disappeared onto the roof of the car. I shied back, petrified. I wasn't sure I could hold on against the wind. Hell, I wasn't sure I could do it even if the train was standing still.

"Hurry!" Isabelle yelled, punctuating the command with a sharp movement of her arm.

"Why?" I shouted back. "Why can't we stay here?"

I thought I heard her say something about the sun, and then she jerked her arm again. I'd no idea what she had planned, but like it or not, there was no way I was going to hang around here alone. I handed up the knapsack, smothered my fear as best I could, and edged toward the opening.

Standing where Isabelle had stood, I clung to the chain for dear life, my hand squeezing the metal links so fiercely it was painful. I didn't want to let go, but in order to step outside and get a grip on the slats, I had no choice.

It may have been the middle of the night, but the moon provided more than enough light to reveal things I'd rather not have seen. The long shadows and the spectral silhouettes rushed by at a wicked pace. I looked away from them and reached for the edge of the opening. The wind burned my face as I swung out and fumbled for hand and footholds on the slats. I was shaking, the sensation in my limbs electric, my nerves burning white hot.

Suddenly I was clinging to the side of the railcar, holding on for all I was worth, the screaming wind doing its best to dislodge me and fling me to the ground. I closed my eyes and pressed my cheek against the cold steel of a slat, forcing myself to raise my hand, inching it up, fingers groping for purchase. Blindly I found the slat above and grasped it tightly, my hand aching from the strain. I moved my foot and planted the toe of my boot on a strip of steel, and when I thought I was as secure as I'd ever be, I levered myself up.

It seemed like I was out there for hours, my progress infinitesimal, but finally my right hand came into contact with the protruding lip of the roof. I dared to open my eyes and immediately wished I hadn't. My face was pointed toward the front of the train, looking down the length of the track, and in the glow of the engine headlight, I could see something mountainous looming, a black wall rising out of the landscape. As I stared at it, my eyes tearing from the wind, the train whistle blew a resounding blast, and the light at the front of the engine vanished.

"Hurry!" Ticket screamed from above me.

Isabelle scrambled across the top of the railcar toward me and shouted, "Tunnel!"

I didn't need the explanation — I'd already figured it out for myself. But I was panicked, and as I tried to pull myself up, I lost my footholds. Suddenly I was swinging against the side of the railcar, holding on with my right hand and flailing about, trying to reach up and grasp the edge of the roof with my left.

I looked up ahead, saw the dark outline of stone rushing toward me. "Bloody hell!" I cried, but it was lost in the shriek of the wind and the whistling of the train.

Isabelle reached me in that moment and grabbed my free hand. With one mighty heave she hauled me up, yanking so hard I thought she was going to tear my shoulder from its socket. I howled in pain as I slammed onto the roof, sprawled on my back. Ticket had already flattened herself against the top of the railcar, and Isabelle snapped prone on her stomach, hugging the roof as though she were trying to bury herself in it.

In an instant the sky vanished, and the world went darker than I could ever recall. The sound of the train rushing through the tunnel was like thunder, the *click-clack*, *click-clack* a raucous, nonsensical Morse code that hammered in my skull. I could feel the close proximity of the tunnel walls and the ceiling overhead, the rush of hot air that swirled turbulently around us.

The tunnel seemed to go on forever, but at the speed the train was moving I suspect we were in there for less than a minute. When we emerged, it was like exploding from the barrel of a gun; suddenly the blackness of the night didn't seem quite so black.

Still shaking from my close brush with death, I dared to lift my head and look around. I stared out across the long-abandoned countryside, which was a crumbling ruin that even in the dark bore the aftermath of war — craters and rubble and a landscape that had been dimpled by bombs and scorched by fire. I realized then that that was exactly what it was, that we were almost certainly moving through some of the territory that had been hit hardest by the rain of V-3s in late 1945 and the subsequent invasion by Hitler's forces.

I lay back, closed my eyes, and listened to the train as I tried to calm my nerves and overcome the surge of adrenaline that had my heart galloping. Rather than dwell on the fact that I'd almost died, I set my thoughts to a past I'd never been a part of. I tried imagining what it must have been like in those dark days, when most of the non-Immune population had died from Gomorrah and those that had been transformed had been ripe for induction into the Führer's legions of Undead soldiers.

I pictured millions of Nazi vamps flooding the shores of North America, pushing the Immunes back into the continent, slowly chipping away at their numbers. Cities had fallen like dominoes, and the land had been laid waste by endless carpet bombings and a succession of increasingly horrific battles.

But the horror hadn't been all one-sided. I was more conscious of that now than ever.

I recalled one of my history lessons from school and my teacher saying: "There are a few ways you can kill a vamp, but most of them aren't all that easy. You can chop of their heads; you can burn them until they're ash; you can expose them to sunlight; you can drive stakes through their hearts; you can even use a crucifix — though generally it serves more to ward them off than to incapacitate them. Immunes tried all these, to varying degrees of success, but in the end it was our own blood that proved the most effective weapon for killing the enemy."

Our own blood.

In this world, everything seemed to revolve around blood. Unfortunately, by the time of the last conflict — the Battle of Cypress Hills, in Alberta, Canada — there hadn't been much of it to spare. The Immune population had dropped precipitously. At the beginning of that battle there'd been a million Immunes left; in its wake, fewer than eight hundred thousand. It was at that point that it became apparent to all involved that it was only a matter of time before humanity would be wiped from the face of the earth.

But then, when the Nazis could have completely annihilated us, they hadn't. Instead, they'd offered up the truce. Unfortunately, even in the wake of peace, there'd still been plenty of suffering to be had. By the time Immunes had reached Haven, they'd numbered fewer than five hundred thousand. In the first few years of settlement, that number had steadily dwindled until we'd finally managed to turn things around and had begun the slow process of rebuilding.

I opened my eyes again and pushed myself to a sitting position, staring out at the passing landscape, at the scars of the past that were slowly fading from view. *No sense in dwelling on it*, I told myself. But knowing what I knew, that the truce had come at the expense of human blood, it was hard not to.

"Sophie!"

I turned to the others and looked blankly at Isabelle.

"We have to make a plan," she said.

I nodded dully. "Yeah. Right. So what is it? What are we going to do?"

"Where are the guards located?" Isabelle asked Ticket.

"A few are in a car at the front, behind the engine, but most are in the caboose." Ticket pointed back along the train.

"What does it matter?" I interrupted. "We should be worrying about getting off this bloody thing as soon as we can."

Isabelle shook her head. "That's impossible. We'll just have to find a place to lay low and ride it out."

"You can't be serious!" I said.

She grinned wickedly. "What's the matter, honey? You afraid?"

"You're damn right I am. You might be virtually indestructible, but I'm not."

"The thing is, kid, you don't know *what* you are. Maybe this is your chance to find out."

"I can do without knowing," I said, making no effort to conceal my feelings. "I just want to go home."

It was the first time I'd articulated that thought, and not for the first time did I remind myself that I'd made a mess of things by coming here. If I'd done what I'd been told, I'd still be back in Haven living my life the way I always had, blissfully ignorant of things I was frantically wishing I didn't know. Instead, I found myself cross and frightened and hopelessly out of my depth.

"Just make sure you keep out of this," Val had told me. If I hadn't been such a mule-headed idiot, I'd have listened to him. Sometimes other people really do know what's best for us.

"We've been traveling for a few hours now," said Isabelle. "We're hundreds of miles north of the city. Do you honestly think we could trek all the way back and make it there in one piece?"

I didn't answer.

"Look, even if we could make it, we'd still have to face the Gestapo. They're probably turning the city upside down looking for you."

"They're on this train, too!" I shouted. "I need to get on a Haven ship or to the Embassy —"

"You can't seriously believe that would stop the Nazis?" Isabelle said, cutting me off. "We're talking about the Third Reich, Sophie. And besides, there are probably people in Haven who'd be just as happy to see you vanish into the Nazi black hole."

She was right, of course. But that didn't make me any less furious with her.

"We don't have any other options," she continued. "The way I see it, we tough it out until this thing gets to wherever it's going, then see how things go from there. Until then, we need to find somewhere a bit more hospitable. We're headed north, and if Ticket is right and this train keeps traveling for two or three days, then it's going to get mighty cold in a few hours."

"Oh, that's just great!" I said. "I thought we were doing this so I *wouldn't* freeze to death!"

"Don't worry." She flashed a grin. "I have a plan."

"It had better be a damned good one," I said under my breath.

But regardless, it wasn't like we had an alternative. Isabelle was right: even if we could have stopped the train in the next few minutes, we'd have still been stuck hundreds of miles from the city, and trekking all the way back through that wilderness was an impossibility. It would take days — probably weeks. And while there might not be any vamps or humans out there, in all likelihood there were plenty of animals. Possibly even dangerous ones. All the things the virus hadn't killed . . . and all the things it hadn't changed. Maybe some things nobody even knew about. The only thing we knew for certain was that no other species had been killed or transformed by Gomorrah, which meant they'd had decades to grow more numerous and expand their territory.

"Let's go," I said at length. "I'd rather be inside than stuck out here."

Isabelle went back down into the railcar to conceal as best she could any signs that we'd been there. When she'd finished, we headed forward, scuttling across the tops of the railcars, leaping from one to the next in the line of thirty or so.

The train passed through ghost towns, blasting past dilapidated stations without slowing its pace. The skeletal remains of buildings were bleak reminders of a world that had once been; now it was littered with the rotting corpses of a dead civilization. These were the graveyards of a human past, a past when humankind had been on the brink of greatness. It had all sputtered and died because of something too small to see with the human eye.

We'd gone forward a dozen or so cars when we came to one that wasn't like the others. It didn't have slats on the sides but instead reminded me of one of the passenger cars on the electrics in Haven — except with all the windows covered by heavy blackout shutters. We climbed down a ladder and stepped onto the small platform projecting from the rear of the car and found ourselves facing a door with a small window near the top, almost at eye level.

Isabelle tried the handle, but it was locked. She thumped the window with her fist, striking it hard, but to no avail. "I need my gun," she said. She dug into her knapsack and pulled it out.

"You're going to shoot your way in?" I said, giving the weapon a dubious look.

"Don't be ridiculous. That only works in the movies."

"Then what? You think someone's in there?"

She shook her head. "No. It looks empty. There're just some boxes of stuff stacked to the ceiling."

Ticket took a peek when Isabelle moved aside and said, "It's the equipment they're always shipping. The lab stuff."

"Are we really going to be any safer in there than where we were?" I argued, glancing back the way we'd come.

"Look, kid, I promised Val I'd look after you," Isabelle said.

"What happens when we get to the end of the line?" I asked.

"I told you," she snapped, "we'll cross that bridge when we come to it. Don't ask me questions I can't answer." She closed her eyes, seemingly trying to calm herself.

My cheeks burned, and yet again I felt like a scolded child.

After a moment, Isabelle went on in a more measured tone: "I'm not going to lie to you, but we have to get there alive before we can think about anything else."

"Fair enough," I said.

She glanced to the east, to where a distinct, crimson glow was forming along the horizon. "We have to hurry. In a few minutes the sun will be up."

I looked in the same direction and felt an even deeper chill, one that had nothing to do with how far north we were.

"Stand back."

Ticket and I retreated out of the way as Isabelle gripped the gun by its barrel and used it like a hammer to strike the thick glass of the window. At first nothing happened, but she kept it up, delivering a flurry of blows, and eventually a starburst appeared. Before long there were several spidery cracks reaching to the edges. Then the window abruptly gave, shattering inward.

But it had taken longer than we'd expected — too long.

In an instant the sun breasted the trees. Shafts of amber light pierced the leaden gray of dawn, streaking toward us like a flight of loosed arrows. Beside me Ticket gasped. I turned and saw her throw up her hands to instinctively shield her face from the searing illumination.

When I looked at Isabelle, I saw the exposed flesh of her face beginning to redden; even as I watched, it started to blister. In a matter of seconds, lesions would appear. A few minutes after that, the two of them would be burnt chunks of flesh, and I'd be on my own.

Isabelle staggered and fell to her knees, weakened by the sunlight. "The door," she gasped, raising a hand that was now mottled with wounds and beginning to smolder. "The lock . . . inside . . . hurry."

I leapt forward and reached through the broken window, ignoring the jagged edges of glass that cut into me as I groped blindly, grasping at anything I could reach.

Next to me, Ticket groaned and collapsed. I couldn't help glancing down at her — wisps of smoke were rising from her body, and her face and hands were cratered with hideous sores. I turned my head away, sickened, and fumbled for the latch with a renewed sense of urgency.

At last I felt something — a protrusion just above the door handle. I gripped it with thumb and forefinger and twisted until I heard a faint click. As I pulled my arm out of the opening, the glass sliced deep. A hot flash of agony raced up my arm, and a stream of blood gushed from the wound. I blinked at it stupidly, then grabbed the handle of the door and pulled. It was stuck fast, but I strained with all my might, and suddenly it gave way, sliding aside with a noisy rasp.

There was no time to spare. I tossed the knapsack inside, grabbed Isabelle, hauled her into the shade of the interior, and dropped her to the floor. When I went back for Ticket, I struggled to lift her, gasping from the pain in my arm. It took all I had to hoist her up and carry her into the railcar.

By then my arm was covered in blood. A long, ugly gash extended from armpit to elbow. I removed my jacket, unlaced the top I was wearing, and gingerly slid it off my shoulder. Then I eased my arm out of the sleeve and peeled back the cloth like a second skin.

The sight of so much blood made me unsteady. I was afraid I'd pass out and bleed to death on the floor before I could stem the flow, so with trembling hands I pulled the knapsack to me and rummaged about inside, searching for a first aid kit. Unfortunately, Isabelle hadn't thought to bring anything that prosaic. Not that I could blame her. What use would a vamp have for such a thing? I gave up and lurched to my feet, tottering uncertainly as I made my way over to the boxes stacked in rows on either side of the car. I clawed at one, tore it open, and found it filled with vacuum tubes, the kind you'd find in a TV or radio. Another contained a machine, the purpose of which eluded me.

Finally I opened a box filled with glass beakers and test tubes nested in cotton batting. Grabbing a fistful of the packing material, I pressed it against my wound, panting through clenched teeth as pain flamed in my arm. It felt as if someone had taken a red-hot poker to it.

The batting was soon soaked in blood. I dropped it, gathered more, and pressed it in place, watching in horrified fascination as red tendrils snaked their way through the fibers, turning them a deep crimson.

More batting. More blood. I was beginning to panic, afraid it would never stop. Sweat stung my eyes, blurring my vision and making it difficult to see. I tried to wipe it away with my left forearm while still compressing the wound, but moving my head was a mistake.

The world spun around me, and I felt myself falling, slipping away into the abyss.

CHAPTER 30
BLOOD, SNOW, AND MEMORIES

It's my seventeenth birthday, and I'm waiting for him.

I glance at the watch on my wrist, the one Aunt Amelia gave me for my birthday. It's after eleven, and he has promised to come before midnight. I've just spent most of the evening celebrating with Camille and some friends at Castelano's, and now I'm waiting. I sit alone on a bench across from St. Paul's, which, for all its grandeur, is an inferior copy of the original. A few electrics hum past; a streetcar rolls by, its bell clanging.

In the warm evening air couples out for a stroll drift along, men stealing glances my way. Every one of them. It's so odd, and the way they look at me is unsettling. I've started noticing that more. "You're a young, attractive woman," Camille has told me. "And you're available. So get used to the ogling."

Farther down Wellington I hear the single half-hour gong of the clock in the Peace Tower.

11:30 p.m.

I'm beginning to think he won't come. Worrying he won't. It's my seventeenth, and I want to share it with him. It's a milestone — the anniversary of our first kiss, a year of changes. And today, in the eyes of the Haven government, I am officially a woman. I can get married, have children, vote, do any number of things I couldn't do yesterday.

Any number of things . . .

I'm thinking about him. I feel as though I've always known I loved him. Even that first time, when I wasn't yet fourteen, I sensed he and I were somehow fated. It sounds so corny, but it's true. We belong to each other. We were meant to be. And tonight I want him to know it. Tonight I can truly show him.

"Are ya all right, lass?" a beat cop asks, stopping in front of the bench and giving me a solicitous look. He's old. Older than my father.

"Fine," I say. But I'm not fine. I'm angry and hurt and disappointed. "I'm just waiting for my boyfriend."

But he's not coming.

"Mind showing me your ID, lass? Ya look a little young to be out past curfew."

A day ago he would've been right, but tonight I'm "street legal," as Camille put it at my party — no more having to dodge police and Neighborhood Patrol.

I fish in my sequined black clutch, take out the ID, and hand it to him. "I'm seventeen," I say. It's redundant; he can see it on the card.

He grins and hands it back. "Well, now, so ya are. And a happy birthday to ya, lass."

I force a smile, but it comes out sad, and a tear breaks free and rolls down my cheek.

"Sure you're okay, now?"

I nod, a tiny jerking motion, too afraid to speak, certain I'll sob if I do.

"Well, be careful now. Stick to the main arteries if you're walking. The lights, ya know. Safer that way." He gives me a concerned look, then tips his hat and saunters on, glancing back at me every now and then until he's out of sight.

11:50 p.m.

He's still not here. I think maybe he's forgotten what day it is, how important it is. I'm trying not to get upset, trying not to make a big production out of it, but it hurts. He should remember; vampires never forget. But I make excuses for him: he's lived nearly eighty years; he's known other loves; he's a man.

How can I expect him to see things the way I do? I think. He's my first love, my only love. I know in my heart I'll never have another.

11:59 p.m.

I try not to cry, but I can't help it as I wrap my shawl around my bare shoulders and slowly get to my feet. I'm wearing the wide-skirted strapless black chiffon dress and strappy heels Camille gave me for my birthday. They're stunning, and I feel stunning in them. The way I wanted to be for him.

I listen for the clock, and there's a whisper of movement behind me.

"Sophie."

I turn, and suddenly I am in his arms, and he is kissing away my tears. His lips find mine. Electrics whiz by, the streetcar bell clangs, but nobody is here but us. The universe has shrunk to two.

I don't know how long it lasts; it feels like forever. Then our lips part, and I breathe as though it's something new to inhale and fill my lungs.

"I would never forget. Not *this* day. Your birthday. Our anniversary." He smiles. "You're a woman now. *Officially*," he adds. There's laughter in his eyes and so much more.

I cup his face in my hands, touch my forehead to his, and close my eyes, breathing in his scent, savoring his touch, feeling myself drown in him, my heart beating against his chest.

"I don't ever want it to end — you and me," I say. "It doesn't have to, does it? We can make it work, can't we?"

He doesn't speak, just kisses me. It's odd, though; I almost feel a sadness in it. I wrap my arms around him and hold him close. Down Wellington, the Peace Tower clock signals the hour.

Midnight. A new day.

* * *

I opened my eyes, and for a fleeting moment I thought I was there, with him, lost in forever. "Val," I whispered.

"Sorry, kid. It's just me."

"Izzy?" I blinked and shifted my gaze toward her voice. I was lying on the floor of the railcar, looking up at her, feeling like a bus had run me over.

"Thought you were toast," she said from where she squatted beside me.

I uttered a feeble laugh. "You, too — literally."

"Yeah. Thanks for that." She grinned, unconsciously touching a healing lesion on her cheek.

"No problem." I closed my eyes and took a deep breath, remembering my seventeenth birthday again, wishing for Val. "What happened?"

"You almost bled to death."

I frowned and tried to sit up, regretting I had the moment I did. My brain felt like it was bouncing around inside my skull, and I was immediately overcome by a wave of nausea.

"Take it easy," Isabelle said, putting a hand on my shoulder. "You lost a lot of blood."

I tried to raise my right arm, but I might as well have been trying to lift a car. Rolling my head cautiously to one side, I could see the crude bandage that had been fashioned from more of the batting and strips of leather from the knapsack.

"You're healing fast," said Isabelle. "You should be up and about in a few hours."

"How long was I out before —" My gaze drifted to my arm again.

She shrugged. "There was an awful lot of blood on the floor when I recovered. I'd guess it was at least a few minutes."

"And since then? How long have I been unconscious?"

"Maybe three or four hours. The sun is well up. Well, for this far north, anyway."

"How much longer till we get to wherever it is we're going?"

"It's going to take longer than we thought," Ticket said. She moved into view, sullen-faced. "The train is moving slower now. I think we're on older tracks — prewar stuff."

"Why would they build whatever it is so far from everything else?" I asked.

"Precisely because it *is* far from everything else," said Isabelle. "The Nazis know they have enemies inside their own ranks. If you want to make a place secure, make it difficult to reach." She smiled scornfully. "We know that better than most, I'd say."

She was talking about Haven, of course — although we knew now that any notion that the islands were safe was nothing more than an illusion.

"Still seems a bit extreme," I said.

"Maybe you'll change your mind when we get there," said Ticket.

I lay back and closed my eyes, listening to the train. "Do you have a plan?" I asked Isabelle.

"There's always a plan," she said, grinning wryly. "I just haven't figured out what it is yet. And whether it'll work when I do is another thing altogether."

She wasn't kidding. It didn't take her long to come up with something, but as simple as it was, I had my doubts about its practicality.

"Okay, I've got it. We uncouple the caboose before we get to the base," she explained some time later. "That gets rid of most of the guards. Then we set fire to this car" — she indicated the one we were in — "and hide atop one farther back until we're inside the base. The fire will serve as a diversion, attracting everyone's attention and giving us a chance to get off and find a place to hide."

"And after that?" Ticket asked.

Isabelle shrugged and spread her hands. "We're making this up as we go along."

"*We?*" I said.

She glared at me. "Look, something is bound to present itself."

I wasn't feeling anywhere near as confident. "And if it doesn't?"

"It will," she insisted with the sort of brazen assurance I recognized in myself.

I didn't argue further, but I worried that there were too many unknowns, not least of which was what we were going to do if we made it inside the base. There was no way we could avoid detection for as long as it would take to ready the train for its return to New York. Even were security lax because of the base's location, I doubted it would be nonexistent.

But as grave as my misgivings were, I couldn't help but be reminded of something Grace had been fond of saying: "Beggars can't be choosers." And at the moment, we were surely the most beggarly lot around.

* * *

It wasn't until early evening the following day when we got our first look at our destination. We had climbed atop the car and were huddled together against the icy wind, staring ahead through a night that seemed eerily animate beneath the beatific light of the moon.

The train had passed beyond much of the boreal forest, and the land before us lay open and white and forbiddingly desolate. It was the first time in my life I'd seen real snow. Under the starlight, it was alien and unnatural, as though someone had painted the vast tundra with a layer of silver dust. New York City had been foreign and difficult to adapt to, but at least there had been a certain familiarity. This was altogether different. It was as though we'd journeyed across the galaxy and landed on another planet.

The temperature continued to drop precipitously, and I was reminded of the stories Grace had told me when I'd been younger, the tales of her childhood on the prairies, when winter had been harsh and even a fire hadn't been enough to hold the bitterness of the cold at bay. I'd never been able to truly picture it until now; I'd never imagined that a place could be so insufferably frigid.

Grace had also mentioned how much shorter the winter days had been relative to the summer ones and that the farther north you went, the more prolonged the darkness became. Above the Arctic Circle, there was even a period when the sun didn't rise for several days. Though we'd not been that far north for all that long, I was already conscious of how much closer the sun was to the horizon and how much shorter the day seemed as a consequence. With that floating in the back of my mind, it suddenly occurred to me why the Nazis had built a base way up here.

"It's the sun!" I blurted out.

"What?" Isabelle said. She lowered her binoculars and glanced at me as though I'd gone insane. "What the devil are you talking about?"

"The reason they put their base so far up here, past the Arctic circle." I hunched against the cold, shivering despite the wads of cotton batting I'd stuffed into the lining of my jacket to help keep me warm.

Isabelle and Ticket stared at me.

"Don't you see? Not only is the base so remote that it would be difficult for anyone to get to, it's also far enough north that even at this time of year there must only be a few hours of sunlight. And there'll be even less in the days ahead with the winter solstice coming. Perfect conditions for vamps," I added, forgetting for a moment just who I was talking to. "They wouldn't be bothered by the cold, and they could walk about outdoors nearly all day without having to worry about being burnt to a cinder. At least for a while. It makes them far less vulnerable. And when spring comes in the north, they simply switch their operations to Antarctica, where the days would be getting shorter there."

"I suppose there's a certain logic to it," Isabelle conceded. "But does it really matter?"

I opened my mouth to say something but bit back the words. I had thought myself so clever for figuring it out, but her lack of enthusiasm was a pin pricking a balloon. I was deflated; my eureka moment now seemed empty and meaningless.

Ticket put a hand on my shoulder and grinned at me reassuringly. "I think it was a brilliant deduction."

"Thanks," I said quietly.

"And I think we've other fish to fry," Isabelle said, going right back to studying the base.

I tucked my hands into my armpits and squinted in the same direction. From this distance, the Nazi facility was nothing more than a glitter of tiny yellow stars on the horizon. Isabelle passed me the binoculars; with them, I could just make out the shapes of watchtowers and buildings. One of the latter was clearly an airship hangar. Closer to us there were lines of fences topped with barbed wire, a series of concentric circles that grew closer and closer to the core of the base.

So much for lax security.

"They weren't fooling around with this place, were they?" I said.

"No," said Isabelle. "There's definitely something important in there — really important."

The train was moving slowly enough by then that it would have been possible to jump without risk of injury, but there was little point. There was nowhere to hide in that wide-open space. It was vast and flat from horizon to horizon — not a single tree in sight. Whether I liked it or not, our best chance for survival was to hope that Isabelle's plan worked.

Even so, I remained less than optimistic.

When we were still minutes from the outermost perimeter, Isabelle turned to us. "We should get ready," she said.

I nodded, dour-faced; beside me, Ticket flashed a tentative grin. I wondered what sort of thoughts were running through her head at the moment. If we were caught and the Nazis discovered she was a Jew, just what would they do with her? I shuddered, blocking it from my mind. *It's not going to happen*, I told myself.

"Time to go," said Isabelle.

"Are you sure about this?" I asked. "Why don't we just hide in the train and wait until it returns to New York?"

She looked exasperated as she said, "Are you serious? Look at that friggin' place. There must be hundreds of soldiers there. Maybe thousands. Chances are, a lot of them will be swarming over this thing the minute it's through the gate. There's nowhere on board where we could hide that they wouldn't find us. And the moment they look inside this railcar —"

"All right! All right!" I threw up my hands in defeat. "I get the picture."

"We have to have a diversion. It's the only chance we have of getting off."

"I still don't like it," I said. "They're going to know something's afoot. They'll start searching for us."

"They'll be occupied with the fire," Isabelle insisted. "They'll want to rescue their precious cargo before anything else."

"We'll still be stuck on the base."

"I told you something would present itself. You saw the airship hangar."

"I think you're grasping at straws."

"Do you just want to surrender to them?" she asked.

I sighed and shook my head. "Of course not. I just . . . I just hope you're right about this."

"Look, I don't want to get caught any more than you do," said Isabelle.

Ticket took my hand. "Come on," she said, giving me an encouraging look. "It'll be fine." But I could tell she was as nervous as I was.

We left Isabelle to work on the diversion and started swiftly back across the railcars. Within minutes, we reached the caboose and climbed down to the hitch that joined it to the rest of the train. Ticket set to work while I leaned out from behind the railcar and kept watch. The first line of fencing was almost upon us, and the lights of the base gleamed brightly beyond it.

"Ready?" Ticket asked, standing astride the hitch.

I took another look forward, peering around the corner of the car, then glanced back at her and nodded. "Ready as I'll ever be," I said.

Ticket pulled a lever, and there was a pronounced *pop* and *hiss*, followed by a soft clinking sound as the hitch came apart. She hopped back onto the small platform beside me, and the caboose began to slowly drift away from us, losing momentum as we pulled forward.

I watched it a moment longer, then turned my attention to the length of train ahead. Wisps of smoke were beginning to rise from the railcar where we'd parted company with Isabelle, rapidly thickening to an inky smudge against the dark sky. As the fire spread and the train neared the base, I saw Isabelle's silhouette against the flames. She was racing across the tops of the railcars, leaping the gap between each as she headed in our direction.

Ticket and I climbed back atop the last car and flattened ourselves against the roof. A moment later, Isabelle joined us, and the three of us lay against the cold steel, peering forward into the night, watching as the flames completely engulfed the railcar far ahead, casting a dancing, ethereal glow across the snowy landscape.

We were now a good mile from the ditched caboose, almost within the borders of the base. Behind us, the discarded railcar was a smear of black barely perceptible through the blizzard of snowflakes that came in off the plain and swirled about through the air. I thought I could hear shouts coming from that direction, but they were so indistinct I couldn't be sure they weren't just my imagination.

Ahead there was a sudden burst of brilliance as searchlights cut through the veil of night and snow. Alarm bells rang, and voices rose in the darkness. It sounded frenzied and frantic, and just the sort of confusion we needed.

The final car of the train rolled into the base and beyond the security gates. From our position, we could barely make out the phantom forms of soldiers and officers running helter-skelter in the snow, shouting and screaming orders to put out the fire that was quickly consuming the train.

"Let's go!" Isabelle said, now brandishing her pistol and lugging the knapsack over one shoulder.

Terrified as I was, I didn't hesitate. I leapt off the top of the railcar and into the snow near the edge of the tracks. The impact knocked the breath out of me and rattled my bones. Ticket dropped down beside me and helped me to my feet, half carrying, half dragging me with her as we followed Isabelle through the falling snow toward the enormous bulk of the zeppelin hangar.

"We're lucky," Isabelle said in a hushed tone. "The new snow will cover our tracks."

"Yeah, lucky," I muttered. "But what about the fire you set and the caboose? They're going to realize those *weren't* accidents."

She shrugged, feigning indifference, but she wasn't fooling anyone. "It's done," she said. "We needed a diversion, and I gave us one. At least it will keep them occupied for a while."

"You hope." I glanced back at the raging inferno, beginning to think Isabelle was even more irresponsible than I was. Irresponsible and overconfident. It was a lethal mix, and one I feared would get us all killed.

"Look, we just have to get to the airship, and we should be safe. There are plenty of places to squirrel away in those things."

"If there even *is* an airship, Izzy. What if there isn't? All we've seen is the hangar," I pointed out. "That doesn't mean there's anything inside."

She just shrugged again, but I caught the anxious look in her eyes. "There *will* be," she said. "There has to be."

When we reached the hangar, we stuck as close to the shadows as possible, making good use of the cover afforded by the storm. Behind us the sounds of pandemonium receded, deadened by the massive barrier of the building and the thickening snowfall.

Before long we came to a door set within the sheet-metal wall of the hangar. When Isabelle tried the handle, she found it unlocked. At first I thought it odd but then realized that with barbed-wire fencing, a remote location, and a small army protecting the place, there wouldn't be much point in locking it.

Single file we stepped inside, out of the snow and the worst of the cold. Ticket came last, closing the door behind her, sealing out the biting arctic wind. Trembling, I dusted snow off my clothes and hair, my heart sinking as I looked up and around. The building was as empty as a raided Egyptian tomb.

For a moment all I could do was stand there, staring into the gloom. As my vision adjusted, I could make out the cavernous expanse of the hangar's interior. It was like standing in a colossal cathedral, the ceiling a vaulted sky of curved metal beams and white paneling shrouded in mist and shadow. It was immense, but an airship like the *Eva Braun* would have only inches to spare. Too bad she wasn't here.

"That settles it," I said, my sharp whisper frighteningly loud in the vast hollow. "No bloody airship." I turned an accusing eye on Isabelle.

"Don't sweat it," she said.

"Don't sweat it?" I squeaked. "Really? What the heck are we going to do now?"

Isabelle turned slowly about, surveying the interior. Her tough façade was firmly in place, but she had to be worried. This wasn't working out the way she'd thought it would. "This whole camp is important to the Nazis," she said.

I gave her a surly look. "Yeah, I think we've already established that. So what?"

"So, you don't spend all this time and money building a hangar like this just to have it sit empty most of the time."

"Even so, it could still be days or *weeks* before an airship arrives," I said. "We don't have a hope in hell of staying hidden that long."

"We might not have to," said Ticket. She'd wandered over to a workstation set off to one side and was flipping through a leather-bound book she'd found on the desk. "According to this maintenance log, the flights are weekly. The last one went out six days ago." She looked up at us. "I'd say they're about due."

"Not in this weather," I said.

She shrugged. "They'd already be on their way." She snapped the book shut. "They'll just wait till this clears to take off again."

"And what do we do in the meantime?" I asked.

"We find a place to hole up and wait," said Isabelle.

"You make it sound so easy."

"You make it sound so hard," she countered. "Don't fret so much, kid." She patted me on the shoulder and offered a grin.

We moved deeper into the hangar and soon came upon a door that opened onto a stairwell. With Isabelle leading the way, we descended below the permafrost. At the bottom, we discovered a long concrete tunnel that stretched straight off into the distance for hundreds of feet.

We started down it, continuing until we came to a heavy steel door at other end. There was no handle, nor any visible means of opening the door, but from beyond it we could hear a deep electrical hum. Isabelle put her ear to the metal barrier and wore a look of concentration as she listened. I did likewise and thought I could hear the sounds of machinery.

"No unauthorized personnel beyond this point," Ticket read, translating the German words painted on a nearby metal sign.

"Maybe it's just the power station for the base," I suggested.

"Maybe," said Isabelle, but I could tell she wasn't convinced. She stepped back and surveyed the wall around the door, searching for something.

"There has to be a way of opening this," she insisted.

"Maybe from the other side," I said.

"Then why would there be signs on *this* side?"

It was a good point, but I didn't care. "Look," I said, "I think we should go back. I'm not sure we want anything to do with whatever's behind that door. The last thing we need is to run into somebody."

"She's right," said Ticket.

Isabelle stared at the sign, then nodded. "We still need somewhere to hide."

We stood there, looking back the way we'd come, all three of us in silent agreement that we didn't want to retrace our steps. By now things might have settled down on the base; the hangar could be crawling with Nazis.

But before we had a chance to make up our minds one way or the other, there was a sharp *clang* from behind us. The three of us jumped back a pace. No one dared speak. Ticket and I melted into the shadows beside the door, while Isabelle sank back and pressed herself flat against the concrete wall on the opposite side, whipping out her gun and aiming it at the door, finger on the trigger.

The door shuddered, and there was a grinding of metal on metal as the sheet of steel, thick enough to stop several pounds of TNT, slowly shifted and moved to one side. The electrical hum we'd heard rose by degrees as a rectangle of light slid across the floor and slowly widened. A shadow expanded into it, and a moment later an armed guard walked out into the tunnel, his gun slung over his shoulder, his head bent downward as he rummaged in the pockets of his gray jacket.

Ticket and I squeezed tighter into the corner of the tunnel and remained as still and quiet as church mice. I held my breath, glad of the noise that masked the beating of my heart. Across from us, I could just make out Isabelle, poised and waiting for the opportunity to strike.

Lighter in hand, the guard remained unaware of us as he lit a cigarette and inhaled deeply. He closed his eyes and titled his head back a bit, and in that one moment of vulnerability, Isabelle struck.

She was lightning quick. She had to be. Pound for pound the guard probably outweighed her two to one. Had she not had the advantage of surprise, he likely would have beaten her senseless before she'd even had a chance to touch him. But she had her knife out and slit his throat from ear to ear before he could utter a word. The blade made a neat *snick* as it sliced through the white flesh, clear through to his larynx. Thick dark blood oozed from a wound that would have killed a human in an instant. But of course it barely slowed the vamp. Silenced though he was, the guard fought back, lashing out at Isabelle and knocking her against the wall.

I stood there, petrified, but Ticket dove into the fray, leaping onto the guard's back and digging her fingers into the gash, tearing viciously at the flesh. If his throat hadn't been filled with blood, I'm sure he'd have screamed, but as it was, all that came out was a hideous gurgling.

The guard staggered about in a frenzy, Ticket clinging onto him determinedly, fingers like claws in his wound. As he tried to throw her off, Isabelle advanced and stabbed him in the chest, again and again, until his jacket was saturated.

The joint attack weakened him, but there are only a few ways you can kill a vamp. I wondered if Ticket and Isabelle had the emotional courage to do it, but my doubts were unfounded. While Ticket pulled back on the guard's head, forcing his mouth open, Isabelle jammed the barrel of the pistol down his throat as far as it would go and fired.

What happened next will remain imprinted on my mind for the rest of my life.

Both Ticket and Isabelle fell back, withdrawing as the guard started to convulse from the effects of a bullet infused with Immune blood. His body shook with a violent spasm, his limbs jerking wildly, his head twisting with such ferocity that I thought it would become detached. Smoke began pouring from every orifice and wound, as though he were burning from the inside out. His body began to shrivel, contracting rapidly, the flesh withering, wrinkling, cracking. More smoke and soot floated up and billowed in the air as the guard disintegrated. Finally there was nothing left but a pile of ash and his bloodied uniform and weapon.

We stood staring. It was the first time I'd ever actually seen a vamp die; by the looks on Isabelle and Ticket's faces, it was not the first time for them. I felt like I was going to throw up.

"Listen," said Ticket, cocking her ear in the direction of the airship hangar. "Someone's coming."

"Quick," Isabelle said. "Help me clear this up." She quickly gathered the soiled uniform and stuffed it in the knapsack, then scooped up the guard's machine gun and grenades. Ticket and I kicked the ashes to the corners, doing the best we could to erase the scene of the crime.

"Come on," Isabelle said, heading for the open door.

"In there?" I asked, hesitating.

"Got any better ideas?"

I didn't, so I followed on her heels as she disappeared into the room beyond. As I stepped over the threshold, however, I froze and stood there, slack-jawed. "What on earth," I gasped. Beside me Ticket stood equally astonished.

It was like nothing I'd ever seen. We stood on a catwalk that encircled the inside wall of an immense cylindrical cavity; the whole thing must have been at least four or five hundred feet across and plunged more than two or three thousand feet into the earth. In the gloom below us, there were more catwalks, one atop the other like the layers of a cake, each bounding the interior walls of the complex.

In the center of the space, a large metal structure, bristling with pipes and machinery, extended from a domed ceiling above us to the shadowed depths of the abyss beneath our feet. Narrow bridges of steel connected it to the catwalks at regular intervals, like the spokes of a wheel.

Lights dotted the enclosure, resembling stars in the deepest depths, so that when I looked over the edge of the catwalk it was as though I were peering into outer space. The effect was dizzying, and I gripped the railing fiercely, afraid I might topple over and plummet to my death.

The sound of machinery filled the air, mechanical and electrical in nature. Through the metal tubing of the handrail I could feel a steady vibration that seemed to radiate throughout the entire complex.

"What is this place?" Ticket wondered aloud.

"I think we've come to the end of the line," said Isabelle. "This is where they bring the cargo in the containers."

"And do what with them?" I asked.

"Worry about that later," Ticket said. "We've got other problems." She pointed below.

I looked down and spotted several white-coated figures moving on the catwalks, stopping now and then to consult gauges and flip switches. Occasionally they formed groups and chatted for a few moments before parting and moving off to other duties. Here and there, I spotted guards, and the sight of them made me instinctively step back into the shadows. Ticket and Isabelle did likewise, and the three of us stood shoulder to shoulder in silence, unsure of how to proceed.

The door we'd entered through was still open, and I glanced back to it with a sense of yearning. But I could hear voices in the tunnel and knew we weren't getting out that way. I turned my gaze to the catwalk and saw stairs farther around the curve. Without waiting to consult Isabelle or Ticket, I bolted toward them, driven by the impulse to escape.

"What the hell are you doing?" Isabelle demanded as she caught up with me and grabbed me roughly by the arm, wrenching me to a halt.

"Finding a way out of this bloody mess," I said, barely stopping myself from adding, "that *you* got us into."

But I knew it wasn't her fault; it was mine. It was my stubborn insistence on finding the truth that had brought us here. She had never really wanted to be a part of it; I was the one who had badgered her into coming.

Without a word, Isabelle pushed past me and led us to the level below, sticking to the shadows and moving as discreetly as possible. Where the walls above had been solid concrete, here we found deep alcoves lined with rows and stacks of devices that bore a striking resemblance to the equipment we'd seen on the train. But these were much larger.

I stepped into one of the alcoves and scraped at the frost coating the glass on one of the units. There, lying stretched out, floating in some sort of gelatinous goo, was the naked body of a young man. His eyes were closed, his face expressionless. He hadn't a single hair on his body. Tubes led into his nose, and some sort of respirator was fitted to his mouth. There were intravenous lines in both his arms. Electrical leads led to circular rubber pads on his chest and temples. As I watched, he took a breath, his chest rising slightly, the noise of the air escaping his lungs a faint soughing through the respirator, barely audible above the hum of surrounding machinery.

"Goddammit, Sophie! We don't have time for this," Isabelle hissed, grabbing at me.

I shrugged her off. "I have to see," I said. "I have to know."

I bent to the cylinder below. Like the one above, a man lay inside, as immobile as the first, hooked up to tubes and wires like his companion. Another of the cylinders revealed a woman, her face deathly pale, bearing scarcely any sign of age. I couldn't tell whether she was eighteen or forty. She might even have been older. Like the men, she was hairless and suspended in a transparent medium. A panel on her unit indicated her rate of respiration, her heartbeat, and her brain activity. The latter was little more than the basics; she was essentially brain-dead, kept functioning by the machinery in which she was enclosed.

I straightened up and turned slowly about, staring at the cylinders in wild-eyed horror. There must have been thousands of them. Tens of thousands. Maybe more.

"It's a factory," I said, aghast. "A goddamn giant blood factory."

CHAPTER 31

HELL IN EARTH

I'd been raised to believe that vamps had no souls; but at least if you didn't have a soul you couldn't sell it. In Haven we'd done that and worse.

Of course, the evidence had been there for me to see for quite some time. I'd had most of the pieces of the puzzle long before this moment, so maybe it shouldn't have come as such a shock to finally see the truth. But a part of me had been hoping I'd somehow be proven wrong, that things wouldn't be as bad as they were.

Now there was no getting around it, and it was impossible not to feel utterly wrecked. I had lived a lie. My life, along with everyone else's in Haven, had been nothing but a fabrication, a cruel and bitter joke. We weren't free at all. We never had been. And we weren't better than our enemy; we weren't more principled or moral. They were doing whatever was necessary to survive, and apparently so were we.

We were nothing more than different sides of the same coin.

We feared the vamps because of what they were, but at one time they'd been ordinary people. Sure, they'd done terrible things since, but so had we.

Their excuse was the virus.

What was ours?

* * *

Perhaps madness seized me. I don't know. In those first moments when I realized the sheer enormity of what had been happening all these years, the world turned upside down and inside out. I couldn't make sense of anything.

What's the point of clinging to what we are, I wondered, *if in the end we're no better than the thing we fight so hard not to be?*

I no longer knew who I was or where I was. I just knew I had to get out of there. I wanted to run, but I couldn't. I felt paralyzed. Numb. This place had clearly been here for decades. The Nazis had probably started building it about the time the surviving Immunes had started building Haven. The two went hand in hand. One couldn't exist without the other. We were two parts of the same evil.

"Come on," Isabelle said softly. She put a hand on my shoulder, infinite compassion in that touch. "Come on, honey. We have to get out of here before someone spots us."

I turned, struggling against tears, not really seeing her. "What am I supposed to do?" I asked, my voice breaking. "Now that I know, what am I supposed to do?"

I felt so lost and alone. I wanted someone, anyone, to make everything right again, to make this go away. I wanted Val. Surely he could fix it — even though I knew in my heart he couldn't. In one way or another, he was a part of it. He couldn't exist without it, and that made the pain all the more unbearable.

"Sophie, we have to go," said Isabelle.

"What am I supposed to do?" I asked again.

She took me in her arms, and I rested my head on her shoulder as she stroked my hair and said, "I'm sorry." I could hear tears in her voice and the sharpness of her own anguish. "I'm sorry about this . . . about everything."

I realized, then, that this was just as difficult for her as it was for me. To know your continued survival came at such a price, in such a way, had to be devastating.

"They're people," I said, looking to the machines containing the bodies.

Isabelle shook her head, and her voice hardened. "No, they're not, honey. Not anymore. They're more dead than I am."

She was right. There was nothing human about the thousands held prisoner in this place. They'd ceased to be alive long ago. They were merely empty vessels serving but one function. It wasn't as though we could revive them, awaken them from whatever slumber they'd fallen into. And even if we could have, once outside of the containers, Gomorrah would quickly seize hold, killing them outright or transforming them.

There was no escaping the fact that they'd never be anything more than what they were right now. In the lottery of life, they'd never even had a ticket.

If I'd had a bomb large enough, I'd have blown the place to kingdom come. I felt the grenades hooked to the munitions belt Isabelle had thrown over her shoulder. They would barely put a dent in a place like this, but they'd be a start.

Before I had a chance to act, however, there was a shout from below. I looked down several levels and spied a white-coated figure standing on a catwalk. He was pointing upward, and initially I thought he must have spotted us, but his attention was focused elsewhere.

The three of us rushed to the rail and looked up toward the doorway through which we'd entered the facility just in time to catch a dark blur of movement that vanished into the shadows. Alarm bells started ringing in a deafening chorus and overtop this, the ascending wail of sirens. Far beneath us we heard the clatter of booted feet.

Isabelle swore under her breath. "That's torn it," she said. "We've got to split. *Now.*"

"Too late," Ticket said, pointing to our exit. Soldiers were pouring in through the opening and fanning out.

"Dammit!" Isabelle scanned the catwalk, saw what she was looking for, grabbed my hand, and took off. I gave her a bewildered look. "The stairs," she said, her words all but drowned out by the sirens. She jabbed the muzzle of the machine gun toward her feet. "There has to be another way out down there somewhere."

I wanted to protest that even if there was, and even if we managed to reach it, it would likely be sealed shut and well guarded by now. But any hope is better than none. And we certainly couldn't stay where we were.

We raced down to the next level, which was identical to the one above. As we moved along the catwalk, darting from shadow to shadow, I saw something steal into an opening up ahead.

"What was that?" I asked, pulling back from Isabelle.

"What was what?"

"*That.*" I pointed to a vague shape that was moving in the recesses of an alcove.

Isabelle could see far better than I in the gray light, and judging by her expression, something was terribly wrong. "No, no, no!" she said, shaking her head in frustration and anger. "Dammit! Not *here*, for pity's sake! Not now."

She started forward again, moving with a renewed sense of urgency. More soldiers appeared on the catwalks above, and far below, I heard someone barking orders. Our chances of escape were fast diminishing.

When we reached the alcove, Isabelle ducked inside and skidded to a halt just beyond the threshold. Ticket and I stopped behind her and stared over her shoulder with equal measures of astonishment. Before us a woman knelt beside one of the cylinders, her hand on the glass as she stared in through a patch she'd cleared in the surface frost. She looked thoroughly bedraggled — as though she'd not bathed or changed her clothes in weeks or months. Her outfit was torn and soiled, her blond hair disheveled and greasy. Her fingernails were chipped and encrusted with dirt and blood, and she looked to be more feral animal than anything approaching human.

When the woman turned her face to glance our way, I gasped and staggered back a step. Lit by the pale red glow of the nearby instrument panels was an older version of Isabelle.

"Mom?" I said, reeling from the shock.

"Mary," Isabelle said, moving a step closer. "You shouldn't be here."

Mary didn't even seem to register us. Instead, she turned back to the cylinder, stroking it with one hand and cooing softly as she stared down at the eternally silent figure within.

"Mary, you have to come with us." Isabelle spoke sternly, as a mother might to a wayward child. She approached cautiously, reached out, and put a firm hand on her sister's shoulder. Mary lifted her head and looked up, a thin mewling cry escaping her.

"What's wrong with her?" Ticket asked.

"She's not right in the head," said Isabelle. "She's been like this since the birth."

Ticket glanced at me, but I ignored her. "How on earth did she get here?" I asked, my voice unsteady and barely a whisper. I hated that I could hear the horror in it.

"The train is the only way to get here. But how would she have hidden and avoided the sun?" asked Ticket.

"I told you before," said Isabelle, "she's not like any of us. She has none of our weaknesses."

Ticket looked confused. "But why come *here*?"

Isabelle didn't answer immediately, instead bending down to examine the cylinder and its occupant. "She must think this is her son," she said, a cheerless look on her face.

"Her son?"

"From before she was changed." Isabelle grimaced and shook her head, her features congealing into a rigid mask.

"How could she know?" Ticket sounded bewildered and frightened. "How could she know it's her son?"

"I've no idea, dammit! I don't even know that it *is* him. Val always said her son was an obsession with her, that losing him nearly destroyed her." Isabelle clenched her jaw and looked at Mary. "That's why we've had to keep such a careful watch on her, keep her locked up. But she's bent on escaping and trying to get back to Haven." She shot me a telling look.

I wondered how many occasions that had happened. Judging from Isabelle's reaction to Mary's appearance here, probably more than my aunt cared to admit. Almost certainly that time in the library, when I was fourteen — my mother had put the journal there. And a few years later, when Camille had been murdered. And the night in the Margolliean, of course. But who knew how many other occasions? Val had said Mary was clever, and it didn't seem she'd any problem taking care of herself. Apparently she was more than capable of eluding both the Nazis and the Haven authorities.

I looked down at the body in the containment unit, feeling an eerie sensation as I considered the possibility this might actually be my brother. But as if she'd read my mind, Isabelle said, "She's just crazy." She gestured to the unit. "This doesn't mean anything."

"But what if it does?" said Ticket. "What if this really is her son?"

"It doesn't matter," Isabelle said. "He's just a lump of flesh."

"But still . . ."

Isabelle stood up, trying to pull Mary with her. "I don't care, dammit! We don't have time for this." She seemed poised on the edge of panic. "We have to move. *Now!*"

I studied my mother, feeling an emotional pull, a powerful sense of connectedness, and thought there must be some things that are instinctual. Maybe there were connections made in the womb that transcended scientific calculation, connections that might even reach across time and space. Maybe that was what had brought Mary to this place.

But there might be another, simpler explanation. I recalled what Val had said about her protecting me. "I don't think she came here for her son," I said. "At least, not just for him. I think she may have been following me. Back in New York, at the train station, I thought I heard something following us. And then there were those footsteps atop the container we were in."

"Why would she follow *you*?" asked Ticket.

"Why else?" said Isabelle. "She was doing what mothers do. She was protecting her own."

"I think she's been doing that from the start," I said, more to myself than the others. What I didn't say was something I still didn't like to admit — that that protection had come at a terrible price. Camille had died because my mother, in her crazed state, had likely mistaken my best friend for a young Amelia — the Lady X of her past. Mary must have been terrified the same thing that had happened to her would happen to me, especially now that I was close to the age when I'd have to get married and bear children.

But there was more to it than that.

"She wanted me to know the truth," I whispered, thinking out loud. "The whole truth. I think she's been trying to steer me in this direction all along. She wanted someone to know what was going on. She wanted someone to believe her."

"That's all well and good," Isabelle said irritably, "but we can't stay here. We have to get going." She pulled on Mary again, commanding her to leave.

I watched the interplay between the sisters and realized that this must have been the sum of their relationship for such a long time. And yet, even madness hadn't broken their bond.

"Mary, for God's sake, we have to go," Isabelle said. "You can't stay here. It's not safe."

Mary stared at us vacantly. Then her gaze drifted and fixed upon the cylinder, lingering there for a moment before sweeping over the rest. She rose slowly to her feet, like something ancient uncoiling. Then she buried her face in her hands and wept.

"Mom," I whispered. I couldn't hate her for Camille. I couldn't hate her for the truth. Tears spilled from my eyes and ran down my cheeks. I pushed past Isabelle, hesitated a step from my mother, then threw my arms around her and drew her tight against me.

She didn't respond, didn't hug me back. She just seemed stiff and cold and a million miles away. But still I held her. To touch the woman who had given birth to me, to know she was real, no matter the circumstances, was an indefinable sensation. Monumental.

But it was all too fleeting.

"I hate to break up the reunion," Ticket said, glancing over her shoulder at us from where she stood in the entrance to the alcove, "but we've run out of time."

I turned and saw more soldiers moving along the catwalk in our direction. Before I could even make sense of the danger we were in, Isabelle unhooked a grenade from the munitions belt she was still carrying and hurled it in the direction of the soldiers. "Get back!" she shouted as the grenade hit the catwalk and rattled along it.

There was a blinding flash and a bang so loud it made my ears ring. The explosion shook the ground beneath my feet and ripped up several yards of the catwalk, turning it into an impassable stretch of pretzeled steel.

On the other side of the gap, soldiers sprawled, their flesh incinerated. Some would heal soon enough, but the closest vamps were charcoal. Even their physiology couldn't resurrect them from that state. Beyond them, however, dozens remained unscathed. They leveled their guns and began shooting at us.

Bullets splatted against nearby concrete and ricocheted off the railing and catwalk. Behind us, the glass of one of the cylinders shattered and a slurry of goo streamed out, cascading onto the floor at our feet. The body inside began to jerk and shudder, wracked by some sort of seizure. Then, as quickly as it had started, it was over, and I knew that this was one living corpse that had at last found peace.

Isabelle raised her machine gun and fired a burst at the soldiers. "Go!" she ordered. She stepped from the cover, unleashing a fusillade.

Ticket squeezed past her, and Isabelle pressed a pistol into her hand as she went. There was a nervous look in the girl's eyes as she took it, then without a word she turned and sprinted away.

I tugged at Mary, but she remained rooted to the spot. "Mary!" I pleaded. "You have to come."

Mary threw off my grip and shook her head, her stringy blond hair flying out from her head in a bright halo, her eyes burning with an animal-like rage. She threw her head back and screamed, her face a map of torment as she clutched handfuls of her hair in her hands.

"You can't do anything for him," I said. "He isn't your son. He's just —"

"Leave her." Isabelle reached for me and hauled me from the alcove. "She can take care of herself."

"No! Damn you!" I couldn't leave my mother behind. I broke free and went back.

"Sophie!" Isabelle turned, the machine gun cradled in her hands. "Get out of there, for God's sake!" She unleashed more rounds and started to retreat.

"Mary, please." I held out a hand, coaxing her to follow me. "Please. You have to come with me. I won't leave without you."

Mary stared at me, and I wasn't sure she actually saw me. But then something inside her seemed to shift. Her expression altered, and she appeared almost lucid, aware of everything that was going on around her. She hoisted me off my feet and set off after Isabelle, carrying me as though I were weightless as she loped along with a bounding, feline grace.

Machine gun rounds peppered the walls all around us, filling the air with a blizzard of concrete chips. We went down another flight of stairs, dashed through the shadows of another level, and came up against more soldiers. Isabelle and Ticket fired indiscriminately into the advancing squad, forcing the soldiers to withdraw. Drawing another grenade, Isabelle tossed it far along the catwalk, turning more metal into an abstract sculpture of bent and twisted ruin.

I was beginning to panic. There was no way forward, and the avenue of retreat was sealed off by the advance of more troops. Our only open route was a narrow bridge connecting the catwalk to the enormous pillar at the center of the complex. We fled onto it, Ticket and Isabelle keeping up a steady barrage. But the guards weren't easily deterred, and a hail of bullets whistled past us.

The mechanical structure that occupied the center of the facility seemed incredibly far away, but despite the best efforts of the soldiers, we made it there intact. Equipment hummed noisily around us as we hunkered down, the majority of it truck-sized pumps that were pushing vast quantities of liquid through enormous pipes. Frost encrusted everything within reach, and the air was almost as frigid as it had been outdoors.

"We can't stay here," Isabelle said, checking her gun and the munitions in the belt.

"There has to be a way down," said Ticket. "If we can get to another level . . ." But she didn't finish. We all knew that even if we made it there, we'd still face the same daunting task of finding a way out. And even if we got outside . . .

Mary set me down, and I turned to face her. My grip on her hand tightened, and she lifted her eyes to mine, a cryptic grin shining through the grime that covered her face as she pulled free of my grasp. She raised her hands behind her neck, and for the first time, I noticed the silver chain she wore. She took it off and held it out to me — a crucifix.

I stared at it, astonished. "You're really not like them, are you?" I whispered. I saw now that my mother lived somewhere else entirely, halfway between heaven and hell, in a place inhabited by one.

"I don't understand," I said as she pressed the crucifix into my hand.

Mary raised her hands to my cheeks, and for a moment, as I peered into her eyes, I saw no madness. Only heartache and sorrow and a hunger for what should have been and never could be again.

I looked down at the crucifix, a sudden realization dawning on me as I studied it. It was no simple piece of jewelry. It was the crucifix my father had mentioned in his notes — the evidence on the body in the alleyway that he'd taken that New Year's Eve. That was why he'd been so upset when he'd seen it there at the crime scene. It was the same crucifix for which there'd been a receipt in the cabinet. The one my mother had written of in her journal.

I hadn't put the two together at the time because when I'd read my father's notes I hadn't known my mother was alive. But now I understood. She had left the crucifix at the crime scene because she'd known my father would recognize it and understand who'd put it there. And now I knew why Father had taken it that night. If he hadn't, it might have exposed a secret he'd been keeping for years from the very government he worked for — that Mary was alive.

Cherkov had *been the victim in the alleyway*, I realized. Mary had staged the murder to ensure that my father and Val would show up at the crime scene. But it was more than that. It had also been her way of telling the others involved in the experiments that they and Cherkov were no better than the monsters they were fighting. Maybe it had even been a warning to them that they could be next.

"It was you, wasn't it?" I said to Mary. "You killed Cherkov. And this" — I held up the crucifix — "was the clue you left for Dad."

Mary lifted a hand and looked around, as though to indicate the facility we were in.

"You wanted Cherkov to die as a vamp because of what he did to you," I said aloud, giving voice to my thoughts. I hesitated, looked straight at her. "You wanted revenge."

My mother nodded, then shook her head vehemently — as if to say yes, but that there was more to it than that. Her expression shifted, hardened, and she put a finger to my chest.

"Me?" My breath caught. "You did it for me?"

She nodded.

"To protect me? So I wouldn't become another of his victims?"

She nodded again.

I glanced down at the crucifix, feeling the weight of all it signified. "But how on earth did you get it back? I mean if Dad had it —" I stopped and stared at her in open-mouthed disbelief.

Her eyes shone with tears again.

"Oh, my God! You were there," I said. "Dad wasn't just babbling that day at Clarkson. Somehow you got in there, and he gave you this."

My mother closed my fingers over the crucifix, leaned forward, and kissed me with cold lips. Then, without warning, she took off.

"No!" I cried, leaping to my feet. "Come back!" I tried to go after her, but Isabelle tackled me from behind, pulling me back into our limited cover as a hail of bullets perforated the air.

I squeezed my eyes shut and tightened my fist, the outline of the cross digging into my palm. In my mind's eye I could see the words engraved on the back: *Our Love is Eternal.* I put it around my neck, an odd sensation washing over me as I felt the metal between my breasts, as cold as silver, as hot as blood.

Suddenly a rising scream, like the death cry of an enraged animal, rent the air. Shouts and shrieks of panicking soldiers echoed throughout the complex. Chaos and carnage. Not far away, the rattle of machine gun fire was deafening.

"She's creating a diversion," Isabelle said. "It's now or never." She got up and cautiously poked her head into the open. When the coast was clear, she led the way out.

We found a ladder and climbed down to another level, then took flight across one of the bridges to the catwalk. Above us the screaming died down and the guns fell silent. I tried not to think about what that meant. There were soldiers everywhere — hundreds of them. And however strong and fast Mary might be, I doubted she could overcome them all.

A door ahead of us held the promise of escape. Isabelle tried it, but it wouldn't budge, so she used a grenade to knock it off its hinges. Beyond the billowing dust and acrid smoke, a long stairway angled up, terminating in another door. My legs were burning as I ascended, and I worried I wouldn't make it. Ahead of me, Isabelle and Ticket burst through the door and rushed out into the glacial night. A moment later, I followed. Behind us, I heard someone shout a warning that sounded like, "Halt!"

But we'd already stopped dead in our tracks.

Two dozen guns were trained on us. And as we stood there in the swirling snow and the blinding glare of searchlights, an officer stepped forward from behind the assembled soldiers. At first I couldn't make out who it was, but when he spoke, I recognized him immediately.

"Well, Fräulein Harkness," Colonel Müller said with a superior chuckle. "You have indeed given me a merry chase. But now I think you are exactly where we wanted you."

CHAPTER 32
AHRIMAN

How do you torture a vamp? There aren't many ways, but during the war, Immunes discovered some particularly nasty methods and employed them with great zeal. Perhaps not surprisingly, the most effective of those came from our own bodies.

Early on in the war, Immunes stumbled upon the fact that their blood was fatal to vamps, and someone discovered that if diluted, it could prolong the death of any vamp you exposed it to. Long enough to torture the hell out of them and get whatever information you wanted — though Immunes hadn't always done it for information; some had simply done it because they could. One miniscule, watered-down drop at a time did the trick. It was ultimately fatal for the vamp, but before death, there were the unspeakably cruel and unbearably slow moments. It's difficult to believe anyone with a conscience would employ such a tactic.

"War does strange things to people," Father had said when I'd once broached the subject with him. It had been in the early days of my relationship with Val, and I had been eager to uncover as much as I could about vamps. "Sometimes you simply don't have the luxury of a conscience. Not when the lives of the people you care about depend on the information you seek."

"It doesn't seem right," I'd said, disgusted by the whole notion of it.

"You have to remember that Immunes were fighting for more than just their lives. They were fighting to preserve the last of humanity," Father had said. "And besides, they didn't see it as torturing *people*. Vamps were —" But he hadn't been able to put it into words, and in the end he'd said, "You do what you have to do for the greater good. There's no sense in being hidebound by morality and ethics and finer principles if in the end the enemy wins, and you're all dead."

In the wake of our capture, I soon came to realize the vamps had learned a lot from Immunes.

Over the course of the next few days they tortured Ticket and Isabelle, and I've little doubt as to how. I could hear the two of them screaming, a sound so truly horrific that I sat huddled in the corner of the wooden cell they'd locked me in with my hands over my ears, wishing I could block out the cries and going half mad because I couldn't.

On the third day, they brought Isabelle inside and threw her in with me. Her body was a battlefield of scars, and when I saw her, I was afraid she was already gone. But she let out a quiet moan, and I went to her, gathered her in my arms, and spent the next few hours trying to ease her pain.

"Tell me about your life in Haven," she said after a while. She lay with her head in my lap while I gently stroked her hair. "It's been so long for me that sometimes I think it was only a dream."

So I told her. I told her about my life and my dreams back home — the life and the dreams that now seemed impossibly far away and inaccessible. I told her about my father, and how he would take me up to the Parliament Buildings each New Year's Eve and we would watch the fireworks with thousands of other people and hope for a better future — a future absent of fear and hardship, ripe with the promise of freedom and better days to come. I told her how he had taught me to drive in little Peppy, and how, when I had first gotten my license, we had celebrated by going to The Casbah, a little open-air restaurant by the edge of Resolute Bay, where I had had a platter of shrimp for dinner and peach melba for desert.

"I remember that place," Isabelle said, a dreamy smile on her lips. "I used to love the lobster." I could see her trying to remember the taste.

I told her about school at Humberton, about the classes I did well in and the ones I didn't like. We both chuckled at how poor I was at German.

"Do they still make you wear those silly uniforms with the knee-high socks and those awful shoes and the ridiculous ties?" she asked. I nodded, and she laughed, so I told her about how Camille had gotten into trouble for shortening her skirt and wearing a pink tie instead of the school's emerald green.

When I spoke of Camille, about how we were so different and yet so alike — sisters in every way but blood — I cried, and Isabelle took my hand, holding it until the moment had passed.

I told her about the things I loved to do, like curl up in bed on a Sunday with a cup of coffee and the windows open and the warm breeze blowing in the scents of the sea. I told her how I liked to soak in a cool bubble bath on a hot day, cold lemonade in reach, and a good book in hand. I told her that I liked to walk barefoot on the beach and watch the sunset and think of places far beyond the horizon that I'd never seen.

Isabelle sighed softly. "I miss the sun."

And then I told her about Val. I told her about the night of our first encounter, about our first meeting in the library, our first kiss on a park bench, waiting for him on my seventeenth birthday, and the many other moments we'd shared. I told her of how we'd once danced in the rain and swum in a moonlit sea. I told her of how we'd sometimes watched the stars, and he would tell me of his life before the Fall as though he were talking about another person. I told her I loved him — despite the truths I'd found. I told her I couldn't imagine life without him and that I wanted to be with him forever — or for as long as it was possible for me to live with a man who would never age another day.

I wasn't sure she actually heard any of it, until I fell silent, and she said, "He loves you, you know. Not the way he loved Grace or the way he loved Mary. He knew when he was changed that he'd lost Grace forever. He knew Mary could only be a moment; that she'd last like mist on a Haven morning, burning away under the sun. But with you he knew he'd found something special."

"Are you sure?" I asked, wanting her words to be true — not sure whether they were. "How can I be any different? He'll go on forever, and I'll —"

I didn't want to voice it, because it seemed so pointless. Isabelle had joked about the possibility of me being immortal, but I'd been aging normally since I'd been born. It didn't seem likely that would change anytime soon.

It might be that I wasn't like other Immunes. Maybe I was something else . . . something in between — not quite belonging here, not quite there. But I wasn't sure that meant Val and I could ever be anything more than just a dream.

"Val has risked everything for you, Sophie," Isabelle said softly.

"What do you mean?" I asked.

"He's worked hard to get to where he is in the Nazi hierarchy, just so he'd be in a position to help the rebellion. But now all that may be lost."

"How?"

"By coming for you. He'll do anything to save you — even though that'll probably mean exposing his role as one of the leaders of the rebellion."

"I never meant —"

"Of course you didn't. Maybe if he'd been more open and honest with you from the start . . ."

She was right, I thought, there'd been too many secrets. But not just Val's. All around me people had been keeping me in the dark, lying to me. My father. Grace. Aunt Amelia. The government. Maybe they'd all had their reasons, but in the end it had all led to this.

I couldn't help but wonder how different things might have been had I known the truth from the beginning. I certainly wouldn't have been sitting with my dying aunt, locked up in the frozen wastelands of the Arctic. And I wouldn't have been facing the very real possibility that I was soon going to die.

As if she'd read my thoughts, Isabelle said again, "He does love you. You have to know that in the end that's the only truth that matters."

"And I'm just supposed to forget all the secrecy and the lies?" I wanted to say. But I didn't. Because in the end she was right — regardless of what the rational side of me said, when it came to Val, it was all about what I felt in my heart. However much I tried, I could never get beyond that.

Grace used to have a saying, though I don't think she'd have ever applied it to Val and me — some things are just meant to be.

Isabelle and I remained wrapped in our silences for a long time after that, until finally I said, "What will happen to us?"

"I don't know," Isabelle replied. "The world is changing. A lot of vamps are tired of Hitler and the Old Ones, and the Nazis can't hold back the tide forever. The world will be different, one way or another."

"Then there's hope."

"There's always hope." Her voice was far away, her gaze distant. "I saw it once, long ago."

I wasn't sure what she was talking about, and in her current state, I doubted even she knew. "I'm sorry I got you into this," I said.

Isabelle tried to shake her head but didn't have the strength. "We all make our choices," she said. A jolt of pain racked her, and she cried out, thrashing in my arms as I held her tighter.

Finally she was quiet again, but I could tell she didn't have long. She must have known it, too, because she said, "I wish things could have been different. I wish we'd had a lifetime to know one another. There are so many things I should have told you. About what I saw in my dreams. About what's coming. About *her.*"

"My mother?"

"No. The girl in my dreams." With that, she went silent and still, and I knew she was gone. I held her close and waited until she turned to dust.

* * *

Ticket died a day later.

At the break of dawn I heard her last scream.

The guards took me outside and forced me to watch, to stand there as the sky brightened and the land was illuminated by the first fingers of sunlight reaching across the snow. The days had been getting shorter, but it only required a brief interval of sunlight to do the deed.

The Nazis had bound her to a post out in the middle of the base, exposed to the open plain, in the direct line of sunrise. She looked horrific. Even worse than Isabelle had been. It was obvious someone had taken perverted pleasure in torturing her with every conceivable means.

It was unconscionably inhumane, but then, I reminded myself, the Nazis weren't human anymore. Maybe they never really had been.

As the sun breasted the horizon, barely peeking above it, the dawn took her. Light engulfed her body, burning her, and finally turning her to smoke and ash. It was over in minutes — though my memory of it would last an eternity.

The wind carried the dust away and scattered it across the snow until all that remained of Ticket was a gray smudge. It was as though she'd never existed at all — except I knew she had. She may have been a vamp and enemy to my people, but Ticket had also been a person, and I couldn't help but hate the ones who'd done this terrible thing to her.

* * *

I must have been alone in my cell for more than a week after that before the guards came and got me, though in truth, I can't be sure it wasn't longer. The only indication of the passage of time was when they brought me meager rations of food and water. The food came at what I assumed were regular intervals, and though I tried to keep track of it, I soon lost count. The cold and my hunger made me lightheaded and unfocused.

I kept thinking of Ticket and Isabelle, and the tears would come, followed by the sobs, until I would collapse, thoroughly spent. They would still be alive had it not been for me. How could I pretend I hadn't had a hand in their deaths?

I slept a great deal, despite my best efforts not to. My unconscious hours were hounded by nightmares. I dreamed of being infected, of something growing inside me, and each morning I awoke feeling nauseated. It was all I could do to prevent myself from retching, and I began to worry I was coming down with something. I thought of my mother being infected with Gomorrah while she was pregnant with me, thought of her in her madness, and the chill that ran through me was worse than the arctic cold.

I was almost frozen by the time the two soldiers who'd come to retrieve me hauled me to my feet. They held me between them while two others kept machine guns trained on me. It might have been laughable under different circumstances — them thinking I was a threat worthy of that much security. I was so stiff with cold and weak from hunger and dehydration that I could barely walk, much less fight my way past four armed vamps.

The soldiers half dragged me down a dimly lit hallway, out a door, and into the snow. For a moment I was afraid this was it — they were going to toss me outside the camp, onto that snow-swept plain, and leave me to die of exposure. Or maybe just stand me up against a wall and shoot me.

I was too feeble to consider making a break for it and could do little more than hang limply between the two men as they bore me to another building. It was dark out, and I wondered what time it was. Morning or night? Did it matter?

Out the corner of my eye, I caught sight of a departing military airship rising skyward. It was emblazoned with a giant swastika, its jet engines burning brightly, casting a steady blue-white glow against its silver hull. It was the sort of ship Hitler might use, were he to travel. Of course, the Führer was renowned for never leaving Berlin, which made me wonder who that ship might have carried here. Someone quite powerful.

The soldiers took me inside and bore me down a wide corridor running the length of the building's interior. Off this were several doors, most of them open so that as we passed I could see vamps at work within the rooms beyond. They were all military and mostly men, engaged in what appeared to be tedious office work. As we passed each room, those within came to a standstill and stared at me, their faces inscrutable blanks.

At last we arrived at the end of the hallway. A brass plaque was mounted on the door, the word *Commandant* precisely etched into the polished surface. One of the guards knocked, and from the room beyond came a muffled command in German.

The two men lugged me into the small antechamber and snapped to attention in front of a simple wooden desk. The uniformed man seated behind it was bent over some papers, pen in hand. He stopped writing and looked up, did a sloppy "Heil Hitler," then surveyed us indolently before waving us through the doorway to the left of him.

By now the warmer air inside the building was beginning to thaw me out, but the feeling was far from pleasant. My skin felt as though it was on fire, and my fingertips and toes burned with an ache that made me clench my teeth.

When we entered the commandant's office, he was standing near the window, peering out into the darkness. Moving with an economy of motion, he glanced our way and watched as the guards brought me forward. He looked me up and down, then uttered a brusque command, prompting the guards to deposit me in a chair. The sensation of sitting comfortably in a relatively warm environment after spending so long huddling on an ice-cold concrete floor was quite extraordinary. I might have sighed had I the energy.

The commandant gave the guards a dismissive gesture, as though shooing away a fly, and they retreated from the room, leaving the two of us alone. I had expected Müller, but he was nowhere to be seen.

The commandant went to a sideboard and poured a cup of tea, then came over and held it out to me. I wanted to refuse it, but he seemed to anticipate this and said, "It is not a weakness to take it, Fräulein. Please."

My hands were shaking as I grasped the cup and saucer, silently grateful, trying not to spill too much as I sipped the scalding liquid. It burned all the way down into my stomach and made me cough and splutter, but the effect on my psyche was nothing short of magical.

"You're far from home, Fräulein Harkness," the commandant observed in a conversational tone. He settled on the edge of his desk, looking relaxed and nonthreatening. Looking almost sympathetic. "How is it you ended up here?"

"Got on the wrong train?" It was probably not the best idea to be flippant, but I said it for Isabelle's sake, because it was the sort of response she'd have given.

The commandant shook his head, as though pitying me. "Herr Müller seems especially interested in you, Fräulein." He paused, pulling out a lighter and cigarette, never taking his eyes off me as he lit up and inhaled. "His is not the sort of interest one wishes to court, I can assure you."

I drank more tea; he exhaled smoke. Then he said, "You seem to have landed yourself in a very unusual and difficult situation."

I didn't say anything, just stared back at him, cold and hungry and so exhausted I was almost beyond being frightened anymore. Almost.

"I'm not sure what's to be done with you," the commandant said, drawing on the cigarette again and looking pensive. "Sadly for you, I'm not the one to make the decision on the matter."

The teacup chattered against the saucer. I wasn't sure I wanted to hear what he had to say next, but at the same time, I wanted him to say it and get it over with.

"There is someone who has just arrived here to see you," he continued.

I glanced over my shoulder, expecting whoever it was to be standing there, but the room was empty save for the two of us.

The commandant gave me another pitying look. "Our guest prefers to be with you alone." He said it as though it were not the sort of thing he'd want to endure himself. He stubbed out his cigarette and stood, clicking his heels together and bowing decorously. "Good luck, Fräulein." And then he left.

It was a long time before I heard the door open again. I resisted the impulse to turn, and sat stiffly in the chair, staring straight ahead, the cup and saucer rattling. I heard movement and felt something pause behind me. An old and powerful presence swept through my body. I felt a suffocating dread, and at that moment, I'd have liked nothing better than to have been outside dying in the cold rather than in that room.

Unbidden, images flashed in my mind — thousands of years of darkness, war and pestilence, famine and flood, all rolled into one. A different sort of vampire, feeding off the misery of the masses, lurking in the shadows, appearing only when men came together in fury and clashed with sword and gun and the engines of war and destruction.

Darkness moved past me. There but not there. Real and yet illusion. It settled into the chair the commandant had vacated and lifted its cold gaze to mine. Dark eyes in the bloodless face of a hairless head stared at me. Of course I'd seen that face before, in those old photographs of Hitler during his rise to power and in the days and years that followed. His shadows. Some even said that they were the men who controlled him — if they were even men at all.

An Old One.

So that was who had come on the military airship.

"Miss Harkness," the creature purred. His voice sounded like dust and ash; it stank of rot and decay. "At last we meet. I am Ahriman. I've waited long for this moment. Waited so very long to meet the one who will finally provide us with what my brethren and I have for centuries sought." The blood-red lips turned up at the corners, conveying malice and triumph and sadistic delight.

I sat watching him, trying not to show the fear I felt and failing miserably

"I must say, I had expected Cherkov's little abomination to be rather more impressive."

The words were like a blow. Cherkov's abomination? Did that mean his experiments on my mother had actually been targeted at the baby she'd been carrying? Targeted at me?

"What are you talking about?" I said, my voice a reedy warble. "How do you know about Cherkov?"

Ahriman laughed. "Oh, my dear, surely you must realize — *we* made Cherkov. We supplied him with the means and the direction to pursue his research. And he served us well. First in the prisons and concentration camps in Germany, then in North America, and finally in Haven."

My head spun as I tried to decrypt the true meaning of his words. "What . . . what do you want with me?" I heard myself ask.

"Want?" He gestured with hands that looked like claws, the fingers long and thin, capped with nails that had been honed to points. "You were created to serve but a single purpose, and when that's done, well . . ."

Created? My pulse escalated, and it felt as though all the oxygen had been sucked out of the room. "I . . . I don't believe you," I said, struggling to get the words out.

"Of course you don't, my dear." The reptilian smile deepened, darkened. "You would prefer to continue living in the fantasy that you are merely the product of an act of love; a moment between two people that ends in the creation of another. But it's far more complicated than that. You might say we are as much your parents as the man and woman who conceived you. It would be fair to say that as we created Cherkov, he, through Gomorrah, had a hand in creating you. Without us, you wouldn't be what you are."

I wished I'd had the courage to ask him what that was, but all I could do was sit there, eyes glued to him, even though I so badly wanted to look away.

"You see, Miss Harkness, for us you are the beginning of the end of a long quest. One that has taken us thousands of years. It's that quest that has kept the peace between Immunes and vamps for more than five decades."

"So you're the ones who were *really* behind the truce?" I said.

"Of course. If that imbecile Hitler had had his way, he'd have hunted down every one of you and destroyed his own kind in the process. Haven would not exist had we not intervened."

"And you knew about the non-Immune babies and the blood all along." It went without saying that they wouldn't care about where the blood came from.

"You must understand," Ahriman continued, "that it was never our intention for Gomorrah to spread throughout the world.

That was an unfortunate accident. It was only ever supposed to be used on limited sections of the population. But once it was loose, we understood full well what it would do. We realized that if all humanity died, then so too would we. Fortunately, as the numbers of non-Immune humans dwindled, it was brought to our attention that Immune women in our North American concentration camps were consistently giving birth to non-Immune babies. We pursued the matter immediately, setting Cherkov up to oversee the operations."

"But why the truce?" I asked. "Why not simply round up the rest of the survivors and keep them in prisons? You could have forced the women to reproduce." After all, I thought, it had almost come to that in Haven.

"Oh, believe me, we tried that. But the results were far from satisfactory. The non-Immunes born there that we managed to preserve were neither suitable as productive sources of blood, nor viable subjects for Cherkov's other experiments. At best, he was able to keep a few of them sustained for short periods of time before they succumbed to the virus and became worthless in all respects. The simple fact is that conditions in the camps were too stressful, the risk of infection too immediate. So we decided upon an alternative."

"The truce," I said.

He smiled, and it was as if what little warmth had been in the room was instantly devoured by the vast desert of ice and snow that surrounded us. "There is an old saying, Miss Harkness — one catches more flies with honey than with vinegar. Hence Haven. A different kind of prison — though I think even you must see by now that it's a prison nonetheless. But so long as your countrymen believed themselves free, they continued to produce what was required, and that was all that mattered to us. The more non-Immune children kept from dying in the womb, the greater the source of blood and the greater the number of test subjects Cherkov would have to work with. That naturally increased his chances of eventually succeeding in the experiments that would ultimately result in you." The smile appeared again. Cold. Sinister. *Inhuman*. "Haven succeeded beyond our expectations.

"From the beginning we knew that so long as we were patient, it would be only a matter of time before Cherkov would give us what we desired. There were, of course, numerous dead ends. Decades of experiments that came frustratingly close but not quite close enough. And then, finally, success. After thousands of years of waiting for the right combination of genetics to come together with the virus, we had what we needed. It took us millennia to guide humanity to that point, to the evolution of a creature neither wholly Immune, nor entirely vampire." He leaned forward across the desk, his deep-set eyes an unfathomable black. "My dear, you don't realize how truly unique you are. You are the means to an end. With you, we'll finally obtain what we've pursued for all these years."

I shook my head. "I don't know what you think I am, but I'll never help you."

"How quaint. You actually believe you have a choice."

My blood ran cold, and the chill that penetrated me reached deeper than anything physical. "What are you going to do to me?" I asked.

"Oh, my dear Miss Harkness," he said, his voice full of menace and shadows and all the things that haunt the darkest parts of our souls, "it has already been done."

I couldn't stop shaking, and it had nothing to do with the temperature.

"There are just a few loose ends to wrap up, and then this will all be over." He glanced toward the window. "We're just waiting upon the traitor; once he has arrived, we can be on our way."

"Traitor?" I could barely bring myself to say the word, because I knew who it was, and it broke my heart to think I'd done this to him.

Ahriman settled his bony elbows on the arms of the chair, touched the fingertips of opposing hands together, and peered over them at me. "You must understand that we have left little to chance," he said. "We couldn't afford to. We've been watching your friend for quite some time. Of course, we could have arranged his demise on any number of occasions, but then we'd have never benefitted from his relationship with you, nor would we have uncovered the true extent of the rebellion."

Those words cut deep, and the truth hit me — if I'd never become involved with Val, he might still be safe.

"It's interesting how things work out, isn't it?" Ahriman carried on, reveling in my despair. "Your attachment to Valentine was so convenient for us — though I must confess he almost failed to meet expectations. We nearly had to have our agents rescue you back in Haven, but in the end you did the job for us. Of course, you eluded us in New York, but thankfully you were considerate enough to come right to our doorstep." He leaned back in his chair with a smug look. "You're a very resourceful young woman."

Not resourceful enough, I thought, *or I wouldn't be here.*

"And now you've led the traitor straight into our hands. It could not have worked out better had we planned it."

"You're using me as bait," I said.

Ahriman shook his head. "You undervalue yourself. The capture of the traitor is no longer of consequence to us. You're all we ever truly desired. It was only so long as you remained beyond our control that the rebellion was a concern. But now it's merely a sideshow we engage in to satisfy our host, Herr Hitler."

"Please," I whispered. "If it doesn't matter to you, then let Val go. If he comes, it's only because —"

"He loves you?" The Old One made a terrible sound. I wasn't sure whether it was laughter, but I shrank from it and felt all hope flee.

"I'm going to enjoy our time together in the days ahead," Ahriman said, slowly unfolding himself from the chair and rising. "I'm going to enjoy it very much."

He started toward the door, but paused and looked back. "We'll continue this later," he said. "I'm sure you've many questions. But for now, I must go make preparations to receive our next guest."

CHAPTER 33
REVELATIONS

Back in my cell, I scarcely slept that night. My nerves were shot, and every time I thought of the things Ahriman had said, I became so terrified that I broke down. My whole body quaked uncontrollably as I sobbed and fought the storm of emotions inside me. I kept wondering what it meant that I'd been *created* and what it was the Old Ones wanted with me. There was no pretending that it could be anything good.

On those occasions when exhaustion took hold and I did drift off, I slept fitfully, plagued again by the dreams of something growing inside me. It was during one of these periods that I was awakened by the sounds of jet engines. Another airship had arrived, and there was a great deal of commotion as it landed at the base.

I had a pretty good idea why — it was carrying the "traitor."

Why did you come, Val? I thought. *You had to know it was a trap.*

Of course I knew exactly why he had come. It was for the same reason I'd have gone to the ends of the earth for him. When you love someone, you'll do anything to save that person when they're in danger. You don't think about the risks. Or if you do, they're secondary to what's really important.

Perhaps had I given that more thought in the first place, I'd have never begun all this. Now it was too late, and I could only hope that love and my foolishness wouldn't prove to be the downfall of us both.

* * *

In the morning they came and took me to the big hangar. There were lights gleaming the length of the building, small squares of yellow illumination that stood in stark contrast to the jet-black sky.

As I staggered over the threshold, I gasped at the sight of the behemoth moored within. The *Eva Braun* seemed even larger than when I'd stood below her at Kensington Aerodrome, moments before I'd embarked on the adventure that had irrevocably changed my life.

I had no idea where we were going, but with Val aboard, it was in all likelihood Berlin. Hitler would want to see the traitor in person, and no doubt a grand spectacle would be made of Val's execution. Fear and intimidation had always been the Nazis' forte, and they spared no opportunity to engage in it.

The soldiers led me to the gondola, where a set of metal stairs abutted an open door on the starboard side of the airship. They prodded me from behind with their guns, motioning me up the steps. There were several officers and crewmen busily at work inside, most with their backs to me as they prepared for flight. As I paused in the doorway to watch them, the captain turned, and I saw that it was Clauswitz. For just a moment my heart soared, then one of my escorts gave me a hard shove from behind and sent me sprawling. Suddenly all activity ceased, and a dozen faces turned in my direction.

The gondola fell deathly quiet, and for a moment everyone just stared. Then the first officer and Clauswitz exchanged looks, and the first officer stepped forward. One of the soldiers shouted at him and made a threatening motion with his gun, but the first officer barked back, eyes flashing with anger. Then he bent to help me to my feet.

“Fräulein,” he said, that single word overflowing with meaning and emotion.

“Thank you,” I whispered. I glanced to the captain, and he gave me a solemn nod and offered a pallid grin.

Another of the soldiers said something to the crew in the gondola. I couldn’t quite understand what he’d told them, but it clearly infuriated them. Suddenly there was chaos as crewmen began shouting and waving their fists, their faces clouded with rage. Some of them tried to attack the guards, held back only by those who saw the futility in the exercise.

Clauswitz bellowed, the sternness of his voice commanding, and everyone froze. The captain spoke to the soldiers, and there was no mistaking the harsh dressing down he was giving them. But if they were intimidated they certainly didn’t show it — belligerence was written on their faces, anger burned bright in their eyes, and they kept the muzzles of their guns trained on the crew.

Someone seized my arm and propelled me roughly forward. We moved through the ranks of the crew, who reluctantly drew aside, and it was then that I experienced what few, if any, in Haven would have believed possible.

“Fräulein,” the first crewman said. He removed his cap, held it over his heart, and bowed at the neck. “Fräulein,” said the others, each in turn, pulling their caps from their heads and mimicking the first.

I met the gaze of each as I passed, seeing in their eyes sadness and sympathy and a respect that left me more conscious than ever that the world was far more complicated than I had ever imagined. Val was right — it wasn’t just black and white.

I recalled what Clauswitz had said on the voyage to New York, about how his men thought of me as someone special. They had pinned such hopes on me. Unreasonable hopes, it seemed, because it was clear I was in no position to change the world. I was in no position to do much of anything at all.

The guards took me to the passenger quarters, but outside of the soldiers and crew, there was no hint of another soul aboard. One of my escorts opened the door to a first-class cabin and shoved me inside. I stumbled, falling to my knees, and as I struggled to my feet, I heard the firm click of the lock behind me. When I tried the door handle it was useless, confirming my status as prisoner.

Frustrated and anxious, I went to the port and pressed my face against the sloping glass, peering out into the hangar, not quite sure what I hoped to see. Maybe something that would actually inspire hope. But there was none to be had; outside, what little movement there was amounted to nothing more than soldiers milling about and the ground crew priming for departure.

I gave up watching and went to the head. It had been days since I'd washed and used a real toilet. I stripped off the clothes Isabelle had given me back in New York — another lifetime ago — and stepped into the shower. The feel of warm, clean water sluicing over my body was sheer ecstasy, and I stood there for minutes, trying to wash away more than the grime, my tears blending into the fall of the artificial rain.

After the shower I inspected myself in the small mirror above the tiny metal sink, staring at the girl looking back at me, but barely recognizing her. She was pale and gaunt, her short black hair wet and spiky, her eyes full of torment and sorrow. The effect on the latter was especially pronounced thanks to the dark half-circles underneath. The faint line of a fading scar extended from armpit to elbow on the inside of her right arm, the flesh slightly puckered and pink. Between her breasts lay a crucifix, suspended from a silver chain that encircled her slender neck.

How could I have changed so much in so short a time? I wondered. The changes were more than superficial — more than *physical*. Something inside me had broken, and I doubted it could ever be fixed.

I had witnessed things no one should ever have to see. I had experienced things no one would ever want to. I thought of the thousands of bodies floating in suspended animation, pumped full of drugs, fed through a tube, constantly being relieved of blood by creatures with less real heart than machines. I thought of Isabelle and Ticket vanishing before my eyes, lost to me forever. I thought of the Old One, Ahriman, for whom the word evil hardly seemed adequate. And I thought of Val.

Val coming to rescue me.

Val caught in a trap.

I stared at my reflection a moment longer, and just as I was turning away, I caught a hint of something in my eyes. It was like a flicker of light. Iridescence. I was immediately reminded of how Val's eyes sometimes looked. But when I bent closer, I saw only what I'd seen all my life, though now with added layers of distress and maybe the shadow of defeat.

Wrapped in a towel, I stepped from the washroom. The patter of drops dripping from my hair produced a faint, uneven rhythm on the floor as I stood motionless. I could feel the distant thrum of the engines through the soles of my bare feet. A carafe had been set on the small foldout table, and I crossed over to it and poured myself a glass of water. I drank it back in huge gulps, and after about three or four glasses I didn't feel so much thirsty as bloated — yet still the pangs of hunger gnawed at me.

I tried not to think of food and turned my attention to my clothes. The outfit Isabelle had given me was caked in blood and reeked of too many days spent in captivity. It was torn in a few places, and some of the stitching was beginning to part along the seams. In short, it had seen better days.

So have I, I thought.

On the canvas chair beside the table lay a carefully folded uniform. Someone must have put it there while I was in the shower. I picked it up and examined it, feeling a tightness in my gut. It was black and neatly pressed, and on one sleeve a red armband with the swastika was prominently displayed. I dropped it like it was something foul — I suppose for a Havenite, it pretty much was.

Exhausted and weak, I pulled down the sheets and climbed into bed, snuggling deep beneath the blanket, sighing at the sumptuousness of the soft mattress and the warm fabric that cocooned my body. Before I knew it, I'd fallen into a deep sleep.

Sometime in the early morning I awoke, and for a few moments, I imagined I was on the flight from Haven to New York and that everything I'd experienced had been nothing more than a dream. But then I saw the tattered clothes and knew the nightmare was all too real. I wrapped a sheet around me and went to the port, and I stood there and looked out into the early hours of the new day. I had slept through the launch of the airship, and now, far below, I could see the glitter of ice in the starlight and the black ragged lines of the leads that threaded through it.

I went back to bed and curled up under the blanket, but I couldn't sleep. Even the hypnotic murmurs of the ship, with its thrumming jet engines and constant tremor, didn't help. I was too awake with the thoughts that circled in my head: the life I'd once had, the discoveries I'd made, and what would happen to Val.

It always came back to Val.

He'd figured in my life at so many critical junctures. He'd been there when my mother had been pregnant with me. He'd been there the night of Cherkov's murder when things had begun to change between my father and me. He'd been there when my best friend had been killed and when I'd needed help finding my way through the darkness of my despair. He'd been there for my father's funeral and had taken care of me in the aftermath of Grace's death.

And then there'd been all those other times when it had been enough just to be with him, to touch him, to know he loved me and had made my life the sort you never want to end.

I was certain he was here now, aboard this airship. I could feel it. He was here because of me, and it might be the last time for both of us.

Grace had called Val our curse, but maybe we were his.

Somewhere, far away, I thought I heard a cry. Feral. Distraught. A woman's scream, filled with anger, sorrow, and lamentation. It resonated with my heart, echoing what I felt so deep within me. It was almost certainly my imagination, yet for a moment, I dared think it might be Mary. I hadn't seen her since the day I'd been captured, yet I couldn't bring myself to believe she was dead — even though all reason said she had to be. It was difficult to imagine how she could have survived what had happened at that Nazi base. Lying in bed, I thought about her and about the sacrifice she had made. A sacrifice made in vain, because all her efforts to protect me had come to naught.

I blinked back tears and wiped at my eyes. Just when I'd found my mother, I had lost her again. I'd barely had a chance to get to know her. I would've liked to have had the opportunity to reach the point where I could have told her I loved her and known in my heart that it was true. Now that would never happen — surely that was worth a few tears.

If I could shed tears for my mother, it went without saying that I could shed them for Val. My thoughts shifted in time to him, and I wept for the love I'd had and the love I might never have again. My father had told me that in the end Val would only bring me pain. I was beginning to think he was right.

* * *

This high up we caught the sun earlier, and when I awoke again, the brilliance of the clear daytime sky filled the small cabin with an airy, ethereal glow. Yawning, I lay there for a few moments, gathering myself and working the lethargy of sleep and sadness out of my system. I wished I could lie there all day and pretend this was some sort of vacation, that at the end of it all I'd be back in Haven, and everything would be the way it had been before — Camille and Val; my flat and school; visits with Grace and trips to see my father.

With great reluctance I rose and shuffled into the head. A wave of nausea seized me, and I promptly vomited into the toilet. I knelt there, heaving and gasping and spitting out bile.

What was happening to me? Up until the past few days I'd never been ill in my life, yet I'd now been sick several mornings in a row. *It's just stress*, I told myself. *You've taken a beating and you're an emotional wreck.* Hell, even thinking about some of the stuff I'd seen turned my stomach.

But deep inside, I knew it was more than that. This wasn't an emotional reaction; it was something else. I thought of my mother's journal, of her descent into madness, and couldn't help but wonder.

As quickly as it had come, the nausea passed, and I cleaned myself up and got dressed. I looked at myself in the mirror, clothed in the Nazi uniform, and almost wanted to be sick again.

This is what we could have been, I thought. *If not for Haven, we'd all be Nazis.* Except now I knew the truth — Haven was a lie, and we were all just slaves. Maybe we were no better than they were. Maybe we were monsters, too.

I breathed deep and tried not to think about it, but I might as well have tried to stop the world from turning.

I tested the door to my cabin and discovered they had unlocked it sometime during the night. When I opened it, there was a guard standing just outside. He didn't so much as blink when I stepped out, merely lifted his machine gun and pointed the barrel down the narrow corridor. The instructions seemed straightforward enough, so I made my way toward the first-class dining lounge, moving warily, expecting at any moment to be told to go back. But none of the soldiers I encountered threatened me, and before I knew it, I was in the lounge.

For a moment I just stood at the entrance and surveyed the neatly arranged tables, recalling the trip from Haven with Mrs. Hassan, Harry Trager and his posse, and the businessmen who had thought me so charming. I half expected them to appear, but the place remained deserted, the tables barren, save one.

I wove a path through the other tables and sat down behind the spotless charger plate and polished silver cutlery. As if on cue, the door to the kitchen opened, and a human steward stepped forth. He hesitated a moment, apparently not recognizing me, and I could see the look of surprise and confusion on his face. "I'm not one of them," I wanted to say, but the words stuck in my throat, because when it all came down to it, I didn't know what I was.

I turned to him so he could see me more clearly, smiled my warmest, and whatever his initial impressions, they were quickly set aside. He visibly relaxed and was soon about his business, grinning back at me as he advanced smoothly to the table and took up a post to one side of me. With a flourish he presented me with a menu and said, "May I recommend the pomfret, mum? It's done in white wine hollandaise, with lightly braised almonds and sun-dried tomatoes."

It sounded delicious — although I was so hungry he could have offered me rat-on-a-stick, and I'd have probably eaten it. I hadn't had a decent meal since leaving the *Eva Braun* back in New York, and that felt like a lifetime ago.

"Yes, I'll try the pomfret," I said, my mouth watering in anticipation.

"Very good, mum," he said, taking back the menu. "And to drink?"

"I'd love some coffee," I said, giving him my most endearing look. "Blue Mountain blend if you have it."

"Of course, mum." He stiffened to attention, made a slight bow, and retreated to the kitchen. I couldn't help noticing the faces staring out the round windows of the metal swinging doors, watching me as though I were something exotic. Rumors must have abounded, and I could only imagine what thoughts were going through their heads.

The steward brought my coffee and left me to it. I inhaled and was instantly transported back to Sunday mornings in my bed. I was on my third cup when he returned bearing a silver tray of steaming food. He stopped beside the table and placed a plate before me. "Pomfret a la hollandaise, mum."

After having been nearly starved to death for days, I could barely restrain myself. The only thing that kept me from gorging myself like a pig was the thought of being sick again. I knew I'd probably end up puking my guts out if I rushed things. So I measured my pace and tried to savor each morsel, ever conscious of the eyes watching me from the kitchen.

By the time I finished the fish, I was on my fifth cup of coffee. The steward came to clear away the dishes and offer dessert. I couldn't resist. While I waited for him to return, I sat cradling my cup in both hands and watching the ice fields that passed far beneath us.

I closed my eyes, drank in the scent of the Blue, and tried to picture myself where I belonged. But the sad thing was, I wasn't quite sure where that was anymore.

* * *

That evening, the vamps came out.

A soldier came for me in my cabin and escorted me to the first-class observation lounge. There were armed guards posted at the entrance and more inside. In the far corner, Ahriman sat in a wing-backed leather armchair, holding court and sipping from a stemmed glass. There was a chair positioned opposite him, and though I couldn't see the vamp seated there, I had the gut feeling it was Val. Or maybe I just wanted it to be.

When he saw me, Ahriman set down his glass and rose. "Miss Harkness," he said, executing a mock bow.

This brought the other vamp quickly to his feet. He turned to me, and I blurted out, "Val!" There was such pain in my voice it almost surprised even me.

Val's jaw tightened, but he didn't say anything.

"Why?" I asked. "Why did you come?"

"You didn't leave me much choice, Sophie."

I felt the sharp sting of guilt, bowed my head. "I'm sorry. I'm so sorry."

Val's face displayed a surfeit of emotion that bewildered and frightened me. I'd been expecting the Val I knew from Haven — the self-assured man, bold and confident, with all the answers, whatever they might be. In the back of my mind, I'd been telling myself that once we were together again, he'd figure some way out of this. But the Val in front of me looked beaten, as though the fight had gone out of him, as though he were resigned to his fate.

We stood there, the three of us, a silence hanging over us. Ahriman seemed in good spirits, studying us with a jocular eye, judging our reactions to one another. He wore an air of triumph, taking pleasure in our misery. "Perhaps we should sit," he said, indicating another chair. "I promised you answers."

I didn't think he cared one way or another that I had answers to my many questions. There seemed little doubt the Old One fed off our suffering. He was like one of those cheesy villains in the old Hollywood films I used to go to see with Camille, gloating over his victory and reveling in his genius as he watched the victims of his machinations squirm, helpless to do anything. This was all grand theater to him, and we were a captive audience with nowhere to run and hide.

With every word, with every gesture, it was like he was digging a knife into us, then twisting it to increase the agony. It might all have been a Shakespearian drama had it not been so tragically real.

I looked to Val and saw no spark of hope. If Ahriman's goal was to crush our spirits, then he was succeeding. I wanted Val to say something. I wanted him to take me in his arms and tell me everything was going to be okay. But he just stood there, waiting for me to be seated.

Finally I eased myself into the chair and sat rigid with fear. I watched Val and tried to gain some sense of what he was thinking, but his eyes betrayed no secrets, spoke no truths. I wondered if he blamed me. He had every right. He had warned me — even pleaded with me — not to pursue it. I hadn't appreciated the risks then, hadn't realized what it would mean for the two of us. Understanding had come too late, and now I'd pretty much driven a stake through the heart of the man I loved.

"Relax, Miss Harkness," said Ahriman. "Your suffering will soon be over." He grinned with delight.

I focused on Val again, but he kept his eyes fixed on the Old One. I needed him to look at me. Just one glance, one brief glimpse that would give me cause to hope.

"All journeys must come to an end," Ahriman continued, more to himself than to either of us. He held his glass of blood aloft, level with his eyes, inspecting it in the warm light from a nearby wall sconce. "Ours is closer now than it has ever been since the day we were exiled to this world."

Exiled?

He took a leisurely sip, and I cringed and looked away. Though I'd seen Val drink blood on a numerous occasions, seeing Ahriman do it was another thing altogether. He clearly enjoyed it. Watching him, I had a sense of a long history of humans being stalked, hunted, and drained simply for the pleasure of it. There were suddenly images in my mind similar to those I'd seen when I'd first encountered him: dingy city streets wrapped in the mantle of night, the pale smooth flesh of a woman's neck, white fangs gleaming in gaslight, lips painted with blood. My stomach heaved, and I closed my eyes, fighting for air.

"It's time for celebration," Ahriman announced in a flamboyant manner. "The long imprisonment of my people is ended. The genius of Cherkov has at last been realized." Stone-like eyes bore into me, and I felt myself shrink under their licentious inspection.

I still didn't understand what he was talking about — other than that I was somehow an integral part of it. Flinching under his gaze, I averted my eyes, studying the patterns in the aluminum floor.

"A pity the good doctor was murdered before he could prepare you for us," Ahriman said, continuing to gloat over his victory. "Had not fortune shone upon us, all might have been lost — especially since there were some in Haven who began to suspect how important you were to us. They figured out Cherkov's work was about more than ending Gomorrah, that his was another agenda and that he served two masters." He smiled at me again. "Knowing that, I suppose one can't blame some of your countrymen for trying to kill you, Miss Harkness. I'm sure by their way of reckoning, it was better you be dead than fall into our hands."

That there were people in Haven who wanted me dead was obviously no surprise. I only had to think back to the night in the library, the car crash with Havershaw, and the gunman in the hospital to be reminded of that. But even so, I continued to struggle with accepting it. Maybe it was a bit naïve of me to think that after all we'd been through, humans would be beyond such things. After all, what was being done to non-Immune babies was surely a testament to how immoral we could be.

"Fortunately Haven is a divided kingdom," the Old One continued, oblivious to my consternation — or perhaps simply enjoying it. "As riven as the Third Reich when it comes to loyalties." He looked pointedly at Val before turning his attention back to me. "Others on the islands were far more pragmatic than your would-be assassins, driven more by necessity and greed than any overarching sense of morality. They ensured you weren't lost to us — proving once again that greed will always trump even the highest of principles."

"I don't believe you," I said. I felt like I was standing inside a building that was crashing down around me. "No one in Haven would work for you."

"And yet we are here, in the moment at hand, waiting upon the future you offer. What does that tell you about your fellow countrymen?"

I didn't answer, and inside of me I felt as though something important, something that had been essential to me, had curled up and died.

"What can the girl possibly mean to you?" Val asked through clenched teeth.

"You can't even begin to imagine, *boy*," said Ahriman, spitting out the last word as though it were an expletive. "She is a means to an end." He looked away, out the windows nearest him, his mood shifting. When he turned back, there was something almost tragic about him. For a moment, it was as if he were something else and not evil incarnate — something that might actually possess feelings.

"You know the myths about us," he said, looking back and forth between Val and I. "You've no doubt heard the stories about how we came to be, that maybe we're from another world. Well, there is always a kernel of truth in even the most outrageous of tales, and in this one there is a great deal.

"We've been trapped on this world for longer than I care remember, struggling to find a way back home. We're exiles. Prisoners. Banished here because we dared to defy the rulers of our world. Because we had the courage of our convictions."

I sat stunned, and looked to Val, thinking what I was hearing had to be madness. Surely Ahriman didn't expect us to believe any of it.

"You doubt my words," said the Old One. He chuckled, a horrid, foreboding sound. "Don't worry, whether you believe matters not. All that's important is that from the moment we arrived here, we haven't stopped trying to return home. If not for the weaknesses of humanity, we'd have done it far sooner. For far too long the people of this world failed us. They'd neither the intellectual nor physical capacity to help us accomplish our goals. And then came the age of science, and not long after, Hitler. How fortuitous and refreshing to find a man with no moral inhibitions. A man willing to cross the borders of ethical behavior and march boldly into the territory of the immoral and profane. And with him came Cherkov, for whom only the data mattered, no matter how it was obtained. Cherkov devised Gomorrah using the blood of myself and my brethren as a basis for the virus. It was a means to accelerate the process of creating an individual who could serve our needs. But the man was careless and infected a population already ill with influenza." Ahriman spread his hands. "You know the rest."

Horrified, I said, "You were willing to destroy an entire world to get what you want?"

"It's not *our* world," he replied, as though that were sufficient justification.

"You really don't care?"

He laughed again. "You think your world is unique, child? Nothing could be further from the truth. There is an infinite number like it in an infinite number of other universes. Why should we care if one is destroyed? It is nothing in the grand scheme of things."

I thought he was completely off his rocker. Other worlds like this one? He might as well be suggesting the world in Camille's stupid book was actually real.

"Your skepticism is not unexpected," said Ahriman. "You're such a myopic, narrow-minded people. You cannot see past the smallness of your own existence."

"So this was all about me?" I said. "The war, Cherkov, Gomorrah, the truce, Haven, the babies . . . it was all just to make *me*?"

"Oh, Miss Harkness, do not flatter yourself. You are only important insofar as being the bridge between what your mother was and the child we have sought."

I stiffened, blinked, and turned to Val, bewildered. "What . . . what's he saying?" I asked him, terrified. "He doesn't mean —"

"That you bear a child?" Ahriman clapped his hands and laughed with childish delight. "But of course that's what I mean."

I stood up, thunderstruck, and fell back into my seat as my knees buckled. The throbbing of my heart was so intense I thought it would burst through my chest. I was dizzy and wanted to be sick, and then I was.

The whole notion of what he had just told me was so repulsive and terrifying that all I could think of was getting rid of this thing. I wanted to claw myself open and rip it out. There was a monster growing inside me! How could it be otherwise? Anything the Old Ones were a part of had to be monstrous.

Oh, God! Oh, God! Oh, God! This can't be happening! It was all just a nightmare, and I was going to wake up and find I'd dreamt it all. I'd wake up and be back in Haven at the beach house, waiting for Camille to come home from her date. *Oh, please, God, make this just a dream. Make it not real.*

I was sobbing, gasping for air, thinking I was going to die and wishing I would. I sat hunched over, arms wrapped around my waist, my head bowed to my knees. Val put a hand on my back, said, "Sophie, it's all right. You're going to be all right."

"Are you out of your mind? How can this ever be all right? How can *I* ever be all right?"

"Sophie . . ."

I flinched, jerked away from him. "Don't," I said.

Across from me, Ahriman studied me in a fascinated silence. "Don't be so hard on young Valentine, Miss Harkness," he finally said. "He was ignorant of what Cherkov was really doing. And he could not possibly have imagined the objective was to create a hybrid capable of bearing a child whose blood will help us return home."

I lifted my head and saw the tortured look on Val's face. But as pained as his expression was, he didn't look quite as shocked by this as I would have expected him to be.

Ahriman continued, as if he found great pleasure in hearing his own voice. "After so many experiments, you, my dear" — he turned to me — "were the first to prove a viable candidate. You alone have proven capable of bearing children. Only you have the perfect set of genes. You are the one success after so many failures. You can't begin to comprehend our joy when Cherkov told us he had finally given us what we had so long desired."

"You can't think it will end here, Ahriman," Val said in a low voice.

"And why not? We have the girl."

"When the rebellion —"

Ahriman cackled dismissively. "The rebellion? Do you think we care about your petty little power struggle? Don't you understand that nothing you do in this world is of consequence? Nothing matters to us but this girl and the child within her. Besides, your foolish little rebellion was finished before it even began. Two of its best lieutenants are gone. Others will join them soon enough. And then, of course, there's you. Imagine what will happen when you're executed before the entire world. How courageous do you think your friends will be when they realize that even someone with so many party connections can't save himself from the guillotine?"

"Rebellions have a life of their own, beyond the work of a single individual," Val said. "Cut me down, and others will rise up in my place. We number far more than you can possibly imagine."

"I daresay," Ahriman agreed. "But again, what care I, now that I have what I want? Let that fool Hitler worry about the divisions within his ranks." He stared hard at Val.

"You won't win," said Val.

"Oh, but I already have, my dear boy."

I stayed bent over during their exchange, clutching at my gut, wondering if this was how Pandora had felt when she'd opened the jar the gods had bestowed upon her and released all the evils into the world. At least in her case, however, hope had remained intact. For me, there was no longer any to be found.

"We haven't reached Berlin yet," Val said.

Ahriman laughed. "And you imagine that at this late stage someone is going to come riding to your rescue?" He snorted. "How charming. It seems you've lived among the humans far too long, Valentine. Having faith in miracles is a human frailty."

"I won't let you harm her," said Val, his hands balled into fists.

"Do you honestly believe you could stop me, were that my intent? But rest assured, Valentine, once you are dealt with, your precious Miss Harkness will remain in good health — at least until she has served her purpose. Beyond that . . . well, I really don't care."

CHAPTER 34
FALLING DARKNESS

"It has to be a lie," I said to Val, forcing myself to an upright position. "I can't be pregnant. It's impossible. It's only ever been you and me, and you're —"

Ahriman sat languidly in his chair, wearing a look of mild amusement. "Really, Miss Harkness, take a moment to reconsider," he interrupted. "You recently spent some time in a hospital in Haven, did you not?"

I stared at him, clutching the arms of the chair so fiercely that had they been made of wood I might actually have torn them apart. "How . . . how do you know that?"

"Come, come. Have I not made it clear by now that we have allies in Haven? It's true they may not have been witting allies, but it's amazing what people will do when given the proper incentive. Oh, let us say" — he gestured airily — "being led to believe they're working for some greater good. If they imagine they're carrying on the work of Cherkov, as indeed they are, well . . ." He spread both his arms. "Too bad for them the end results aren't — how would you Havenites put it? — as advertised."

I cringed as the Old One laughed, and Val said, "Someone along the line must know the truth."

Ahriman grinned, all teeth and savagery. "Someone does. There are plenty of rich and powerful people in Haven who wish to remain that way. They're the sort who would turn a blind eye to what was being done to one of their own if they thought it in their own best interests to do so."

"You're lying!" I screamed. But as soon as the words had left me I was struck by the realization that he might very well be talking about Aunt Amelia. I remembered that night in the hospital after my accident with Peppy and Havershaw. I'd seen Aunt Amelia and the gunman conversing. She'd been upset — angry or at least annoyed. Maybe that meant she'd been angry at the attempt on my life.

Or maybe that's just wishful thinking on my part, I thought. Clearly Aunt Amelia had something to do with shipping non-Immune babies to the Third Reich and stood to lose a great deal if *that* ever became public. Even if she hadn't wanted me dead, maybe others she'd been working with had. Maybe someone in that inner circle of the rich and powerful had given the gunman orders that had countermanded hers.

Even were that true, it was still hard to believe Amelia would help the Old Ones. She had always strongly advocated taking back the planet and making it a world exclusively for humans. But I also knew she was the type of person who would do almost anything to achieve her goals — even if that meant conspiring with the enemy.

The more I thought about it, the more I'd the impression of wheels within wheels, with the right hand unaware of what the left hand was doing and vice versus. Somewhere along the line, the government was involved. They had to have been party to the trafficking of non-Immune babies — it was part of the truce. My head spun with thoughts of it. It was all so Machiavellian.

Would the government have tried to kill me, then? I wondered. I didn't want to think so; to go down that road was to realize there was nowhere in this world I was safe. I squeezed my eyes shut, wishing I were back home in my flat and that I'd wake up and find out this had all been a nightmare.

"Right now I suspect you're wondering who tried to have you killed on Haven," said Ahriman.

I looked up at him, incredulous.

"Don't be so surprised, Miss Harkness. You're as easy to read as an open book."

"You know who they are," I said, rage overcoming my fear for just a moment.

He made an offhanded gesture. "It hardly matters now. Suffice it to say that there are those who would have you silenced for what you know and what you mean to us, and there are those who would save you for that very reason — because they understand your value. I imagine they're the sort who believe they can use you as a bargaining chip."

"A bargaining chip for what?"

He shrugged. "Who can say?" But I had a feeling he knew far more than he was letting on. "All that's important is that you're here, and we'll soon have what we want. We've been monitoring you for years, and our patience had been growing thin. But now all is well, though admittedly when you were shot it didn't look so good. As things stand, however, that proved rather fortuitous. Once you were in hospital, it was a simple matter for one of Cherkov's followers to execute the necessary procedure. Such are the marvels of modern science."

"You're crazy!" I heard the shrillness and mounting hysteria in my voice, and I couldn't rein it in. I still wanted to believe he was lying about the whole pregnancy thing, but I could feel it inside me. Not just the sickness but something else.

"You've been feeling ill in the mornings lately, have you not?"

I gawked at him, telling myself he only knew because they'd been spying on me. Unconsciously I put a hand to my stomach and imagined I could feel something there. It was ridiculous, of course. There hadn't been enough time. Not even enough time to be experiencing morning sickness, surely. But who knew what sort of thing it was that was growing inside me? All I could picture was some monstrous creation of the Old Ones, an atrocity as heinous as they were. A scream started deep inside me, and I had to fight to throttle it. Not for the first time did I fear I was slipping into madness, falling into the nightmare my mother had been trapped in since before my birth.

"This can't be happening," I moaned.

"And yet it is," said Ahriman. He laughed cruelly. "You humans are so weak and predictable."

I turned to Val. "Did you know about this?" I demanded, tears stinging my eyes, lips trembling.

"No. Of course not!" He glared at Ahriman as he spoke. "This is the first I've ever heard of it, Sophie. I swear."

I wanted to believe him, but there was something about the look in his eyes that gave me doubt. There were just too many secrets. Apparently there always had been.

"Well," said Ahriman, "I have so enjoyed our conversation. It has been truly invigorating, and while I'd love to stay and chat some more, there are a few minor details I must attend to before we reach Berlin. I'll leave you lovebirds to sort this out."

I watched the Old One rise from his chair in an eerie, inhuman manner. He stood and bowed again, mostly from the neck. "Before I go," he said, "I thought I might leave you a gift. You'll find it most edifying." He snapped his fingers, and a soldier stepped forward to hand him a book. Ahriman put it down on the coffee table in front of me, and I glanced at the cover — *No Haven for Darkness*. "There are some truths far stranger than fiction," he said, tapping the book. And then he was gone, disappearing so swiftly that for a moment, I thought I must have blacked out.

Val and I just sat there, locked in our silences, trying not to look at one another.

"I'm sorry," I said at last, meaning it even more than the first time I'd said it. "I truly am. I didn't mean for it —"

"Oh, Sophie," he said wearily, "it isn't your fault. I should have done a better job of protecting you."

"You tried. I just didn't listen."

"Just like your father. Like Mary."

I had promised myself I wouldn't ask, but I couldn't stop myself from saying, "Did you ever love me, Val?"

He looked at me with such anguish that I felt foolish and ashamed. I hated myself for the doubts I'd had. I got up and went to him, sat on the arm of his chair, and cradled his head in my arms. He put his arms around my waist, holding me as though he were afraid I might suddenly disappear. I stroked his hair and laid my cheek against the top of his head; for the longest time we just sat there, saying nothing, yet speaking volumes in the way we simply touched.

"I've really messed things up, haven't I?" I said at last.

"We're not in Berlin yet. And despite what Ahriman said, maybe there are such things as miracles."

"But what can we do?"

"Whatever it takes. We can't let this ship reach Berlin. No matter what, Sophie, we can't let Ahriman succeed."

I closed my eyes and nodded. "I know," I said. "And if it means —"

He pulled away, lifted his gaze to mine. "I could never do that."

"There may be no choice. And surely it's better that I —"

"No." He shook his head vehemently.

"Val —"

"No, Sophie. I'll find a way to save you. I have to."

"How are you going to do that? Look around. We're constantly being watched." My eyes darted to the vamps stationed at the lounge entrance. "There are soldiers all over the ship, and half the crew are vamps. I don't know how you even managed to get this ship here in the first place. And with Immune crew on board, at that."

"I commandeered it," said Val.

I wasn't as surprised as I thought I should be. "No one tried to stop you? They didn't know you were . . ." My shoulders twitched in a hint of a shrug. "You know?"

"I left the Embassy before any message to that effect came in."

"You put yourself and the crew at risk just for me." It wasn't a question, and implicit in it was reproach. I didn't want their lives weighing on my conscience.

"There was no choice, Sophie."

"Of course there was. And now what are you going to do? Look at us. We're captives of that lunatic monster."

"I came here to save you," said Val, "and I will."

"You're just one man."

"Clauswitz is no Nazi, and his people are loyal to him."

I nodded, recalling their reaction when I'd first come aboard. "Okay. Fine. But that still leaves the soldiers. I've seen at least a dozen of them. And they're armed to the teeth."

"I didn't say it would be easy."

"It's impossible," I said. "You'll just —"

"Get myself killed?" Val grinned wryly. "I'm already dead."

"You know what I mean." I scowled at him.

"Better that than you ending up with those monsters. That can't happen, Sophie."

"I can't lose you just to save myself. It doesn't work that way, Val."

He looked more serious than I'd ever seen him. "This is about more than us."

I nodded, chagrined. He was right, of course. The Old Ones couldn't win. There was no scenario in which I could see the result of that being a good one. "What do you want me to do?" I asked.

"Stay out of trouble."

"I'm not just going to sit in my cabin."

"That's exactly what you're going to do. It's the safest place for you to be until I come for you."

"And what if you don't?"

"I will."

"And then what?" I wasn't sure how much of this he'd thought through, and it was impossible not to think of Isabelle and Ticket and what our rashness had led to.

"I just have to get rid of the Old One," Val said. "After that —"

"Get rid of the Old One?" I stared at him in disbelief. "Are you crazy? You make it sound like a walk in the park, but you're no match for him. You told me yourself they're not like other vamps. They're stronger, faster, more agile. And you've seen him; you've listened to him. He's insane and utterly ruthless. He won't hesitate to kill you."

"And I won't hesitate to do likewise."

"Val . . ."

He looked at me earnestly. "Once Ahriman is out of the way, Clauswitz will bring the ship down in Stockholm. There we can transfer to another flight that'll take us back to New York."

"Okay," I said, hesitating. "But what if —"

"Nothing will go wrong," he insisted.

I wasn't so convinced. "But if it does . . ."

"We're going to be all right," Val said, but I wondered if he honestly believed that.

"If we get back to Haven, where do we go from there? What becomes of us?" *How can there be an* us*?*

"You're not like the others, Sophie," he said. "If you didn't realize it before, you certainly must now. I've always sensed it, knew that what happened to Mary when she was pregnant with you had made you something special."

"I'm what Cherkov made me, Val." My voice was small, frightened. "What the Old Ones want. For all we know, I could be another monster. What if what happened to Mary happens to me? And what about this . . . this *thing* inside me. . ." My stomach clenched, and I fought down a wave of terror.

"Listen to me, Sophie. You have no reason to be afraid. Years ago, when I was helping Isabelle, there was a boy going through the same thing she did."

"I know," I said, remembering Isabelle in my arms. "She told me about him — Jason."

"Yes. And he told me . . . he told me things about myself he couldn't possibly have known. And then he told me about my future. And about you."

"Me? What are you talking about, Val?" I felt a different kind of fear. "How is that even possible?"

"I don't know." He looked at the book Ahriman had left on the table. "All I know is that it has something to do with *that*."

"That?" I glanced at the book dismissively. "But it's just a story. Surely you don't believe any of it."

"Sometimes it's enough just to believe. Sometimes you have to have faith."

"But it's not real. I've read that book, Val. It's nonsense. It's just some guy's barmy ideas."

"It was real enough for Isabelle and Jason. They saw the world in that book when they were a part of Cherkov's experiments. And they said Cherkov believed them."

"Are you listening to yourself, Val? You're sounding like Ahriman. You can't make choices based on a fairy story."

"Look," Val said, "whether it's true or not doesn't matter right now. Only this moment is important." He bowed his head to my hand, kissed it. "I want you to know that only with you have I ever believed I could be happy. You and I —"

"What about Grace? And Mary?" It was impossible to mask the doubt I didn't want to have.

"No, Sophie. Only *you*."

"Val . . ."

"I'd planned to make your eighteenth birthday one neither of us would ever forget." He looked up at me, hope and passion in his eyes.

"But now . . ." He essayed a grin, but it was meager and despondent. "Now this may be our only chance, and I want to know."

"Know what?" I asked.

"What would you have said?"

My heart skipped a beat. "I'm not sure I understand."

"When I was crossing Canada after the plague hit North America, I helped a girl who told me I'd one day meet the woman who was meant for me. She gave me this to give to . . . you." Val dug into a pocket, withdrew his hand, and held it before me. He uncurled his fingers, revealing a ring nestled in his palm.

I gasped and put a hand to my mouth, staring at the ring, then at him. I was caught between a valley of sorrows and the highest summits of joy. A mournful little laugh escaped under my breath, and I felt tears beginning. I leaned into him, put my arms around his neck, and whispered my answer in his ear.

He put a hand to my cheek, kissed me, and pressed the ring into my hand, folding my fingers over it. "That's all I needed to know," he said.

We kissed again, but out the corner of my eye, I caught a glimpse of *No Haven for Darkness* on the table and a chill ran up my spine. What did it mean, and why was it so important to so many people? It kept showing up like a bad penny, and now I was beginning to think it was the catalyst for everything. In a way this whole thing had started with it.

But how could it be real? How could any of what's happening right now be real? It's all just madness.

And I was afraid of how it would end.

I felt the ring in my hand, the warmth of the metal against my skin. Small as it was, the enormity of its physical and emotional weight was crushing. It felt as though I was carrying the world upon my shoulders.

I closed my eyes and tried to picture the day when I'd wear that ring with pride and joy. But somehow all I saw was darkness.

CHAPTER 35
FIRE AND ICE

I lay no claim to having much experience with flying, but when the loud bang echoed throughout the ship from stem to stern, I knew something was wrong.

The violent tremor that passed through the *Eva Braun* in the wake of the explosion rattled the deck and bulkheads and swept right through me, bringing me quickly to my feet. I hurried to the port and pressed my face to the glass. The pitch black of the night sky was lit by an inferno that had erupted from the long strut belonging to one of the aft engine mounts. The flames screamed from the ragged end like a blowtorch, fluttering at the tip and curving back under the force of the airship's momentum.

I stared at it, for a moment bewildered, until I realized that what puzzled me was what I *didn't* see — the pod of the jet turbine itself. The entire engine was gone.

I watched the fire, aghast, and then realized with even greater horror that it was working its way up the strut. There was another explosion, not as pronounced as the first, but now a billowing cloud of incandescence threatened to set the entire fabric covering of the ship's hull ablaze.

The zeppelin shuddered again, the vibrations becoming constant, and beneath them I could hear the whine of the remaining engines.

The deck shifted under my feet, and I staggered. Outside the window, the horizon seemed to be sinking as it passed out of view.

The ship began to shake and rattle, the metal around me groaning in protest as the whole thing pitched. I fell against the door, getting my breath knocked from me. Gasping in pain, I fumbled for the handle and discovered I was still locked in. Terrified and trapped, I began pounding with my fists, yelling and screaming at the top of my lungs for someone to let me out.

I thought I heard people moving in the hallway and redoubled my efforts to attract their attention. Somewhere overhead I heard a sharp twang, followed by metal banging on metal, the noise reverberating like thunder.

"Help!" I cried, hammering the door with enough force to dent it. "Someone let me out!"

I gripped the handle again, yanking on it, and felt the door give a little. I pulled harder, but the handle tore loose, and I crashed back onto the bed, still holding the handle in my hand, staring at it dumbly.

"Sophie!"

I rushed to the door, shouting as loudly as I could. "Val, I'm in here."

"Get back!" he warned. I stepped toward the glass port and watched in stunned silence as the door was smashed inward, torn off its hinges. Val stood in the opening, holding out a hand to me. "Come on! We have to hurry."

"What's happening?" I asked, taking his hand and letting him lead me into the hallway.

"We're losing altitude," Val said as we struggled toward the stern in the company of a dozen crewmen. "Looks like we'll hit ground in the next few minutes. We don't want to be down here when that happens."

We came to a door at the end of the hall, and beyond it, I could see a stairway leading up into the vast envelope of the ship. It was darker there, the path lit by the feeble glow from low-wattage bulbs.

I gripped the railing tightly as I climbed the stairs, trying to pretend I wasn't as afraid as I felt.

"Is this your doing?" I asked Val.

He shook his head. "I'm trying to save you, not kill you. This'll bring the whole ship down. We'll be lucky if we survive."

More Immune crewmen joined us, mostly stewards, cooks, and cabin personnel. Noticeably absent were the officers and engineers, as well as the riggers, who I imagined were up above us somewhere. They'd be in the shrouds and amidst the gas cells that filled the vast interior of the ship's hull, working alongside their vamp counterparts in a bid to save the ship.

The *Eva Braun* shuddered again, metal creaking, wire shrouds and stays humming with tension as they were stretched to the limit. Far off, toward the tail end of the zeppelin, I heard the shriek of tearing metal. Shouts filled the air, and when I looked up and back, I saw men pouring forth from one of the passageways that tunneled through the gas cell closest us. The catwalk they were on twisted and came apart, a section of it falling, narrowly missing us as it pierced the fabric of the hull below. Bodies dropped from above, tumbling toward us. Some managed to grab hold of cables or girders, but others vanished through the ragged tear and were swallowed up by the night.

"This way," said Val, pulling me after him.

We'd only gone a few yards when a figure loomed before us. Val's grip tightened on my hand, and even though I couldn't see who was ahead of us, I knew it had to be Ahriman.

Val retreated a step, pushing me back, his head turning quickly from left to right, searching. But there was no other way forward.

"Val —" I started to say.

I felt him tense, sensed his consternation. "Sophie, you've got to go back," he said. "You've got to get away from here."

"I'm not leaving you!" I cried, clinging to his arm.

"You have to. I've got to settle this, and I need you to be safe."

Safe? In a ship that was on fire and headed for a crash landing on the ice? Was he insane? But I knew what he meant — he couldn't focus on Ahriman if he had to worry about me.

There were so many things I wanted to say to him, but there wasn't time for any of them. "Come back to me," I said as he let go my hand and stepped forward.

Val glanced back over his shoulder, nodded, and then moved faster than I would ever have imagined possible. He leapt toward the Old One, and in the anodyne light, I saw the flash of an ironwood blade.

The airship shifted, throwing me hard against the opposite rail. I grappled for a hold as the catwalk collapsed beneath me, severing cables and shrouds. Wires whipped through the air, slicing through the fragile skin of a gas cell and decapitating a vamp soldier as he tried to flee. Another was chopped in half.

I screamed, but Val was too far away to hear me, battling Ahriman high up in the airship, the two of them leaping from strut to strut, climbing up cables, racing along catwalks, swiping and clawing at one another.

I found myself alone, clinging with an iron grip to the catwalk, which was now held in place by nothing more than a solitary piece of metal. As I searched for a more secure position, the *Eva Braun* heaved herself skyward, her bow rising higher as the stern sank toward the ice. The catwalk jerked and slipped, and there was a sharp *crack!* as it tore loose. I plummeted with it, screaming as I held on for dear life. The mass of metal breached the fabric skin and plunged into the night sky, taking me with it.

I thought for certain I was dead, but the tangle of metal bars and pipes snagged on the airship's frame. With a bone-jarring jerk, my descent was brought to a halt.

The wind howled about me, icy cold, and my eyes watered as I squinted forward, seeing nothing but black sky and stars. I turned my head and was horrified to see a wall of flame licking at sections of the stern. Below was the arctic desert, far closer than it should be, yet still a good two or three thousand feet away.

My grip on the catwalk intensified, even as the metal shuddered and slipped again. Getting back inside the ship was my only chance for survival, and with that in mind, I steeled myself and began to inch my way upward.

It seemed like I climbed for hours, but finally I was within striking distance of the dark opening in the hull. Pieces of fabric fluttered and flapped in the wind, tantalizingly close. I stretched, straining, reaching out, groping for a handhold. But before I could secure myself, the catwalk gave way and fell earthward again. I cried out, snatched blindly, and somehow managed to seize a fistful of cloth. It started to tear, but a hand extended from within the ship and grabbed mine, hauling me up into the *Eva Braun* in one fluid motion.

"Thank you! Thank you," I gushed as I sat rubbing my sore wrist.

A hand touched my face, and I looked up and found myself face to face with Mary.

I couldn't believe my eyes. My mother. I had thought her dead but wished otherwise. Somehow, against all odds, she had survived and managed to remain hidden all this time. But then, I suppose, she was good at that. After all, she'd been doing it for years: eluding Val and Isabelle; somehow getting herself to Haven; avoiding detection. Was it really any surprise she would show up now?

Mary led me forward, climbing the increasing incline of the ship as the bow continued to rise. Smoke was now swirling up past the intact gas cells, the access tunnels through their centers acting like chimneys through which a roiling black cloud spewed forth.

I looked for Val, but saw no sign of him. I started to turn back, but Mary simply threw me over her shoulder and carried me away as though I were a child.

The bass rumble of another explosion rolled over us, and the ship groaned, shaking even more violently. Mary found a stairway and ascended to a catwalk that was pitched so steeply it was a wonder she could even stand. The ship was almost vertical when we reached the last set of steps, but Mary was undeterred and crawled up it as though it were a ladder. I tried not to look down, but even still, I caught glimpses of the hull glittering with fire, the fabric evaporating like lit tissue paper, leaving behind only the skeletal frame of the ship.

Somehow we made it onto the docking platform, and Mary carried me up through the hatch and onto the prow of the airship. A scorching wind howled around us, clawing at us as though it were trying to rip us free and toss us into the sky.

Mary set me down and I staggered, reaching out to grasp the docking probe for support as the stern of the airship struck the ground, crumpling in a shriek of tortured metal. The *Eva Braun* seemed to slowly vanish, like an ocean liner sinking into the sea. Her airframe collapsed, and her fabric skin exploded, creating a roaring maelstrom of flame and burning embers that billowed in all directions. As we clung desperately, the ship shook herself to pieces. Waves of searing incandescence rolled outward from the base of impact, spreading across the ice and snow, oozing like rivers of lava. The remaining half of the ship slewed drunkenly to one side and toppled over.

We were thrown clear, flying head over heels through the air, landing beyond the perimeter of the flames. I slammed into deep snow, the wind knocked out of me. Beside me, Mary alighted with catlike poise, quickly scooping me up in her arms and carrying me away as the last of the wreckage rained down around us, clanging and banging, shrieking and thundering in an expanding inferno.

A couple of hundred yards from the edge of the crash site, Mary stopped and set me down. I stood there in the snow, staring in stunned silence at the remains of the *Eva Braun*. Survivors staggered around in the shadow of the wreckage, silhouetted against the vivid blaze of burning kerosene. They looked dazed and confused; some were seriously burned or otherwise injured. I wanted to find Val, but as if she could read my mind, Mary held me tightly, her eyes beacons of maternal consternation, bright with emotion.

Finally it all caught up with me. My legs gave way, and I collapsed. The last thing I saw was my mother's face, her lips moving as though she were trying to say something. But I couldn't make out what it was, and somewhere in the back of my mind, I recalled Isabelle saying that Mary hadn't really spoken since the day she'd left Haven more than seventeen years ago.

CHAPTER 36
EXSANGUINATION

"Fräulein."

I opened my eyes, blinking torpidly, not sure where I was as I tried to overcome the lethargy that wanted to drag me back down into unconsciousness. Reddish-yellow firelight flickered and danced nearby, beating back the cold, offering refuge from the dark. Wreckage rose in the background, a forest of twisted struts and girders. A field of stars burned in the heavens, and then a face loomed, cast in shadow. It took me a moment to recognize Captain Clauswitz. He flashed a grin and said, "I'm glad to see you're all right."

"What happened?" I asked. I sat up, the blanket covering me falling into my lap. "How did I get here?"

He scratched his head. "We didn't get a very good look at her," he confessed. "She kept her distance, but she made certain we knew you were there when she dropped you off."

"Where did she go?" I jumped to my feet, tottering uncertainly, still groggy.

Clauswitz put out a hand and steadied me. "You need to rest," he said, concerned.

"I need to find her."

"She went back out there." He pointed into the darkness, to the ice and snow and forbidding emptiness. "There's nothing you can do for her."

He was right of course, but I was still reluctant to give up so easily. I squinted at the shadows beyond the light of the flames, hoping I might see something, some hint of her. But if Mary was there, she was well concealed by the jet of night and the icy desolation that seemed to stretch on forever.

I sat down and picked up the blanket, wrapping it around my shoulders and bending toward the fire the crew had built, drinking in its warmth. After a moment or two, I lifted my head and looked about, surveying my surroundings in more detail. The flames had died down, and we were camped in the lee of the wreckage, next to the remains of the control gondola.

The gondola was covered with tarps and blankets, ready, I assumed, to serve as shelter for the vamps when morning arrived. For now the crew had gathered around the fire they'd made. When they spotted me observing them, they lifted their heads and looked at me, faces grim with resignation. Many of the Immunes wore improvised bandages stained with blood. They looked beaten by their ordeal. The vamps were in much better shape, the soot on their faces and the ruin of their clothing the only signs of the trauma they'd been through. Judging by their small number, however, a great many had perished in the disaster.

I reached out my hands to the fire, my body craving the heat, sucking it in greedily as I surveyed the circle of survivors again. As I looked from face to face, a sense of dismay crept over me, threatening to overwhelm the relief I'd felt upon realizing I wasn't alone.

He wasn't there.

"Was there no one else?" I asked Clauswitz.

"We haven't finished searching," he replied, but I could tell from the look on his face and the tone of his voice that he didn't expect to find anyone alive. "It's quite a mess in there." He nodded toward the wreckage. "We're taking a break, but we'll try again. At least until sunrise."

I looked to the east, then back at the wreck, my pulse quickening. If Val was somewhere in all that mess, I had to find him before the first rays of dawn ripened the sky. If I didn't . . .

That wasn't an option. I couldn't even entertain the possibility of *not* finding him.

"Is there a chance of rescue?" I asked the captain.

"We managed to get off a mayday before we went down," he told me. "Our location and situation. I'm sure they must have heard it in Stockholm. Lufthansa will probably have a ship in the air already, heading for us as we speak. If we're lucky we'll all be back in civilization within a day. Surely no more than two."

"Good," I said, huffing a frosty cloud of breath, not really certain whether it actually was good or not. I wrapped the blanket tighter, tucked my hands under my arms, and shifted closer to the fire, trying to gather strength. I had to start looking for Val, but I was freezing; I felt sick and weak and just wanted to lie down and sleep.

"You need to rest," the captain said.

Trembling, teeth chattering, I shook my head. "I'll be all right," I said. "I have to find him."

Clauswitz took off his jacket and draped it over my shoulders. I looked up at him in surprise. He merely shrugged and said, "You need it far more than I do."

I gratefully drew the coat closer around me and sat in silence, shivering, unable to think of anything other than Val. I had to get up. I had to find him.

You should be worrying about Mary, I told myself. But I had the feeling that wherever she was, she'd be all right. She was resourceful, a survivor. And as mad as she might be, she was resilient and determined. Those were qualities that had helped her protect me over the years — regardless of who or what had threatened. So many times when I'd needed her most, she'd found me, and I knew in my gut, she'd never stop. When I was little, my father used to tell me that my mother was watching over me, my guardian angel. I had thought he meant it in a spiritual sense, but his words had turned out to be far more literal.

When at last I mustered the strength to stand and walk, I donned Clauswitz's jacket, threw the blanket over my shoulders, and joined the other able-bodied in combing the wreckage. The *Eva Braun* had been twelve hundred feet long, but the debris field was no more than half that length. The largest and most difficult-to-access portion was the initial point of impact. Half the ship had been compressed into a crazy, chaotic forest of metal that was virtually impenetrable. If anyone had been in that section of the ship when she'd hit the ground, it was doubtful they'd survived.

The Immune crew had salvaged some flashlights from the gondola emergency kits, and having commandeered one of these, I began poking through the skeletal remains of the airship. I was of two minds about this — one part of me desperately wanted to find what I was looking for, while the other was terrified I would. What if I discovered he hadn't survived? What if he had turned to ash and what remained of him was now lost amidst the charred remains of the airship?

I shuddered and pushed the thought to the back of my mind, determined to focus on the positive. But after an hour I'd just about given up hope. Despondent, I tried to reconcile myself to the fact that he was gone and had started making my way back to the gondola when someone called out from what was once the airship's passenger section: "Found someone over here!"

Heart beating like a drum, I picked my way through the confusion of girders and trusses, ducking under bent struts and warped metal beams, avoiding the tangle of cables and shrouds. Others converged on the site, and together we began to shift the debris, heaving away sections of battered paneling, digging out the body that lay beneath.

Even before we'd finished, I knew it was Val. I pushed past the others, falling to my knees beside him, reaching out to him with tremulous hands. I thought I had my miracle, and tears of elation spilled down my cheeks. But as the last of the wreckage was lifted away, I saw the silver hilt of a dagger protruding from his chest.

I reached out and touched his face, waiting for a response. "Val," I whispered, pleading. "Please. Please wake up."

He opened his eyes, and I let out a cry of relief. "There you are," he said in a faraway voice. His eyes shifted to mine, and he attempted a grin.

"You're going to be all right," I said. "We're going to fix this. You'll see."

He stared at me, unfocused, then seemed to pass out.

Clauswitz knelt opposite me and looked at the hilt of the dagger. "It missed the heart," he said.

"That's good," I said, clinging to hope. "That means he's going to be all right, doesn't it? He can heal from this, can't he?"

The captain gave me a pained look. "If it were just the knife wound, Fräulein . . ."

"I don't understand." I was frantic. "It's just a knife. Vamps can be shot and not die." I shook my head and said again, "It's just a knife."

"I know this kind," said Clauswitz. "A blade of ironwood, soaked in blood." He looked at me soberly. "*Immune* blood, Fräulein."

"No. No, he's going to be okay," I insisted, running my trembling hands over Val's face and chest.

Slowly and carefully, Clauswitz withdrew the blade, and as it came free, I saw the smooth black surface of the polished ironwood. It was the same sort of handcrafted dagger that had once been common to Immune soldiers during the war. Driven through the heart of a vamp, it was as good as any wooden stake — the effect was just as final and irrevocable. Soaked in Immune blood, even a scratch would eventually be fatal to a vamp.

I recognized the blade almost immediately, recalling my father's description of it from the night he and Val had found it buried Cherkov's body. I could see the words etched into it — *Now, I am become Death.*

I began to shake uncontrollably, and a sound formed deep in my throat, breaking free as a wail of despair. I pulled Val into my arms, hugged him to me, his head to my bosom, and buried my face in his hair, sobbing.

"Val, wake up!" I cried. "Please wake up. Don't leave me. You're the one who's supposed to live forever. Come back. Please come back. You promised."

"Sophie." His voice was faint. Fainter than a whisper.

"Val." I pressed my face close to his, felt his cold lips against mine.

"Sophie," he breathed into me. "There was so much I needed to tell you."

"I don't want you to go," I said through tears. "I can't make it without you."

"You will. You have to. For Chloe's sake."

"Chloe?" I said, confused.

"Your daughter. Jason . . . he told me about her. I never thought it would be this way . . . never realized the Old Ones were behind it . . . never thought it would be this soon . . . thought you'd have more time. But you have to know . . . it's important you keep her safe. Whatever it takes. She's the only one who can stop them."

"Stop who? Val, I don't understand."

"The Old Ones."

He shuddered, a spasm wracking his body. "You are my sun," he said. And then he was still.

I knew he was done, that that was it. I bent to Val and gently kissed his forehead, his eyelids, his lips. When I'd finished, I lowered him back onto the bed of wreckage in which we'd found him. It was better this way; it would destroy me to watch him turn to ash and dust and nothingness.

And yet I lingered. Perhaps in my heart, I believed in miracles. I wanted one now, wanted him to come back to me. But there would be no such thing for Val. He lay there, silent and still — at peace, perhaps, in a way he hadn't been since the day he'd been transformed. I knelt there and watched him slip away until he was gone forever.

The other survivors stood in silence as I wept. After a few minutes, they drifted away, one by one, leaving me to suffer my heartache in solitude. Only Clauswitz remained, standing off to one side at a respectful distance, watching over me.

The sounds of the crew picking through the wreckage floated on the cold breeze, but I wasn't really conscious of them. Even when they shouted that they'd found another survivor, I didn't pay attention. I was vaguely aware of Clauswitz leaving me, and it was only when he returned minutes later that I realized they'd found something significant.

"Fräulein," he said, as he approached from behind. There was compassion in his voice but something else as well. Apprehension? I didn't care. I didn't care about anything. Val was gone, and I couldn't accept it, couldn't make myself believe it.

"Sophie," Clauswitz said. He laid a hand on my shoulder. "You must come. There's something you must see."

I lifted my head, the effort a great labor, and turned to look up at him. "It wasn't supposed to be this way," I said in a fragile voice, sniffling back the tears, choking on the sobs. "He's supposed to be immortal. We're supposed to be forever. He promised me."

"Even vampires can't be forever," the captain said. "The Old Ones, they think they are. They think nothing can stop them. But they're wrong. Something can. Someone will."

I didn't know what he meant, though somewhere in the dense forest of my grief I recalled Val's words about Chloe — my daughter. The one I didn't yet have. The one I might never have.

The one Ahriman said they'd been seeking.

I wanted the captain to go away, to leave me alone with my sorrow so I could just cry and cry and cry until I couldn't cry anymore. I couldn't do anything else. I couldn't bring Val back, and crying was the only weapon I had against the agony of loss. It was the only thing to fill the emptiness.

"Please," Clauswitz said.

I took a breath and tried to steady myself, to hold back the vast reservoir of pain. Finally Clauswitz took my hand and helped me to my feet, leading me over a heap of charred metal where some crewmen were clearing away debris. I felt a mix of horror and fury as I realized they'd found the Old One.

Trapped beneath beams, tightly imprisoned, he too looked finished. I climbed up to where the others were and stared down at him, trying to gain some solace from his death.

"At least you will be safe," Clauswitz began. But before he could say anything more, the Old One's eyes flashed open, and he glared up at us from within his cage of twisted wreckage.

"So," he said, sneering at me, "you survived, despite the best efforts of your lover to kill us all."

I wanted to flee, but I didn't. I was silent, trying not to be afraid, trying to feel only the hatred I had for him. Some of the vamp crew moved closer to me, as though to protect me, and Clauswitz put a hand on my arm. "He will not have you," he whispered.

"Get me out of here!" Ahriman shrieked, struggling against the metal that enclosed him.

None of the soldiers had survived the crash, but the vamp crew was standing about. Clauswitz gave no orders, however, and it was only when Ahriman roared another command that a couple of the vamps, perhaps more intimidated by the power of an Old One than that of the captain, moved obediently into action. They lifted the last of the beams that pinned him and pulled him free of the tangle of wreckage. Ahriman looked incredibly old and fragile, his skin a ghostly white and papery thin. He had several injuries and was clearly weakened by them. It was a stunning contrast to what he'd been when I'd first encountered him.

Now would have been the time to kill him, if any of the vamps had had the courage to do so. Had they been part of Val's rebel forces, they doubtless would have. But as it stood, they were simply too frightened of the Old One, even with his diminished strength, to risk taking him on.

"Blood," Ahriman demanded. He moaned and sagged against some twisted struts. Someone passed him a flask, which he snatched and greedily drank from. "More!" he howled, tossing the empty flask aside. "I need *fresh* blood!"

"There is none," Clauswitz said, moving to place himself between me and the Old One. "We must wait for the rescue flight. It should be here within the day."

"The day? You think I can wait that long, you fool?" Ahriman turned unsteadily, focusing on some of the Immune crew. "There's blood aplenty here." Before anyone had a chance to react, he moved in a blur, leaping past the vamp crew and alighting in front of a human, his long fangs bared.

"No!" Clauswitz shouted. "He is an Immune! You can't."

But if Ahriman understood what the captain was saying, he showed no sign of it. He snatched up the man and sank his teeth into the hapless victim's neck. The poor wretch struggled and screamed and then went limp. The other humans scattered, and even the vamps shied away from the Old One, dropping back amidst the wreckage.

When he'd finished, Ahriman stood there clutching the lifeless body, eyes wide with animal lust. Had he been an ordinary vamp, he'd have died within seconds of consuming that much Immune blood. But Old Ones were unlike all other vamps, and so he stood, looming large, more threatening than ever. With an effortless flick of his wrist, he pitched the dead crewman aside as though the man were nothing more than a rag doll. "Bring me the girl," Ahriman said. His face was a map of madness, and insanity burned in the depths of his eyes.

"It's the Immune blood," Clauswitz said, pushing me back, still holding his ground in front of me. "It's already beginning to destroy his mind."

I kept backing away, putting as much distance between the Old One and myself as I could.

"Give me the girl!" Ahriman roared. "I shall have the blood of her child. I shall not be denied the return to my home." He stalked forward and easily swept Clauswitz aside with a swipe of his arm, sending the captain crashing into nearby wreckage. The rest of the crew scattered, vanishing into the shadows, unwilling to take on an Old One whose power far exceeded their own.

I shrank back in terror, stumbling blindly through the remains of the ship.

"Fräulein!" Clauswitz shouted. He staggered to his feet, one arm hanging motionless at his side, his back hunched as he limped forward. He tossed me the ironwood dagger with his free hand. It spun through the air, end over end, the silver handle flashing in the starlight. In the same instant, Ahriman leapt toward me.

I reached for the dagger as the dark mass of the ancient vampire descended upon me. The cold metal of the hilt struck the palm of my open hand, my fingers snapping closed around it as I swung my arm up and thrust the blade into Ahriman's chest. He smashed into me, and his momentum carried us backward, head over heels, the two of us separating and falling to the ground on opposite sides of a wide clearing in the debris.

Had Clauswitz been uninjured I'm certain he'd have seized the opportunity and finished the Old One off himself. But the captain moved with difficulty, clearly suffering. He limped to where I lay, stunned and breathless, and took hold of me, hoisting me to my feet and supporting me as I struggled to regain my equilibrium.

"You're hurt," I said, stating the obvious.

He ignored that and said, "You should leave him to me." He jerked his chin toward Ahriman. "The blood he drank is destroying him. With the wound you just inflicted, he may be weakened enough for me to overcome him."

I shook my head. "You're in no shape to fight him."

"I'll heal."

"Not fast enough."

"Fräulein . . . Sophie, you cannot beat him." Clauswitz glanced to where Ahriman was already beginning to move again. "He is no ordinary vampire."

"And I'm no ordinary human."

The captain opened his mouth as if to say something but seemed to think better of it. Perhaps he knew that in the wake of Val's demise, this was one argument he couldn't possibly win.

I looked east, to where the first blush of dawn was brightening the sky, turning the black to a pale, iridescent blue. "It's too late for any of you to do anything," I said. "You don't have time. This is my fight now."

"Fräulein . . ."

"It's okay," I said, trying to sound brave. "He's mad. He doesn't realize he's out of time, too. I just have to keep out of reach for a few more minutes."

"It would take less than that to kill you," Clauswitz said.

Ahriman was starting to rise, lumbering to his feet, his hand reaching to his chest. Though I had missed his heart, it was only a matter of time before he was done. But there was still fight in him yet.

"You have to go," I said to Clauswitz, giving him a shove. "The sun . . ."

"You should run," Clauswitz urged as he backed away.

"I will," I lied. But I had no intention of leaving. Ahriman was weakened, and I wanted my revenge. I didn't care if I died in the process. He'd already killed the most important part of me; there wasn't much more left.

I looked east again. "Get going," I said. "Now! Please."

The captain nodded grimly, perhaps understanding — if reluctantly — that this was something I had to do. "Very well," he said. The sorrow in his eyes reflected unbounded desolation, and he lingered, hesitant to abandon me. Finally Clauswitz put a hand on my shoulder, giving it a gentle squeeze. "Take care, child." It was as if he were saying goodbye for the last time. Forever. And maybe he was. He turned and vanished into the shadows.

By now the ancient vampire had dragged himself to his feet and was leaning against a shattered strut. He clasped the hilt of the dagger in one hand. "You can't win," he said, the glare in his eyes boring into me as he slowly pulled the blade free and flung it aside. "I have lived for thousands of years. Better foes than you have tried to slay me. All have failed."

"I won't," I said, spitting the words at him as I backed away, maneuvering into the open. "You're nothing more than a monster. A fairy tale told in the night. The darkness we fear. You don't belong here. You don't belong on this world."

He nodded in his odd, bird-like fashion. "You are right about that, girl," he said unevenly, as if it were a monumental strain to enunciate each word. "And now you will help me escape. The blood of your child will release me from my exile."

"I don't think so."

"You have no choice."

"There are always choices," I said. *Just not always good ones.*

I was in the middle of the clearing now, and over my shoulder, the shimmering liquid edge of the sun was on the cusp of cresting the horizon. All I had to do was keep Ahriman exposed long enough for that light to do what I knew I couldn't. I turned and ran toward it.

Ahriman flew through the air, sailing high above and landing in front of me with a loud *thud*. The ground trembled, and I skidded to a halt, panting, heart racing.

"Don't be foolish," the Old One said, rolling his tongue sinuously across his lips. He drew himself up, and in the dark, he seemed to be a giant, monolithic in stature. "You cannot escape me, Miss Harkness. I am faster, stronger, superior."

"Maybe," I agreed, taking a step back. "But I'm not the one you have to worry about. She is."

Ahriman whirled around, but it was too late. Mary was on him and tearing savagely, her hands like claws as they ripped into his flesh, gouging and slashing. He yowled in rage, trying to throw her off as they tumbled across the snow, leaving a spotted trail of dark blood in their wake.

I looked beyond them, toward the horizon, willing the sun to rise and praying Mary could hold him long enough.

Just a few more minutes.

They fought back and forth, two titans locked in gladiatorial combat, tearing up the ground around them, each landing telling blows, until Ahriman, fueled by his growing insanity, gained the upper hand. In one furious motion he threw Mary off, hurling her through the air and into a pile of wreckage.

"Mary!" I cried, wanting to rush to her side.

But Ahriman turned toward me again, his eyes filled with a bloodlust that would not be sated until he had what he wanted.

I ran.

Behind me I heard him careening across the clearing, smashing aside debris, roaring his defiance. I scrambled up a heap of mangled girders and struts, clawing for handholds, desperate to flee. But Ahriman slammed into the pile above me and grabbed me in one large hand. His long fingers encircled my neck, sharp nails biting into my skin, drawing blood as he held me high above him and bared his fangs. A strangled scream escaped me as I flailed and tried to kick free.

The Old One snarled at me. "I shall not be denied," he said. "I shall have the child's blood and be done with this world." He opened his mouth wide, fangs gleaming, wet with saliva.

Tears streamed from my eyes, and I felt myself fading. I stole a glance past Ahriman and saw a gleam of blinding light flickering along the horizon, igniting the snow with its distant flame. I just needed a few more seconds. If I could hold on that long, I was saved. All I needed was a diversion.

I fumbled blindly for the chain about my neck and tore the crucifix free. With the last of my strength, I swung my arm and drove the stem of the cross as hard as I could into Ahriman's neck. He screeched in agony and released me, staggering backward, clawing at his neck as it smoked and burned and bubbled with putrefaction.

Past him, sunlight raced across the arctic desert, a gleaming golden army, shredding the darkness, flaring against crystals of ice and snow. It struck the metal debris and sent shadows leaping into the west. Duralumin flared bright, as though on fire.

The light struck Ahriman like the blade of a sword.

The Old One unleashed a sound like nothing I'd ever heard. It was inhuman. Unearthly. Rage and torment consumed him, and he thrashed about, tearing at his body as if trying to rip the sunlight from his flesh.

I scuttled through the wreckage, seeking cover as he crashed through girders and struts, now driven completely berserk. I had thought it would take minutes, but the process was over quickly. Ahriman's flesh turned red and blistered. He began to smoke and peel, entire chunks of him falling away. His face transformed into an unrecognizable landscape of eructing sores that quickly turned to black soot and a powdery gray ash. He became skeletal as flames engulfed him, and his screams rose into the early morning air.

And just like that it was over.

All that remained of the nightmare were bits of clothing and a greasy gray residue. Smoke drifted up from the pile, rising in the morning sunlight and vanishing on the wind.

He was gone, and I felt none of the satisfaction I'd thought I would.

Amidst his remains I found the crucifix. I bent and picked it up, the broken chain coiling over my hand. Staring at it, I felt empty . . . and alone.

I heard the clatter of metal and looked over to where Mary had fallen. She got to her feet, a shadow against the backdrop of a brightening sky. She had several wounds, and her clothing was even more tattered than before. She looked terrible, yet I had never seen a more welcome and wonderful sight.

I faced her and smiled sadly, new tears springing to my eyes and rolling down my cheeks. I started toward her, slowly at first, then breaking into a run and throwing myself at her.

"Mom," I said, hugging her tightly, burying my face against her neck and weeping into her shoulder. She put her arms around me, holding me and stroking my hair, making sounds that seemed like soft, soothing whispers.

For a long time we remained like that, bathed in golden sunlight, the two of us reborn. Mother and daughter, two of a kind.

Bound by blood.

CHAPTER 37
HOME

I sat in the observation lounge and peered anxiously through the large windows, monitoring the approach of the dark smudge on the horizon, watching with soaring spirits as it spread wide and seemed to rise up out of the sea. It grew taller the closer we got, until I could make out the tip of the Blue Mountains, thrust skyward like a monument to defiance.

I rose and moved closer to the railing, clutching it tightly and bending toward one of the open ports on the starboard side. The three main islands of Haven loomed. From afar they seemed insignificant. Dots on a map. But in my heart, they were immense.

As the *Hindenburg III* sailed closer, the familiarity of the landscape unfolded before me on the broad canvas of the ocean. There was Point Pleasant, jutting northward, and above it tiny Brute Island. We passed south of the latter, and I could see Dunington, squatting on the south shore of Central Island, at the mouth of the Goddard Strait.

The airship turned north, nosing toward Resolute Bay. Below us, eclipsed by our shadow, fishing boats and yachts bobbed on the rolling swell that swept toward the islands. We began to lose altitude, and as we did, I could see Caelo through breaks in the clouds, the city gleaming brightly beneath a midday sky.

Other passengers had risen from their seats and were crowding the rail on either side of me. They chattered excitedly, captivated by the sight of their homeland. But none could be anticipating a return as eagerly as I.

Days ago I wouldn't have imagined it possible that I'd ever see this place again. Now I was only minutes from setting foot in the only place I knew could ever be home. It was almost too good to be true, and I wanted to pinch myself to make sure it wasn't a dream, that I wasn't still a prisoner of the Old One and just imagining this.

But Ahriman was gone forever, and though there were other Old Ones, I had eluded them for now. Thanks, in no small part, to the agency of Clauswitz and the crew of the *Eva Braun*.

The crash had been nearly two weeks ago, and I was still reeling from all I'd lived through since I'd left Haven. In my heart I knew nothing would ever be the same. I couldn't just walk back into the life I'd had. The same people who'd tried to kill me before I'd left were still there. The threats remained, and I had no idea what I was going to do about them. I needed help, but I didn't know whom to trust.

And then there was the hole inside of me. It was an emptiness that Val had once filled, and nothing could take its place. When you lose someone you've loved as deeply as I loved him, you know that life will never be normal again. Normal for me was waking up each day knowing he was there. Normal was the assignations at night, the long talks and longer walks, the hugs and kisses, the laughter and whispered promises. Normal was my heart skipping a beat when he said my name and my stomach doing little somersaults when he touched me. Normal was me believing we could be forever, that somehow it could work.

But he was gone. Nothing I could do would ever change that. I had to live with it, though I couldn't imagine how. I was still crying myself to sleep each night.

As we passed over the Third Reich Embassy, a sharp stab of pain lanced through me. I couldn't help but think of the night Grace had died. Val had held me in his lap, and we had watched the stars through the open window. The memory was almost too painful to bear.

I swallowed a sob and looked toward the city again. The day captain's voice boomed over the intercom, announcing we'd be landing shortly. I leaned into the open port once more, staring down as the earth seemed to rise toward us. It couldn't come fast enough.

We passed over the houses of West Borough, heading into the wind. The engines whined, and the entire ship trembled. I felt the vibration through the soles of my sandals and thought of the *Eva Braun* again. Captain Clauswitz had arranged everything after the crash, using his contacts in Stockholm to get me clothes and to parlay a trip back to Haven using a fake ID and visa.

No one on the airship that had rescued us from Norway had questioned me when I'd boarded along with the other survivors. They'd assumed I was crew. Sophie Harkness, for all intents and purposes, had died when the *Eva Braun* went down, and Clauswitz had done nothing to disabuse them of that notion. He had done most of the talking, spinning a plausible yarn about the explosion and the subsequent crash, his story a mix of fact and fiction — though mostly it had been a matter of omitting details that might have caused difficulties for all of us.

It had been enough to satisfy the rescue team, and when we'd reached Stockholm, Clauswitz had made contact with the underground and his people in Lufthansa, and now here I was. For a while, at least, I was dead to the world. Dead to the Old Ones. Dead to my enemies in Haven. In some ways, even dead to myself. How long that would last, I'd no idea.

The engines changed pitch as we fell toward the grassy field of Kensington Aerodrome. The massive hangars materialized before us, silver-gray monoliths that overshadowed everything and made me think of the Nazi base in the far north where Isabelle and Ticket had died, and I had discovered truths that would have been better left buried. I shuddered and brushed the memories aside, concentrating on the familiarity of what lay below. Everything was bright and green, a studied contrast to the gray concrete and rusted steel of New York City and the barren white wasteland of the Arctic.

I couldn't help smiling, feeling elated. Was this how the first settlers had felt when they'd arrived in Haven shortly after the war ended in '48? They must have imagined themselves finally safe in a world that had become increasingly hostile, protected by the vastness of the sea.

I recalled reading in school of how people had wept; some had fallen to their hands and knees and kissed the ground. At the time I hadn't really understood the intensity of such emotion, but now I saw it clearly.

We're so few against so many. Yet we must live life as though we're billions. Because now I knew the truth — that this isn't what our world should have been. And impossible as it may seem, we have to keep believing that somehow it can be changed, that we can make it better, make it what it should be.

Perhaps it'll only take one person to start things in the right direction.

I put a hand to my stomach and wondered if she could really be that one.

The one to save us all.

* * *

As I stepped from the gondola and set my feet on the grass, I paused and looked around. Other passengers walked by, paying no attention to their surroundings, but I crouched down, sitting on my heels to put a hand on the grass. I spread my fingers in the moist blades, feeling them press back against my skin. How could such a simple sensation carry so much meaning? It was a metaphor for all I could have lost, and a reminder that sometimes we take things too much for granted.

A gentle breeze blew in from the sea. Warm, luxuriant, and filled with promise, it caressed and teased, like a lover's gentle touch. I thought of Val again and felt the weight of my sadness as the void within me grew larger.

"Cheer up, luv," one of the ground crew said as he passed me. "Yer home now, you are. Nothin' to worry 'bout."

I smiled feebly at him and moved on, falling in line behind the last of the passengers heading into the terminal. As I went through the main doors, I glanced back at the zeppelin. In the shadows, I caught sight of what I was looking for, a familiar figure melting away from sight. I watched her and smiled. My guardian angel on the job.

Inside the terminal, I waited to go through customs. The officer who checked my ID barely gave it a passing glance before handing it back and waving me on with a quick, "Welcome home." Beyond customs was the arrival lounge where all the passengers sat and waited until our luggage was off-loaded.

It seemed such an ordinary world. So mundane.

I could get used to mundane. Whether I'd get the chance was another story. However much I might think of this as home, I had come back to a world I wasn't sure I belonged in. There was really nothing for me here — no family, no friends, no Val.

And then there was the matter of the truth.

I looked out the windows and thought of all those people in Haven going about their daily affairs, oblivious to the house of cards on which their lives were built. How would they feel if they knew the truth?

You can tell them, I told myself. *You have to tell them.* But then what? What became of us all after that?

I retrieved my luggage and went in search of a cab. As I stood on the concrete terrace in front of the terminal, an electric drew up to the curb, stopping sharply in front of me. The driver leaned across and wound down the passenger window. "Can I offer you a lift, Miss Harker?"

The use of my alias caught me off guard. I bent down, squinted inside, and found myself face to face with Inspector Havershaw. "Is this business or pleasure?" I asked, lifting an eyebrow inquisitively.

"There can be no question that driving a pretty young woman home is anything but pleasure," he said with a laugh.

"Why, Inspector, I do believe you're flirting with me."

Havershaw blushed and lowered his eyes a moment. When he looked up again, the humor was absent. "I've a few things I'd like to discuss."

"Ah." I felt reality close in, accompanied by the grief that had been my constant companion lately. "That sounds rather serious."

"It is. It's about your future."

"Do I have one?"

"That's up to you." He gave me a pointed look.

"Then I guess you're driving me home."

The inspector got out of the car, tossed my bag in the boot, and held the passenger door open as I removed my hat and slipped into the vacant seat. He gave me an odd look, and I touched my hair self-consciously, "I thought I'd try something different," I said by way of explanation.

"Very nice," Havershaw said, gently shutting the door. He hustled back to the driver's side and jumped in, gunning the motor and turning out into the road. I waited for him to speak, but he remained tight-lipped until we'd cleared the aerodrome grounds and were motoring along Republic.

"How did you know I was arriving today?" I asked. "How did you know I was arriving at all?" It worried me that he did, because it meant others might also be aware of my return.

"I didn't," he said. "I received a message from a Captain Clauswitz a few days ago. He told me to keep an eye out for you, so I've been checking the passenger manifests daily. I had them forwarded to my office."

"I wasn't aware they were so liberal about giving those things out."

The corner of Havershaw's mouth quirked up. "A silver badge and a bit of official-looking paper can work wonders."

"Let me guess, you told them you were looking to catch a nefarious criminal."

He chuckled. "Something like that."

"And my alias?"

Havershaw shrugged. "Mina Harker?" He looked at me and smiled. "I have daughters, remember? Right now the oldest is hooked on *Dracula*. Personally, I think we have enough vamps without having to read stories about them. Anyway, when I saw that name on the manifest I figured it was worth checking out."

"And I thought myself so clever choosing that for my pseudonym," I said, an unsettled feeling growing in my gut.

"Don't worry. I doubt there are many people who would have got it."

"You did."

He didn't have a response to that and purposefully set his eyes on the road.

I stared ahead, my anxiety mounting. I didn't want anyone knowing I was back. Not that it mattered in the long run, I suppose. I couldn't hide forever. At some point my enemies in Haven were likely to find out I was alive and well. I looked at Havershaw, thinking it rather ironic that he might be the only one I could trust.

"I had a visit from your vampire friend," he said, the words like pointed barbs. "Just after you left for New York. You might have informed me you were going, by the way."

"I wasn't aware I was required to."

"It could have been interpreted as fleeing prosecution."

"I wasn't under arrest," I pointed out.

"Still . . ." He scowled, the dark lines of his wrinkled brow forming canyons of annoyance.

I didn't say anything, just sat looking ahead, my hands folded in my lap.

"Why did you go?" he asked.

"I guess I was afraid. I thought I could find answers. I thought maybe I . . ." I didn't finish.

"And did you?"

"Find answers?" I smiled at him, but the smile was a wound in my face. "Some. Enough. Maybe too many."

He cocked an eyebrow. "You don't like making things easy for me, do you, Miss Harkness?"

"What would be the fun of that?" I asked drily.

Havershaw grinned and shook his head. "You're certainly your father's daughter."

"Thank you." I looked out the window at the passing houses. *If only they knew,* I thought. *If only they knew the truth.*

"So what did he want?" I finally asked, trying to control my voice.

"What?"

"My friend. The one who visited you. What did he want?"

"To talk about you."

I felt tears and dabbed at the corner of my eye as I fought them back, refusing to give in to them.

"He was quite anxious," Havershaw continued, "and under a great deal of stress. He seemed to believe he'd made a mistake."

I closed my eyes and put a hand to my heart, felt the heavy beat of it under my breast. "I made the mistake," I whispered. I knew that now. I should never have run away; he should never have come after me.

"He asked me to watch over you when you returned."

The ache in my chest swelled. Val must have known he wasn't likely to return.

Havershaw glanced at me with inquisitive eyes. "It appears you've made enemies in high places, Miss Harkness."

"So it would seem."

"And do you know who they are?"

I could have told him everything, but I just said, "Corporate leaders. The blue bloods. Maybe the president." I tried to smile, to make it seem like a bit of a joke. "The usual suspects."

"It's hard to believe."

"Yes, I suppose it is." I glanced at him. "*You* don't have to."

He didn't respond at first, then said, "You've got yourself into something deep."

"The deepest." I grimaced. Deeper than he could ever imagine, I was sure. I looked outside, watched the buildings, and thought of the people again. How lucky they were in their ignorance. How happy. Did I have the right to rob them of that?

My mind drifted back to *No Haven for Darkness*. In the fictitious world of the novel, Samantha Jarvis was just a girl caught up in a web of intrigue. One day she had an ordinary life, and then, just like that, she awoke into a nightmare. By the end of the tale she was in a position to change the world. All because of circumstance. All because of things beyond her control.

I hadn't really understood her before, but now I did. We were two of a kind.

"So where do we go from here?" I glanced at Havershaw, waiting.

"That depends on you," he said.

I narrowed my eyes. "How does that work?"

"You tell me why you need protecting, and I decide whether you do."

I scoffed and shook my head. "Thanks, but no thanks. I'll manage somehow. I already have a guardian angel. Besides, telling you what I know would end up making you as much a target as I am."

He shrugged. "I've already survived one shooting with you."

"The next time you might not. And you have children . . . a family."

Havershaw glanced at me, bemused.

"You're still not convinced."

"This is Haven, Miss Harkness. It just seems . . ."

I looked at him pityingly. "That's what makes it worse."

"I'm not sure I understand."

"You've a lot to learn," I said. "Do you remember that murder I mentioned to you in the cemetery? The one my father was called to? It was in an alleyway, on New Year's Eve, 1999."

"What does that have to do with this?" Havershaw asked.

"Everything."

Before I knew it, I was telling him my story. The abridged version, at least. After all, I didn't have a right to ruin his life the way I'd ruined my own and so many others.

* * *

That night, there was a guard outside my door and a police electric parked across the street. In the end I hadn't argued; it would have been stupid to pretend there was nothing to worry about. But I wondered how long this could go on. How long before Havershaw and his men were forced to abandon me? And then it would be just Mary and me. Despite what I'd said to Havershaw, I wasn't sure that was enough.

As I got ready for bed, I looked around the flat and thought how different it was now that everything had changed. I'd been so excited the day I moved in, so happy to be independent and to have a home that was truly mine. It had been my first place, and I'd made it my own. Now it was just rooms filled with far too many painful memories — Grace, Camille, Val.

I knew I couldn't stay. Even a night or two was probably risking too much. In fact, it was probably foolish to have come here at all. But I had nowhere else to go. Once, not so long ago, I might have gone to him and hidden out in the Embassy. I'd have let him take care of me. But that was over. It was never going to happen again.

I couldn't even sleep in the bed, because I remembered him there. I remembered the time we had lain together and he'd whispered the same words he'd said to me when he'd died: "You are my sun."

If only we had both realized at the time how bitterly ironic that would become.

I gathered the sheets and took them into the other room, curling up on the settee to sleep. But sleep didn't come. Most of the night it seemed I just lay there, staring out the window, watching the stars and recalling how he had held me and how safe I had felt in his arms.

I didn't know how I was going to make it without him, yet somehow I must. There was no other option. "Life goes on," Grace would have said — even if sometimes we wished it wouldn't.

The tears came, and this time, I made no effort to stop them. They were all I could give him.

CHAPTER 38
THE BODYGUARD OF LIES

The phone woke me.

I lay there listening to it ring, not sure if I should answer. What if it was someone calling to see if I was back? Amelia knew my number and where I lived. If I answered, I might be setting myself up as a target again.

After a dozen rings, the phone fell silent.

I sat up and felt the crushing weight of the new day already settling on me. I'd no idea what I was going to do. After the crash of the *Eva Braun,* it had all been about getting home. Nothing else had mattered. I'd kept telling myself that I'd work things out once I got to Haven.

Now I was here, and I didn't have a clue.

The phone started ringing again, and this time, it didn't seem it was going to quit. I went into my bedroom and stood in front of it, looking down at it, listening to it go on and on. I was just reaching for the receiver when it stopped.

Surely they'll give up now, I thought. I turned away and was just about in the loo when it rang for the third time. *What if it's Havershaw?* I thought. *If I don't answer, he may think something's wrong. But if I do, and it's not him . . .*

I picked it up and put it to my ear.

"Miss Harkness?"

I stiffened. "Who is this?"

"I'm Mrs. Balder, the president's personal secretary. President Mallory requests that you see him at your earliest convenience."

"I beg your pardon?" I gripped the handset tighter.

"The president would like to discuss some matters of national urgency with you," the woman said. She sounded impatient, and I conjured an image of her as middle-aged, the sort who was prim and proper and without a shred of humor. "A limousine will be sent to pick you up this morning at eight thirty, if that's all right with you," she went on.

I rubbed at my forehead and scrunched my eyes shut, trying to concentrate.

"Miss Harkness?"

"What time did you say?" I asked.

"Eight thirty. It's seven fifteen now. That should give you plenty of time to get ready. Can I confirm you'll be able to make the appointment?"

"Uh, yes. I guess so." I couldn't see that I'd much choice.

"Thank you. President Mallory will be expecting you. Good day, Miss Harkness."

"Uh, yeah. Thanks . . . I guess." But she'd already hung up, the sharp click a rude bark in my ear. I held the handset before me, staring at it with a mixture of belligerence and apprehension, then set it back in its cradle.

That settles it, I thought. *I'll have to find another place to stay.* My life was in this flat, and that had driven me back like a moth to a flame.

It was obvious I'd been an idiot to gamble on returning here. Sentiment had no place in survival. I should have just gathered a few of my things and gone somewhere else. Where, I'd no idea. It wasn't like I had the resources to go stay in a hotel. In fact, I didn't have a clue how I was going to make my future work. I'd come back to Haven because there'd been no alternative, but now that I was here the breadth and scope of my dilemma was overwhelming.

Maybe Havershaw could find me somewhere to hide out. Maybe I should have asked him to do that in the first place, because if the president knew where I was, then it was possible Amelia knew as well. And even if she didn't, it was likely only a matter of time before she did.

"There's nothing to be done about it now," I said aloud, feeling far less cavalier than I sounded.

A little more than an hour later, I stepped out onto the sidewalk in front of my flat and found a black limousine waiting. Two flags fluttered on small metal staffs that stuck up from the left and right front fenders — one the flag of Haven, the other a dark-blue, gold-trimmed rectangle bearing the presidential seal.

There were already university students out on the street and in the Quad, and they regarded me curiously as the chauffeur hastily moved to open the back door. The car was a twin of the Mercedes Val had always driven in, and I kept thinking of him as we drove down University Avenue, kept remembering the many times we'd spent in the back of his car and the things we'd done.

Before long, the chauffeur drove down an avenue lined with acacia trees. At the end of the road stood Government House, the presidential residence. It was a sprawling stone manor with a copper roof that bore the verdigris of age. The car rolled to a stop just in front of a broad flight of sandstone steps, and a doorman rushed to help me out.

I stood there for a moment, looking up at the mansion, recalling the only other time I'd been so close to it. That had been back in sixth grade, on a field trip. Camille and I had had a grand time that day, one that still stuck in my memory.

A very efficient-looking middle-aged woman dressed in a black suit and black stiletto pumps met me at the top of the stairs. Mrs. Balder, the president's personal secretary, I assumed.

"Come this way," she said. She set off through the heavy front doors and led me into a vast foyer. Marble busts were arrayed about it, and large portraits of dour-faced subjects hung on the walls in heavy, gilded frames.

I followed her down a wide hallway lined with more artwork, passing plainclothes PSS agents, none of whom I recognized from my father's days as chief of the service. At the end of the hall was a set of paneled oak doors. Two agents stood to either side, rigidly attentive. Mrs. Balder ignored them and knocked on one of the doors. Without waiting for a response, she opened the door and stepped inside. I hesitated, not sure if I was meant to follow. But she reached out, grabbed me roughly by the arm, and hauled me inside.

The door clicked shut behind us, and we stood there side by side, silent as mice. Across the room, a man sat at a broad, ebony desk, his attention focused on several papers he was in the process of signing. It was a place I'm sure everyone in Haven knew well enough. After all, it had been on television plenty of times: the office of the President of the Republic of Haven.

The president looked up and stared at us, carefully laid aside his pen, then pushed back his chair and rose to his feet. He stood before a floor-to-ceiling window that looked out onto sprawling floral gardens. With the light shining in behind him, it was difficult to make out his features, and for the briefest of moments, he resembled Ahriman — when the sun had backlit the Old One before turning him to ash and dust.

"Miss Harkness to see you, Mr. President," Mrs. Balder announced.

"Thank you, Marion," President Mallory said, inclining his head in acknowledgement. "That'll be all."

"Yes, sir." Mrs. Balder made a slight bow and withdrew, opening the door quietly and slipping out with scarcely a sound. Even the *click-clack* of her heels seemed subdued as she retreated back down the hallway.

The president stepped out from behind the desk, holding out a hand in greeting. I tentatively shook it, feeling as though he were evaluating me with his warm, firm grip and his steely gray eyes.

"It's been a while since a Harkness stood in this office," the president said, his voice far too buoyant. He sobered a bit, and added, "Your father was a great man. Loyal and the best at what he did."

I didn't know what to say, so I just nodded modestly and waited. Mallory turned and gestured to a chair in front of the desk. "Please have a seat, Miss Harkness." Without waiting to see if I'd obey, he returned to his own, settling into it with an easy familiarity.

I sat down stiffly, pulling the hem of my skirt toward my knees. Even though I'd put on one of my posh outfits for the occasion, the ostentation of the room made me feel underdressed.

"Would you like something to drink?" Mallory asked.

My mouth was dry, but I'd already had more coffee than I should have and didn't think it would go over well if I suddenly announced I had to visit the loo. Besides, I was so nervous I didn't think I could swallow anything, so I shook my head and said, "I'm fine, sir." It sounded like my voice hadn't been used in years.

"Very well, then perhaps we should get down to business."

Business. I knew what he wanted to talk about; there couldn't be any other reason for me to be here. On a subconscious level, I'd been rehearsing this conversation for some time, trying to picture it and work out what I was going to say. In my imagination, I was strong and confident and made my point without hesitation. But what I felt right now was anxious and queasy and incredibly small.

"You were in the Third Reich," the president began.

"Yes." There was no sense denying it.

He seemed to consider his words. "And how did that work out for you, Miss Harkness?"

I chewed at my lip and looked away, my face coloring. I felt like I was in the principal's office at Humberton, having to explain why I'd skipped a class.

"Not so well, did it?"

"No, sir," I replied.

"I had a long chat with a friend of yours not so long ago."

"Sir?"

"The vamp."

Val!

"It was quite an illuminating conversation, I must say."

I sat still, watching him, waiting.

"You realize you've created something of a problem for me."

"I didn't start this, sir."

Mallory's eyebrows shot up, then lowered again. "No, that's true. It started a long time ago. Before you were even born. But running off into the heart of vamp territory alone was foolhardy and irresponsible. If half of what my sources say is true, you're damn lucky to be alive. Do you have any idea how close you came to causing irreparable damage to our relations with the Third Reich?"

"That wasn't my intention."

"Wasn't your intention, Miss Harkness? Then what exactly *did* you intend when you joined forces with vamp rebels and infiltrated a high-security base in Nazi territory? Do you realize you could have been shot as a spy?"

I'd never really thought about it that way. I didn't even know there were spies anymore. "I was trying to find answers, sir," I said.

"Answers?" the president said, his voice flirting with anger.

I shrank at the sound of it, but kept going. "Somebody killed my father, Mr. President. They killed my grandmother, and they were trying to kill me. I wanted to know why. I thought maybe if I did, I could protect myself."

"Your father died in a fire caused by his Alzheimer's. Your grandmother died in an accident. And the police say the incident on Coast Road was probably just some farmer shooting at gulls."

"What about the hospital, sir? And the library."

"The library had nothing to do with you. You were just in the wrong place at the wrong time. And as for the hospital —" Mallory consulted a paper on his desk, then looked across at me. "You'd suffered trauma and had sedatives in your system. Hallucinations weren't out of the question."

I didn't argue; it would have been wasted breath.

"Look, Miss Harkness," the president said, clasping his hands together and leaning on the desk, "I don't doubt you're earnest in your beliefs, but we can't have our citizens gallivanting about, creating all sorts of trouble, because they think there's some sort of conspiracy going on."

"I saw them," I said.

Mallory froze and straightened. "I beg your pardon?"

"I saw the babies, sir. The one's that aren't supposed to exist. We've always been taught that all non-Immunes are stillborn, but it's a lie, isn't it? I saw where the vamps keep the ones that live beyond the womb."

For just a second or two, the president looked shell-shocked, but he quickly recovered and ran a hand over his hair. "Look, I don't know what you *think* —"

"I know what I saw, sir," I interrupted, amazed by how bold I was. The blood rose to my cheeks, and I felt my skin prickling with heat.

Mallory sat back in his chair and let out a sigh. "Do you know why we're here, Miss Harkness? Here on these islands, I mean."

"Because of the truce."

"Yes. The truce. Without it there'd be no Haven. There'd be no human beings left on the entire planet."

"If we didn't give them blood —"

"Let me finish!" he barked.

I shut my mouth and waited.

Mallory blew out a breath. "Look, we're here because of what a few courageous people managed to achieve more than fifty years ago. And make no mistake about it, Miss Harkness, it was a monumental achievement. It was the salvation of humankind."

"I don't know how you could make such a deal," I said, disgusted.

"I didn't," he said, lifting his hands imperceptibly. "But the men who did were only doing what they believed was in the best interests of humanity. It was the only way out of an untenable situation. There were no other options. They knew we couldn't fight any longer; if we had we'd have been wiped out. So they accepted what the vamps offered. It was far better than the alternative."

"I don't know how you can say that, sir. They agreed to stealing babies and shipping them off to the vamps. How can that —"

"Those babies aren't Immunes," he said. "There's no chance of them surviving."

"But they do," I insisted. "I saw them. Adults in tanks, being drained of blood. They could be changed. They could become vamps."

"No, they couldn't. Do you think we're idiots? Procedures are performed on all the babies that are shipped out."

"Procedures?" I didn't like the sound of that.

"Our doctors have become quite adept at making sure those offspring will never exist in anything but a vegetative state," President Mallory said. "Outside of the containers they're kept in, they'll die."

I couldn't find the strength to say anything. I must have looked appalled because he said, "Look, my wife lost a child. Almost every woman on this island who has had children has. Our second son was born without immunity to the virus. He made it out of the womb alive, but after that . . ." He sighed again and lifted his hands. "It's the way it has to be."

"Does your wife know the truth?"

"Of course not. She's not privy to that information. Few are, for obvious reasons."

"And you've never wanted to tell her?"

"Of course I have. But I took an oath, just like every man who has held this office."

"Maybe I should do what you can't," I said.

Mallory's face darkened. "Do you honestly believe people will be singing hallelujah and heaping praise on you if you go out there" — he jerked a hand toward the window behind him — "and reveal what you know? Think again. They'll despise you for making them feel guilty. Believe me, everyone is much happier not knowing this particular truth."

"How can you believe that?" I asked.

"Because I've been at this game a lot longer than you, and I can tell you unequivocally that it would only hurt them, Miss Harkness. Once they knew the truth, they'd feel obligated to do something about it. And that would mean making hard choices, choices none of them would want to make. In the end the results would be the same. They'd choose to survive, just as the men who made the truce in the first place did. Those few lives we sacrifice are a small price to pay for the future of millions."

"I don't know how we can think like that," I said.

He wiped at his face and sat silently a moment. "You know," he said at length, "I used to be like you. I was full of self-righteous indignation. I was going to be principled, and I was going to tell everyone we were living a lie. But I soon realized there's no room for idealism when we're talking about survival. Without the truce there is no future. Not for us. Not for Haven."

"Shouldn't we at least be given a say in that?"

President Mallory shook his head. "The instruments of democracy can extend only so far. It has to be enough that the people are given the chance to elect their leaders. Having done that, they have to trust we'll act in their best interests, that the choices we make will be for the good of all."

"They can't make a valid choice about leadership if they don't know the truth," I argued. "They should know the truth and be allowed to make their own decisions."

"They wouldn't want that responsibility." He gestured dismissively. "People vote for politicians like me because they don't want to have to make the tough decisions. They don't want to get their hands dirty. They're quite happy to have someone else bear the burden."

"Even if that's true —"

Mallory made a sharp gesture to silence me. "I'm not trying to pretend I like this situation any more than you do. But I have to do what I feel is best for the country. No doubt there will come a day when my predecessors and I will have to answer for the things we've done. History will judge us; it always does. And I'm sure many will condemn us for our choices. After all, it's easy to be critical with the comfort and security of hindsight. But I think even our worst critics — if they're honest — will acknowledge that we did what we had to do. It was the only thing we *could* do. "

"I don't believe that," I said. "There has to be another way."

"I'm not a cruel man, Miss Harkness. But the fact is, the vamps need human blood to survive, and the only way Haven can continue to exist in relative freedom is to supply them with what they need. If we don't, then they'll destroy us."

"And themselves in the process," I said.

He nodded slightly. "Maybe. But more likely they'd just tighten the noose around us and turn Haven into a prison camp."

"Isn't it one already? The Old One said the only reason they permitted Haven to exist was because the concentration camps had proved ineffective. If that's the case, they won't try that again."

"A lot has changed since the war," he said. "The Nazis have technologies that didn't exist back then. Don't underestimate their capacity for evil."

"So that's it, then? We just accept this?"

"For now. But Haven is hope, Miss Harkness. So long as it exists, we have a chance to take back what's ours. The vamps may think they have us by the short hairs, but since the day we arrived here, we've been working on a way to defeat them. One day we will. But for now, we live with the untenable." Grim-faced, he set his eyes on me. "They're the enemy, and they've never stopped being the enemy."

"What about Cherkov?" I said.

The president flinched and made a face. "The problem in making a deal with the devil is that you have to suffer the consequences. I don't think anyone was ever happy about Cherkov, but they understood it was a small price to pay. It was better to have him here, where it was possible to monitor what he was doing. And without Cherkov, there might not have been a truce. He was the one who perfected the technology that kept non-Immune babies alive, and he was working on a way to stop Gomorrah, maybe even reverse what it had done."

"But he created Gomorrah!" I countered. "He worked with the Old Ones in the concentration camps. He was a monster."

"Yes, but a brilliant one. Don't you understand, Miss Harkness? Gomorrah is everywhere. What Cherkov was doing for us wasn't merely about the possibility of saving a few non-Immune babies. It was about creating a means to destroy Gomorrah outright. If we can do that, we can end the tyranny of the Third Reich and rid ourselves of the vamps forever."

"But how?" I asked. There were things Ahriman had said that had hinted at this, but it seemed to me it bordered on the impossible.

Clearly Mallory didn't think so. There was a glint of enthusiasm in his eyes and a bit of a feral grin when he said, "As I'm sure you understand, Immunes have survived Gomorrah because we're genetically immune to the virus. If that immunity becomes compromised at any point, then we become susceptible to the virus."

I thought of Isabelle and the others like her — thought of her last moments, in my arms, and how that should never have happened to her. I wanted to say as much, but Mallory didn't give me the chance.

"Without immunity one of two things happens," he continued. "You either die or you become a vamp. As you're well aware, most everyone who was infected during the Fall, some two billion people, died because they lacked the antibodies Immunes produce. Their cells were overcome, and their bodies simply shut down. The rest, the vamps, were a little luckier. Instead of destroying their cells, Gomorrah took control of them."

"And transformed them," I interjected.

He nodded. "The same thing would happen today to non-Immune babies. One in ten would be transformed. The rest would die."

"That still doesn't —" I began, but he raised a hand to silence me.

"Let me finish," he said. It wasn't a request.

I sat still, waiting.

Mallory drew a breath and was sober-faced as he looked across at me. "We now know that if you remove Gomorrah, those who have been transformed will die. Their cells have become dependent on the virus to the point that they simply can't exist without it. That's why Immune blood is poison to them. It destroys the symbiotic link to the virus. Cherkov understood this; he brought us closer than anyone ever has to using our own natural defense against the enemy. But unfortunately, we've no means of weaponizing Immune blood on a grand scale. We need to be able to spread it throughout the world the way Gomorrah was transmitted, and for that we need a way to catalyze a transport mechanism. A virus to kill the virus, if I understand our scientists correctly. But to create such a thing, we need the original stock from which Gomorrah was created."

It sounded convincing, but I knew the truth — that was not all Cherkov had been doing. In fact, he probably hadn't been doing any of that. But how would the president react if I told him the experiments on people like Isabelle and Jason had been about something else entirely? That all that protocol stuff — the checklist of symptoms and characteristics — had been a sham. That it had just been a way of ensuring that any Immune who got sick and fit a certain pathology would become a subject in Cherkov's experiments. That Grace thinking she'd been helping her daughter and doing right by Haven had been part of a web of lies.

It hadn't been about saving non-Immune babies from the virus. Nor had it been about wiping out Gomorrah and the vamps along with it. But I doubted Mallory would believe me if I told him what Ahriman had said — all that stuff about somehow being transported to another world. It still sounded crazy. And maybe it was. Maybe it was just some cock-and-bull story that Cherkov had come up with to string the Old Ones along. Maybe nothing he'd said to anyone had been the truth. Maybe when it all came down to it, he'd just been trying to save his own neck by making people believe he was onto something. And maybe, at some point, he'd even begun to believe it himself.

I opened my mouth to speak but stopped short. Saying out loud any of what I'd been thinking would surely lead Mallory to believe I was batty. But still, I had to try. "Cherkov was also working for the Old Ones when he was here," I said.

Mallory didn't look at all surprised. Instead he nodded and said, "I know."

I blinked, caught off guard. "And nobody thought to stop him?"

"Sometimes, Miss Harkness, you have to take a little water with your wine. In the beginning, no one really cared what else Cherkov was doing, so long as Haven got what it wanted. I'll admit, had it been my choice, I might have been inclined to put an end to his collaboration with the Old Ones. But by the time I came to power, Cherkov was firmly ensconced, and there were too many others who wanted to see the end results of what he was doing for the enemy. They thought that, whatever it was, they could take it and control it and possibly use it against the Old Ones."

Mallory was staring straight at me, and there was no mistaking the implications borne in that look — the president knew about me. He knew what I was or at least had some inkling of it.

In barely more than a whisper, I said as much. "You know about me."

"Only recently," he confirmed. "Your friend had his suspicions. That's why you're here. I know the Old Ones are interested in you and that you're connected to what Cherkov was doing for them. Why they're interested in you and what that connection is . . . well, that's another question altogether." He stared at me expectantly.

"I don't know the answer," I lied.

The president grinned, as if to say he knew I wasn't telling the truth.

There was a long silence and the air seemed to grow thin. "So what happens now?" I asked at length.

"Your father understood well enough how dangerous this business is," Mallory said. "He understood what it means to be loyal to his country. He knew what it meant to serve with honor and dignity."

"You want me to keep silent."

"Yes."

"I don't have a choice, do I?"

"No. There are people looking for you, Miss Harkness. Powerful people. Some would kill you outright because of what you know. And then there are those whom I suspect have some awareness of your connection to what Cherkov was doing for the Old Ones. They may even know more than I do." He looked tellingly at me. "And if that's true, they may want to exploit you. Use you as a sort of bargaining chip with the Old Ones, as foolhardy as that might seem. In either case, they won't stop until they've found you."

"You're the president," I protested. "Surely —"

"I'm a servant of the people," Mallory said. "There's only so much I can do. If I had any sense, I'd probably dig a hole, put you in it, and have you buried for good. But I don't believe in burning my bridges. Besides, I owe your father, which means that so long as I'm in office, you'll be protected. But you have to understand, Miss Harkness, even a democracy like ours has its limitations. Money breeds power, and the islands have more than their fair share of very wealthy people. The sort of people who will go to great lengths to get what they want. They won't let anyone stand in their way, and they're not above doing pretty much anything to achieve their ends.

They may not be vamps, but when it comes to morality and ethics, they are peas in a pod."

"So I'm just supposed to go back to my old life and pretend nothing happened while guards follow me around everywhere?" I asked incredulously.

There was a bleak look in the president's eyes, and he shook his head. "I'm afraid that's not possible. Even as we speak, arrangements are being made to secure you."

I stared at him, shocked. "You're putting me in prison?"

"No, though you may come to think it one. You'll be given a handler and a new identity. The life you had, Miss Harkness, is over. You can never go back. You will never be what you were before all this started. And I suspect you'll only ever truly be free again when we have a breakthrough against Gomorrah."

I sat there, stunned. I'd never truly thought it would come to this, though upon reflection, I probably should have. After all, when you considered the whole situation, how else could it end? Other than me being dead.

Suddenly telling everyone the truth about the truce seemed such a small, inconsequential thing. I wished I could have turned back the clock, but I couldn't. I had to deal with what I had, regardless. Unconsciously I put my hand to my stomach.

"I'm sorry," said Mallory. "This is the way it has to be."

I nodded meekly.

"Please believe me when I tell you that I'm trying to balance what's best for you and what's best for Haven. Right now your enemies have no idea where you are. Though returning to your flat was not a very smart move. I've taken care of that, however. We're moving someone who looks like you into it and creating an appropriate cover story. If anyone pokes around, they'll discover that our operative is the new tenant who just took up residence yesterday."

"And if somebody finds out the truth?"

"Better hope they don't, because if they do, I can't promise I can protect you."

I felt the wind go out of my sails. "Is that a threat, Mr. President?"

"That's just a fact, Miss Harkness. You can't escape the realities of the world we live in. It is what it is."

"For now."

"Yes." He nodded wearily. "For now. But I would consider your future, if I were you. The children you'll have, above all else. Haven is far from perfect, but at least it's a place to grow up in. Give your offspring that chance."

I almost gasped, afraid Mallory knew I was pregnant, but then I realized he was probably speaking in generalities, assuming that at some point I'd have a child. It was a natural enough thing in Haven. But eventually he was going to find out about Chloe, and then what? If he understood what *she* meant to the Old Ones, that it was *her* and not me they were after, would I still be able to count him as an ally? After all, it was clear he would continue the practice of shipping non-Immune infants to the Third Reich, despite what I'd told him. And while he might not be willing to turn *me* over to the Old Ones, there was no guarantee he'd have any such compunctions when it came to my daughter.

If I hadn't accepted it before, I had to now — I was out of my league. The other players in this game were far more adept than I, and it was going to take every resource I had to keep Chloe and me safe.

There was a gentle knock at the door, and Mallory straightened himself, regaining his placid demeanor, suddenly a different man altogether. Gone were the worry and the fear skirting the surface; now he was all good humor and bonhomie.

The door opened and Mrs. Balder stepped in, halting just beyond the threshold. "Your nine thirty is here, Mr. President."

"Thank you, Marion. We're just finishing up here." He turned to me, forcing a ragged grin. "Thank you for coming, Miss Harkness," he said, rising to his feet and offering his hand again.

I got up, shook hands, and said, "You're welcome, sir." But I was glad to pull my hand free and equally glad to be leaving. There's nothing like deception to sour a relationship.

"The limousine will take you to your flat," the president said as I reached the door. "You'll have half an hour to pack whatever you can take in two suitcases."

"Where will I be going?" I asked meekly.

"I don't know. I won't ever know. Only your handler will."

I looked back at him. "Will it always be like this?"

"One day the world will be the way it's supposed to be."

"And what way is that?" I asked.

"The way it was without *them*, Miss Harkness. Good luck."

I opened the door and brushed past Mrs. Balder, walking toward the foyer as quickly as possible. Outside, the limousine was waiting. I got in, feeling trapped, a cold tide of fear rising in me as the car carried me home for the last time.

When we pulled up to the curb in front of my flat, the driver jumped out and hurried around to open the door. He offered a hand to help me out, and as I stood I came face to face with him and started. "Wilson," I said. "You're working for the government now?"

"Always have been, miss," he said.

That admission stung, and I thought of all the people I'd met in my life and wondered how many of them had been a conduit to the president's office.

"So are you my handler, then?" I asked.

Wilson shook his head. "No, miss. He'll be here soon." He tipped his hat, looked apologetic, then turned and strode back to the driver's side of the car. As he opened the door, he hesitated, seemingly searching for the right words. "Master Valentine asked me to keep an eye on you, miss. He was worried about you."

"So I gather." I made an effort to smile. "He was good at worrying about me, wasn't he?"

"Yes, miss. He cared a great deal for you."

"Too much," I said quietly.

"Oh, no, miss. He would never have agreed with that. He was a good man — as vamps go. I'm sorry about what happened to him."

"So am I." There was a little hiccup of sadness in my voice.

"You could have done worse, miss."

Before I could respond, a black BMW pulled up just behind the limousine. Wilson glanced at it and said, "That would be for you."

"Oh."

"You take care, miss." With that, he climbed into the Mercedes and drove away.

I stood there, feeling alone and desolate as I watched the limousine disappear down University Avenue. I touched the ring on my finger, the last thing Valentine had given me that day on the airship, just hours before he had vanished from my life forever. A symbol of a bond that might have lasted an eternity had we been given a chance.

EPILOGUE

There are so many questions in life, and yet I have answers to none.

How can a person become so lost? I wonder.

All I know for certain is this — I hold the truth within me.

Maybe it should all die with me, for regardless of everything that has happened in the past few weeks, nothing has really changed. The world I stand in today is the world I stood in yesterday, and it will probably be the world I stand in tomorrow. It's only that I see it differently that makes it seem other than what it was. And who's to say I see it the way it should be seen? Maybe Mallory is right. Maybe the not knowing is everything. Maybe it makes the untenable tenable.

But my greatest fear isn't the terrible truth I have to live with. It's something else. It's this thing within me. This child — this daughter of mine. The Old Ones want her because they believe her blood will somehow allow them to escape back to wherever it is they came from in the first place. I don't know whether to lend credence to any of that. Cherkov was a madman, and the Old Ones could be just as crazy. Certainly it all sounds insane. But then, I remind myself, there was a time when we thought vampires were just stories, and look how that turned out.

Maybe the sanest thing to do would be to destroy my child. End it all now, so no one ever has a chance to have her. Neither the people in Haven who want to use her against the Old Ones, nor the Old Ones themselves. But even as I think that, I hear Val's words telling me to protect her, that somehow she's going to save a world.

I don't know what to do. All I do know is that there isn't much time. The baby is changing me by the day, and all I can think of is my mother and the madness that consumed her, and wonder if I, too, am becoming darkness.

ACKNOWLEDGEMENTS

I live in other worlds. Every day I climb a flight of stairs, sit down behind a keyboard, and type for several hours on end. I submerge myself within environments that exist only in my head and don the personas of characters to whom I have contrived to give life. I live and breathe their trials and tribulations, and for days and weeks and months on end, I am content to do nothing more — be nothing more. But eventually the story comes to an end, and I resurface into the real world. At that point, like most writers, I am driven by the desire to share the conjurings of my imagination with a wider audience. That audience is you.

Anyone who has gone through the process of getting published for the first time will tell you it isn't always easy, that it can be fraught with difficulty, and that, on occasion, it is beset by episodes of frustration and despair. Writing the book is often the easy part, but delivering its words to the world at large requires the work and commitment of many other people.

By the time a book ends up on the shelves in a bookstore, a large cast has taken part in its production. The author is the start, and you, the reader, are the finish. But it's all those people in between who allow the beginning to meet the end. Without them, without their dedication and belief in an author and his or her work . . . well, the manuscript would probably remain on the hard drive or buried in the bottom of a desk drawer gathering dust.

Among the many people who conspired to nurture and mold *Becoming Darkness* into what it is, there are, of course, the usual suspects — my parents, my siblings, assorted nieces and nephews, dear friends, my agent, and my editor.

I don't think you can be a writer without first being a reader, and both my parents encouraged me to read long before I ever went to school. My mother also inspired in me a passion for writing. She had yearned to be a writer herself, and actually had some poems published in her youth. Though World War II and parenthood intervened and took her along a different path, for much of her life she remained an ardent letter writer. She lugged a portable Remington typewriter (which, incidentally, was not so portable) almost everywhere she went — through the jungles of the Belgian Congo in the 1950s, and later into Pakistan, Iran, and Tanzania. It was on that very machine that I wrote my first story (when I was eight), and from that moment on, I knew I wanted to be a writer.

We are the sum of the people we encounter in life and the many experiences we endure. My brothers and sisters — Brian, Elaine, Terry, Carolyn, and Michael — all contributed in no small measure to making me the person I am today, and that plays a significant part in my writing. At various points in my life they have been instrumental in sustaining me and have made me truly grateful that I belong to a large family. I cannot imagine existence without them — past, present, or future.

Of course, my siblings have blessed me with a whole slew of nieces and nephews – Ashley, Erin, Nicholas, Jennifer, Daniel, Reese, McKee, and McKinlee — who have also influenced me in many ways and have allowed me to see the world from a perspective I might otherwise not have had.

Life can be very lonely for a writer, which makes friendship especially important. For that I am truly appreciative of the role Gerhard (the Great) Klemm and Richard Roberge have had in maintaining my spirits during those occasions when I may have felt somewhat beleaguered and perhaps even a little disillusioned. Their unceasing optimism convinced me that the attainment of my dream was within my grasp so long as I continued to believe in myself.

Most writers, I am sure, will agree that a good agent is fundamental to success, and in that I am truly fortunate that Kelly Sonnack saw potential in my first draft and took a chance on me. I cannot express enough my gratitude for all that she has done to help me mold this book into a better work and find it such a good home.

It doesn't seem there are enough good things I can say about the people at Switch Press. They are consummate professionals who have made the entire experience of bringing this book to production an absolute pleasure. Alison Deering, who edited my manuscript, made the process of rewriting it both painless and illuminating, and I know the book is far better for having had the benefit of her guidance and wise counsel. More importantly, I am a better writer for having benefited from her insights. Many others in various departments at Switch Press have contributed to steering this book toward becoming what I always dreamed it would be. To each and every one of them, I thank you.

They say it is not the destination so much as the journey that matters. This has been a fine journey indeed, and I hope it is but the first of many to come. I thank you, the reader, for having accompanied me on at least part of it.

LINDSAY FRANCIS BRAMBLES was born in Ottawa, Canada, in 1959 and spent a large part of his childhood and youth living and traveling overseas in countries such as Pakistan, Iran, Kenya, and Tanzania. Although he occasionally attended traditional schools, most of his education was gained through correspondence courses and the life experience of living among other cultures. As a child in Iran, Lindsay produced a weekly newspaper, which kindled what would become a lifelong interest in writing. In 1989, he won first prize in the Pine Cone II Science Fiction Convention writing contest for his novella "Zero-Option." He has worked in a variety of fields, from construction to childcare while pursuing a vocation as an artist and writer and is currently hard at work on several new projects.